From Ashes to Honor

Loree Lough is a master at weaving deeply honest and heart-rending portrayals of the human condition, set against breathtaking backgrounds that make you feel you're actually there. It must be as much fun to be one of Loree's characters as it is to read about them, because she takes them on journeys that twist and turn and leave them wanting more—and does it with grace and conviction. She's one of today's true storytellers.
—CARLA BUCKLEY, author of the bestselling *The Things That Keep Us Here*

In *From Ashes to Honor*, talented author Loree Lough puts us in the minds of first responders who courageously met the threat to our nation on 9/11. It's a believable, gritty, and sometimes humorous story that captures the haunting echoes of the horrific attacks.
—DEAN ECKMANN, F-16 Flight Lead, 119th Fighter Wing, Detachment 1 Alert Site, Langley Air Force Base, NORAD first responder to Washington, DC on 9/11.

One of my favorite things about Loree Lough's books is that she really *gets* that God weaves the tapestry of our lives with many thin threads, and that each has a purpose. The characters in *From Ashes to Honor* are perfect examples of lives drawn together across many miles by one fragile and unseen connection. Lough's masterful tale draws the reader in by grit of pure emotion and compelling storytelling. Highly recommended!
—SANDRA D. BRICKER, award-winning author of laugh-out-loud fiction for the inspirational market, including *The Big 5-OH!*

From Ashes to Honor is truly one of the most captivating books I've ever read. Story and characters. Characters and story. That's what it's all about. Loree Lough's eidetic writing style makes the reader see, hear, feel, taste, and smell what's going on. In other words, she doesn't take the story to the reader, she brings the reader into the story. A must read and a permanent addition to anyone's library.
—KEN FARMER, veteran actor (*Silverado, Logan's War, The President's Man*), producer/director (Timber Creek Productions), coauthor of *Black Eagle Force* with Buck Stienke

September 11 is a date forever branded onto the minds and hearts of Americans, especially the courageous first responders who risked—and, in some cases, gave—their lives to save others. In *From Ashes to Honor*, bestselling author Loree Lough weaves a deeply honest and heartrending portrayal of the effects of the tragedy. As always, she has masterfully woven together a powerful storyline, believable characters, and "you are there" descriptions of the disaster, and artfully balanced each with knee-slapping humor and beautiful images of the Chesapeake, DC, and New York. No wonder Loree's stories have earned hundreds of awards!
—LYNN SPENCER, author of *Touching History: The Untold Story of the Drama that Unfolded in the Skies Over America on 9/11*

Other recent books by Loree Lough

Suddenly Daddy/Suddenly Mommy (2 full-length contemporary romances)
The Lone Star Legends series:
    Beautiful Bandit, Maverick Heart, Rio Grande Moon
Prevailing Love series (3 full-length contemporary romances)
Tales of the Heart series (3 full-length historical romances)
Love Finds You in Paradise, Pennsylvania
Love Finds You in North Pole, Alaska
Be Still . . . and Let Your Nail Polish Dry (devotional with Andrea Boeshaar, Sandra D. Bricker, and Debby Mayne)

FROM ASHES TO HONOR

Book 1 of the First Responders Series

Loree Lough

Abingdon Press fiction
a novel approach to faith

Nashville, Tennessee

From Ashes to Honor

Copyright © 2011 by Loree Lough

ISBN-13: 978-1-4267-0769-8

Published by Abingdon Press, P.O. Box 801, Nashville, TN 37202

www.abingdonpress.com

The persons and events portrayed in this work of fiction
are the creations of the author, and any resemblance
to persons living or dead is purely coincidental.

Cover design by Anderson Design Group, Nashville, TN

Library of Congress Cataloging-in-Publication Data

Lough, Loree.
From ashes to honor / Loree Lough.
    p. cm. — (The first responders series ; bk. 1)
ISBN 978-1-4267-0769-8 (pbk. : alk. paper)
    1. First responders—Fiction. 2. September 11 Terrorist Attacks, 2001—Psychological
aspects—Fiction. I. Title.
PS3562.O8147F76 2011
813'.54—dc22

                                            2010053762

Printed in the United States of America

1 2 3 4 5 6 7 8 9 10 / 16 15 14 13 12 11

To my heavenly Father—the author of all relationships—who blessed me with this story idea. To my loyal readers, whose friendly letters keep me on the path to publication. To my husband, daughters, and grandkids, who tolerate (and support) my oddball work schedule. Special thanks to dear friend Sandie Bricker, who goaded me into sending this series proposal to our beloved editors, Ramona Richards and Barbara Scott, and to Barb, for believing in it enough to issue contracts. To all first responders, whose courageous service and sacrifice keeps us safe. Most of all, this novel is dedicated to every man and woman—whether in New York, Pennsylvania, or Washington D.C.—whose example reminded every American of the real meaning of patriotism, bravery, and valor on 9/11.

Author's Note

If you're old enough to read this, September 11, 2001, is a day you'll never forget. And if you're like me, you'll never forget where you were and what you were doing when news of the attack on our great nation reached you. If you close your eyes, you can probably see the horror that befell New York, Shanksville, and Washington, D.C., on that terrifying and tragic day.

Before that infamous date, 9-1-1 represented the numbers you dialed when injured, afraid, or threatened, believing—even as you pressed the digits—that help would reach you soon.

Right this minute, in police and fire stations all across our land, brave men and women are checking and re-checking every piece of equipment in preparation for the next emergency that will deliver them to the line of fire. And when the crisis is over, they'll return to their posts and start it all over again, to ensure they'll be alert and ready for the next call.

I find it remarkable that the courageous firefighters, police officers, EMTs, and search-and-rescue team members respond to our calls, never knowing as they speed toward our homes and businesses whether or not *this* call might be their last—and yet they go.

Their brave dedication prompted me to ask myself: Just how does one properly thank those who risk their lives every time they roll away from the stationhouse, sirens blaring, strobe lights flashing? How do we show our gratitude to the professional life-savers whose skills lead them to find lost children, save accident victims, and carry unconscious victims from burning buildings, all while making life-and-death snap decisions that affect every patient delivered to the ER *and* their concerned loved ones, as well?

Unable to come up with a satisfying answer, I felt called to write "The First Responders" series. It's my hope that through these stories, we'll all learn a little more about our nation's silent heroes. The novels will serve as my humble and heartfelt thanks to each daring man and woman who utters this prayer (written by the Reverend Robert A. Crutchfield):

Father in Heaven,
Please make me strong when others are weak, brave when others are afraid, and vigilant when others are distracted by the chaos.
Provide comfort and companionship to my family when I must be away.
Serve beside me and protect me, as I seek to protect others.
Amen.

I hope you'll write me (c/o Abingdon Press) to share your own 9/11 and first responders stories. Until then, may the good Lord shower you and yours with joys too numerous to count!

Blessings,
Loree

Prologue

They cried to the Lord in their trouble,
and He delivered them from their distress.
Psalms 107:6

New York City
8:40 A.M.
September 11, 2001

As on every morning, the sweet scents of cinnamon and mocha mixed with drugstore aftershave and pricey cologne. And, as on every morning, Austin ordered a large black coffee with a shot of espresso.

A strange vibration rumbled above the whir of blenders, busily whipping milk into froth for cappuccinos and lattes. A New York City trash truck, or another fender bender? he wondered as his cell phone chirped. It only took a quick glance at the caller i.d. to inspire a low groan.

Eddy smirked. "Your brother?"

"Third time this week."

"Sheesh. And it's only Tuesday."

Becky, the counter girl, held out one hand. "That'll be a buck fifty, cutie pie."

Austin handed her two singles and told her to keep the change.

"Let me guess," Eddy said. "He wants you to get a safer job, one with a more predictable schedule, so you can spend more time with your mom."

"Bingo. All I can say is, thank God for unlimited minutes. The two messages he left yesterday?" Austin pocketed the phone and cut loose with a two-note whistle. "To call 'em long is an understatement."

"You know what they say about paybacks."

"What?"

"Well, all *I* can say is, rambling messages must be in the Finley DNA."

"Bite me," Austin said, grinning as Becky handed him his coffee.

"No, seriously, Finley." He looked left and right and waved Austin closer, as if preparing to divulge a state secret. "Listen up, dude. There was a big story about birth order on the news this morning." He shrugged. "This stuff with Avery? It's all 'cause he sees you as his baby brother."

"Aw, gimme a break. He's five stinkin' minutes older than me."

"Big difference, five minutes. Made him *ju-u-ust* older and wiser enough to become a hot shot Wall Street investment banker." He gave Austin the once-over, from close-cropped blond hair to spit-polished black shoes. "And develop the opinion that he needs to watch over you. Y'know, since you're only one of many tiny little cogs that make the City's gears—"

Austin chuckled. "Yeah, well, you can *both* bite me."

Becky wiggled a forefinger at Eddy. "Your turn, honey pot."

He leaned a forearm on the counter and frowned. "Holy moly, Beckster, you gotta quit partyin' all night, 'cause—shoo-eee and wowza, dudette—you are some kinda green around the gills this mornin'!"

She blew a baseball-sized purple bubble and popped it with her front teeth. "Some days it's hard to believe you found a woman willing to marry you."

Eddy snickered, then ordered decaf with double cream, pretending not to hear as Austin and the rest of his cop pals agreed with Becky. The good-natured taunting came to a halt when a second rumble shook the windows and rattled the mugs, stacked pyramid fashion on glass shelves behind the counter. For a blink in time, the West Street Coffee Shop fell completely quiet. Then a chorus of buzzing cell phones, radio bleeps, and the sputtering of dispatchers summoning all available personnel to the World Trade Center ended the eerie silence.

Amid the clamor of cops and firefighters charging into the street, Austin disregarded a second call from his twin. Tossing Eddy the keys to their cruiser, he growled "You drive for a change. I'm afraid I'll take my bad mood out on some 'Got my license in a gumball machine' sightseer at Battery Park."

Siren blaring and lights flashing, they peeled away from the curb. "Smart decision," he said, honking and shaking a fist at the slow-moving taxi that blocked him from the destination, just half a mile away.

Emergency vehicles, city buses, cabs, and limos joined the rows of cars and delivery vans that rolled to a dead stop. "What's the holdup?" Eddy demanded. "Can't those clowns see that the light is green?"

"I hate these stupid tests. It'd make a lot more sense for the big shots at city hall to do stuff like this when the roads aren't clogged with traffic." Austin shook his head. "But no-o-o, we've gotta put on a good show for the tourists."

"Guess we can't complain about getting paid to sit on our duffs."

"Yeah? Well, *I* can complain, about these exhaust fumes for starters."

The radio buzzed and hummed with steady static, and Austin beat a fist on the dash. "Oh. Great. Now this piece of junk decides to die, leaving us clueless about what's going on at WTC."

"I hate to break it to ya, pard, but you were clueless before we—" Eddy draped his upper body over the steering wheel and looked up. "What—Is—*That*?"

Squinting, Austin scrubbed the inside of the windshield with the heel of his hand. "Turn on the defogger, genius."

But the murk was *outside*. Fierce, roiling white smoke stained the blue early-autumn sky. "I have a feeling this is no ordinary test," he said grimly. "We'd better hot-foot it the rest of the way."

"You're right. Ain't like we're gonna block traffic."

Side by side, the partners jogged toward the Towers, and the closer they got, the harder it became to see through the smog.

"Must be one heckuva fire to make a mess like this."

In his pocket, Austin's cell phone buzzed, and he ignored it for the third time in five minutes. When he got hold of his twin later, man, was Avery gonna get a piece of his mind.

1

New York City
10:00 AM
January 2003

"Would you agree that the 'watched pot never boils' maxim applies here?"

Austin looked up from his watch and hid his annoyance behind a grin. "May I remind you, Doc," he said, slow and easy, "that you were fifteen minutes late for the fifth time in a row, and, as usual, wasted another five tidying your desk before we got down to business." He shrugged one shoulder. "I'm only trying to make sure those high muckety-mucks at headquarters get their money's worth outta these sessions."

"How noble of you, particularly under the circumstances."

Translation: The Department put him on desk duty, and that's where he'd stay until the doctor deemed him fit to hit the streets again. That fact galled him, but he'd grind his molars to dust before he'd give her the satisfaction of scribbling "easily provoked" in his file. "They're just going by the book. I've got no beef with that." A bald-faced lie, but no way he intended to admit it to *her*.

She leaned back in the too-big-for-her chair. "If you think hostility will get you out the door faster, you're sadly mistaken."

Hostility? He looked left and right, as if to say "*Me?*"

Lifting her chin, the doctor added, "A talent for double-speak might be useful on the streets, but it won't get you anywhere with me."

First hostility and now double-speak? In Austin's mind, she'd just confirmed the old "You need to be half nosy and half crazy to become a shrink" theory.

"Cooperate here," she said, tapping her desk blotter, "and maybe I can help you get back out *there.*"

The only person who'd ever talked to him that way—and got away with it—had been Principal Buell. Well, Buell and Lieutenant Marcum, who cornered him in the bullpen six weeks earlier with a snarly "You're at the end of your rope, Finley. See the department shrink, *this week,* or you're through."

The threat made him call to schedule that first appointment, then arrive on time five weeks in a row—more than he could say for Dr. Samara. It also explained why he'd stretched his patience to the breaking point, and why he hadn't provoked her by admitting what a waste of time it was, nattering on and on about *feelings.* He didn't acknowledge that wearing stylish business suits instead of a burqa didn't fool him, because everything—from her name to her green-rimmed brown eyes and sleek, dark hair—branded her a Muslim. It galled him that she wielded the power to end his career, especially since, for all he knew, her kinfolk were 9/11 terrorists. But he didn't tell her that, either.

"You've been dancing around these police brutality incidents in your file long enough, don't you think?"

That haughty tone—a regular thing with her, he wondered? Or had she adopted it to tick him off, see if she could make him lose it, right there in her office? Well, if she wanted to play the game that way, she'd best prepare to learn a thing or two about scoring points.

He sat up straighter and cleared his throat. Because if she intended to talk about those, she'd better be prepared to cite the dozens of commendations he'd earned in the line of duty, too. But just as he started to make the point, she said "Eight separate incidents in the eleven months since 9/11."

Technically, there had been ten, but the first two had occurred in the first weeks after the terror attack, and the lieutenant had agreed not to put them in Austin's file. Knowing Marcum, he'd added both to cover his own butt after the third perp-cop confrontation, providing this arrogant little smartmouth yet another arrow in her "Get the Hothead to Hang Himself" quiver.

Her expression and posture reminded him of the black and white photo he'd found, researching Sigmund Freud for a Psych 101 assignment. In it, the doctor sat in an overstuffed wingback, fingers steepled under his bearded chin, wearing that same self-important smirk. Why would the little fool want to emulate a man whose theories had been debunked by his own contemporaries?

"Surely you have *something* to say in your own defense."

Austin pinched the bridge of his nose, hoping to buy time. Time to summon the patience not to let her have it with both barrels. Time to remind himself that he'd always been a good cop, and his actions didn't *need* defending. So he'd roughed up a few perps—thugs who'd beat their wives, robbed hardworking shopkeepers, got into gunfights in the streets and killed innocent folks. If it took a little "police brutality" to get animals like that off the streets, so be it! But that wasn't what she wanted to hear. *Just play the game*, he told himself, *and keep your cool.*

It dawned on him that he might be going at this all wrong. Maybe under that smug, buttoned-up exterior beat the heart of a "badge groupie," like those he'd charmed in cop bars from the Bronx to Manhattan. Austin rested his left ankle on his right knee and linked his fingers—not too tightly, lest she see it as a symptom of agitation. "You forgot to swear me in, counselor."

One perfectly plucked eyebrow disappeared under thick, gleaming bangs. "I beg your pardon?"

"'In your own defense'?" Austin chuckled quietly. "Seriously? You sound more like a lawyer than a shrink."

"I've never been overly fond of the term 'shrink.'"

"Ah." He grinned. "Maybe you prefer 'wig picker.'"

To that point, her practiced expression hadn't changed much, but the subtle narrowing of her eyes and lips didn't escape his notice. In place of the "Gotcha!" reaction he'd expected, it made him nervous, and, much as he hated to admit it, a little afraid of what she'd tell Marcum.

If only he could go home, numb his brain with a little Jim Beam! Lately, he'd been moving in two speeds: Too Fast, and Off, like the windshield wipers on his beat-up pickup. It took more and more booze to knock him out, and mega-doses of caffeine to jack him up again. Maybe he ought to just tell her that, because what could it hurt to blast her with a dose of grim reality?

Austin leaned forward, elbows on knees and hands clasped in the space between, until no more than two feet of cluttered desk separated their faces. "Y'know, I *do* have something to say in my defense." He mimicked her earlier move, and aimed his forefinger at the window. "I'm a good cop, and I *belong* out there, not in here." He paused, more to ratchet up the courage to continue than to give her time to mull over his words. "And I think you know it as well as I do."

"Your dedication to the department has never been in question."

She might as well have said "The sun is shining" or "It's Tuesday." And then *she* leaned forward, too, and he caught himself pulling back to put more space between them. As he wondered how she'd read *that*, she said, "May I be perfectly honest with you, Austin?"

Her silent scrutiny unnerved him, but he couldn't afford to let her see it. So he matched her steady gaze, blink for blink. She tilted her head, and for an instant, he got a glimpse of the human being behind the stodgy title. If he'd ever seen a more appealing smile, he didn't know where. It was almost enough to keep him from noticing that she'd completely ignored his statement.

Almost.

"As my sweet mama says, 'Honesty is the best policy.'"

As quick as it appeared, her smile vanished, like the whiff of smoke blown from a spent match. "You're seriously mistaken if you think you can charm your way out of the hole you're in."

Score one for the doc, he thought, frowning. Because that's exactly the way he'd been feeling since 9/11, like he'd fallen into a deep, dark pit with no flashlight and no way out.

"So be frank with me."

Austin cringed. In his experience, when people tucked the word 'frank' into a sentence, he'd best prepare for the verbal sucker punch that would follow.

"Why are you so angry?"

The question caught him by surprise, jarring him nearly as much as the left hook he'd taken on the jaw a couple weeks back, trying to cuff a drunk driver near the Brooklyn Bridge. "I'm *not* angry!" he ground out. Enraged, maybe. Even incensed. But angry? He nearly laughed out loud at the absurdity of it.

But he couldn't very well admit it, now could he? At least, not without opening his own personal can of worms, the one that barely kept a lid on the bitterness and resentment born on 9/11. The one where he'd tried to stuff the memory of his brother's final cell phone call, ignored by Austin as a chorus of radio blips summoned every available first responder to Ground Zero.

It took every bit of his self-control to keep his butt in the chair. He wanted to get to his feet, stomp around her messy little office. Wanted to slam a fist onto her cluttered desk and bellow, "Yeah, I'm angry. Who *wouldn't* be?"

But he sat still and kept his mouth shut, because only the most self-centered schmuck would moan and groan about his own misery when thousands of others had been hit much harder, had lost far more than he had.

So, yeah, he was angry, all right, and it made him the meat in a Life Sucks sandwich:

If he admitted it, she'd send for the men in white coats. If he didn't, she'd think he didn't have a handle on his rage, which would probably inspire the same outcome. Still, he needed to tell her *something* if he hoped to put these blasted pick-his-brain sessions behind him, once and for all.

Her pen, scritch-scratching across the top page of his file, caught his attention. Just as he looked up, she met his gaze. "Are you angry because you feel guilty?"

"Guilty?" he echoed. "What in blue blazes do I have to feel guilty about?"

"You're alive, for starters, and many of your comrades aren't."

Score another one for the doc, for making him admit he *was* ticked off, big time. For reminding him that when finally he returned to his third-floor walk-up on September fourteenth, he carried the grisly images of mangled bodies with him.

Mental pictures of cop and firefighter pals and hundreds of uniformed officers he'd never met, all buried under smoking debris with badges and kids' tiny sneakers, women's high heels and spit-polished Wingtips.

Just tough it out, he'd told himself, and the pictures will fade. But all these months later, he saw it as clearly as he had that day. He'd never been a nail biter, but every cuticle glowed red and raw now. Never experienced a tic, either . . . until he developed a few of his own. And though he'd quit smoking years ago, Austin burned through a pack a day. When memories of the thousands who fell that day shuffled through his head like a deck of gory playing cards—and it happened at the weirdest, most unexpected moments—steely determination had been the calmant that put a stop to head-to-toe tremors.

What happened that day stirred up a lot of differing emotions, but guilt at having survived? That sure as heck wasn't among them!

The voice mail from his brother, played for the first time on the fourteenth, after showering and wolfing down a bologna and mustard sandwich, after looking at his most recent credit card bill, after checking his email? Oh, he felt plenty guilty about *that*. Because Avery, knowing full well that he'd never get out of his office in the North Tower alive, wanted to spend his final moments with his twin. And when Austin didn't pick up, he'd launched into a trembly voiced rendition of the Lord's Prayer. He got as far as ". . . for Thine is the kingdom . . ." before an ear-blasting explosion cut him short and—

"What a horrible thing to carry around in your head all this time," she interrupted.

The look of shock and disbelief on her face mirrored the ache that had clutched his heart.

"Have you talked about this with anyone else? A relative? A clergyman? *Someone?*"

Until she asked the questions, Austin hadn't realized he'd said it all out loud. He glanced at his watch. Last time he'd looked, it had been one thirty-five. Now the dial read one thirty-seven. He'd interviewed enough witnesses to know how much could be divulged in two short minutes.

Confused—and flat-out annoyed with his lack of self-control—he got to his feet, slapped a hand to the back of his neck and began to pace. He'd wanted to be a cop since junior high school, when two somber-faced cops informed him that his dad had been shot in a convenience store holdup. They could have left him alone to deliver the dismal news to his twin and their mom, but they didn't. And when they promised to check in with them often, Austin chalked it up as just another one of those well-meaning but empty promises grown-ups sometimes made. But he'd been wrong. Separately and together, they returned every few weeks, sometimes to throw the football or teach the boys how to catch a pop-up fly, other times to mow the lawn or fix a leaky faucet. *That's* the kind of cop he'd worked so hard to become. If his maniacal blathering cost him his job, what would he do with the rest of his life?

"Please, sit down, Austin. We still have ten minutes left before—"

That first day, while waiting for her to grace him with her company, he'd paced off the space, and estimated her office at eight-by-ten feet. Right now, it seemed hot as Hades, and half that size. "Gotta go," he said, flinging open the door.

It slammed into a shoulder-high stack of books, and for a moment, Austin could only stare as it swayed to and fro, exactly as the Towers had, milliseconds before collapsing in a sky-blotting plume of roiling black smoke. A colorful "Come to Jamaica" brochure stuck out about halfway down the pile, and for a blink in time, it reminded him of the brightly colored tail section of the jetliner that had pierced the first building.

He reached out to steady the pile a tick too late. Novels, textbooks, and a copy of *How to Build a Birdhouse* clattered to the floor. Feeling stupid and clumsy, he dropped to his knees and began shoving them, one by one, onto the nearby bookshelf. "What kind of idiot piles books behind a door!" he bellowed, tugging at the how-to book, wedged under the door. After several futile tries, he got up and kicked it shut with enough ferocity to rattle her black-framed diplomas and degrees against the wall.

Trembling and sweaty, he faced her. "Was that another one of your cockamamie *tests*?" He drew quote marks in the air, raised his voice an octave to mock her. "'Let's see how riled up the crazy cop will get if the tower of books falls down around him, reminding him of the day when—'"

She grabbed his wrists and held on tight. "I give you my word, Austin," she said. "I'd never do such a thing."

For a long, silent moment, she gazed into his eyes, and in that moment, she looked every bit as vulnerable and helpless as he felt. Without the doctor-patient wall between them, they were just two people. A man and a woman who, like so many others, were forever changed by that dreadful day.

Her expression softened to a slow smile. "Thanks," she said, nodding at the tidy row of books he'd arranged on the shelf. "I've been meaning to do that since I moved in here."

As he stared at their hands, he couldn't help thinking that maybe he really *did* need therapy, because he would have sworn she'd grabbed his wrists. When—and *how*—had their fingers become so tightly linked? He'd been a cop for years, for crying out loud. Why hadn't he *noticed*? And why were his eyes smarting with unshed tears?

If he didn't get out of there, and fast, he'd get the psychological treatment he seemed to need, all right . . . in a padded cell, wearing a jacket with no arms.

He strode purposefully toward the elevator and thumbed the Down button hard enough to make him wince. From the corner of his eye, he saw that she'd followed him. Saw the Exit sign, too, and for a second, considered racing down the stairs instead of waiting for the car to reach her floor. But the image of once-normal and civilized people, screaming and crying as they crawled over one another to escape the Towers, stopped him dead in his tracks. He didn't need a shrink to tell him those were normal reactions to a thing like that, but he sure wouldn't mind knowing long it would take before he could ride in an elevator or climb a flight of stairs without breaking into a cold sweat as his heart beat double-time.

"I'll see you on Thursday, ten sharp. And I promise to be on time."

Austin stepped into the car and, facing her, lit up the number One. "So, did you get everything you needed from your little experiment?"

"It wasn't an experiment, or a test, or anything of the kind." Her tiny hand formed the Boy Scout salute. "I give you my word."

Only the image of her, bent over his file and scribbling "It is my professional opinion that Officer Austin Finley should be relieved of duty" kept him from barking "Yeah, right".

"So I'll see you on Thursday, then?"

Nodding, he thanked God that the elevator doors hissed shut when they did, because if Dr. Samara hadn't already gathered enough "Crazy Austin" trivia for her file, his traitorous watery eyes and trembling lower lip would have sealed his fate, for sure.

2

February 2003

$\mathcal{M}$ercy stared at the calendar page and sighed.

Twenty years ago today, her placard-waving feminist mother announced, "If I can sail alone from New York to Annapolis, why, I'll feel whole and fulfilled and powerful for the first time in my life!" Even at ten, Mercy heard underlying message, loud and clear: *Being your mom isn't enough for me. I need more.* Lots *more.*

Angry and hurt, the pouting pre-teen made herself scarce when her mother left for the family sailboat, docked at Fire Island, and remained unavailable for the phone call made from a Baltimore marina. Unfortunately, she'd been there when the Coast Guard informed her dad that *The Sea Wind* had gone down in the stormy Atlantic, because it forced her to add "guilt" and "regret" to the list of emotions roused by her mother's never-ending pursuit of freedom.

Her father wasted no time dragging her to a psychologist. By the time the second session concluded, Mercy had outfoxed the so-called child specialist and put a quick and permanent end to the meetings. The only good thing to come from therapy had been Mercy's unquenchable thirst for knowledge about the human psyche, for it put her on a career path that led to numerous degrees and diplomas, and filing cabinets bulging with positive outcomes for her patients.

But even as her patients confessed sins and exposed fears, the successful Dr. Mercy Samara struggled. Not with the proper diagnosis and treatment for their disorders, not with which medication—if any—to prescribe. Her conflict? Hypocrisy, because though she'd taught herself to conceal mistrust and cynicism behind a sunny smile, Mercy never learned how to shed the resentment and bitterness that clung to her heart and mind like the destructive barnacles that fixed themselves to *The Sea Wind's* hull.

Frowning, she did her best to shrug off the negative sentiments. She had work to do, and nothing good could come from wallowing in the past. Perhaps if she got the most disagreeable task out of the way first, the gloomy aspects of the anniversary would fade into the background.

Mercy reached for a thick manila folder that said "Austin Finley" on the tab. Opening it, she flipped through dozens of pages, meticulous notes she'd typed up after every one of his sessions. On page seven, she'd described nightmares that often interrupted his sleep. Page ten documented the blinding migraines and stomach aches. Thirteen listed bad habits he'd once overcome that had returned with a vengeance since the tragedy.

She flipped to the last page and stared at the blank form. Here, the Department's decision-makers expected her to cite the reasons why, in her professional opinion, Officer Finley could return to active duty—or provide a detailed explanation for the reasons she believed he shouldn't. Try as she might—and she'd spent hours studying his file, searching for a legitimate way to get him back to work—Mercy couldn't avoid the ugly truth: Austin Finley was the proverbial powder keg personified, and if allowed to continue on his path of self-destruction, the detonation would destroy him and anyone who made the mistake of getting too close to him.

Of all the first responders she'd treated for post-traumatic stress disorder—and there'd been nearly a hundred since the attack on the World Trade Center—why had she let Finley get under her skin this way? The analyst side of her brain recited rational, clinical reasons, but the *woman* in her couldn't forget the raspy edge that hardened his pleasant baritone when he told her about his brother's cell phone message. Yes, other patients had lost comrades and brothers-in-arms on 9/11, but this one? *This* one believed he deserved to suffer for ignoring that call, because in his mind, it was penance for letting his twin die, alone and afraid.

Mercy fired up her computer and called up his file. If she believed in God, the way her father did, this would be a very good time to pray. She'd pulled out all the stops, hoping to give Finley permission to go back to the work he clearly loved. But neither sympathy nor empathy could change the cold, hard fact that her decision would ultimately protect the department, the citizens of New York, and most important of all, Finley, himself.

Her father had a favorite adage, and it amazed her how often and how well he could make it fit nearly every situation: "Two wrongs don't make a right."

Fingers flying over the keyboard, she typed her final conclusions onto the form, saved the data, and printed a copy for his file. And as her pen hovered above the signature and date lines, Mercy sighed.

"Ah, Papa," she whispered, pressing the pen's nib to the page, "if only you'd taught me a wise old saying that could ease the sting of doing the right thing."

3

August 2009

*L*ike every morning, Austin woke to the screeching of gulls and waves, gently lapping at the hull, and thanked God for the peace of mind that had become as much a part of his life as the briny scent of the Chesapeake. Quite a difference from the spite and malice he carried home on the day he slammed his badge and gun on the lieutenant's desk! One of these days, he'd screw up the courage to call Dr. Samara and thank her, because if she hadn't recommended permanent desk duty, he'd probably be toes-up in some untended grave instead of banging his elbows in the minuscule shower stall . . .

Purchased sight unseen for five hundred dollars, the old tug required another twenty grand to be moved from Wisconsin's Lake Michigan to Bullneck Creek, and fifteen thousand more to make her habitable. Until his move to Maryland, he'd shared a third floor Manhattan walk-up with two other bachelor cops, and what the trio knew about real estate could fit in one shirt pocket. Before docking in the narrow inlet of the Patapsco River, Austin had known even less about boats.

But like the EMT certification that lured him from New York, scars collected retooling the engine and muscles built by varnishing wood and polishing brass had been earned the hard way. Both the career and his floating home delivered a sense of accomplishment, but few things filled him with more pride than the name, applied one Old West letter at a time in a bold, broad arc across the stern:

One Regret.

When asked why that, instead of something more work- or water-related, he recited the same answer: "At the end of every day, there's sure to be at least *one* thing I could have done better."

Coffee mug in hand, he scaled the ladder leading to the pilot house, where, for decades, a short list of stalwart captains had stood to guide unwieldy vessels into an assortment of ports along Lake Michigan's shores. The 360° view made him feel like the ruler of a watery kingdom that stretched from the Bay to the Patapsco River to this private cove on Bear Creek. His one regret? That his twin would never enjoy the Van Gogh–like sunrise that blended orange and yellow into the cloud-streaked azure sky.

Stepping through the narrow door and onto the upper deck, he filled his lungs with briny air and, forearms on the glossy brass rail, surveyed his domain. Melancholy wrapped round him as, holding the steaming mug high, he toasted the horizon. "Here's to you, Avery," he said into the salty wind, "may you always—"

"Ahoy, Finley!"

Austin turned toward the eardrum-piercing voice. "Mornin', Flora." Grinning, he lowered the cup. "Don't tell me Bud's still in his berth. . ."

Her brittle cackle skipped across the mirrored surface of the water. "I keep telling him if he intends to sleep his life away, I'll have no choice but to move in with the good lookin' young paramedic next door."

Much as he enjoyed the company of his elderly neighbors, Austin sometimes wished he'd chosen a more remote place to tie up, because regardless of season, Flora squawked the same greeting every day, no matter what time he rolled out of his bunk. Half a dozen times, thinking it had been his cabin lights skittering across the water that roused her, he'd climbed to the pilot house without so much as a candle to guide him. But not even full-out darkness deterred her. Small price to pay, he supposed, for fresh-baked chocolate chip cookies in the winter, homemade ice cream during the summer months, and amusing conversation all year long. "You flatter me," he said. "I'm off to work in a few. What're your plans for the day?"

Even from a distance of twenty yards, he could see the bend of her arthritic finger, pointing west. "Into town to restock the pantry," she said, loosing another guffaw. "Hopefully I can rouse that lazy husband of mine and get him to help me toss groceries from the car to the dock."

"Aw, the exercise'll do you good," he joked. "Besides, poor ol' Bud hasn't been retired all that long."

"Next Tuesday it'll be *six years*, I'll have you know!"

His tug doubled their schooner in width and length, yet he couldn't imagine sharing it 24-7—for six years—with *anyone*. "Well, I'd better hit the road. Have a good day, kiddo."

"Will do. And you stay safe out there, y'hear?"

Three years earlier, the Callahans' firefighter son had died when the roof of a blazing building collapsed under the weight of his heavy gear, so they understood better than most the dangers of Austin's job. "Give my best to Bud."

"I'm making shrimp Creole for supper . . ."

Because she knew he had no family, Flora made sure they shared one meal a week, sometimes more; and much as he enjoyed the "your turn—my turn" feasts, Austin looked forward to his solitude. Tonight, he planned to watch a Tom Selleck movie on TV and hit the hay early. *Think fast, Finley.*

"Thanks, Flora, but I'll be getting in kinda late. The captain said if I don't get caught up on my reports, he'll put me on KP duty for a month." He gave a final wave, knowing, even as he ducked back into his pilot house, that when his shift ended he'd sneak onto his boat to spare her feelings. Again.

He heard her voice, fading as he descended the ladder: "All right then, I'll save the leftovers for you."

Grinning, he shook his head, because something told him that by six bells, he'd be eating shrimp Creole at the chrome and red-marbled Formica table in Bud and Flora's narrow galley.

And he wouldn't have it any other way.

4

Mercy hated wishing her life away, but she could hardly wait for the construction crew to finish up. The old brick structure felt cold and drafty between November and March, and stifling the rest of the year, especially on her side of the building.

A humid blast of air sneaked past the crumbling caulk of the dingy tilt-out window nearest her desk, and she reached for a bottle of spring water. "Patience," she muttered, unscrewing the cap, because in no time she'd exchange the stack of sweat-blotting paper towels on the corner of her desk for the portable heater that would have her reaching for hand lotion, instead.

All things considered, she had very little to complain about. The drive from her end-of-row townhouse in Baltimore's historic Fells Point neighborhood took a pleasant fifteen minutes, now that students with drivers licenses weren't on the roads; and because school wouldn't officially start for another three weeks, she could wear capris and flip-flops, a tank top and a ponytail instead of her traditional flowing skirts and blouses. In New York, she'd never owned a home or a car, never had a pet, and since resigning from the department and moving here at the insistence of her college roommate, she had all three—and a gratifying job as a guidance counselor, as well.

Her work day began like every other, with a cheery welcome from the gray-haired cop assigned to the main entrance. "Mercy, Mercy, Mercy," he sing-songed Billy Crystal style, "you look *mah*-velous this morning, simply *mah*-velous!" He'd delivered the same greeting every morning of the three years she'd been affiliated with the high school. Would there ever come a day when she *didn't* blush as she thanked him for the compliment?

Mercy hurried to her office, passing a bank of pea green lockers, then a row of pasty yellow ones. *Who chooses these nauseating colors?* she thought as a line of sickly coral lockers came into view. For the time being, at least they looked clean and tidy. What a pity that by the third week of classes, chips and dings, fingerprints and lipstick would dull the semi-gloss sheen. As her sandals click-clacked over the polished linoleum, she thought of her own high school days, when metal detectors and policemen at the door were unheard of, and when parents ambled in and out of schools without the need to sign a book, or submit to being frisked by an armed guard. Her mood brightened slightly as she heard her father's gruff voice comparing the scenario to the dictatorship he'd grown up in.

Memories of her dad could be happy and lighthearted—and could just as easily lead to dark and depressing thoughts. Mercy consciously focused on the peculiar layout of the tiles. If the blue squares led to the main office or the science lab, they might have made sense. Instead, a row here and a row there merely connected with pink and green squares, or formed ridiculous zigzags across the floor, as if they'd been designed and slapped into place by a crew of drunken construction workers. In her high school, teachers insisted that kids going north stay on one side of the hall, those headed south on the other. "No running allowed!" was an all too-familiar shout. No wonder these kids moved from classroom to classroom between periods like dizzy cattle, recently turned loose from weeks in a too-small corral!

In most ways, kids weren't so different than they'd been back then. That first week of September, they'd change their minds about courses they'd chosen the previous spring, or if a teacher who'd earned a reputation for sternness appeared at the top of their schedules, they'd swap classes to be with their friends. By May, graduating seniors called in "sick," while juniors scrambled to sign up for next year's prerequisites. Sophomores with an eye on college gathered up every available pamphlet in the guidance office, and those bound for vo-tech made appointments to learn which tradesmen were looking for apprentices to work the second half of every school day.

Her duties as a counselor were as varied as the teens themselves. Occasionally, Mercy was called upon to advise pregnant girls, or kids whose parents were divorcing. Sometimes, she found herself going to bat for youngsters caught red-handed with drugs or alcohol. Always, she made a point of underscoring the dangers of tobacco. She befriended the new transfers, put athletes with sub-par grades together with tutors, scolded bullies—and gave pep talks to their victims.

But even when the principal demanded Mercy's input on decisions to suspend or expel a student, the pressures and stresses of the job didn't come close to what she'd faced as a police department psychiatrist. Until 9/11, Mercy had loved the work so much that she didn't even mind the low pay and long hours, because—

A quiet knock interrupted her reverie. A moment later, Abe Archer, the Owl's assistant coach, stuck his head into her office. No doubt he'd come to collect on the promise she'd made before school ended for the summer. He stood in the doorway, grimacing and waving his arms in a futile attempt to stir up some cool air. "Cheese and crackers, girl, and I thought it was hot down in the locker room! How do you stand it?"

Mercy laughed. "Easy. I pretend this is my own private sauna."

Shaking his head, he said "Well, more power to you." Then, "We're ready for you."

Where had the hours gone! Last time she'd checked, the big clock above the door said ten, and now the hands pointed to the eleven and the three. "Let me grab my clipboard," she said, shoving back from her desk, "and I'll meet you on the field."

Winking, he fired off a smart salute and closed the door as Mercy gathered her things.

She'd suggested at the start of last year's football season that maybe with a few pointers the team could "psyche out" their opponents. So she studied their opponents and watched the Owls practice, and taught them how brain power, in combination with savvy plays, could win out over brute force alone. At first, her idea received noisy skepticism and scoffing from the coaches and the boys on the team alike. Never one to back down from a challenge, Mercy convinced them to at least give it a try. "If it doesn't work, I'll take you all out for pizza!"

As things turned out, she treated them to deep-dish and thin crust . . . to celebrate making it into the playoffs. This year, they wanted to get started even earlier, with the hope of winning the championship.

By the time she arrived on the field, the team had already split into "shirts" and "skins" to practice their new plays. The boys on the bench made room for her while on the field, their teammates grunted and groaned as big padded bodies peppered the grass.

Abe and Coach Jordan paced on the sideline, shouting insults and instructions in equal measure. Jordan blew his whistle so long and hard that his face turned beet-red, inspiring the kid beside her to lean closer and whisper, "Is it possible for a person's face to explode?"

Laughing, Mercy said, "No, but I have a feeling if it's physically possible, your coach might just qualify for an entry in the *Guinness Book of Records*."

Jordan's croaking bellow overpowered the boy's response. "Winston! For the luvva Pete! We went over this not ten minutes ago: Twenty-four, zig right . . . blue. Twenty-four, zig right . . . blue. *Got it*?"

"Got it, coach."

The face mask and mouth guard made it tough to read offensive tight end's reaction, but on the next play he leaped into the air, hands outstretched to catch the pass. Healye, the defensive safety, looked like a locomotive as he chugged across the turf, dirt and grit spewing from his cleats. He battered Winston with such force that the sickening sound of the impact rolled across the field like an ocean wave.

Mercy jumped to her feet now, too, watching the scene unfold like a slow-motion replay:

Winston's body, bent at an awkward angle, seemed to hover in mid-air for a moment before it hit the grass with a sickening *thud*. Then he tumbled and rolled several times, and when at last he came to rest, he looked like a human pretzel. Nothing moved, save the rise and fall of the number fifteen on his chest.

By the time his stunned teammates gathered round, Abe had already dialed 9-1-1.

Jordan took a knee. "Don't touch him, boys. And stand back, for the luvva Pete!"

Abe snapped his cell phone shut. "We're in luck. Dispatcher said there was a false alarm right up the street. The ambo's just around the corner."

"Couple of you boys open that gate," Jordan barked, pointing at the chain-link fence that surrounded the field.

Half of the Owls ran toward the road while the rest stood, green-and-gold helmets dangling from sweaty, trembling fingers, staring at Winston's motionless body. Mercy stepped up and ushered them aside.

Healye used his sleeve to blot his eyes. "He gonna be OK, Dr. Samara?"

Before she could respond, the quarterback said "Man. I sure hope he won't be paralyzed for life, like the kid in that *Friday Night Lights* movie."

She slid an arm around Healye's shoulders and led him away from the group. "This is football," she stated. "Everybody knows it's a rough game and that you were only doing your job. What happened was just . . . just a freak accident, but I'm sure Winston will be fine." She smiled, but her heart wasn't in it. "He probably just got the wind knocked out of him."

Healye nodded, but his demeanor made it clear he wasn't buying a word of it.

"Do you hear sirens?"

"Yeah, thank *God!*"

Mercy gave him a sideways hug. "Don't you worry. Before you know it, Winston will be back on the field, giving you a run for your money."

"Maybe." Then, "Should we say a prayer or somethin'?"

It had been a long, long time since Mercy believed in the healing power of prayer. She considered citing studies and news reports that outlined what the high courts had decided on public prayer, but thought better of it. If calling on an uncaring, unresponsive heavenly power brought these kids a moment of peace, what harm could it do?

When the boys gathered close and bowed their heads, they stood and waited, their silence making it clear they expected *her* to do the honors. Thankfully, the approaching ambulance saved her from having to concoct a believable entreaty.

The EMTs whipped the vehicle around and backed as close to Winston's stock-still body as possible, kicking up dust and bits of dried grass as they lurched to a stop.

Two EMTs jumped from the cab. "Did anybody touch him?" asked the driver.

Mercy read "McElroy" on his name tag as the coach answered "Nope, and he hasn't moved—not so much as a pinky—since he hit the ground, either."

The paramedics grabbed a backboard and raced to Winston's side. She saw the flash of scissors as they slit his shirt from hem to neck, a blur of white as the cervical collar snapped into place. Next, they eased him onto the board and carried him to the truck.

The tallest EMT climbed in beside the boy, and, after covering Tommy's face with a clear-plastic mask, adjusted the dials of the oxygen tank. Round disks were taped to the boy's broad, hairless chest to monitor his vitals, and a needle inserted into a blue vein on the back of his hand. Immediately, glucose trickled from a bulging bag.

When he turned to thump the snaky length of flexible tubing, the breath caught in Mercy's throat, because she would have recognized those long-lashed blue eyes at thirty yards, even in a crowd at Penn Station. Thankfully, he seemed far too busy to notice her.

"What hospital you takin' him to, mister?" Healye asked.

"Bayview." Before anyone could fire off another question, McElroy added, "And if any of you follow us over there, you're to drive the speed limit, you hear? We don't need another patient in the ER!"

Austin met Healye's teary eyes. "You the boy who hit him?"

Healye nodded.

"Well, don't worry, son. We'll take good care of him, and so will the staff at the hospital. You've got my word on it."

McElroy slid behind the steering wheel, revved the engine and fired up the siren as Austin climbed into the back with his patient. He grabbed the left door handle and pulled it shut with a bang. Reaching for the right one, he met Mercy's gaze. "*You're a long way from home,*" he said, grinning as he slammed it.

5

After delivering the battered football player to Bayview, Austin and his partner hung around for the traditional fifteen minutes, just in case the attendings had questions. They were leaning against the counter, sipping strong, stale coffee and chatting with the ladies in Admitting when the coaches and a couple dozen Owls poured into the ER waiting room.

Jordan marched forcefully up to them and crossed both arms over his chest, reminding Austin of his own football coach. "So what's the prognosis, boys?"

"Last we heard," McElroy offered up, "his vitals were strong and steady."

"That's a good sign, right?" Abe put in.

Austin opened his mouth to answer when he spotted Dr. Samara passing through the double sliding doors. She looked like a little kid in her ponytail and sporty get-up. How old could she possibly be, he wondered, doing some basic math in his head. Even if she'd graduated from college and med school early—and it wouldn't surprise him a bit if she had—she couldn't be less than thirty.

Seeing her on the field, looking at the boy with wide-eyed concern, reminded him of the way she'd looked at him the day he lost his cool and blathered nonsensically about the hours and days after 9/11. How many times had he made up his mind to call her, give her a piece of his mind for signing the form that changed the course of his life?

Too many to count, especially during those first agonizing months after he'd quit the force. Caring for his mother in the last year of her life had one positive outcome: It shamed him out of his self-centered self-pity. Taught him a thing or two about faith, too, and by the time his mom joined the angels, he had faced the ugly truth that freed him of bitterness and resentment . . . because he had nothing and no one but his own reckless behavior to blame for the demise of his career.

When he saw her standing behind the ambo, a dozen things shot through his mind, from how gorgeous she looked to what had put her on that football field, hundreds of miles from New York City. He thought of the long-overdue apology he owed her for the brusque speech he'd delivered at the conclusion of their last session.

But he had time now.

He'd worked with McElroy long enough to know it could take him five minutes to deliver his "Bayview is affiliated with Johns Hopkins, so the kid couldn't be in better hands" speech. Austin took advantage of the moment and strolled over to where she stood, looking confused by the painted arrows that usually failed to keep people from getting lost.

"Hey," he said, more than a little surprised at the slight tremor in his voice.

"Hey, yourself."

It had been years since he'd been this close to her. He'd almost forgotten that despite being barely bigger than a minute, she had the largest, longest-lashed eyes he'd ever seen. Pocketing his hands, he said, "So . . . what're you doing here?"

"I'm here to check on my student, of course."

She sounded incredulous, as if she expected that somehow, he'd know that important fact. Now, in addition to wondering what she was doing in Maryland, he wanted to know why she'd left the police department. *Couldn't handle the nutjobs like you . . . ?*

Austin cleared his throat. "You're a teacher now?"

A soft laugh prefaced her response. "Hardly!" She adopted a slightly more serious expression to add, "It isn't easy to admit, but I don't have the patience for lesson plans and paper grading." She sent him a half smile and shrugged. "So these days, I'm a guidance counselor."

Her matter-of-fact response reminded him of the way she'd conducted ninety-nine percent of their sessions. Only once had she allowed him a glimpse of the *real* Mercy Samara. Reminded him, too, that she had a talent for putting music to even the most ordinary words.

Both perfectly arched brows rose as she nodded toward the ER's double doors. "I suppose it's too soon to expect a report on Tommy."

What *was* it about her! Back in their "session" days, he'd spent most of his time searching his mind for ways to get her off his back. And now all he only wanted to erase that worried look on her face. "I, ah . . ." He jerked a thumb over his shoulder. "I could go back there, see what I can find out, if you like."

"Oh, would you?" Now those big, dark eyes focused on the team and the coaches, gathered in a tight semi-circle around McElroy, still singing the praises of the staff. "I'm sure an update will ease their minds, too."

The hospital's entry doors slid open to admit a couple whose curly blond hair and green eyes identified them as the injured kid's parents. Austin walked toward them. "Mr. and Mrs. Winston?"

The man made a half-hearted attempt to extend a hand in greeting, but the woman held tight, preventing it. "Where's our boy?" she demanded.

He'd have to be deaf not to hear the brittle fear and worry in her voice. He'd seen that *look* before, too. Unfortunately, it identified her as the type who'd faint dead away at the first sight of her son, connected to monitors and tubes. Last thing the poor kid needed when he regained consciousness was a hysterical mama hovering over him. Austin definitely didn't envy the doctors and nurses who'd have to contend with *this* two-legged tiger.

He raised a hand, traffic-cop style, hoping they'd read it as their signal to stay put. "Let me find out where he is," he said, backpedaling toward the exam area. "Soon as I know something, I'll be back."

As he shoved through the double doors, he saw Mercy approach them. The Winstons didn't know it yet, but he'd had years to figure out that they couldn't be in better hands. And when this latest family crisis ended, he'd find a way to tell her exactly that.

6

Mrs. Winston blotted her eyes on a pink tissue. "I *knew* this would happen if he played football," she whimpered. "I don't know why I let your father talk me into signing those papers. Just look at you. Why, you look as though you were hit by a bus!"

"I sorta was," Tommy said. "That's been Healye's nickname since last season."

"Don't be a smart-mouth."

"But Mom, it's true. Just ask my coach or any of—"

"If I *ever* have the displeasure of seeing your Mr. Jordan again," she sniffed, "he won't soon forget what I have to say about his so-called *coaching* skills!" She aimed her next barb at her husband. "Well, are you happy now?"

Her husband heaved a resigned sigh and hung his head. "Lorna," he droned, "the boy tried out for the team because *he* wanted to, not because I played the game in college."

"Oh, fine," she huffed, dropping onto the seat of the green vinyl chair beside Tommy's bed. "If lying to yourself eases your conscience, then by all means—"

"Hey, guys," Mercy interrupted, "will you join me in the cafeteria? It's been a long, tiring afternoon, and I'm sure you could both use a break."

Mrs. Winston simultaneously crossed her legs and arms—a not-too-subtle hint that she intended to stay put, and woe to the person who tried to change her mind. But Mercy could be stubborn, too, when the situation demanded it.

She stepped between Mrs. Winston's chair and Tommy's bed. Patting the boy's hand, she said, "Didn't I hear you say earlier, Mr. Winston, that you haven't had a bite to eat since breakfast?"

He sent her a tiny, grateful smile. "That's right."

"And I'm sleepy," Tommy said. "I could sure use a nap."

Mercy winked at him. "Y'know, you do look a little pale."

And so it was agreed. They'd join Mercy just long enough to grab a quick bite, giving their son a chance to rest up after his ordeal.

Neither parent spoke as they rode the elevator down to the first floor, and the uncomfortable silence continued as they stood, waiting their turn to choose between chicken, meatloaf, and burgers. Finally, at the end of the line, as Mercy paid for all three meals, husband and wife agreed on something. "You shouldn't have, Dr. Samara."

"It's my pleasure," she said, meaning it. It would have been worth five times the dollar amount to get them away from Tommy's room.

The Winstons sat with their backs to the windows. The darkness outside gave the glass the appearance of black mirrors. Mercy sat across from them, and, ignoring her reflection, slid her tray across the speckled Formica table. "You've done a wonderful job with Tommy," she admitted. "He's a delightful boy."

Tommy's mother looked so young and pretty when she smiled. Mercy hoped the little spiel she seemed determined to deliver wouldn't erase it.

"About five years ago," she began, "my dad was injured on the job and spent six grueling months in the hospital, so I know how stressful and exhausting it can be for family members. Fortunately," she said, draping a paper napkin over her knees, "Tommy will be home by this time next week. Even so, you'll need to pace yourselves, maybe alternate visits, so one of you can rest while the other is with him."

Mr. Winston didn't need convincing, as evidenced by his agreeable grin. But if the thin-lipped grimace on his wife's face was any indicator, it would take a little more work to persuade her.

"I'm sure the doctors have already explained that he'll need a lot of one-on-one care after he gets home. Might be a few weeks before he can get himself into and out of bed without help, and he's a big boy!" She poured a dab of mustard onto her hot dog. "I wish somebody had advised *me* to take advantage of my dad's round-the-clock hospital care!"

If she'd had to guess, Mercy would have said *Mr.* Winston, not his wife, would agree with her. "You make a good point," the woman said. "He *is* a big boy!" She looked at her husband. "What do you think, honey?"

"I think Miss Samara is an angel, that's what I think." He kissed his wife's cheek, then grinned at Mercy. "I detect a slight New York accent. Were you born there?"

"Actually, I was born in England. My parents met when they were students at Oxford, and after graduation, they were both hired by . . ." Though proud of their chosen careers, Mercy sidestepped the truth. ". . . a government agency."

"What kind of name is 'Samara'?" Mrs. Winston asked. "Jewish?"

At times like these, she wished she'd followed her father's example. On the day he became a U.S. citizen, he'd changed his name from Samara to Samuels. After 9/11, he changed careers, too, and traded the prestige and salary of a U.N. translator for a demanding job as a delivery boy. But try as he might to out-run the suspicion and mistrust aroused by his dark skin and jet-black hair, he couldn't escape the prejudice of a population still hurting because of the actions of his former countrymen. To this point, she'd been nothing but pleasant, blaming Mrs. Winston's rudeness as the unsavory result of her concern for her son. She'd do her level best not to appear rude, but she would *not* answer the woman's question.

"Heavens," she said, pretending to read her watch. "I had no idea it was so late!"

She got to her feet and shouldered her purse.

"But you haven't had a bite," Mrs. Winston said. "You're going to let all this food go to waste?"

Mercy felt no need to answer that question, either. "I should have checked the time before I sat down. Feel free to help yourself. Or bring the tray to Tommy. As you pointed out, I hardly touched it!" Then, in a slightly less brittle tone, she added, "My poor cat will think I've abandoned him." Shoving her chair under the table, Mercy waved. "It's been a delight visiting with you, though I wish we could have gotten acquainted under better circumstances."

She'd been rambling and knew it, but seemed powerless to stop the steady flow of words. "I'll stop by in a few days to see Tommy," she added, picking up her tray. "My neighbor's husband subscribes to *Sports Illustrated*. If he has any old issues lying around, I'll bring them, to give Tommy something to do besides watch TV."

Shut up, Mercy. Just—shut—up!

"Thanks for supper," Mr. Winston said.

"Yes, thank you," his wife agreed.

"My pleasure!" *Liar*, she thought, making a beeline for the door. Nothing about this day had been pleasurable.

Head down, she rummaged through her purse in search of her keys. For months now, she'd been threatening to buy a new one, something smaller, with pockets and compartments and zippers where she could store her wallet and cell phone and sunglasses. And a clip to hold her keys! Tomorrow, first thing, she'd go to the mall and—

Mercy never finished the thought, because she plowed straight into Austin Finley.

7

$\mathcal{A}$ustin stared at the ceiling, wondering how a woman half his size managed to put him flat on his back.

"Ohmygoodness!" she said, kneeling beside him. "I'm so sorry. Are you all right? I'm sorry," she said again. "I'd just had the most uncomfortable—" She waved a hand in front of her face, as if shooing an annoying mosquito. "Silly me. You don't want to hear about that!" Laughing, Mercy added, "I was looking for my keys. Didn't even see you out here. Are you all right?"

"I'm fine," he said, levering himself onto one elbow. "Dumbfounded that somebody no bigger than a minute packs such a wallop, but otherwise, I'm OK."

Austin pretended not to notice when she held out a hand to help him up, because no way a gal her size could stand him upright again. He got up and started dusting himself off, and to his surprise, Mercy helped him. Her little hands, patting his back, his chest and upper arms, were unexpectedly strong. And warm. Whether she stopped because people were staring or because he was staring, he couldn't say, but it took every ounce of self control he could muster to keep from saying, "Don't pay them any mind."

"What're you still doing here?" they asked in unison.

"Just stopped by to check on the football kid," he said while she sputtered, "Trying to give Tommy a minute's peace from his hovering mother."

Then she faced him and pointed into the cafeteria. "Were you going in there for coffee?"

"Yeah," he said, nodding. "Thought I'd grab a sandwich to eat on the way home." But he sensed a warning in her words, and added "Why?"

"Trust me. Don't waste your money. The coffee's so thick you can stand a spoon in it. You'll get a fresher cup at the Double T Diner."

Instinct made him lick his lips. "I'd suggest we head over there together, but I take it you've already eaten."

She waved the question away. "I put a bunch of stuff on my tray, mostly so the Winstons would follow suit, but I didn't eat a bite." Another giggle, and then, "Truth is, I'm starving."

He'd dated his share of women, here in Maryland and back in New York, but not one had made his palms damp and his ears hot. Hadn't made his heart beat double-time, just by *looking* at him, either.

He'd better make a decision, fast, because if she kept looking up at him that way, blinking those oh-so-perfect brown eyes, he might just have to kiss that oh-so-perfect mouth. He'd always been drawn to tall women, blue-eyed blonds and brassy redheads who wore bright lipstick and ebony mascara. The top of Mercy's head barely reached his shoulder, and while she had curves in all the right places, he'd hardly call her buxom. He saw her as smart and funny, and—as evidenced by what she'd done for Tommy—big-hearted, too. He could do worse, he supposed. A whole lot worse. "You want to meet me over there? Or, I'm happy to drive you, bring you back here so you can pick up your ca—"

"Well, well, Dr. Samara," Mrs. Winston said, "I take it you've called a neighbor to feed your cat?"

Austin grinned at her. "You don't strike me as the cat lady type."

Mercy laid a hand on his forearm and answered the woman. "I was just getting ready to give Mr. Finley, here, directions to my place. We're old friends—knew each other in New York!— and he hasn't seen it yet."

Friends? Austin bristled slightly at the term, because like it or not, he wanted to be more than just her friend.

Tommy's parents exchanged a knowing smile, then hurried into the elevator. "You kids have fun, now," Mr. Winston said.

Last thing they heard before the doors slid shut was Mr. Winston's hearty laughter.

Austin waited a moment before saying "Was that invitation for their benefit, to get rid of them quicker?"

"No." She shrugged. "Makes no sense to pay for food when I have leftover spaghetti and meatballs in the fridge." Another shrug. "It'll save you having to drive me all the way back here to fetch my car afterward."

Meaning she *would* have let him drive her to the Double T? The notion made him smile.

"Besides," she continued, "as those kids so astutely pointed out, we *are* grownups."

He played along with her. "With strict instructions to have fun."

She pulled a tablet from her purse and grabbed the ball-point clipped to his shirt pocket and started scribbling. "In case we get separated," she said, tearing off the top page and tucking it into his pocket.

Not a chance that's gonna happen, he thought as she put the pen back where she'd found it.

What a difference from their heated exchanges in her tiny office! A mental image of it flickered through his head, making him wonder if her house was just as cramped and cluttered. But he didn't bother asking, because he'd find out soon enough. He'd always been a realist. And a bit of a pessimist, too. Surely this newfound ease between them wouldn't last, so what did it matter if her place looked like a sty? Because no way he'd spend a lot of time over there.

The admission disappointed him more than he cared to admit, souring his good mood.

When they reached the stairwell leading into the parking garage, Mercy said, "Do you have a GPS?"

"Nah. I only live a mile from the station, and there's a GPS on every truck." He held the door, and as she stepped into the garage, added, "Never saw much point in investing in one."

Mercy sighed.

"What . . . ."

"That's my car over there, Mister-Map-in-His-Head," she said, pointing at a plain gray sedan. "Without a GPS, I'd spend half my time driving in circles around the city. Fells Point is gorgeous on foot, but it's confusing as can be when you're behind the wheel."

If he'd read her address correctly, she lived on Merchant's Row, an easy commute to I-83 by way of Fleet and President Streets. Making a part-time job of getting lost? It seemed the only trait Mercy shared with other gals he'd known. "How do you get to work?"

"Boston Street to Dundalk Avenue to Holabird."

"Ah, and then a quick shot to Delvale . . . ."

"Right."

What in the world had gotten into him? He could count on one hand the number of times he'd wasted this much breath on small talk—especially with a woman—and have fingers left over. Since his days in therapy, he'd become a bit of an armchair shrink, and now he blamed his behavior on the emotions aroused by seeing her in person after so many years of picturing her in his head.

She unlocked her driver's door and opened it. One foot in and one out of the car, she said, "See you over there, then."

Mercy didn't wait for him to find his pickup. Instead, she headed for the exit like a woman being pursued by a bad guy. Is that how she saw him, thanks to those borderline temper tantrums in her office?

Borderline, my big fat foot, he thought, pocketing both hands as he headed for his truck. Everyone, it seemed, from his folks to his twin and now his coworkers had found occasion to accuse him of making mountains out of molehills. So maybe he was reading too much into the look on her face, the one that wavered between regret and concern. Construction on I-95, or traffic between here and her house could just as easily have inspired it as the invitation—and his acceptance of it.

Stomach grumbling as he turned over the engine, Austin wished he'd taken a few minutes to grab a bite, because those corn flakes he'd wolfed down at breakfast didn't have much sticking power. Should he stop and pick up something on his way to Fells Point, save her the bother of heating up the leftovers? Couple of crab cake sandwiches sure would hit the spot. Then again, what if Mercy hadn't gone as nuts over the traditional Maryland staple as he had? What if she was one of those unlucky people with seafood allergies? Better to play it safe, he told himself, and grab a pizza. And he knew just the place to get one, too.

8

Rather than wait twenty minutes for the deli to bake a fresh pizza, Austin bought one of the cheese-only pies, already warming under a heat lamp. The scent of spicy sauce and yeasty crust assaulted his nostrils during the final miles of his drive. He hoped he wouldn't have to park too far from her townhouse, because he might just devour it before he got a chance to ring her bell.

He'd half expected that Mercy would live in one of the old row houses that resembled New York's brownstones. Austin did a double-take when he read the address above her blue-painted steel door. The porch light illuminated six matching concrete steps, and lit a chrome buzzer, as well. He pushed it, then leaned his backside against the black wrought-iron railing, his gaze scaling the three-story brick façade. Tall, many-paned windows—trimmed in the same shade of steely blue—sparkled in the warm glow of the street lamp. Evidently, she'd entered the house by way of the garage, because mail poked out of the mailbox.

He'd barely plucked it from the box when the door swung open as if propelled by a fierce wind. In the enormous slate-floored foyer, she looked tinier and even more like a kid than she had before.

"Thanks for grabbing my mail," she said, tossing it into a big oval bowl on the narrow table against the wall.

He held out the pizza box. "To save you the trouble of dirtying a pot and plates . . . ."

"Wow. Heroic, and thoughtful, too." Shoving the door closed with her keister, she relieved him of the box. "What's your preference, living room sofa or kitchen table?"

Austin shrugged, feeling like a red-faced schoolboy on his first date. "Your house, your choice."

Mercy led the way into the kitchen, her flip-flops slapping the soles of her feet with every tiny step. After plopping the pizza box onto a four-by-six-foot slab of black granite that topped a cherry cabinet, she said "Let me grab some plates and napkins and something to wash the pizza down, and we can watch the news while we eat." Almost as an afterthought, she tacked on, "Unless you'd rather watch something else—"

"News is about *all* I watch," he admitted. Then, "Wow. This is some room. Did you design it?"

Her laughter echoed in the big space. "You must have me confused with someone who understands color and layout. I bought the place furnished, sight unseen—unless you count photos on the Internet. All I had to do was unpack my clothes and a few personal things, and voila, home."

"How long have you been here?"

She grabbed a couple of bottles of mineral water from the restaurant-sized fridge and stood them beside the pizza. "Going on three years, now." She flipped open the lid, then took a spatula from the row of utensils hanging beside the sink. "I had an apartment before this."

As if on cue, his stomach growled.

"Help yourself," she said. And as she padded down the hall, tossed over her shoulder, "This was really nice of you!"

She sounded surprised that he could be anything but surly and sarcastic. But rather than dwell on it, Austin dogged her heels. He stood for a minute, waiting as she grabbed a tiny remote. One button turned on the overhead lights; another raised a wide flat-screen from a box made of the same burled wood as the foyer table. Flopping onto the middle curve of the black leather sectional, she kicked off her flip-flops. "Please, make yourself comfortable."

"So . . . ," he said, biting off the point of his pizza, "what made you leave New York?"

She'd fixed her attention on Channel 13 as anchorman Vic Carter announced the latest item about a former child star's latest prison sentence. Unscrewing the cap of her water bottle, her gaze slid to Austin's. "I'll tell you if you'll tell me."

"Ladies first," he agreed.

Mercy took a dainty sip of her water and took her time putting the bottle on the table in front of the sofa. Crossing her legs Indian style, she wrapped a ribbon of cheese around her forefinger. "Too many bad memories up there." A long pause followed her statement. "First, the . . ." She sighed, shrugged, and popped the cheese into her mouth. "After my father was killed," she said around it, "I really had no reason to stay."

Killed? He wanted to ask how the man had died, but her dour tone and the sadness that tinged her big dark eyes kept him quiet.

She brightened slightly to say "Your turn."

Nothing Austin could say about his reasons for moving to Maryland would surprise to her, so he began where the two of them had left off. "My mom and I held a memorial service for Avery about two weeks after 9/11. And about two weeks after that, she was diagnosed with cancer. Fought like a trooper for years, but eventually I had to put her in hospice." He could have given her a list: No job to speak of, no family, no real friends, so why stay? Instead, Austin repeated, almost word for word, what she'd said a moment ago.

"After she died, there wasn't anything to keep me there."

From the look on her face, he expected her to say something sweet and sympathetic. Last thing he'd wanted was for her to feel sorry for him, so he quickly added, "Besides, I was getting bored, living off the money my rich uncle left me."

His flippant remark more than lightened the mood.

"You have a rich uncle?" She slid one cushion closer to his and snickered. "Do tell . . . ."

Oh. Right. Like the gal who could afford *these* digs is impressed by a guy with money in the bank. Austin looked into her warm, smiling face and thanked God that the cold, clinical psychiatrist had left the big city. If she'd been a little more like *this* back then . . .

What a ridiculous thought. Of course things would have turned out exactly the same way. And he had no room to complain. His life here in Maryland had been better in every way than the one he'd left behind. If it took leaving the police force to make him admit that, so be it.

He remembered the dozens of times he'd considered calling her to say how bad he felt about the many out-of-line things he'd said and done. Why not now?

But the anchorman launched into a story about the upcoming tenth anniversary of 9/11. Images flickered on the screen, each with a different angle of the pillars of smoke, black and threatening and taller than the towers had been. The footage was followed by the image of the bright white beacon, rooted at Ground Zero and stabbing into the heavens like a silvery sword, a symbolic promise that on this hallowed ground new buildings would rise in honor of those who died on that history-making date.

"What a load of crap," he snarled, tossing his empty paper plate onto the coffee table. "Do they really think any of us are *buying* this baloney?"

"What baloney?" She scooted closer still.

Austin pointed at the TV, where tourists waited in long lines to catch a glimpse of the flattened plot that had once housed two of the most impressive structures ever built. "*That* baloney. Nothing will bring back all the innocent people who were slaughtered that day. What a colossal waste of electricity, lighting up the sky with that . . . that *baloney*. Like we're a bunch of colicky babies who can be pacified by the sight of a bright light." He balled up his napkin and tossed it onto the table beside the plate.

During the silence that followed his tirade, he drove both hands through his hair and braced himself for the psychobabble that would no doubt spew from her lips.

"You're right."

Well, he certainly hadn't expected *that*. Nor had he expected the simple report to stir up a myriad of emotions—from anger to pain to bitter regret—that pinged from his heart to his head to his soul. He'd pushed himself hard, and because he had, Austin could finally ride an elevator and climb long flights of stairs without breaking into a sweat. He held tight to the hope that one day, news like this wouldn't wake hard memories, either. "If you're wondering if it'll ever go away, completely," she said quietly, "I'm afraid it won't. The pain gets dimmer, but gone?" She shook her head. "Nope. Never."

She said it like someone who'd lost a loved one during the bedlam. The notion knifed through him, making him feel guilty and ashamed and self-centered. Why hadn't he considered that possibility before? She'd said her father had been killed. Had he died on 9/11? It surely went a long way to explain why she'd seemed impatient as he struggled to cope with his losses. No wonder she'd written him up as a head case for storming out of her office after just six sessions of the mandated ten, angrier than when he'd first entered it. During those few hours with him, Mercy came to know him better than he knew himself, yet he didn't know the first thing about her, and he felt regretful about that.

He sat forward and assumed what she'd once termed his "analysis pose," elbows on knees, hands clasped in the space between. "I'm sorry, Mercy," he said, meaning it.

"Sorry? Whatever for?"

He hung his head. "I always knew that the cops and firefighters who survived Ground Zero walked away carrying some heavy emotional baggage. But until now, I never gave a thought to how it might have affected *you*."

When Austin met her eyes, it stunned him to see tears rolling down her cheeks. "Aw, jeez," he said, "what did I say? Whatever it was, I'm sorry. Honest."

Using her free hand, she blotted her eyes on a paper napkin. With the other, she massaged her temple. Lips trembling, she whispered, "It wasn't you. It's just—" She groaned and shook her head. "What you're going through is perfectly normal. I just want you to know that."

Pain had stolen the music in her voice and left her brow furrowed. He wanted to give the comfort she seemed to need—and absorb some, too—by holding her close. But what if, by opening his arms to her, he unearthed memories she'd hidden deep in her heart, instead?

She heaved a huge sigh. "I suppose it can be said that the two of us are resilient, if nothing else."

He mirrored her smile. "Oh? How so?"

"We aren't the type to wallow in self-pity." She grinned and held out her hands, palms up. "Just look how fast we straightened ourselves up after our little pity party. I'd say that's a good thing, wouldn't you?"

She blew her nose, and it made him chuckle that someone as petite and delicate as Mercy could produce a sound on a par with a Mack truck's horn blast.

"What's so funny?"

"Well, you didn't hear *me* trying to mimic a foghorn."

Eyes wide, she gasped, then got onto one knee to look behind him.

"What're you doing?"

"Looking for your mean streak, that's what. I would have bet my fancy remote control it was back there, and every bit as wide as your back, too."

Kneeling on the cushion beside him that way, she was close enough to kiss. Austin grabbed both slender shoulders and gave her a gentle shake, and stared deep into those amazing green-flecked brown eyes. "Mercy, Mercy, Mercy," he breathed, closing his own. He'd almost kissed her that day in her office, and unless he'd been seriously mistaken, she would have let him. If he had a lick of sense, he'd plant one right on those oh-so-perfect lips, right now.

But common sense rose above manly urges and warned him that only an idiot would start up a relationship with his former shrink. *Think of all the ammunition she'd have in her arsenal, using your own words against you every time we have a disagreement.* And history told him there would definitely be disagreements!

"So . . . tell me," he said, releasing her, "how'd you get a name like Mercy? And," he added, looking around, "where's this *cat* of yours?"

9

Mercy bounced over to her original sofa cushion and cut loose with a high-pitched whistle that made Austin cup both hands over his ears. "Holy moly, woman! I hope that mouth of yours is registered as a deadly weapon!"

"Sorry, but you know what they say. . . ."

"What who says?"

"The sages."

"About . . . ?"

"Careful what you ask for."

"Now I'm the one who's sorry."

She grinned. "Why?"

"Because I've completely lost my train of thought."

"That's what happens," she said lightly, "when you have a one-track mind."

A fat orange stripe-tabby waddled into the room, leaped onto the couch, and headed straight for Austin.

"Meet Woodrow, who comes when whistled for and enjoys welcoming guests to our humble home."

After sniffing Austin from ear to elbow, Woodrow swaggered to Mercy and climbed into her lap. Amid her cooing and petting, Austin noticed a four-inch scar that started at the pad of her left thumb and ran halfway up her arm. He leaned forward to see if she had one to match it on the other side, because if she did . . . .

During his career as an EMT, he'd rushed nine patients to the ER—females, except for one—who'd attempted suicide with a slice that ran crosswise on their wrists. If they'd slashed a bit deeper, or had been left alone longer, they might well have died at their own hands. Only one had been determined enough to succeed, mostly because of the elongated cuts she'd carved into her forearms.

It almost seemed that Woodrow had repositioned himself on Mercy's lap for the sole purpose of giving Austin a clear line of vision to his mistress's right arm. Sure enough, an identical white line ran the length of that one, too. He'd read someplace that of all the professionals who commit suicide, psychiatrists were at the top. He remembered that day in her office when the tower of books toppled to the floor, and, thinking it had been a test, he'd blasted her. His roaring had triggered a memory of some kind, and in place of the condescending, long-suffering look he'd expected to see, pain glittered in her dark eyes.

Austin was reminded again that he knew next to nothing about Mercy Samara, police department psychiatrist turned high school guidance counselor. During the seconds that passed as she cuddled and cooed to her cat, his mind went to war with his heart.

Everything about her appealed to him, yet he felt a powerful urge to turn tail and run. For one thing, he'd barely come to terms with his own gloomy past. For another, she seemed at peace with her new life, despite the tell-tale white scars. What if running into him after all this time had opened Pandora's box, and reminded her of the reasons she'd picked up that blade in the first place?

Back off, he told himself. *Just back off and give the poor woman some space.* God knew she deserved a better man than the likes of Austin Finley. Besides, what made him think she had so much as an inkling of interest in him!

She looked up and caught him staring. Flustered, Austin chuckled nervously. "So, before you tell me how you got your unusual name, how 'bout telling how your fat cat got *his*?"

Her left brow lifted slightly, the way it had during sessions, a sure sign that what she said and what she thought were two completely different things. *OK, so you do know a thing or two about her. But that doesn't mean—*

"Woodrow is a small hamlet in Amersham. Sounds stuffy, doesn't it? And when I first met this big ball of fur, that's how he struck me." She stroked the cat's nose and said "Stuffy." Then, "My mother was born there."

"Amersham? As in England?"

Mercy nodded. "She spent the first fifteen years of her life there, dreaming of ways to escape Buckinghamshire."

Interesting, Austin thought. "But she took you there, for family visits, right?"

A strange expression flickered across her face. Regret? Resentment? His questions were answered by the brittle edge to her voice when she said, "Mother died when I was ten, before I was old enough to figure out that she didn't want to go back. Ever."

He didn't see himself as the curious type, but Austin found himself considering all the ways Mrs. Samara might have died, especially after hearing that Mercy's father had been killed. Woodrow ambled across the couch cushion between his mistress and her guest, and promptly made himself comfortable in Austin's lap. Grinning, he scratched behind the cat's ears. "Now that the story of how this guy got his name has been told, why don't you tell me how you got yours."

"Have you ever looked up the word 'mercy' in the dictionary?"

"I guess it must have been on a list of vocabulary words or a spelling assignment back in grade school." Woodrow's hearty purring reached his ears, broadening his smile.

"Most folks think it means forgiveness," she said, "and it does. But it also means compassion. My mother's parents didn't approve of her relationship with my dad. They even went so far as to threaten to disown her because of his heritage."

So her folks were prejudicial bigots. "Good thing they're not around to meet me, then," he said. But his laughter died a quick death when he realized what a silly comment might sound like to Mercy. "It's just . . . with my, uh, with my past issues, and the reasons I left the department and all, they might get the idea I'm—"

"No, you would have passed their litmus test. With flying colors."

Austin didn't get it, and said so.

"You could be a Brit with those blue eyes and blond hair. But even Irish or Scottish would have been more tolerable than—"

"They didn't like—" He paused, not knowing how to refer to her father's nationality without sounding like a bigot himself.

"Don't be afraid to say it. I'll grant you it's a four-letter word, but not one of the unacceptable ones. At least, not in *all* circles." She slid closer, her tiny hands manipulating his lower jaw. "Arab," she said, exaggerating the pronunciation. "Aah-*rub.* Go ahead, now you try it."

"Arab," he echoed, feeling every bit like the ventriloquist's dummy. "But you're not getting off the hook that easily. No way. Nuh-uh. All this skirting the question has me more curious than ever."

"Curious? About?"

He saw the teasing glint in her eye, and it made him want to kiss her for the second time since he'd arrived. Oh, who was he kidding? He'd wanted to kiss her that day in her office, when she took hold of his wrists and swore that she hadn't been testing him. The truth of it? He really *did* want to know why her folks had named her Mercy. "About the reason your parents chose such an unusual name for their only daughter."

"Who says I'm an only child?"

Another bit of proof that he knew diddly about her, but Austin decided to call her bluff. "You did."

"Oh." She shrugged. "Actually, I have a half-brother. We've not kept in touch, I'm afraid."

From her expression, Austin couldn't tell if she'd written the rules that kept her and her brother apart, if it had been the brother's doing, or if it had only been a matter of miles that separated them. But something in her voice made him think Mercy would have liked more time with her only sibling.

"Mom was quite the free spirit in high school. Afterward, too. Ran around with hippy types, spent a few summers in communes, a few more following some rock band through Ireland. How she knew who fathered her 'love child' is anybody's guess, but Leo lived most of his life with his dad in London. A week at Christmas or in the summertime didn't give us much opportunity to bond."

"Spared you the whole sibling rivalry nonsense, at least."

"I suppose." She sighed. "Leo became a plastic surgeon, just like his father. You wouldn't believe his patient list—rock stars, movie moguls, politicians and their spouses. He's in great demand at the London Bridge Hospital, and—"

"London Bridge Hospital? You're kidding," he said, grinning. "Right?"

She held her hand up as if swearing an oath. "I'm as serious as serious can be. It's a lovely old building on Toohey Street, and yes, it's near *that* London Bridge."

"But I thought they moved it to Arizona or something."

"The original, ornate version, yes. But the city rebuilt it, naturally. How else would people get from one side of the Thames to the other?"

He chose to ignore the bored tone that told him she'd covered this ground before, many times. "When was the last time you saw him? Your brother, I mean."

A deep furrow formed between her eyebrows. "March 2003," she said dully; "not long after you turned in your badge and gun."

How could she have known *when* he resigned . . . unless she'd checked up on him? The notion touched him. Confused him, too. Now he regretted even more that he hadn't called to apologize for walking out without so much as a phone call, if only to see how *she* was faring. He'd never been able to figure out what, exactly, happened between them as they'd stood, hands and gazes united by the common bond of tragedy, but Austin knew he'd never forget that moment. Had Mercy remembered it too?

"Things never quite returned to normal after 9/11 for anybody," she said, slowly, softly. "For a few years, I tried pep-talking myself into the notion that as a psychiatrist I should be able to handle things better than most. I stayed with Leo for nearly two months, then decided it was time to come home and face the music."

When he stormed out of her office that day, Austin pretty much left the worst of the tragedy behind him. Not so for Mercy, whose job required her, hour after hour, to read anguish on the faces of her patients.

Her shoulders lifted with a dainty sigh. Then she forced a smile and said, "Turns out I developed a real aversion for that music. By year-end, I'd put in my resignation, too."

She'd been so happy, so animated before he opened his big mouth. Austin felt like a heel for making her relive even a sliver of that part of her life. "But we digress," he said, grinning. "You were about to tell me how you came by that remarkable name of yours."

"Oh, I don't know how remarkable it is. In fact, it's a simple story, really." She leaned against the back cushion. "Hard feelings were rampant on both sides of my DNA fence." She held out her right hand, palm up. "Here's Mom, with her illegitimate son." She held up the left. "And Dad, whose ethnicity wasn't at all to her parents' liking." Mercy clasped her hands, then snapped them quickly apart. "None of the parents attended the wedding, and according to legend and lore, my birth provided the merciful balm that allowed them to at least tolerate the marriage."

"Like Romeo and Juliet, only without the gloomy ending."

"If you say so." She waved the notion away. "And what about you?"

"The reason my name is Austin, y'mean?"

Weird, he thought, that all it took was a smile from Mercy to send his heart into overdrive. *Just answer her question, idiot!* "This cat of yours purrs louder than my boat's rusty motor." At least now he could pretend that if she could hear his heartbeat, she'd blame it on Woodrow.

"I have to admit, I'm a bit jealous. He's never taken to a stranger this way before."

"You know what they say about kids and animals . . . ."

"That they're naïve and innocent and easily fooled?"

The sound of her laughter set his nerves to jangling. *If you know what's good for you, you'll get out of here, and fast.*

Instead, he said "When my dad was stationed at Fort Hood, he and his buddies drove to Austin on a three-day pass. Mom was a waitress in the diner where they ate all their meals. Love at first sight, or so the story goes. They were married a few months later—and honeymooned in Austin."

"And Avery?"

It shouldn't have surprised him that she remembered his twin's name. She was smart. And she'd taken notes. But when had she read them last? "Because when my grandmother got her first look at him, she said he resembled an elf. And Avery means 'ruler of the elves' or some such thing."

Mercy giggled. "I love it!"

The modern teak-and-stainless clock on the stone wall above her fireplace chimed nine times. "Wow," he said, setting Woodrow aside, "how can it be nine o'clock already?"

She stood, too, and lifted a flat-eyed Woodrow into her arms. "He isn't very happy with you for disrupting his nap."

"Sorry, Woodie ol' boy, but me 'n' my lap have to work the first shift tomorrow."

The cat responded with a bored yawn, and, turning his back on Austin, snuggled deeper into Mercy's arms.

"Guess I'd better hit the road."

"It's been—pleasant."

Why the hesitation? he wondered.

". . . the pizza, conversation, learning how you got your unusual name," she added, joining him on the porch.

Austin felt like the bobble-head Cocker Spaniel that once perched beneath the rear window of his grandpa's Oldsmobile. "Yeah, yeah it was nice. Real nice." Disappointment drummed in his heart when she didn't invite him back. But what was stopping him from suggesting that they get together again?

He knew the answer even before the question fully formed in his head. Austin needed time to process the unsettling up-

and-down emotions she'd stirred in him. Time to figure out if being around her felt so good—well, *mostly* good, anyway—because he'd been alone too long, or if Mercy could be "the one"?

That's just plain crazy, he thought, jogging down the steps. Last thing he needed was some woman—one who knew almost every detail of his life, no less—messing with his head. Worse yet, with his heart.

From the sidewalk, he looked up into her angelic face, and before he knew it, Austin heard himself ask if maybe she'd like to share another pizza with him, soon, at his place next time.

Mercy tilted her head as the hint of a smile lifted one corner of her mouth. "You know, I don't think I've ever been on a fully functioning houseboat."

Not exactly a "yes," but then, she hadn't said "no," either.

"Good, good," he said, hoping as he backpedaled toward his truck that he wouldn't trip on a crack and end up flat on his back. Again. "OK, then. I'll give you a call, and we'll set something up."

For the past year or so, the driver's door of his pickup squealed something fierce every time he pulled it open. Until tonight, it had never bothered him enough to drag out the oil can. But when its racket drowned out the last words Mercy uttered before she closed her front door, he decided to take care of the problem. Tomorrow. The minute he got home from work.

And when he finished with that, he'd scrub the tug from stem to stern, so that every square inch would sparkle when she visited. Then he'd ask Flora to suggest a recipe that would wow Mercy without exposing his complete lack of culinary skills. And make a quick trip to the discount store for place-mats and matching napkins for the deck table, so that if nature cooperated on the night of her visit, he could serve the meal topside, and share his incredible 360° view of Chesapeake Bay.

So much for worrying about whether or not it was a good idea to move the relationship forward, he thought, pulling into his parking space in the marina lot. He had a feeling it would take days to get the picture out of his mind: Mercy, mimicking Princess Di's parade wave as she mouthed, "See you soon!"

10

Sometimes, all it took to bring on ugly, unsettling dreams was a short clip on the evening news, describing the respiratory illnesses that were ravaging so many of the 9/11 first responders, or maybe an item about a new monument being erected in memory of the innocents slaughtered at Ground Zero, the Pentagon, or the grassy field at Shanksville. This time, Austin blamed the hours he'd spent with Mercy—the one person who had witnessed his weakness, seen him at his lowest after the tragedy—for uprooting the painful thoughts.

More than likely, though, it had been Cora's number in the caller i.d. block of his phone, and the blinking light that told him she'd left another long and rambling message. Dismissing Avery's message that day taught him a lesson—and left him paranoid about ignoring calls, especially from people he cared about.

And he cared a whole lot about Cora and her boys.

Kneeling in the hot ashes after the cave-in, he'd bloodied all ten fingertips trying to pry Eddy free of his steel and concrete prison. Somehow, he found the strength to beg Austin to check on his wife and sons from time to time. "Don't be an idiot," he'd teased. "Just hang on, and you can look after them yourself, just like you always have."

But they'd both passed the department's mandatory CPR classes, and knew full well that Eddy wouldn't last until help arrived. Austin cracked a molar that day, gritting his teeth to keep from bawling like a baby as he made that promise. "Couldn't have asked for a better partner," Eddy whispered, and then his eyes went blank and cold. Austin had been seeing that in his dreams ever since, and didn't doubt for a minute that he'd keep right on seeing it until he joined Eddy in heaven.

Hard experience had taught him that tossing and turning wouldn't get him anywhere. So he had put his sleepless hours to good use, sanding the decks, polishing brass, painting and staining the cupboards and cabinets. If not for nights like this, it would have taken twice as long to turn the neglected old tug into a home he could treasure.

Austin padded into the galley to start a pot of coffee, and while waiting for it to brew, showered and dressed. After making up his bunk, he filled his favorite mug and carried it to the pilot house.

Yawning, he stood at the rail, watching as shimmering ripples danced across the surface of the night-black water. The familiar *quark-quark* of a night heron slid from the shadows, making him wonder what had disturbed its nest.

"Yo, Finley."

Austin instantly recognized the raspy whisper. "Yo, yourself, Bud." He glanced at his wristwatch: Three fifty-two a.m. "What're you doing up at this hour?"

"I could ask the same question," the older man said, and quickly added, "I'm trying to escape Flora's snoring." He stood at attention. "Say, is that fresh coffee I smell?"

The wind was blowing due north, not south toward the Callahans' schooner, so it wasn't likely the scent had snagged a breeze and drifted across the water. Smiling, Austin said, "Sure is."

"Hot dog! I'll be right over."

"Meet me up here. I'll have a mug poured and waiting for you when you get here."

For the past month or so, he'd seen the old gent prowling around on the deck of his schooner at all sorts of odd hours. While emptying the coffee maker's carafe into a Thermos, he recalled the frantic night when Bud suffered a near-fatal heart attack. Fortunately, Austin had been on hand to administer emergency CPR and monitor the situation until the ambulance crew arrived. And he'd been available to take Flora to Johns Hopkins, because the way she'd blubbered all the way there, only the good Lord knew what might have happened if she'd driven the distance alone.

The quadruple bypass saved Bud and greatly improved his quality of life, but that had been nearly three years ago. What if his restlessness had nothing to do with Flora's snoring? What if, instead, it was a sign that his ticker had developed a new problem?

Austin carried the Thermos and an extra mug to the pilot house, praying as he went that the Almighty would continue watching over his friend and neighbor. Because if Bud's hospitalization and recuperation had turned the normally resilient Flora into a woman who trembled and wept every time Bud got out of earshot, what would losing him do to her?

He'd barely settled into his favorite sling-backed chair when the older man's white-haired head poked through the doorway.

"Did you add a couple of rungs to that ladder?"

"You ask the same question every time you come up here," Austin said, laughing.

"Well, it sure seems like a longer walk between visits." He grabbed the Thermos. "Say . . . did you hear that night heron earlier?"

Austin watched the steam rise as Bud filled his mug. "Yeah, weird, isn't it, hearing one way over here?"

Bud grunted slightly as he lowered his bulk into a chair that matched Austin's. "Well, the mouth of the bay ain't all that far away, I s'pose." He pursed his lips. "And it is about time for the fledglings to leave Fisherman's Island."

During the years their boats had been docked side by side, Austin and Bud must have shared hundreds of mugs of coffee while discussing the Orioles' lousy coaching staff and the Ravens' latest draft pick. Taxes, the threat of a rent hike at the marina, and of course, the weather dominated their conversations, but they'd never talked in the middle of the night before.

Bud blew across the surface of his coffee, then took a loud slurp. On the heels of a long, satisfied sigh, he said, "Now, that's what I call good java." Then he frowned. "Hard day, son?"

At first, the term of endearment had rattled Austin. Lately, he'd come to like being part of Bud and Flora's family, even if only in a surrogate way. "No harder than most."

"Bad dreams keepin' you up again, huh?"

He saw no point in saddling the old guy with the gory details. He'd done that once, years ago, after coming home from a bachelor party with a few too many beers in his belly. Even half-toasted, he'd seen how upset he'd made the Callahans, and it bugged him just enough to vow never again to utter a syllable about the terror attacks.

"Well," Bud said in the ensuing silence, "no surprise, there. We're comin' up on another anniversary here soon. All that stuff on the TV news and in the papers? Shoo-eee. No wonder it's front and center in your brain."

Austin only nodded. Hard to believe it had been nearly nine years since—

"Talked to Eddy's widow lately?"

"She left a message while I was out tonight." Later, he'd listen to it. It always took a day or two to screw up the courage to call her back.

The non-answer hung between them like a new-spun spider web. "So," he said, "has Flora developed allergies or something? It's too early for her hay fever to kick in. And from what you've said, it does seem that her snoring has gotten a whole lot worse these past few months."

"Dragged the old girl to the doctor day before yesterday. He said more than likely, it isn't pollen or any of the usual suspects. That quack. Fat lot he knows." Bud waved a hand in the air. "At least the fool helped me make an appointment with a specialist for day after tomorrow. Not a minute too soon, if you ask me, 'cause I can't imagine she's getting much more sleep than I am."

Austin sipped his coffee, waiting for the qualifier that would follow Bud's remark.

"If it reminds *me* of a locomotive, pulling into the station, imagine what it sounds like inside *her* head!"

Austin laughed under his breath. But his smile faded when he remembered how his mom had snored deeper and louder as her final days drew nearer. About the only peace the poor woman got came from listening to CDs of a favorite old radio show, *The Bickersons*. He'd heard some of the episodes so many times he'd memorized a lot of the dialog. Bud and Flora often reminded him of the battling comic duo, but despite the Callahans' salty relationship, he knew each would be a living, breathing mess without the other.

"Doc said if the allergist doesn't find anything, they'll arrange a scan of her head." Snickering, he added, "Now let me be the first to say that those will be some interesting pict—"

"Good Lord A'mighty," came a raggedy voice from across the way, "how's a girl supposed to get her beauty sleep with the two of you over there, chattering like a couple of magpies into the wee hours?"

The men exchanged an amused glance, then Bud put a hand to the side of his mouth. "Watch and learn a thing or three about women, young'un. I'll have her eating out of my hand in no time flat." He ended the sentence with a noisy finger snap, and, raising his chin, looked over at Flora. "And exactly how long have you been up and about, my sweet little Flor-de-lee?"

An audible "Ha!" floated to them before she said, "Long enough to want to hurl my black iron skillet in your direction. Maybe that'll quiet the pair of you down!"

Bud leaned closer to Austin and heaved a sigh of resignation. "Just my luck," he said under his breath, "she woke up with a big ol' grump on."

"I heard that, Liam Kyle Callahan!"

Bud clapped a hand over his eyes. "I do declare, a man can't slip anything past that woman!"

"If you'd get yourself some hearing aids—like I've been after you to—maybe you could slip one by me every now and again."

"Women. Can't live with 'em, and can't live *with* 'em."

While Bud chuckled at his little joke, Flora's voice took on a maternal tone. "All right now, Bud, you've kept that boy from his bed long enough. Why don't you drag your hard-of-hearing bones back over here, and I'll scramble you some eggs so he can get some much-needed sleep." Hands on her hips, she tacked on, "Why, I'll bet he's on the early shift tomorrow, or should I say later this morning!"

Austin knew better than to intervene. He'd tried acting as the peacemaker between these two often enough to know that the gesture would only put him in the line of fire. And wasn't it funny, he thought, that despite all that, he sincerely hoped that if God ever saw fit to bless him with a wife, the woman would have Flora's "love your man and gently keep him in check" skills.

Bud drained the last of his coffee and put his mug on the table between the deck chairs. "If I know what's good for me, I'd better hot-foot it over there before she has to repeat herself. My luck, she'll rouse the rest of the marina, and old Betsy will call the cops to report a disturbance." He started down the ladder, stopping long enough to say, "Catch you later, son. You take care out there, y'hear?"

"Thanks, Bud. I will." He pointed toward the schooner and snickered. "And you take care over *there*."

Minutes later, as the Callahans' quiet laughter drifted to him on a sticky puff of air, Austin leaned back, and, eyes closed, grinned. During his first year out here on the water, he must have told himself a hundred times that the next time he bought property, he'd put plenty of space between him and his neighbors. But as the months rolled by, he knew that if he left this place, he'd miss their well-meaning, good-natured involvement in his life. Like it or not—and the longer he knew them, the better he liked it—the quarrelsome duo were all the family he had in the world.

Admitting that made him think of Mercy, who lived alone in the spacious contemporary townhouse that she shared with an overweight cat named Woodrow. She'd gone out of her way to comfort that kid—Winston?—out there on the football field, and went right on consoling and reassuring him, even after the ER staff had worked their medical magic on him. She had the whole nurturing thing down pat, as evidenced by the way she'd calmed the boy's hovering parents. Prettiest little thing he'd ever seen. So why hadn't she married, popped out a few dark-eyed little kids of her own?

The image of her glimmered in his mind so clearly that he could almost touch her. In fact, he found himself wishing he *could* touch her.

The notion unsettled him, and made him realize that at some point before he saw her again, he'd better give the whole Mercy matter a lot of careful thought, because—

Growling under his breath, he got to his feet. "Get a grip, Finley."

Fingers wrapped tightly around the polished brass rail surrounding the deck, he faced east and stared out over the peaceful Chesapeake, where the first signs of sunrise were winking in the cloudless black sky. A perfect morning to see the green flash.

The first time he spotted it, he'd still been knee-deep in reconstruction materials. A nightmare had driven him topside, where he kicked aside sawed-off two-by-fours and spent sandpaper in an attempt to escape the haunting memories. He remembered thinking that one of two things explained what he saw out there on the horizon: Either he'd added sleepwalking to his list of mental maladies, or it had been an optical illusion. By the time he finished knuckling his eyes, it had disappeared, confirming that it had been a figment of his overworked imagination, and he never mentioned a word about it to anyone, not even Bud and Flora.

Its second appearance drove him to the Internet, where he typed countless words and phrases into his search engine until, at last, he learned about the phenomenon that was a result of scattered air molecules. The emerald flare, he read, appeared only under the right circumstances, and lasted little more than a second.

Blink, and you'll miss it, he reminded himself.

He'd no sooner finished the warning than a burst of bottle-green light sizzled across the horizon and vanished in less than a heartbeat. Hoping to catch sight of a second spark—a far, far rarer occurrence, his research had taught him—Austin held his breath and waited.

A moment passed, then another, with no repeat performance. Meaning he'd blinked despite his best efforts not to, or God had decided one flash was enough on this sticky morning. Contentment quickly replaced disappointment as Mercy's face drifted into his head. If she'd been there to share the miracle with him, would her perfect brows have risen in sync with the corners of her mouth?

"Yep, you're losin' your mind," he muttered, facing the pilot house. Besides, hadn't she said that during her childhood, her folks had owned a sailboat? For all he knew, she'd seen the mini-light show dozens of times, and it wouldn't seem like a big deal to her at all.

Grabbing both mug handles and tucking the Thermos under one arm, he headed down to the galley. It had only been a few days since he'd reconnected with her, yet she popped into his head at the weirdest moments. Like when a songbird rang out a melody, or a soft breeze caressed his face. And without exception, he'd catch himself grinning like a knock-kneed schoolboy.

Sweaty palms and burning ears might have been normal in study hall, when he'd done his best not to let any of his classmates see him gawking at the prom queen, but at this stage of his life? No *way* he liked feeling that he'd lost all control over his thoughts *and* his emotions!

After washing Bud's mug and the Thermos, he propped both in the drain board and emptied the last of the coffee into his cup. TV flickering, he stretched out on the sofa and turned up the volume to hear Jamie Costello read the early morning news. But not even stories of robberies gone wrong and the threat of a hurricane skimming the Atlantic coast could distract him from thoughts of Mercy.

When, exactly, had his feelings for her changed from out-and-out disdain to borderline affection? And would the feelings last, or were they—as Bud said every time Austin brought a woman home for a tour of the tug—"Just a flash in the pan"?

The tiny red-blinking light on his answering machine accomplished what the horizon's green flash and the morning news couldn't, and diverted his attention from the former therapist-turned-counselor.

He wouldn't call Cora now—though he would have bet the boat she hadn't gone to bed—because the boys were light sleepers and needed their sleep a whole lot more than she needed to cry on his shoulder. Besides, if he hoped to administer his usual dose of sympathy and patience, he needed a clear head. Better for him *and* her if he stopped on the way home from work, instead, with a couple of bags of the boys' favorite fast food.

He knew exactly how she'd react when she saw the familiar golden arches on the bags, first listing a dozen university studies that stated the negative after-effects of cheeseburgers, French fries, and chocolate shakes, then blasting him with "that stuff is simply *horrible* for growing children!" After a few minutes of the boys' unrelenting pleas, she'd invite Austin into the parlor, where she'd slide the pocket doors shut so the boys wouldn't hear her list the reasons she resented Eddy. And missed Eddy. And wished Eddy had chosen a safer line of work. As usual, he'd pray all the way to her house that he'd wouldn't lose his cool and blurt "For the love of *God*, Cora, get some counseling, why don't you, so those terrific boys of yours can look up *to* you, instead of looking out *for* you!"

He gave God the credit for reminding him what Mercy had said during one of their first sessions, and thanked Mercy for the words that kept his lips zipped: "Not everyone heals at the same pace or in the same way." It had taken him *years* to break free of his alcohol-induced prison of self-pity, and he hadn't been saddled with the care and well being of two impressionable kids. Who was he to judge how she handled her grief?

A shard of sunlight pierced the galley porthole, illuminating the round-faced captain's clock. Austin padded into the companionway and opened its glass-and-brass door. He'd always loved the gritty *whirr-purr* of the key, turning the gears that would keep the timepiece ticking for another day. A small thing, really, yet it gave him a sense of calm reassurance, because he knew he could depend on it to chime every hour on the hour. "Too bad *people* can't be as reliable," he said, closing the door.

On the way out, he grabbed a banana to quiet his rumbling stomach, and, while walking to his parking space, heard the steady *putt-putt-putt* of a boat motor. At this hour, it couldn't be anyone other than Jed Card, heading out to set his crab pots. The retired Marine never expected a big haul, but if he got one, he celebrated like a kid on Christmas morning. Mostly, though, Jed got his kicks from gliding up and down the Chesapeake's shores, checking his lines and offering two or three free Maryland blues to anyone who called the bay "home."

Jed untied his aluminum johnboat from the piling and tossed the thick rope onto the deck. "What're you doin' up so early, Tugger?"

He'd stuck Austin with the handle two days after the tugboat had been delivered to the dock, and except for Bud and Flora, that's what his neighbors had been calling him ever since.

"Same thing you are."

And Jed only nodded. The war-hardened former soldier was but one of the few who understood Austin's peculiar sleep habits—and his deep need for privacy. He could count on one hand—and have fingers left over—how many people had heard his 9/11 story, and if it hadn't been for that night several years ago, before he joined AA and returned to his Christian roots, Jed wouldn't know the details either.

A pang of gratitude clutched Austin's heart. Like Bud and Flora, Jed was, as his grandpa would say, "good people." In a pinch, he could call on any one of them, and they'd come running. Austin may not have a slew of blood kin, but he had the quiet reassurance of solid family ties, thanks to these three. "So tell me, Card, when are you gonna admit you're the only one in this marina who operates on military time?"

"'Bout the time you quit startin' every sentence with the word 'so.'" His boisterous guffaw startled the roosting water birds into a wing-flapping frenzy. Squinting as their downy gull and tern feathers floated into the boat, Jed added, "Either that, or when I get my viking funeral. Whichever comes first." He cackled again. "So . . . ," he teased, "you want I should set aside a few blues for you?"

He blinked away the sunset image of Jed's lifeless body, floating out to sea as flames devoured him and his humble cabin cruiser. "Much as I hate to," Austin said, "I'd better pass, 'cause it's likely I'll pull a double shift today." Waving the banana, he increased his pace. "I'll take a rain check, though."

"Drive safe."

"You bet."

"I'm not talkin' about that bucket o' bolts you call a truck," Jed said. "I mean in the ambo. Take care not to drive it into any innocent civilians, y'got me?"

Chuckling, Austin tossed back, "And you take care not to ram that hunk of tin foil into any *real* boats."

Last thing he heard before turning over the pickup's motor was Jed's robust laughter, and Austin smiled. Despite the dream, his spirits were high, thanks to Jed and the Callahans. His mood rose even higher as he realized that at this hour he'd have an easy drive to the station, and higher still knowing that when he got there, he'd be greeted with a hearty slap on the back and noisy enthusiasm, especially from the lucky night shift guy who pulled the long straw and won the chance to head home a couple hours early.

He tuned the radio to WPOC in time for the last half of an old Garth Brooks tune. Most days, he would have belted out the lyrics, but today, he tapped the beat onto the gear shift knob while making a short list of things that might explain Flora's snoring. Bud's midnight meanderings. Regret that he'd turned down free steamed crabs, Baltimore style.

"Say," he said, giving the steering wheel a light thump, "*that's* what I'll serve when Mercy comes to dinner."

She didn't seem the type who'd go all prissy when faced with the mess, traditional part of cracking into the spice-and-rock-salt–covered crustaceans. And if she did? Well, that would settle things, once and for all. Because what choice would he have but to see it as a sign that she *wasn't* the woman God intended him to share the rest of his life with!

He might have laughed at the image of her, pinkies in the air and nose wrinkled as she recoiled from the rust-colored crustaceans on butcher paper. But his last thought smothered any enjoyment that might have resulted. *The rest of his life?* he replayed. Where had *that* come from? Austin scrubbed a palm over his face and muttered, "Great Scott." Because if he added up all time he'd spent with her—both in New York and here in Baltimore—he couldn't legitimately tally more than a dozen hours. "Oh, you're losin' it, old boy. Definitely losin' it."

Not a big leap from 'losing it' to 'lost.'

Lost in love?

Shaking his head, Austin added to the mental list of things he'd been compiling:

What in this crazy, out-of-control world had put Mercy Samara front and center in his head and way, way too deep in his heart?

11

Mercy dialed Tommy Winston's room number at Bayview Hospital, and, after a dozen unanswered rings, hung up and tried the main switchboard.

"Mr. Winston was released this morning," the operator said, and abruptly ended the call. Which meant in order to retrieve his contact information and arrange a visit, she'd need to drive to the school. Not her favorite way to spend a summer Saturday, but as Tommy's counselor, she felt duty-bound to do it.

After donning jeans and a Yankees T-shirt, Mercy pulled her hair back in a clip and hurried to the foyer, where she stooped to give Woodrow a hearty goodbye backrub. "I'll be back before you finish your kibbles," she said, popping a kiss to his fuzzy brow. He emitted a happy *chirrup* and wound a figure eight around her ankles, then leaped onto the arm of the sectional. "So what do you think," she asked, grabbing her keys and purse, "which will cheer our injured football player more, a CD or a DVD ?"

Whiskers twitching, the fat tabby responded with a breathy "R-rup."

"Maybe I'll buy you a brand new catnip mouse while I'm out, just for being so adorable." And with that, she closed the door behind her, thankful her neighbors weren't out front to hear her talking to the feline as if he were human.

An hour later, she stood on the Winston's front porch, a big sack of fast food in one hand and a small department store bag in the other.

"It's open," called a voice from the other side of the door.

Mercy stepped into the dimly lit entryway. "Hello?"

"In here," came a gruff baritone.

She followed the sound of the voice to the family room at the end of the hall, and found Tommy, surrounded by sports magazines and candy wrappers. "Well, don't you look like king of the castle?"

Grimacing as he sat up straighter, Tommy said, "The folks took my little sisters to the movies. Probably won't be back for hours and hours."

Mercy perched on the corner of the coffee table. "I hope you haven't had lunch," she said, hoisting the bag of burgers. "I wasn't sure if you preferred cheeseburgers or hamburgers, so I got both."

"Wow. Thanks, Dr. Samara. That was cool of you."

"So how are you doing? What's the prognosis?"

"Doin' great," he said around a mouthful of fries. "Doc says if I don't push it, I can be back on the field before the Homecoming game."

Considering that he'd dislocated his collarbone, broken two ribs, and pulled a tendon, the answer surprised her, and she said so.

Tommy unwrapped a cheeseburger, used it to point out all the games and goodies around him, a mischievous glint sparkling in his eyes. "I figure it'll take Mom a week to get wise to me, and then, everything will go back to normal." He slurped his soda. "Until then, I'm gonna enjoy this while it lasts."

Mercy grinned as a big oaf of a dog trotted up beside her.

"That's Odlaw," Tommy said. "Y'know, the bad guy from the 'Where's Waldo' books?"

She ruffled his shaggy fur. "Aw, one look at that face and anybody could see he isn't a bad guy."

"Easy for you to say. You weren't here when he was a puppy, eating everything in sight and tearing up the place." His smiled dimmed when he asked, "Say, would you know how I could get in touch with those paramedics who took me to the hospital? My mom said it looked to her like you were pretty good friends with the tall one."

She could only imagine the rumors that would fly once school started if she confirmed a relationship with the good-looking EMT.

Tommy shrugged. "I guess you think it's kinda weird, huh, that I want to thank them?"

"Absolutely not!" What's *weird*, she thought, is the fact that the mention of his name conjured a distinct memory of their almost-kiss. "I think it'd be a very thoughtful thing to do."

"Yeah, but I'll bet they get stuff like that every day. He'll probably think I'm from the planet Bizarro or something."

Mercy remembered two of the firefighters she'd counseled after 9/11, who'd been completely bowled over by the cards and gifts from the families of those they'd helped that day. "Actually, I think the opposite is true. People probably have good intentions of calling or writing a note to say thank you, but then they get back to the business of living their lives, and before they know it, too much time has passed, and they tell themselves 'What's the point?'"

"That's sorta what I was thinking," Tommy said. He rooted through a stack of magazines and puzzle books until he found a square blue envelope. "It's all filled out, so if you'll be seeing them, could you deliver it for me?"

Mercy's hand went out automatically to accept it. Only when he let go did she acknowledge what the gesture meant: She *did* have a personal relationship with Austin Finley.

"I know it seems lame, maybe even a little bit sissy, but I was really scared that day." Tommy frowned. "Couldn't breathe, couldn't move, couldn't tell them what hurt and what didn't, couldn't even cry about it! I thought I was a goner, for real." He brightened slightly to add, "And then those guys showed up, and the way the tall one said I was gonna be all right, well, I believed it." He concluded with a grin and a shrug. "That's when I relaxed and took a breath. Dad called it melodramatic when I said the dude saved my life. But I know better."

"Austin," she said quietly. "His name is Austin, Austin Finley, and his partner's name is Lyle McElroy."

Nodding, Tommy unearthed a pen and took back the card, then scribbled both names on the envelope. "There," he said, beaming. "Even if they get stuff like this a hundred times a day, I'll feel a lot better, thanking them for what they did. I'm sure Dad would say *this* is melodramatic, too, but I think those two guys are real heroes."

An odd sensation washed over her, and Mercy couldn't help smiling, because it felt good having a hero for a friend.

But was Austin a friend, or something more? That moment on her sofa, when his face hovered so near her own—why, if she'd leaned forward just half an inch, he—

"So what's in the shiny red bag?" Tommy asked.

As she handed it to him, Mercy said, "I didn't know if you'd like a CD or a DVD, so I got one of each." She hoped as he tossed aside the tissue paper that the kid who'd helped her in the discount store had the same taste as Tommy.

His eyes lit up as he looked at each brightly colored plastic square. "Whoa, I've been saving up for this album, and the guys were talking about this movie in the locker room the other day." He met her eyes. "Thanks, Dr. Samara. You're the best!"

"I'm glad you like them," she said, standing. "Well, I'd better get going. Is there anything I can get for you before I leave? Ice for your drink? A snack?"

"Nope. I'm good. But thanks. And thanks for the presents, and the visit. And for delivering the card for me. You really are cool."

"Tell your mom and dad I'm sorry I missed them." She grabbed her purse and slung it over one shoulder. "You take care, OK, and follow doctor's orders, so you really *can* get back onto the field in a few weeks."

Odlaw walked her to the entry, and wagged his shaggy tail as Mercy gave him a final pat. "Go on into the family room, y'big oaf, and keep Tommy company," she said, pulling the door shut behind her.

What a great kid, she thought, sliding behind the steering wheel. Thoughtful and considerate, honest and kind-hearted. If she was ever lucky enough to have a son, she hoped he'd be just like Tommy. Why, she wouldn't be at all surprised if, when school officially started in a few weeks, he made an appointment with her, for the sole purpose of discussing which classes would best prepare him to become an EMT. Not at all unusual for a boy who'd just experienced a life-changing event. In fact, because of his youthful enthusiasm, he could just as easily change his career track, along with the courses he'd chosen to earn credits for graduation.

She glanced at the blue envelope poking out of her purse, and tried to remember what inspired Austin to become a cop. None of the other family members he'd told her about during their sessions had chosen careers in law enforcement. Stumbling onto a bit of information she hadn't uncovered in New York produced a smile. How refreshing to have something to bring up—a bona fide question—when she saw him again. *If* she saw him again.

Traffic on I-95 came to a grinding halt, and she craned her neck to see what had caused the jam up ahead. Dozens of drivers had already exited their vehicles, and milled about between the lanes. Mercy stepped onto the pavement, too, and leaned an arm on the open car door. "What's the holdup?" she asked the man parked beside her.

"Ah, some fool bonehead doing ninety miles an hour on his Harley plowed into the rear of an eighteen wheeler. They'll hafta scrape him offa the bumper, for sure."

A tiny gasp slipped past her lips as fire engines, police cars, and rescue vehicles sped toward the scene.

"That idiot better hope he doesn't survive," the man growled.

And before she could protest, he added, "Must be a dozen or more cars involved in that pileup, and at least three fatalities that I could see—but I couldn't see much." He shook his head. "I know *I* wouldn't want to live, only to find out that my self-centered stupidity killed so many innocent people."

His agitation reminded her of the day her father decided to join New York's auxiliary police force. Gritting her teeth, she forced it from her mind, and aimed her fury at the fellow's hardhearted comment. She supposed anger and annoyance was perfectly normal under the circumstances, but in Mercy's opinion, verbalizing such a thought—to a stranger, no less—was *not*. And she would have said exactly that if the wind hadn't delivered a whiff of burning fuel, and thick black smoke overhead that pointed, like an accusing finger, to the source of the chaos.

Just then, an ambulance screamed past, lights flashing and horn blaring. If she'd blinked as it went by, she wouldn't have seen Austin behind the wheel. Rushing Tommy to the hospital after an accident on the football field couldn't compare to the events taking place a quarter mile up the road. What if, as he worked to extract an injured person from one of the burning vehicles, *he* became a victim, too!

Mercy slammed her car door and ran toward the eighteen wheeler, dodging curious bystanders who stood grumbling about the heat and humidity, arriving late for back yard barbeques and weddings, missing the opening credits of the movie they'd been on the way to see. "I'll run out of gas before they clean up this mess," complained a goateed boy. "I can top that," said one of his friends, "I'll run out of cigarettes!" All three laughed when a third teen added, "At least we have plenty of beer."

Under different circumstances, she might have stopped and given them a piece of her mind, about the hazards of smoking and the dangers of drinking and driving. Might have scolded them for their insensitive remarks, too. Instead, Mercy kept moving, intent on finding Austin, because she needed to see with her own eyes that he was all right.

She passed a young mother, pacing as she jiggled her crying baby. In the SUV ahead of hers, an elderly man tapped the gauges on his wife's oxygen tank. Two kids bickered in the back seat of a minivan while their distraught father threatened to disconnect the cable TV if they didn't knock it off. How strange, Mercy thought, elbowing her way through the whimpering, whining crowd, that they'd focused on their own ordinary, petty concerns, while up ahead, people just like them lay dead or dying.

The breath caught in her throat when she spotted Austin, barking orders to the inquisitive onlookers who'd pressed close, hoping to steal a look at the misery. "Get back!" he bellowed, stabbing the air with a beefy forefinger. "You want to end up like these poor folks?"

Mercy's gaze went automatically to the mangled black Harley, now fused to the semi's right mud flap. A total of eleven vehicles—counting the bike and the truck—seemed welded together, like a deformed and derailed passenger train. The pitiful cries of the injured mingled, making it impossible to tell man from woman, adult from child.

"Get back," Austin repeated, "or I'll flag one of those squad cars up ahead and have the cops haul you off to the can. We need to make room for the copter to set down and—"

That threat did the trick, and the droning throng dissipated. She remembered how Tommy had called Austin a hero. Seeing him in action for the second time in a week gave her no choice but to agree. Everything about him screamed "Hero!" from his authoritative stance to the commanding tone of his voice. How handsome and gallant he looked, branding each stubborn straggler with a get-a-move-on-or-else glare!

She wanted to call out his name, tell him to please be careful, but Mercy wouldn't risk distracting him and possibly putting him in harm's way. She decided to concentrate on the fact that some of the first responders had already left the scene as others prepared to follow. He'd leave soon, too—long before the snarl of cars even began to untangle—and she'd gratefully endure exhaust fumes and the angry shouts of frustrated drivers without complaint, because at least Austin was safe.

Suddenly, she remembered Tommy's card, there on the passenger seat, tucked under her purse. With the windows down, anyone passing by could see it. What if some greedy kid thought it contained a cash gift, reached into the car and grabbed it!

Mercy dashed back to her sedan, hoping with every slap of her flip-flops that she'd find the card untouched, right where she'd left it. When she saw the tiny triangle of blue peeking out from beneath her purse, she leaned against the driver's door and gasped with relief. Why would a simple thank you card, penned by a grateful boy, mean more than her credit cards and driver's license? Why did it seem more valuable than the GPS and digital camera in her glove box, or the laptop on the floor beneath the dash?

In a flash, the answer came to her.

Yes, she'd agreed to deliver it for Tommy, but more significant than that, it provided a legitimate excuse to see him again, in case his promise to call had been nothing more than a polite way of saying "Thanks, but I don't think I'm interested."

He didn't seem the type to give his word and then break it, but she'd been wrong about people's motives before—men in particular—on both personal and professional levels. Mercy learned the hard way that dwelling on thoughts like that would inadvertently led directly to the dark and heartbreaking memories of her father's murder. Closing her eyes, she willed herself to think of something—anything—that would take her mind off the grisly images of the moment he died in her arms.

The steady *whap-whap-whap* of the chopper's blades churned the air above them, kicking up a cloud of dust and road grit. Mesmerized spectators instinctively shielded their eyes with hands and crooked elbows and tight-squinted eyes. Next, a mini-parade of fire engines and ambulances raced by on the shoulder, kicking up more dirt and tiny stones that splattered across all four lanes of traffic. It had been years since Mercy believed in the power of prayer, so it surprised her when she asked God to comfort the families of those killed or injured, and deliver those who'd died to a better place than this brutal world.

"You all right, miss?"

She recognized that voice. What cruel thing would he say this time? That he'd said a prayer, too, asking God to let the man on the motorcycle die a slow agonizing death? "I'm fine," she snapped. *Go away*, she wanted to shout. *Find another callous cad like yourself, and the pair of you can curse the poor biker to your heart's content.* Funny, but when she met his sparsely lashed pale eyes, he didn't look nearly as much like an ogre as she'd first thought. He looked weary, like everybody else caught up in the tragedy. The oppressing heat that rippled from the blacktop dampened his graying hair. A sheen of perspiration coated his face, and beads of sweat peppered the bridge of his nose. Evidently, Mercy and the Tin Man shared some critical DNA, because if *she* had a heart, would she consistently jump to the conclusion that every human being had devious and ulterior motives?

Well, not everyone. Austin had not inspired a single negative thought.

What could it hurt to give this guy the benefit of doubt? "You look a little flushed," she said, reaching into her back seat, and handing him a bottle of vitamin water, Mercy added "It isn't cold, but it'll replace your electrolytes and hydrate you."

A thin smile slanted his thinly mustachioed mouth. "Gee," he said, unscrewing the cap, "thanks."

He leaned close to look over her shoulder, and those old suspicions rose right up again. She flattened against the car and opened her mouth to ask what in the world he thought he was doing when he said, "Just lookin' for angel wings. These days, it's rare to meet a good and decent person, especially in the middle of a mess like this." He toasted her with the bottle. "Thanks."

You must have me confused with someone nice, she wanted to say. But "You're welcome," is what she said, instead.

A pair of uniformed officers approached, alternately shout-ing over the clatter of TV news helicopters. "Get back into your vehicles," said the youngest one, "we're about to move y'all into the left lane and get you on your merry way."

"That's right, folks," said his partner. His right hand mir-rored the left as he pointed toward the median. "C'mon, now. That's the way. Let's go."

"We'd like nothin' better than to go," muttered the gray-haired man. Fortunately, neither officer seemed to hear it when half a dozen of his fellow motorists agreed.

"I wonder where they've taken the people who were hurt," Mercy wondered aloud.

Someone said, "Hopkins, I reckon."

"Nah," a second voice said. "A mess like that? I'd bet my next paycheck they're at Shock Trauma."

"Why?" the man with the water asked her. "You planning to check up on 'em?"

His question made her face burn with a blush. "N-no, of course not. I was just hoping the emergency rooms were equipped to handle so many—"

"You've restored my faith in humanity, young lady," he said. "I'll bet most of these yokels haven't even given the accident victims a thought, except to carp about being held up by the accident. I'm guilty of that, myself. If I could get my foot up that high, I'd kick myself in the bee-hind."

She smiled, even as guilt intensified the flush in her cheeks, because she hadn't asked the question out of concern for the accident victims. She'd asked because of her concern for Austin.

Mercy knew she'd better get busy—and stay that way—if she hoped to find the strength of will to keep from calling his cell phone the minute she got home.

12

*H*e almost wished he hadn't called Cora. *Who are you kidding?* he thought, because there was no "almost" about it.

On the heels of a day like this, he wanted nothing more than to head straight for the tug, stand under a hot and steady spray of water, and hope all the *bad* would spiral down the drain with the dirt and grit and blood. Instead, he'd showered at the station and changed into clean jeans and an Orioles T-shirt, and asked for permission to endure another two hours of misery.

Construction on I-70 slowed the drive to Cora's. And a brand-spanking new cashier at McDonald's fumbled so many orders, the manager had to take over and start everybody's order from scratch, so the trip that should have taken thirty minutes took nearly an hour. He could hope Eddy's widow would be in an upbeat mood for a change. He had a better chance of growing wings and flying the rest of the way to Ellicott City. On days like this, he wished she hadn't taken his advice about moving, so she and the boys would be closer to her parents—and their Uncle Austin.

Then the twins met him on the walk, and he knew nothing could be further from the truth. They greeted him with riotous enthusiasm, squealing and giggling and wrapping their arms around him as if they were still a couple of diapered toddlers instead of eleven-going-on-twelve.

They babbled nonstop, all the way to the covered front porch, where Cora met him with her usual dour expression.

"Hey," she droned, bussing Austin's cheek. "So good of you to stop by. The boys have missed you. They've been looking forward to this all day."

"Good to see you, too," he said, forcing a smile that he didn't feel.

Cora relieved him of the food sacks, and he braced for a lecture about healthy meals versus junk food. She surprised him by saying, "Hard day?"

"Nah. Just your routine—"

"Don't give me that," she interrupted. "I know that *look*."

That part of the scolding, he could handle. In fact, he might consider it a caring gesture from a good friend—if he didn't know better. It didn't surprise him when she added "That's the look I see every time I look in the mirror."

Austin could count a thousand reasons why he missed his old partner, and the care and nurturing of his widow had always kept Cora and the boys at the top—or close to it—of his priorities list. The ebb and flow of Cora's mercurial mood swings had never seemed like a challenge for Eddy, and often Austin found himself wishing the man had left detailed directives, so he'd know how to sidetrack her when self-pity got hold of her head and heart. Unfortunately, Cora didn't come with a "Care and Maintenance of a Grieving Widow" instruction manual.

Of course he felt sorry for her, and sure, he knew that losing Eddy had been rough on her. And packing up the house they'd shared to move from New York to Maryland couldn't have been easy, either, especially with two rambunctious little boys.

But hundreds of people had lost their spouses on 9/11. Surely they weren't *all* still wallowing in self-pity, especially if they had kids. Eddy had been gone nearly ten years. When would Cora learn to cope with the grief and get on with her life, if not for her own sake, then for her boys'?

You're a fine one to talk. Because if it hadn't been for his pal Griff—

"We saw a really bad crash on the news," Raymond said, changing the subject. "Did you take some of those people to the hospital?"

His brain zapped back to the here and now as he admitted that, on any given day, a dozen accidents might foul up the Baltimore roadways, particularly during rush hour. Before he had a chance to ask the location of the one Ray had mentioned, Ricky gave his brother a playful shove. "Shut up, Raymo. Austin doesn't want to talk about blood and guts while he's eating."

Ray screwed up his face and doubled up a fist. "If you don't quit callin' me that, I'm gonna—"

Rick snickered. "My mistake. I meant to call you—"

"Raymond, Richard, *please!*" And Cora, God save her whiny soul, ran both hands through her hair. "Can't I have just one hour without your incessant bickering?"

If her voice seemed shrill to Austin, what must it sound like to the twins, who had to listen to it all day, every day? Their young shoulders sagged as sour expressions replaced their grins. "Sorry, Mom," came their droning monotone.

His heart ached for them. They were only behaving like normal kids, right? Or did it only seem that way to him because he didn't have kids of his own?

Something told him his mindset would be the same, even if he had to deal with them 24-7-365, because he wanted kids, and he'd have a houseful, if he could find a woman who didn't consistently put her own needs ahead of her children's. A woman like Mercy.

Far better to focus on the promise he'd made to Eddy. Like it or not, he'd watch over this woman and these boys, no matter how hard she made it.

Austin clapped his hands once. "I'm starved, so what say we eat!"

Two chairs squealed across the linoleum and the kids dug into the fast food bags, distributing burgers and fries and sodas with the smooth efficiency of a Vegas dealer, chattering the whole time. When Ray got up for extra ketchup, Rick said, "How 'bout grabbin' the mustard, long as you've got your big head in the fridge?"

"We're identical twins," Ray shot back. "If my head's big, so's yours."

"Yeah, but you're four minutes older, so your head's four minutes bigger."

Even Ray had to chuckle at that one, and Austin joined them. He didn't think he could love them more if they'd been his own flesh and blood. To add to his pleasure, the older they got, the more they reminded him of his partner and best friend—a miracle in itself, since they'd only been one when their dad died. Their mannerisms, wry sense of humor, genuine desire to please the people they loved, just like Eddy.

He got a kick out of listening to their exchanges, and marveled at the way their minds worked. Much as he wanted to zero in on them now, he knew he'd better keep a wary eye on their mother. Earlier, she'd claimed to have recognized the worn-out look on his face. Well, he'd seen the one she wore right now, too. At times like these, Cora reminded him of a Mylar balloon, filled too full of helium. Any minute, she'd pop, and the twins would react to the explosion by trading their happy banter for sullen silence.

An idea dawned, and he decided to go for broke. "So Cora, what would you say to joining me for a walk?"

And Cora, true to form, pursed her lips. Oh, how he wanted to say "Keep that up and your face will freeze that way!"

"I have to do the dishes and there's laundry in the dryer, and—"

"Schweetheart," he said in his best Bogart imitation, "yer breakin' my heart." He pushed back from the table, and, standing, held out one hand.

Cora sighed and rolled her eyes. "Oh, all right. I might as well go. I know you, Austin Finley, and *you'll* pester me even longer and harder than these two."

Austin winked at them and adopted a bratty, sing-song voice: "She doesn't know everything."

Now really, he thought as Cora led the way, how sad is it that her kids were out-and-out relieved to be rid of her, even for half an hour or so? Somehow, he had to try again to convince her to see a counselor, harder this time. "So what have you been up to lately, m'dear?"

"Oh, mostly just more of the same."

He refused to join in her self-pity game. "Same what?"

"You know, cleaning and cooking, doing laundry, garden—"

"But last time I was here, you were actually excited about getting a job. Down at the bookstore, right?"

"I can't commit to a work schedule. The boys need me."

Austin groaned. "Aw, now, that's just plain nuts. They're great kids, thanks to you. And you know as well as I do that they can be trusted for a couple hours a week. And who knows? Maybe you'll get lucky, find a boss who'll let you work while they're in school."

She continued walking. "Are you kidding?" she blurted. "You saw the way they went at each other before supper. If I wasn't there to referee, it'd be that times a thousand."

"Will you sock me on the arm if I say that's ridiculous?"

He didn't have to look at her to know she'd frowned. Again. "Cora," he continued, "seriously. You're a *girl*. What you don't know about boys could fill a book. No, not a book. A whole library."

She stopped walking. "Excuse me?"

"My brother and I fought *all* the time. Hurled stuff at each other—including insults—even drew blood on more than a couple occasions." He chuckled. "And we loved every tooth-and-nail minute of it." The memory inspired a crooked smile. It felt good, thinking about Avery without feeling like a low-down heel.

"I'm sure your mother didn't approve."

Oh, go ahead, Cora. Rain on my parade, why don't you. "If she did, it sure didn't show."

She looked genuinely surprised. "But . . . but how did she stand all the *noise*?"

He laughed. "She didn't. She was at work. Spent every hour she could at the local flower shop."

Cora picked up her pace. "It might be nice, putting my teaching degree to use after all this time."

"And if you can convince the boys' principal to hire you, it'd be the best of both worlds."

"Both?"

Eddy often complained, as they rode from one call to another, that sometimes, it seemed Cora worked hard at being *thick*. The longer he knew this woman, the more inclined Austin was to agree.

"So are you dating anyone these days?"

The question brought Mercy to mind, and broadened his grin. "No." Should he tell her about the former Dr. Samara? Nah. Then he'd have to go into the whole story, and Cora would work herself into a snit, saying stuff like "The woman isn't good enough for you" and "Of all the nerve! Who did she think she was, judging you?"

"I might not know everything there is to know about boys, but I know a fib when I hear one." She smiled up at him. "Spit it out, mister. Who is she, and why haven't I met her yet?"

It did his heart good to see that light in her eyes again. Cora had always been a fine-looking woman when she wore something other than a scowl. "It's a long story."

"We can walk around the block again. As you so astutely pointed out, my boys can take care of themselves for an hour or so."

He pocketed his hands. "Well, I knew her in New York. Sorta. And now I know her here."

Cora giggled. "Will you sock me on the arm, the way you did your brother, if I say that's ridiculous? What kind of information is that?"

Shrugging, he said, "It's all I have." For now, he added mentally.

"I remember that paramedic you were dating a year or so ago. Good grief. What a mess *that* was."

Though he agreed, Austin didn't say so out loud.

"Every woman you've dated has wanted you to give up your work. Part of me gets that, because, well, you know, it's dangerous. But part of me is like, well, they knew what you did for a living when they agreed to go out with you. What is it with women, thinking they can change a man?"

"Y'got me by the feet." In truth, Austin didn't understand that, either. "Never entered my head to ask a gal to give up working at the animal shelter or teaching kindergarten."

"I can see how working around animals could be hazardous." She shivered. "All those sharp teeth and claws. But kindergarten? What's dangerous about that job!"

"Are *you* kidding? All those germs? And they don't call 'em ankle biters for nothin', y'know."

"Austin Finley, you're a nut, but honestly? I don't know how I'd have survived all these years. If it hadn't been for you—"

"C'mon, now. Knock it off. You know how easily I blush."

"Yes, yes I do."

He liked the way she said that, with the firm confidence of a friend.

Maybe next time he visited, he *would* share his news about the amazing Dr. Samara.

But he hadn't talked with Mercy lately. Every time he'd picked up the phone, something—work, boat chores, errands, the wreck on I-95, then Cora and the kids—prevented him from dialing her number. He felt fairly certain he'd been the one who'd promised to call, set up dinner on the boat. For all he knew, that parting comment that had been drowned out by his squealing pickup's door had been the dating version of "Don't call us, we'll call you." Besides, the phone lines went both ways, didn't they? If she'd really wanted to get together, she could have called *him*.

Right?

She was a mystery; that much he knew. Happy one minute, quiet and withdrawn the next. Clearly, he had a ton to learn about what made her tick, starting with how her parents had died, ending with how she felt about faith, and God, and everything that came between. If this thing between them continued, he needed to understand the events and experiences that shaped her into the woman she'd become. How else could he provide emotional support?

On the other hand, if it took solving a passel of riddles to bring their relationship to the next level, at least Mercy—unlike the women who'd come before her—was worth the effort.

So he fine-tuned his plan:

Next time he visited Cora, he'd tell her about Mercy—provided he had anything to tell.

13

*T*hey got the preliminary "hellos" and "how are yous" out of the way, then launched into an abbreviated version of the weather forecast—Austin quoting WBAL's John Collins, Mercy citing the version Marty Bass delivered on Channel 13. Following a short silence, Austin said, "Sorry I haven't called before now." And chuckling, he added "If you want the truth, I forgot who was supposed to call whom."

Mercy loved the sound of his laugh—deep and hearty and wholly masculine. A smart woman would figure out how to inspire more of it. "No problem. I figured you were busy. Or working some off-beat shift. Or both."

"So, when's it convenient to have that dinner I promised?"

If she'd been talking to any other man, Mercy would have put him off a day or two, to ensure he wouldn't get the idea she'd kept all her nights free, in case he called. But she could hardly call Austin "any other man."

"I guess that depends."

"On . . . ?"

"Whether or not you've stocked up on the ingredients to *make* that dinner you promised."

He paused only slightly before saying "I guess that depends."

All her life, people had been telling her she needed to play more, work less. What could it hurt to play along? "On . . ."

"On whether or not you're 'pro' steamed crabs or 'con.'"

"Oh, pro. Definitely!"

"Ah, she's a woman after m'own heart."

"Say, isn't 'Finley' an Irish name?"

"Yes'm, 'tis."

"Then I'm flabbergasted that—"

"Flabbergasted? Such language!"

"—that you can't do a better brogue than *that*."

Another hesitation, and then "You know the old saying, 'Honesty is the best policy'?"

"Uh-huh."

"Well, it's bunk. Wouldn't have killed you to *pretend* mine is the best Irish accent you've ever heard, bar none, to protect my fragile ego. Y'know?"

"Fragile, indeed. Why, if I had to guess, I'd guess the only fragile thing about you is your—"

"OK. All right. That's *it*. No crabs for you."

Mercy threw back her head and laughed, and oh, how good it felt! "I take it back, I take it back! You're the most sensitive, fragile, easily hurt human being on planet Earth." And now she paused. "Am I forgiven? Will you still serve steamed crabs tonight?"

"Sure. I'll pick you up at—"

"Don't be silly. I'm perfectly capable of driving to your place. Just tell me what time to be there and give me some directions, and—" What did a dinner guest bring her host with an entrée like that? "What can I bring? Rolls? Wine or beer? Dessert?"

"I don't drink."

Had she imagined it, or had his voice taken on a gritty tone?

"But I keep a few bottles in the fridge, for guests who do. So, unless you have a favorite brew—"

She remembered how he'd been written up by his lieutenant for coming to work hung over. On more than one occasion. Marcum made a point to tell her that, in his opinion and by every other measure, Austin was an alcoholic. If he'd kicked the habit, she sure didn't want to be the one to tempt him back to it.

"Seriously. Doesn't bother me a bit—any more—to be around people who, ah, imbibe. Besides, I know almost as well as native Baltimoreans that crabs and beer go together like—"

"A hand and a glove?"

He laughed. "I was gonna say salt and pepper."

"Or socks and shoes."

"A horse and carriage."

The lyrics of an old Frank Sinatra song echoed in her head, but no way she intended to top his comeback with "love and marriage."

"You win," she said.

"Don't sound so surprised. I win far more often than I lose."

If he thought she planned to ask "Win *what*?" well, he had yet *another* think coming, that's what!

Once they'd rounded out the conversation with arrival time and directions to the marina, Woodrow walked a figure-eight around her ankles. "Just enough time," she told him, looking at the clock, "to whip up a cheesecake for dessert." She bent to scoop up the cat. "You think he likes plain, or blueberries on top?"

The feline answered with a musical chirrup, and leaped from his mistress's arms.

"Plain it is, then."

An hour and a half later, Mercy set the dessert on the stovetop to cool as the phone rang. With any luck, Austin wouldn't view her change of mind as a "This is what life would be like if we were married!" hint, because in place of the cheesecake, she'd made—

"As I live and breathe, you're *home*," said the voice on the other end of the phone. "It's as though you disappeared from the face of the earth!"

She would have recognized that oh-so-proper British accent anywhere. "Leo! Oh, my goodness, it's good to hear from you. And ironic, too, because I've been thinking a lot about you lately."

"Uh oh."

"Only good things, of course."

"Despite those horrible pranks I played on you when we were kids?"

"Forgotten! Well, except for the time you blindfolded me and made me eat a cicada. And the time when—"

"Seems to me you haven't forgotten at all." Laughing, Leo added, "But just listen to me, telling the family psychiatrist about should-be-buried memories and the hidden meanings behind them." Another chuckle, then, "I have to see a patient in five minutes. It's reveal day, don't you know, so there's a higher than normal price if I'm late. But I digress. The reason I called, sister dear, is that I have a few weeks' vacation time coming. And I haven't seen you since you were here in . . . how long has it been, three years now?"

"Something like that," Mercy said, hoping Leo wouldn't bring up the reason she'd gone to London.

"How would you feel about putting up with a middle-aged English houseguest for a few days?"

"You want to come *here*? Oh, wow, Leo, that's wonderful! I'd love to see you, and since I have a few weeks, myself, before school starts, I can show you aroun—"

"I'll only say it this once, Mercy dear, and only out of deep affection and genuine caring, so bear with me, won't you?"

She listened as he sighed, clucked his tongue.

"Trading your fascinating post with the police department to work with rude, tattooed teenagers? Honestly. What were you thinking?"

"As I've said a thousand times, the job wasn't all that fascinating," she muttered, "and the kids aren't *all* rude."

"Well, there's the bright side, I suppose."

The mantle clock chimed four times, meaning she had an hour to shower, dress, and drive to Austin's. "When is your flight? I'll pick you up at BWI, save you taxi fare, and show you a little bit of Charm City on the way from the airport."

"I haven't made reservations yet. Wanted to make sure you were up for a visit first."

Why wouldn't she be up for a visit? Surely Leo didn't believe that she still suffered from the after-effects of the depression that sent her over edge a few years back. "I love you for being such a protective big brother, but take my word for it: I'm fine," she said in the most upbeat voice she could muster. "It'll be so good to see you! I won't hurt your feelings, will I, if I tell you that I can't chat long? I have a dinner date across town, you see and—"

"Bully for you, sister dear, bully for you! It's high time you put some zest into your life!"

She'd never thought of Austin as 'zesty.' But then, he'd promised to serve steamed crabs. *Can't get much spicier than that!* Grinning, Mercy said "Let me know just as soon as you've booked your flights. Meanwhile, I'll gussy up your room and put your favorite after shave in the guest bath. Is French toast still your favorite breakfast?"

"Does the queen have white hair?" Leo laughed. "Go on, now. I wouldn't want to make you late for your very important date."

Mercy hurried to her room and pulled together an easy-care outfit that wouldn't show the tell-tale signs of a crab-eating frenzy, and in the shower, she pictured her only living relative. He'd been wonderfully supportive throughout her ordeal, spending countless hours listening to her blubber, reassuring her that in time her life would return to normal. He hadn't made her feel the least bit rushed, even when the intended two-week visit turned into nearly eight.

Once she'd remarked that maybe he'd chosen the wrong specialty, because his understanding of the human mind equaled that of any psychiatrist she'd studied under or worked with. "My dear," he'd said, patting her hand, "I'll grant you it takes skill to do what I do in the operating room, but the *hard* work begins long before I pick up a scalpel."

Until then, she'd never given a thought to how much "doctoring" goes into preparing a patient for plastic surgery, whether the operation is scheduled to repair scars and burns, or add and subtract inches in just the right places. Her appreciation of Leo doubled that day, and so did her love for him.

Mercy grabbed her keys and GPS as Woodrow wove a figure eight around her ankles. "Can you believe it?" she said, stooping to scratch between his ears, "you're going to meet my big brother soon!" She slung her purse over one shoulder. "Behave yourself while I'm gone, and I'll give you two treats when I get back."

As she drove toward the highway, she made a mental list of things to buy before Leo arrived. His favorite ice cream. A tube of that ultra-minty toothpaste he liked so much. Some American sports magazines for the guest room.

She wondered what he'd think of Austin, what would Austin think of him. *But it's too early in the relationship to introduce them, isn't it?*

Relationship?

The question distracted her so much that she nearly missed the ramp to I-83.

It was way too early to call it a *relationship*.

Wasn't it?

Mercy shrugged. She didn't know why, but it seemed important to see how the two got along. The only question that remained was what to serve once the meeting was arranged.

Now won't *that* be a Norman Rockwell moment, she thought, picturing her two favorite men, shaking hands for the first time.

Mercy laughed so hard that she drove right past the sign that pointed the way to Austin's marina.

14

Mercy found the only employee at the tiny marina convenience store in the back, stacking toilet tissue on a gingham-covered shelf. "Excuse me, but I'm a little lost. I wonder if you've heard of a houseboat called *One Regret?*"

"Sounds familiar," he said, thumbing his Orioles cap to the back of his head. "Follow me, young lady, and we'll see what we can see."

He led her to the counter, where he slid a book from a tidy shelf behind the cash register, and proceeded to page through it. "*One Regret, One Regret,*" he chanted as his beefy forefinger slid over the listings. "Here we go . . . *One Regret,* registered to Austin Finley."

"Whew," she said. "I drove three miles past your sign before I realized I'd missed the entrance."

"Missed it?" he echoed. "The thing's as big as a billboard." Chuckling, he added, "It is a billboard! How'd you miss something that size?"

Mercy felt her cheeks go hot as she remembered the ridiculous thoughts that turned her into a scatterbrained twit. "Can I bother you for directions from here?"

A dapper gent with a tidy white beard stepped up beside her and said, "Don't trust this old geezer. Why, some days, he needs help finding his way to the door of his own store!"

"Bud, if you didn't pay for all your groceries with cold, hard cash, I'd bar you from the door of my very own store."

"All bark, no bite," Bud shot back. And an aside to Mercy: "He's harmless. Just a little feeble-minded, is all." Then he sandwiched her hand between his own. "Did I hear you say you're having dinner with Austin? Alone? On his boat?"

The heat of her blush intensified. "Um, yes."

Bud gave her hand a gentle squeeze. "Well, doggies! His taste in women is improving, ain't it, Pete?"

"Big time!" Pete put his book back on the shelf. "Much as I'd love to stand here jabbering with you, you old coot, I have work to do. Can I trust you to get this pretty little thing to Finley's slip? No funny business now, you hear, or I'll sic Flora on you."

Mercy didn't quite know what to make of the exchange. Quite clearly, both men had met several of Austin's female guests. She should feel flattered that, compared to the others, they saw her as an improvement. So why did she feel jealous, instead?

Bud's hearty laughter didn't give her much time to bristle as Pete headed for the back of the store. "I'll make you a deal," he said, gathering up his groceries, "you drive me to my boat, and I'll show you where Austin's is."

He looked so friendly and harmless that she didn't give it a second thought. "Is your boat far from his?"

"Oh, not too," he said as she led the way to her car. "If I had to guess, I'd say it's all of twenty yards from my place."

Mercy punched in the digits to unlock the car as Bud stuck out his right hand. "Name's Bud. Bud Callahan."

"Mercy," she said, shaking it. "Pleasure to meet you, Bud."

"Mercy. Now ain't that a lovely name!"

Smiling, she waited until he'd buckled his seatbelt before rolling toward the exit.

"Make this left," he said, pointing, "then follow that little road 'til it dead ends, and go right."

"How long have you known Austin?"

Bud scratched his chin. "Lemme see now, we came here in '98, and unless my memory is fading, he showed up about five years later." Chuckling, he added, "Don't tell him I shared this with you, but most folks around here call him Tugger, 'cause he spent the better part of a year working on beat-up old boat. I think if he hadn't come along when he did, they'd-a sunk her on Lake Michigan so the sea life could set up house on her."

Mercy grinned. She could almost picture Austin on his hands and knees, sanding the decks, stern-faced and determined to make quick and efficient work of it. "You don't call him that?"

"No-no-no," he said. "We met him long before the rest of these yokels did, and he said his name was Austin. We're creatures of habit, the wife and me." Bud shrugged. "Like Flora always says, makes our relationship with him special. And we like to think he feels the same way."

"Well, m'dear, here's our parking pad. You can pull in beside Austin's truck, if you like."

She stopped behind the pickup. "But wouldn't you rather I parked closer to your place, so you won't have to walk too far?"

Bud laughed. "My boat is one hundred and four steps from his. I know, 'cause I've counted."

Grinning, she slid into the space. As they exited the car, Mercy retrieved a rectangular cake pan from the floor of the backseat as Bud collected his groceries. "He told me not to bring anything, but I couldn't just show up with *nothing*." As they neared the walkway between the boats, she said, "Maybe you can join us for dessert?"

"Depends," Bud said with a wink. "What is it?"

"Pineapple upside down cake."

"Land o' Goshen," he said. "The boy's favorite." He regarded her from the corner of his eye. "How'd you get *that* bit of information out of him? Normally, he's more tight-lipped than—well, lordy—I can't think of anybody who says less about himself!"

And that, Mercy thought, is precisely why I can't tell Bud that the subject had come up during one of her first sessions with Austin, as she helped him remember good times with Avery. But even if it hadn't still fallen under the patient confidentiality principles, she'd have kept it to herself. Mercy didn't have to be his therapist to feel protective of him.

"Don't tell anyone I'm sharing this with you," she said, "but I'm a mind reader."

Laughing, Bud turned and headed up the ramp leading to his boat. "I'll see how Flora's feeling, and if she's up for dessert, I'll have her call the boy." He put his arm back, thrust a hand into the air, and waved. "Hopefully, she'll be interrupting something, and he'll say no."

And laughing, he disappeared inside, oblivious to Mercy's reddening cheeks. She stood at the foot of Austin's ramp, wishing she'd inherited her father's swarthy complexion to help hide the fact that she blushed so easily.

"I was beginning to think maybe you chickened out on me."

The voice came from above, and she shaded her eyes to look up. Bent at the waist, he leaned both forearms on the gleaming brass rail that surrounded a small porch-like room high on the boat. "Pass up free crabs? Obviously, you don't know me very well."

One corner of his mustachioed mouth lifted in a wry grin. Oh, how she loved that grin!

"The whole point of this dinner is to get to know you better," he said, straightening. "Stay where you are, and I'll meet you, help you hop over the water gap."

She couldn't have moved if she'd wanted to, because her feet seemed nailed to the weathered wood boards of the walkway. Why had she fussed with her hair, instead of wearing it in a ponytail, or a clip, anything to get it up off her neck, because sudden nervousness threatened to wake beads of perspiration that would flatten her efforts in no time.

Smiling, he jogged toward her, blond curls glistening in the sun. "Thought I said you didn't have to bring anything," he said, taking the cake pan from her.

"I know. But I wanted to."

He balanced the pan on his left palm, pressed the right one to the small of her back. "C'mon, so I can show you around."

When they reached the end of the walkway, she laughed. "You must think I'm dumb as a bag of rocks," she teased, looking at the one-foot space between the boards. "Or more clumsy than a drunken ostrich."

Chuckling, Austin took her hand. "It's just an excuse to do this," he said as she put hers into it.

"Oh, I'll bet you say that to all your women," she said as his fingers closed around hers.

"All my women?"

Mercy might have come back with a teasing barb—if she hadn't noticed the froth of waves slapping at the piling. She froze, and, pointing, said "Is that . . . is that a *stingray* down there?"

Austin peered into the murky water. "Yep. It sure enough is." He gave her hand a tiny squeeze, then let go of it and moved easily to the other side of the opening. "Trust me," he said, reaching for her, "I won't let you fall through, though God knows you're tiny enough to."

Mercy couldn't decide whether she so quickly and willingly took because she wanted to see the inside of his houseboat, or at the unspoken invitation that beamed from his gorgeous blue eyes.

"This thing weighs a ton," he said, nodding at the cake pan. "Don't tell me. . . it's a ten-pound cake?"

Once both feet made it past the gap, she grinned up at him. "They don't call it pound cake because that's what it weighs. It's because in the old days, the recipe called for a pound of flour, a pound of sugar, a pound of—"

He sniffed the pan's aluminum cover. "Do I smell *pineapples*?"

Much as she hated to do it, Mercy wriggled free of his grasp and relieved him of the cake. "It's a surprise. For after dinner." It was her turn to sniff. "Why don't I smell crabs steaming?"

"Because we aren't having crabs, that's why."

He didn't give her time to ask why not. The spring that kept the screen door from swinging freely on its hinges creaked as he opened it for her. "Welcome to my humble abode," he said, bowing slightly as she climbed to steep steps and entered the tug. "From this spot, you can see—well, you can pretty much see all of my humble abode in one glance."

A small, red-speckled Formica table nestled between two high-backed matching benches, and he slid the cake onto it to announce "This is the galley." He made a quarter turn and pointed. "That's the cabin." Another quarter turn. "The stateroom, ah, translation: bedroom. And down the companionway, er, hall, you'll find the head, better known to land-lubbers like you as the bathroom."

She followed his gaze to a narrow ladder. "Is that where you were when you called down to me?"

"The pilot house. Want to see it?"

"I'd love to."

And so Austin led the way up as Mercy wished she'd worn sneakers, to get better purchase on the flat wood rungs. The instant she stepped into the pilot house, she found herself turning in a slow circle. From every one of the dozen or so narrow windows, a different but equally beautiful look at the Chesapeake. "Oh, Austin," she sighed, "how do you ever tear yourself away from this spectacular view?"

"Isn't easy," she heard him say. He stepped up beside her. "So, you like it?"

"What's not to like? It's breathtaking." Facing him, Mercy added, "I'll bet the sunrises are mind-blowing."

"So are the sunsets. That's why we're eating out there." He nodded to indicate a short doorway. "We're standing in the pilot house. When this was a working tug, this is where the captain stood, to—"

"—to pilot the boat, and keep an eye on everything?"

"Exactly."

"And that?" She pointed at the deck, barely visible on the other side of the west-facing windows. "What's that called?"

"The up-deck. Where you came in? I call that the down-deck." Austin shrugged. "And the rest of the stuff beneath your pretty little shoes is just plain deck."

All right, so maybe she'd made the right choice, not wearing sneakers.

"Come see the deck. Earlier, there was an osprey on her nest. Her babies are pretty much grown, but they still sit in it with her. If we're lucky, the whole feathered family will be home."

He ducked through a door barely taller than his shoulders. "Take care not to thump your forehead on the door jamb."

She joined him on the deck and said "Thanks for the tip, Gulliver."

And then Mercy spied the little round table he'd set up in the shade of the pilot house, near the rail. A glass-globed lantern sat in the center of a red-and-white checked tablecloth, its points flapping in the evening breeze. In the middle of each white enamel plate, a matching napkin.

He'd wrapped the silverware in the napkin, placed a big red tumbler at two o'clock next to each plate, and, at the ten o'clock position, a salad bowl. Chunky salt and pepper shakers and a gingham-lined basket of rolls completed the setting. Either he was *very* practiced at entertaining ladies on board his houseboat or a generous and gracious host. Either way, it seemed he saw this as a bona-fide date. And if he ever found out how much time and effort had gone into getting herself ready, he'd have realized that she did, too.

"It's lovely," she admitted.

"Yeah. I know. Sometimes when I come up here, I'm amazed at how fast the hours go by."

She prepared to point out that it was the beautiful restaurant-style set-up he'd created, not the spectacular view that had captivated her when he said "What can I get you to drink?" He tapped the top of a waist-high refrigerator where a stumpy CD player thumped with a quiet tune. He counted on his fingertips. "I have iced tea, lemonade, root beer, cola—"

"Iced tea sounds great. And I love that song!"

"'No More Cloudy Days'," Austin said, grabbing a pitcher from the fridge. "It's been one of my favorites since the Eagles recorded it. I forget the year."

"2007," she provided. "I have the same album. You should hear me belt that one out on the way to work, especially if I'm stuck in traffic! They're probably the only group I'd pay to see in concert. I became an Eagles fan when I stayed with my brother a few years back."

A strange expression darkened his face, but he recovered quickly.

Only Leo and her doctor knew about that awful time in her past, so Mercy didn't know how to explain the peculiar eye contact. Fortunately, it didn't last long.

"Something tells me you have a lovely voice."

"Then something tells you wrong." Mercy laughed as he filled their tumblers. As he put the pitcher back into the fridge, she noticed that he'd placed a bench beside the table, and on it stood an ice bucket and silvery tongs, a covered butter dish, and a shiny red tray that held tortilla chips and salsa.

Obviously, he'd put even more effort into getting the boat ready for her visit than she had to come see it. And if she didn't watch out, tears of gratitude would spoil her careful mascara application, because Mercy couldn't remember when anyone had gone to so much trouble for her!

He added ice to the tea and handed her a glass. "Let's sit and enjoy the sunset," he said, gesturing toward two Adirondack chairs near the rail. He checked his watch. "We have about twenty minutes, by my guesstimation."

Mercy put her glass on the table between the chairs and eased into the one farthest from the water. Had she ever taken the time to watch the sun set? If so, it must have been decades ago, before her memory began to document life events—far too many of them harsh or sad.

"I met your neighbor," she offered.

"Which one?"

"Bud. I passed the marina entrance and had to backtrack, and stopped at the convenience store for directions. He was in there shopping and struck a bargain with me."

"Let me guess: A guided tour to my place in exchange for a ride home from Pete's."

Mercy laughed. "He's quite a character. I hope you don't mind, but I invited him to join us for dessert."

"Don't mind a bit."

"Is his wife ill?"

"Flora?" He sat up slightly, looking genuinely concerned. "Not that I know of. Why?"

"Bud said if Flora was feeling up to it, he'd have her call you, to see what time they should walk over."

Austin's handsome features crinkled with a frown as he said, "It's tough to check on 'em, working the night shift." He nodded. "Would you mind very much if, after we eat, we bring dessert over there?"

"Not at all."

"That way I can check up on her without her knowing that's what I'm doing." He paused long enough to take a long slow swallow of his tea. "Bud was over here couple nights ago, said Flora has been snoring like a buzz saw lately."

For several semesters, it had been a tossup between psychiatry and geriatrics, thanks to serving part of her internship at a nursing home. Maybe she could offer a bit of hope, and put Austin's fears to rest. "Has she talked with her doctor about it?"

He nodded slowly. "Yeah, Bud said something about an appointment."

"Good." She saw no point in adding to his unease with facts about cancer of the nasal cavity. "It could very well be a very normal part of the aging process. Lots of elderly people snore—even those who never did before, and I'm sure her doctor will tell her—" She stopped speaking when a big merry grin broke out on his face.

Austin held up his glass in a silent toast. "I keep forgetting there's an *MD* behind your name, and a *DR* in front of it."

She feigned a haughty demeanor. "I don't know why, when I take advantage of every possible occasion to flaunt the fact that, in order to specialize in psychiatry, I had to earn a medical degree first."

His infectious laughter warmed and delighted her, and Mercy made the decision right then and there to encourage as much of it as possible, as often as possible.

They sat in companionable silence for most part, with Austin occasionally pointing out geese and heron and egrets, various types of gulls and ducks, and the ever-present osprey that, once she landed on the nest not ten yards away, kept a wary and beady eye on the inhabitants of One Regret.

"Looks like rain," she said, eyes on the horizon. "I hope it holds off until after the show."

"It will."

He said it with such authority that she had no choice but to believe it. "Were you a boater before you bought the tug?"

"Nope." He told the story of how he'd bought the boat after seeing photos of it on the Internet, detailing what it had cost to have it trucked to the marina, and how much he'd spent on construction supplies to make it livable. "I don't know much," he said, tapping one temple, "but the little knowledge I've gained came by way of trial and error."

"My dad would have loved you," she said, more than a little surprised that the comment evoked a truly pleasant memory.

"Y'think?"

"He always said that lasting lessons are learned the hard way."

Austin nodded approvingly. "Then I guess I would've liked your dad, too."

That surprised her, and she said so.

"Why *wouldn't* I like him?"

"He was born in Saudi Arabia, for starters."

"So?"

"Used to be a practicing Muslim."

"I hate to repeat myself, but . . . so?"

Mercy matched his grin tooth for tooth as he added, "Didn't you tell me he became a citizen, converted to Christianity out of love for your mother?"

When had she told him *that*? Mercy wondered. "And quit his job as a translator at the U.N. after 9/11, then sold his house on Long Island and bought a tiny condo in Manhattan, so he could live off the proceeds and his savings, and dedicate himself to the Auxiliary Police."

That raised his eyebrows. "But that's an all-volunteer force."

"She shrugged a shoulder. "What happened that day shamed him."

"But why? He wasn't a terrorist. Or a Jihadist. Or—"

"They were Arab-types, and it was enough to make those who were less informed than you jump to conclusions about him."

Frowning, Austin shook his head, and, after another sip of tea, he pointed toward the horizon. He told her about the green flash, adding that last time it had rained he'd seen a fire rainbow.

"Never heard of one," she admitted.

The way he described the rare sighting of the balled-up rainbow, clinging to the underside of a cloud, made her want to see one, too.

"Don't blink," he whispered, pointing again, "and you might catch a glimpse of the flash."

Hard as it was to pull her gaze from his stunning face, Mercy looked west, just in time to see the sun slide—like a golden coin into a slot—from the sky. She heard a tiny gasp burst from her lips, felt her pulse quicken. What a fool she'd been, to allow errands and chores and work-related tasks to keep her from enjoying something so magnificent.

"Amazing what God can do, isn't it?"

God? Of all the things she might credit for the spectacular sight, *God* surely wouldn't be one of them! "I'm a scientist," she said.

"OK, so I admit it: I'm downright redundant. But . . . so?"

"Science is black and white, and demands proof to back up every theory."

"Theory." He nodded, then met her gaze. "Surely that isn't what you think, that God is a *theory*."

He'd dropped plenty of hints about his devotion to his Lord. Mercy didn't know why the question surprised her, but it did.

"Your own father walked away from the Muslim faith—and from what I've read, that can be considered a sin punishable by death in his former world. He must have had reasons for that, good, solid reasons that went deeper than love for your mother."

"If he did," she said carefully, "I never heard them."

"No way I'd turn away from my faith for a woman. Any woman. And I can't imagine he did, either."

Mercy had a feeling she knew where *this* would lead, and she did not want to have this conversation. Experience had taught her that it would only lead to harsh words and hurt feelings for both of them. Why couldn't people just agree to dis-agree on the subject of religion, instead of working themselves into a lather to bring everyone to their way of thinking?

She liked this man. Liked him more than any she'd known to date. But more important than that, she respected Austin. Respected his First Amendment right to believe in God— or not—as he saw fit. But how would she tell him all of that without damaging the connection between them that seemed to grow stronger with every meeting?

Then her stomach rumbled, providing the perfect opening. "Wow. When was the last time you fed that beast?"

"This morning."

She started to tell him that she'd made herself two slices of buttered toast with cinnamon and sugar on top and pretended that the bubbles and ice cubes in her tea had totally captured her attention. Pretended because the last guy she'd dated—a criminal defense attorney—once asked why she felt it necessary to describe everything in elaborate detail. "It's what my clients do," he'd said over the lasagna dinner she'd made for his birthday. "The guiltier they are, the more intricate the details. It makes me wonder what crime *you've* committed."

He'd been kidding—at least about her alleged crimes—but his criticism went straight to the heart. If he ever figured out why she'd rushed him through dessert and ushered him to the door for a cool, not-so-much-as-a-kiss-on-the-cheek goodbye, it didn't show in the four voice mail messages he left that next week. She never called him back, but maybe, she thought now, she should have at least thanked him for teaching her a valuable (if not stinging) lesson in communicating with men. Or, more accurately, in *not* communicating with them.

She put her tumbler on the table between them and smiled, feeling at once victorious and proud for having kept her babbling urges under control, yet again. "Were you just teasing, or are we really not having steamed crabs tonight."

His face contorted with an apologetic wince. "Sorry, kiddo. My supplier had troubles with his boat motor and couldn't check his pots today." He laughed. "'My supplier.' Makes me sound like one of those snooty 'I'll have my people call your people' types, doesn't it?"

No doubt, his 'people' would be *church* people. But Mercy had no intention of opening *that* door again.

"I grilled some big juicy steaks earlier. All I have to do is heat 'em up and warm the baked potatoes and we're good to go."

She scooted to the edge of her chair, eager to do something to busy her fidgeting fingers. "What can I do to help?"

"Hardest part of serving dinner up here is carting stuff up the ladder. Two pairs of hands means fewer trips, so I'll take you up on that offer, m'dear." He got to his feet and gave her a hand-up getting out of the chair.

"I need to get a couple of those for my terrace."

"First of all," he said, "your place is way too contemporary."

They climbed down to the galley floor. "And second of all?"

He winked. "Now *you're* the one who sounds like a 'have your people call my people' type." Chuckling, he opened a round-cornered old fridge that stood only slightly taller than the one up on deck. Like the ancient soft-edged stove, a few chips that stood out in stark contrast to the once-white enamel.

"Where did you find these wonderful old appliances? I can't think of any way to describe them except to say they're positively charming! I wonder if they'd qualify as antiques—not that you'd want to sell them. Do they work efficiently?"

She had to grin at her rapid-fire line of questioning. Well, the attorney had commented on *offering* too much information, not on gathering it.

"I have to kick the fridge now and then to remind the compressor it has a job to do," Austin said, "but the stove is as trusty as an old dog."

"How did you learn to live in such a small space?" she asked as he handed plates and bowls to her. "I mean, you're a big guy. I'll bet it took a year before you stopped whacking your elbows and clunking your forehead on these short, skinny doorways."

Nodding in agreement, Austin chuckled quietly. "Yeah, I sported a few bruises those first six months or so. But it got so I couldn't remember which I got whipping the place into shape and which came from clunking and whacking myself on stuff." Grinning, he stacked two plates and a bowl against his chest. "If you can grab what's left, I think we're all set."

She looked around to see what he'd missed, and grabbed the plate of sliced tomatoes. "Mmm. These look home grown. I'll bet you got them at Lexington Market. That's where I get my produce. And meat. And fish. And just about everything else that's best when it's fresh."

"Nope. Grew these myself. You didn't see the outstanding multi-tiered container I built with my own two hands?"

"To be honest, once I spotted that ray skimming the surface of the water, I didn't see much else."

"Sheesh," he groused. "What a *girl*."

On the upper deck, he put the food down and relieved her of the tomato plate. "Not that I'm complaining, mind you, 'cause Mercy, Mercy, Mercy, you're one girl who's mighty easy on the eyes."

She felt a blush coming on. "Do you enjoy embarrassing me?"

"The truth shouldn't embarrass you," he said, matter-of-factly. Then he struck a match and lit the grill. "Like I said, the steaks are pre-cooked, so I only need to get 'em hot. Unless you like yours well-done."

"No sir. I prefer medium rare."

"No kiddin'?"

"Is that a problem? Because if they're already well-done, I'm fine with that."

"No, it's just that I like 'em medium rare, too."

"Looks like we have music *and* meat in common."

Smiling, Austin nodded. "More tea while we're waiting for the grill to heat up?"

"I'll do it." Tapping a forefinger against her chin, she said "Something is missing."

Before he had a chance to ask what, she added, "Why aren't you wearing an apron? And a puffy white hat?"

My, but he looked adorable, blushing that way!

"I don't own a chef's hat, but I have an apron." He used his chin as a pointer. "Right over there in that cabinet."

Mercy half-ran to the drawer he'd pointed to, and, finding it, carried it to him. "Duck," she said, flapping it.

When he did, she slipped the neck strap over his head.

"Now turn around."

He did that, too, and when she reached for the ties, he grabbed her hands and said over his shoulder "I can't help but wonder what else we have in common."

And then his stomach growled.

"Well," she said, tying the strings in a tidy bow, "there's *that*."

"And let's not forget pineapple upside-down cake," he said, facing her. Hands on her shoulders, he looked deep into her eyes.

For an instant, his gaze lifted, skimmed the Chesapeake's shore. Then he kissed the tip of her nose. "Pop another album into the CD player, will ya, while I tend these steaks?"

Mercy didn't wonder which disks she'd choose, or whether to turn the volume up or down, because her brain had locked on one wish—

—that he'd aimed those mustachioed lips of his an inch *south* of her nose.

15

As they walked toward Bud and Flora's boat, Austin said, "Wish I'd taken a minute to grab the hand truck."

"Hand truck? What's a—"

"You know, one of those long-handled carts on two wheels? The kind moving men use to haul boxes from the truck?"

Mercy wrinkled her nose. "What on earth do you need—" And then she snickered. "I get it," she said, giving his arm a playful slap. "The cake isn't *that* heavy, you big tease."

Man, but he adored this little slip of a thing! Austin didn't for the life of him understand how a guy could go from resenting a woman to being nuts about her in the span of a few weeks. Or how he'd managed to put aside every angry thought and bitter emotion she represented. If she'd give him a sign— even a little one—that she loved God, he'd ask her to marry him. In a heartbeat. Now how crazy was *that*.

"Who's that on my porch?"

Austin leaned down to whisper, "That's Flora. You're gonna love her."

And she whispered right back, "If she's anything like her husband, I'm sure you're right."

The greeting alone took five minutes, and after peeling back the foil wrapper on the cake plate, another five was spent oohing and ahhing about the dessert. She put her arm around Mercy and insisted on taking her on a tour of their boat, leaving Austin and Bud in the cabin, shaking their heads.

"Sounds like a henhouse," the older man said. "Thought I'd left all that behind me in Virginia."

"Ever miss it?" Austin asked, making himself comfortable on the couch.

"Well, since we're both Irish, you'll understand better than most my need to answer your question with a question." Bud poured two cups of decaf coffee, handed one to Austin, carried one to his easy chair. "Why, I bet I'll have the stink of chicken dung in my nose as I draw my last breath. Now I ask you . . . would *you* miss that?"

Chuckling, Austin shook his head. "Who drinks hot coffee when it's ninety degrees outside?

"You 'n' me, that's who," he said matter-of-factly. Then, "What could be taking the gorgeous li'l thing so long?"

"Hey, you tryin' to move in on my girl?"

"Like I could get away with that, with old eagle eye right in the next room!" Bud chuckled, then leaned across the end table that separated his chair from the sofa and whispered, "But I hafta admit, I wouldn't mind getting to know *that* doll better. A whole *lot* better." He sat back and slapped his thigh, nearly sloshing coffee onto it in the process. "She's a treat for the eyes, I'll give you that. Puts me in mind of my Florrie, when she was a century younger, of course." He looked guiltily around. "And if you tell her I said that, I'll deny it!"

"Won't do you any good," Austin pointed out. "She'd believe me in a heartbeat And you know it."

Grinning, he waved away the comment. "Yessir," he said, nodding approvingly, "a real treat. If you have a lick of sense, you'll keep this one, son, and I mean *permanently.*"

Close, Austin, thought, *so* close to what he'd been thinking, just moments ago. "Before she died, my mom gave my brother and me some good advice about women," he said. "She told me never to overlook a girl's most annoying traits and habits. 'Stare at 'em,' she'd say. 'Put 'em under a microscope and study 'em, then ask yourself if you can live with 'em for the rest of your life, 'cause you aren't gonna change the girl—or her faults!'"

"Good advice," Bud said. "Wish somebody would've given me a piece of that advice back when I was a younger man."

"Gimme a break. You're crazy in love with that wife of yours, even after—how many years has it been now?"

"Couple more weeks, and it'll be forty-eight years." Bud shook his head. "But it hasn't *all* been peaches and cream, son. We had our sour years, too. Plenty of 'em. Every married couple does."

"My mom used to say that, too. Right before she told me that—"

Flora burst into the room with Mercy close at her heels. "This girl is a delight, Austin. If you let her get away, well, then you're even more the thickheaded Irishman than I thought you were." She gave Mercy a sideways hug, then clapped her bony hands together. "And now we're off to the galley to fix us all some cake and ice cream."

For the second time since arriving, Bud and Austin were alone in the cabin. "Your secret's safe with me, boy. You soft on this one? Or is she just another notch on your headboard?"

Austin grimaced at the coarse statement. "Good gravy, Bud. Do you always have to tell it like you *think* it is?"

"Yessir, I most certainly do. You wouldn't want me to go to the good Lord with stains on my soul from tellin' lies and fibs, now would you?"

"You're just lucky He doesn't shave points for being unnecessarily crude."

Flora and Mercy returned, each carrying two bowls piled high with ice cream. "We'd have been here sooner," Mercy said, "but Flora thought this would taste better if we microwaved the cake."

"That's right. All warm and toasty." She sat down and balanced her bowl on her knees. "Now why did I hear the word crude when I walked into the room?" She branded Bud with a steamy glare. "You haven't been telling that awful motorcycle joke again, have you?"

"No, I most certainly haven't," he said around a mouthful. "That joke isn't the least bit crude. And by the way? This cake is delicious, young lady! Can you cook, too?"

"Oh," she said, "I can navigate a kitchen fairly well."

Austin thought she looked precious, sitting there blushing like a schoolgirl. How much prettier would she look in a bridal gown and veil?

He grit his teeth, fully prepared to give himself a good talking to when Bud aimed an arthritic finger at him. "I'm tellin' you, son, let this one get away and the both of us will be sorry!"

"Listen to you, Liam Kyle Callahan!" Flora grated. "To hear you talk, every morsel of food that goes into your mouth is as black as charcoal. And just as tasteless!" She reached over and gave his ample belly an affectionate poke. "How do you explain *this* if that's the case?"

"It's a little-known fact," he said, his face expressionless, "but charcoal is very fattening."

The foursome enjoyed a moment of merry laughter.

"Liam Kyle?" Mercy said.

"That's his daddy's doing," Flora answered. "The way his mother told the story, when this silly fellow was a boy, he followed his father around like a puppy and earned the nickname Buddy. Over the years, it got abbreviated, but it stuck."

He'd often wondered how Bud came by the moniker, and, not wanting to pry, never asked. Leave it to Mercy, with her gentle, easy way, to get to the bottom of it within minutes of their first meeting. Even more amazing, she'd done it without sounding like a busy-body.

Maybe Bud had a point. Maybe he *would* be sorry if he let this one get away.

"Would you mind telling your motorcycle story?"

"Oh, Mercy dear," Flora groaned. "You have no idea what you've just done!"

"Hush, Florrie-May. Take a little nap, why don't you, while I entertain our beautiful little guest."

Flora's groan circled the room, then she got up to collect the dessert plates and spoons. "I'll be in the galley," she said, "cleaning up. Somebody call me when it's over, will you?"

But Mercy grabbed her hand, and, smiling, said "Oh, do stay, Flora. I'm almost as curious to see your reaction to the story as I am to hear it!" She relieved her of the plates. "I'll help you with these when Bud finishes. Please?"

The woman had a steel trap mind and a donkey's stubborn streak, so when she sat down and smiled, Austin and Bud exchanged a quick, shocked glance.

"There," Mercy said. "A full house for your story." She sat back and folded both hands on her knees. "Should we applaud, the way they do on that comedy show on cable TV?"

"An intro? Why, I've never had—"

"Don't push your luck, you silly old coot. Just get on with it."

Bud sat forward on his recliner and sipped his coffee, and, clearing his throat, cracked his knuckles. "The way the story goes," he said, donning a thick Irish brogue, "McAfferty and O'Brien was cruisin' down a country road on their motorbike one cold winter's day, with O'Brien at the helm and ol' McAfferty hangin' on b'hind 'im for dear life.

"'I'm freezin', O'Brien!' says McAfferty. 'Ye've got to pull over!' So over t'the side goes O'Brien, who climbs off the bike.

"'Well, St. Brigit's ghost,' says O'Brien. 'No wonder ye're cold, y'big meat head. Yer jacket's on backward!'

"So McAfferty takes off his leather coat, and O'Brien zips it up the back. 'There y'go, now,' says O'Brien, fluffin' the fur around his pal's chin. *That'll* keep y'good 'n' warm as we toodle down the highway!'

"And on they ride, until O'Brien notices the back of his bike feels a bit light, and there's no one clingin' on to his chest as if for dear life. 'Hey, McAfferty!' O'Brien yells. 'What're y'doin' back there!' When there weren't no answer, he pulls over to the side of the road again, and lo and behold, *no McAfferty*!

"So back the way they rode goes O'Brien, until he comes to two farmers, huddled over somethin' in the middle of the highway. When he gets closer, he sees that it's his pal, McAfferty, on the ground between the men. 'Lord of angels,' says O'Brien, 'I can't believe he fell off the back of my motorbike! Is he all right, then,' says O'Brien to the farmers.

"And one farmer shrugs as the other says, 'He was movin' a bit, even talkin' some when we found him, but since we turned his head around the right way, he ain't moved or said a word!'"

Bud's eyebrows rose high on his many-lined forehead and he sat, eyes wide and grinning, waiting expectantly for the laughter to begin. In the fraction of a second that passed, Austin watched Mercy, who looked helpless and bewildered as her gaze shifted from him, to Flora, to Bud, and back again. The poor kid. Unlike Flora and himself, she'd never endured the story before, and had no idea whether or not she'd heard the punch line, or, if she had, what her reaction should be.

Austin searched his mind for something to say that would spare Bud's feelings and solve Mercy's problem, as well. But his mind remained blank.

Her laughter began, slow and soft, like sea foam kissing the shore at the start of high tide. Then it grew, one sweet note at a time, until she'd written a symphony of pure pleasure that filled the room with joy and amusement. It was contagious, too, and despite Flora's best efforts to discourage Bud from ever telling the story again, merriment spilled from her lips, too.

Bud slapped a knee and whistled, then got to his feet and grabbed Mercy's hands. He pulled her from the sofa, and, planting both meaty palms on her shoulders, said "Darlin', you're good for what ails a man's heart. If the good Lord had seen fit to give me a daughter, I would've considered myself blessed if she'd been like you."

There were tears in his eyes when he returned to his chair. Austin swallowed the lump in his throat. Bud had always been the type who'd well up when things moved him, from the sight of the Stars and Stripes flapping in a blustery breeze to hearing an old love song. It had always struck Austin odd that this giant of a man—who proudly displayed battle scars earned as he felled the enemy—never had any trouble showing his sensitive side.

And it got Austin to wondering if *he* had a sensitive side.

He'd teased Mercy, not long ago, about his fragile ego. Her quick mind had come right back with a joke, or tried to, anyway. If he hadn't interrupted, how might she have finished "If I had to guess, I'd guess the only fragile thing about you is—"

Heels propped on the coffee table, he linked his fingers over his belly and sat back to watch Mercy interact with the Callahans. If he didn't know better, he would've said she'd known them even longer than he had, and Bud mirrored her animated face and gestures.

Flora, on the other hand, seemed *off* somehow. A month or so ago, under the same circumstances, she'd have been the life of the party. Tonight, her smile never quite made it to her eyes. She moved more slowly, spoke more softly, as if the brief visit had lasted hours and hours.

He waited for a slight break in the conversation to ask "So, Flora, what did your doctor say?"

"Doctor!" she echoed. "What doctor?"

Austin looked at Bud. "Did you tell me just the other day that she had an appointment?"

His happy expression died, and in its place, the stern frown of a disappointed parent. "Yes, she did," he ground out, "but she cancelled at the last minute."

"Because I overslept," she said defensively.

"But you rescheduled, right?" Austin asked.

Flora looked like a child caught with her hand in the cookie jar. "Not yet."

And Bud looked genuinely surprised. "That isn't what you told *me*."

"I'm sure it was just an oversight," Mercy put in. "In fact, I'll bet it's on your to-do list for tomorrow, isn't it, Flora?"

"Why, yes. Yes it is!"

On her feet now, Mercy added, "Well, I have an early day tomorrow, so much as I hate to, I'd better hit the road."

Everyone stood, including Flora, whose balance wavered slightly. She quickly got her bearings, but not before Bud said "If you don't call the doctor in the morning, *I will*."

"You're such a nag," she said, hugging him.

He touched a finger to her nose. "*Somebody's* gotta look out for you, since you refuse to do it yourself."

Austin slipped an arm around Mercy's slender waist and led her to the door. "Thanks, you two, for the coffee. Call me when you get home from the doctor's tomorrow."

"Wait," Flora said, darting into the galley. She returned carrying Mercy's cake pan. "Delicious as it was, we can't possibly eat all of this," she said. "Please, take it with you."

Mercy accepted it, but headed right back into the galley. "If you'll show me where you keep your storage containers, I'll leave two slices for you and Bud, and Austin can take what's left to the station."

"That's a great idea!" the older woman agreed. "*That's* sure to earn him some brownie points with the rest of his crew."

Again, Austin marveled at Mercy's instinctive people skills. He could have talked himself hoarse without getting that kind of instant cooperation from Flora! Better be careful, he warned himself, *in case she decides to turn those talents in your direction.*

But who was he kidding? She'd won him over days ago when she'd followed his ambulance to the hospital to check on the injured football player.

Moments later, on the walkway between his boat and the Callahans', Austin slid an arm across her shoulders. "You know what?"

Mercy shook her head. "No, what?"

"You're pretty amazing, that's what."

He adjusted his pace, so her short legs wouldn't have to work so hard to keep up with his long ones.

Mercy fiddled with the shiny new sheet of foil Flora had put on the cake pan. "Oh? Because of my scrumptious pineapple upside-down cake recipe?"

"Well, there's that," he said, chuckling. "And then there's your knack for putting people at ease."

"Oh, it's not really a knack so much as a job requirement. But thanks for the compliment all the same."

Affection for her surged within him, and Austin gave in to the urge to pop a kiss to the top of her head. "Y'know what?"

"No, what?"

"I like you, kiddo. I like you a lot."

She looked down at her feet, then out toward the water, and sighed. "And the feeling is mutual."

What inspired the hesitation, he wondered, preceding her words?

"I hope Flora really does call her doctor—"

Had she changed the subject on purpose? Or—

"—because I think you're right. I think something *is* wrong." She fiddled with the tin foil again. "Did you see the way she lost her balance right before we left?"

Yes, he had, but before he could admit it, she added, "Oh, I hope it's nothing serious." She stopped walking and looked up at him. "Will you call me? After Bud tells you what her doctor said, I mean?"

Starlight sparked in her eyes and the moon's glow shimmered around her hair like a white halo. Concern drew two vertical lines between her eyebrows, making him rack his brain for words that would erase them. How could she fret so much about a woman she'd only met, what, ninety minutes ago? The better question: How could anyone with a heart as big as Mercy's *not* be a Follower? "'Course I will."

"Promise?"

"Promise." He'd call even if he hadn't given his word.

Mercy gave one nod of her head and started walking again. "Good."

For the second time in as many minutes, Austin slung an arm over her shoulders. "Mind if I ask you a question?"

He felt one shoulder rise, then fall beneath his hand as she said "Long as you don't mind if I can't answer."

Doesn't take a genius to know that "can't" really means "won't".

"Nope. I won't mind a bit." *Liar,* he thought.

"OK, then, shoot."

"Why is it so all-fired important to find out what Flora's doctor says?"

"You know, I haven't the foggiest idea." She shrugged again. "It's just hard not to care about a woman like that, even given the fact that we only just met."

"I know what you mean. It was the same for me when I met her. Bud, too."

"It's weird."

"What is?"

"This knack they have, for making people feel like they've been adopted by the sweetest old couple in the world."

Was it the music in her voice or the words, themselves, that made his heart feel twice its normal size? "Yeah. I know what you mean." He held open the screen door, and as she walked into his cabin, Austin said "You have that effect on people, too."

"Hey," she said, putting the cake pan on the stove. She rummaged through is cupboards until she found the one where he kept his plates. "I'm barely thirty," she said extracting one, "who you callin' *old*?"

Smiling, Austin leaned against the companionway wall, hands in his pockets as she opened and closed drawers in search of a spatula. It pleased him that she felt comfortable enough to make herself at home. Pleased him so much that an image of her, standing in the same spot—but wearing an apron and a gold band on the third finger of her left hand—flashed through his head. Austin had to blink a few times to shake it.

Now, as she stooped to poke around in the lower cabinets, he wondered what she'd gone on the hunt for this time.

"Ah-ha!" she said, grabbing the plastic wrap. "When I'm finished getting this ready for your pals down at the station, I'll help you wash up our supper dishes."

"You don't have to do that."

"I know, but I want to."

His heart did the bigger-than-normal thing again as he pictured the two of them, side by side at the sink—her washing, him drying—performing the routine household chore of a husband and wife. Why hadn't any of the other women he'd brought here inspired thoughts of wedding rings and domestic togetherness?

Because none had baked his favorite cake? Or because none had bothered to ask what his favorite cake *was*.

Austin watched her blanket the left-over slices and put the plastic wrap back where she'd found it. He had no intention of turning down her offer to help with the dishes, not because he minded the chore, but because it gave him a legitimate excuse to be with her for . . .

. . . for as long as he could find things for her to wash.

Up on deck, Mercy popped another CD into the player, then proceeded to pile plates, glasses, and silverware onto the red tray. While Austin pretended to scrape the grill racks, she hummed along with another Eagles' tune. Would she sing out loud if a favorite song blasted from the speakers? *A guy can hope*, he thought, grinning to himself.

"Austin! Look!"

He turned in time to see her pointing at the sky. "What," he asked, joining her at the rail.

"A shooting star!"

His arm went around her as if he'd been doing it for years. "Where?"

Mercy leaned closer and, taking his hand, used his finger as her pointer. "There, right between—what are those bright ones called?"

"That one's Venus," he said. "And that's Vindemiatrix."

"I'm impressed," she said, pressing into his side.

He opened his mouth to impress her with the names of a few more when she gasped and jumped up and down like an enthused child. "Look! There goes another one!"

Nodding, he said "Yep." But he couldn't concentrate on the stars. In fact, Austin had no desire to look into the sky.

"It's amazing! I could stand here forever, just watching for the next one." She turned slightly to look up into his face. "How do you ever get any sleep, knowing there's a light show, right on the other side of your roof!"

"Some nights I don't. In fact, if I had a dollar for every night I've fallen asleep in one of those chairs—" He chuckled. "Well, I could buy a couple more chairs."

Mercy sighed. "Maybe I'll sell the townhouse and buy a tent and pitch it right here. One with a big clear-plastic window on top of it, so I could snuggle into my sleeping bag and fall asleep, watching the sky. And instead of rent, I could cook and clean for you. Why, it'd be a dream come true!"

He liked to think of himself as a "feet on the ground" kind of guy, the type who poked fun at folks who wished upon the stars. But Mercy's dream produced a silent groan that started deep in his gut and echoed all the way to his heart, because the only change he'd make to it would be to add himself to that sleeping bag—wearing a gold band on the third finger of his left hand that exactly matched hers.

He shook his head again, hoping to shake some sense into it. Or, at the very least, shake the nonsensical idea *out* of it. What he knew about Mercy, he could put in one eye. He needed time, and so did she, to—

"What's going on in that handsome head of yours?"

He'd been daydreaming, and she'd caught him red-handed. "Handsome?" Austin blinked and, grinning, said, "You think I'm handsome?"

She stood on tiptoe to kiss his chin. "Please. Like you're surprised to hear it. I'll bet a hundred girls have said the same thing, on the very spot where I'm standing right now."

His smile faded as he took her in his arms. "You're wrong, Mercy. Dead wrong. No woman has stood where you are. I never introduced any of them to the Callahans. Or grilled steaks for them. Never took 'em up on deck, never watched the sunset, never told 'em to watch for the green flash—"

"Which I missed—"

"Sorry."

Giggling, she rested her forehead on his chest. "And fire rainbows?"

"Nope. Never told 'em about those, either." He pulled her closer, so close that he could feel her heart beating hard against his chest, and much to his delight, she didn't resist.

"Keep it up," she whispered, "and I'm liable to get a big head."

"S'OK. I've always been partial to girls with big heads."

"That isn't what *Flora* said."

"Uh oh . . . I'm almost afraid to ask. What did Flora say?"

"That all of your women have been tall and lithe, blond-haired and blue-eyed. Like centerfold models. Well, except for the redhead. She had a normal figure. Oh, and green eyes."

Funny, but Austin couldn't remember ever dating a red-head, let alone bringing one here.

"How do you suppose she's so up on your type?"

"Who?"

"Flora."

He chuckled. "I dunno. Maybe she's got a telescope aimed this way."

"If that's true, it's only because she's looking out for your best interests. She thinks the world of you, you know."

Nodding, he said, "Yeah, I know. And I feel the same way about her."

"Do you think she's watching us right now?"

The moon chose that moment to slide out from behind a cloud, lighting a mischievous grin lit her gorgeous face. "Probably." Oh, to have the power to read that amazing mind and know what inspired it.

She walked her fingers up his chest until her palms came to rest on his shoulders. Raising herself on tiptoe again, she touched her lips to his. "Then what do you say we put on a little show for her?"

"Put on a—?"

"Just so she'll have a good story to tell the next girl you bring here?"

"Next girl? What're you talkin' about? There isn't going to be—"

Mercy silenced his denial with a long, tender kiss, and for the first time in his life, Austin understood what the poets meant when they wrote about pure, heart-pounding love.

16

Leo had been in town nearly a week, and, except for two breakfasts and dinner the night he arrived, Mercy had only seen him in passing.

"I'm only trying to be a good houseguest," he said when she pointed it out.

"You aren't fooling me, brother dear. You've met a wholesome Maryland girl, haven't you? Is she teaching you why the travel brochures call Baltimore 'Charm City'?"

"I must confess," he said around a mouthful of potato chips, "I'm learning a lot about the place under her tutelage, but 'wholesome' is hardly the word I'd use to describe her."

"And where, exactly, did you meet this unwholesome creature?"

He dumped a few more chips onto a paper napkin. "At the Walters Art Gallery."

"I don't believe it."

Leo shrugged and crunched another chip. "It's true, I tell you!"

"And from the gallery to—"

"—to the B&O Railroad Museum. I had no *idea* how trains moved from track to track. Quite enlightening."

"I'm sure."

"Now, now, now. Sarcasm doesn't become you."

"Uh-huh. So what are your plans for the evening?"

"I'm all yours," he said, arms wide. And after delivering an expansive yawn, Leo added, "If you can keep me awake, that is. And don't bother to blame my late hours, because I'll just be forced to remind you it's jet lag and nothing more."

Eyes narrowed, Leo gave her a sidelong glance. "All right. Out with it. What's going on in that can't-rest-for-even-a-minute brain of yours?"

"I was hoping we might have dinner together, so I could introduce you to a—to a friend."

He smirked. "A friend, eh?"

Mercy nodded and did her best not to let her enthusiasm show.

"How old is your *friend*?"

She frowned. "You know, I'm not exactly sure. Thirty-two? Thirty-five?"

He wrinkled his nose. "Ugh. A tad long in the tooth for my taste, but—blond or brunette?"

She knew as well as he that her "friend" wasn't female, but Mercy went along with the joke, just for fun. "Oh, blond. One hundred percent natural, I might add, with huge blue eyes and the longest, darkest lashes, ever."

"Sounds delightful. So delightful that I'm sure this friend must be short and squatty. You know the type— all butt no body?"

"Quite the contrary. *This* blond is tall." She stretched her arm high over her head to estimate Austin's height. "Six-two, maybe six-three?"

"Goodness," he said, grinning, "must be terribly uncomfortable."

"Uncomfortable?"

"You know, the crick in your spine."

"The crick in my spine?"

Leo looked around the room. "Odd, but this is the first time I noticed it."

"Noticed what?"

"That there's a terrible echo in this room."

"Leo, I—"

"The crick," he explained, wiggling his eyebrows, "from craning your neck to kiss him, of course!"

There had only been the one warm and tender, glorious, mesmerizing, too-short kiss, and it had been anything *but* uncomfortable.

"Mercy, dear. I don't suppose you have you any antacids?"

"As a matter of fact, I do. They're in the medicine cabinet in the hall bath. Why? Has your not-so-wholesome tour guide been feeding you too much rich Maryland seafood?"

"No, no," he said with gusto, "I've thoroughly enjoyed the local fare, and I'm happy to report that it agrees with me quite well."

"Then why do you need antacids?"

"Why, to counteract that sickeningly sweet *look* on your face, of course."

"What sickeningly sweet—"

"The one you got just now, thinking of Mr. Longest, Darkest Lashes Ever's kiss."

Mercy felt the blush creeping from her heart to her neck, and slapped both palms to her cheeks, hoping to hide it before it reached her face.

Leo tossed his paper napkin and hit her square in the forehead. "Oh, don't go all pink-faced on me. I didn't mean to embarrass you, little sister." He chuckled. "Much."

"Then you'll join us for dinner?"

"Why not?"

She resisted the urge to launch into a detailed description of Austin, what he did for a living, how much fun she had in his company—

Cold fear gripped her, because if she knew her brother, he'd ask how they met, one of the most natural conversation-opening questions ever asked. If she answered truthfully, Austin might feel uneasy. And then Leo would, too.

You're putting the cart before the horse, she thought, citing another of her father's favorite expressions. For all she knew, Austin had to work tonight. And with Leo leaving in just a few days, the two might never meet.

"Where will we dine?"

Mercy blinked. "What?"

"Are you planning to fix dinner here, or are we going out on the town tonight?"

"Oh. I-I thought I'd make us something here. That way, if you get tired, you'll only be feet from your bed."

"How very thoughtful of you, Mercy dear." He loosed a wicked snicker.

"Leo, honestly! Austin and I . . . we're nowhere near . . . I couldn't . . . we haven't . . . for all I know, he isn't even interested in me that wa—"

"Heavens to Mergetroid!" he interrupted, hugging her. "Down, girl! I'm your brother, not your father. You certainly don't owe me any explanations." He held her at arm's length. "Though I must warn you, if I get the impression he's a churlish, dastardly sort, I might be forced to break out my black belt." Leo let go of her and assumed a karate stance before unleashing a blood-curdling "H-h-hay-*ya-a-a!*"

"Have I told you lately that I love you?"

Straightening his back, he dusted imaginary dust from his trousers. "As a matter of fact, you haven't." He hugged her again, and, pressing a brotherly kiss to her forehead, said, "It's rather nice to hear, so I won't mind at all if it becomes a habit."

He yawned and stretched. "Do I have time for a nap before I shower and dress for dinner?"

Laughing, Mercy said, "It's barely noon, you big silly!"

Leo checked his wristwatch. "So it is," he said, and padded up the stairs.

When the door to his room clicked shut, Mercy picked up the phone and dialed Austin's cell number.

"Hey!" he said after the third ring.

"Hey, yourself."

"Worked a double shift yesterday or I would've called."

"I figured it was something like that."

"So, what was *your* excuse for not calling?"

She heard the smile in his voice, and it inspired one of her own. "My brother's in town."

"Cool. When do I get to meet Dr. London Bridge?"

"Tonight, if you're free."

"Hold on while I check with my secretary."

Mercy heard the muffled sound of paper-rustling before he came back on the line.

"You're in luck. Seems there's been a cancellation, and I'm happy to say there's an opening in my schedule."

"Be still my heart!"

Chuckling, he said "Where should we take him to eat?"

"He's been running around doing touristy things for three whole days, so I thought it might be a nice change for him to eat in."

"Sounds good to me. Can I bring anything?"

"Just a hearty appetite."

"What time should I be there?"

"Six, six-thirty? I'll put out some appetizers, and we'll eat at sevenish?"

"Sevenish. Got it." Then, "What's for dinner?"

"Haven't decided yet."

"I can bring something, save you the fuss and bother. Does Leo have a preference? Italian? Asian? Mexican?"

"He'd eat a rock if I salted it, but really, it's no bother. It'll be fun, cooking for my two favorite guys."

She didn't know what to make of the lengthy pause. Had she assumed too much from that kiss? Or had something in the atmosphere interrupted their cell reception? "Hello? Did I lose you?"

"No way. At least, not if I have anything to say about it. Just picking myself up off the floor, is all."

"Off the—"

"Had a dream last night that you said those very words. Woke up wearing a grin so big, my face hurt."

Mercy knew exactly what he meant, because if she kept smiling this way, her face would begin to ache, too. "See you at six."

"Five forty-five."

She laughed.

"You think I'm joking?"

"G'bye."

"G'bye."

She could hear him, chuckling on the other end of the phone. "Austin?"

"Mercy?"

"Hang up."

"No, you."

"All right, I will."

"When?"

"Right now."

A second, then two, ticked by.

Austin chuckled. "Well?"

"Well what?"

"I thought you were gonna hang up."

"I was."

"Then, why didn't you?"

"Because—" *Because I can't break the connection, that's why.*

"Weakling."

"Who?"

"Your feet don't fit a limb."

Mercy giggled. "What?"

"Owl? Tree? Feet on a limb?" He laughed. "Killjoy."

"Killjoy?"

"That's right, killjoy."

"Killjoy," she said, trying to figure out what it meant.

"A joke isn't funny if you have to explain it."

"Explain—"

"You can't see me, but I'm shaking my phone. Hard."

"Why?"

"Because I'm hoping it'll put an end to the echo, that's why."

"Echo?" And then she got it. "You're a nut."

And he started singing a commercial she hadn't heard in years. "'Sometimes I feel like a nut, sometimes I don't . . . .'"

"Austin."

"Mercy."

"If I don't hang up, I can't start dinner."

"Then I suggest you do it."

"All right. I will. Here goes."

She'd barely returned the phone to its cradle when it rang.

"I'm crushed," he said the moment she answered.

Laughing, Mercy said "Why?"

"You hung up on me!"

"Guess you'll have to do it this time, so we'll be even."

"I love the way your mind works. Scratch that. I love every-thing about you."

Fortunately, he took her advice and ended the call, because she had no idea how she would have responded.

"—and where did you say I could find those antacids?"

"Good grief! You scared me half to death!"

"I can't believe you didn't tell him."

"Tell him? Tell him what?"

He slapped a hand to his forehead. "If you think *I'm* going to play verbal 'who shot John' and repeat the ridiculous back and forth of that phone call, you've got another think coming." Then, "It's perfectly obvious that you're mad about the man. And that he's mad about you, too."

"You were—you were *listening*? Leo, I'm surprised at you!"

He pointed to the phone, with its still-lit speakerphone light.

Mercy hid behind her hands and groaned.

"Austin," he said, nodding his approval. "I rather like the name. It's strong, simple, unique. And I'm guessing it fits?"

"You'll just have to wait and see."

"Yes, of course. Until 'sevenish.'" He snickered. "That was the first time he bared his soul? Acknowledged his feelings? Confessed his love?"

Mercy groaned and headed for the kitchen. "I have to start dinner."

Leo tagged her heels. "He gave you the perfect opening. Why you didn't tell him that you feel the same way?"

She stuck her head in the fridge. "For one thing, I'm not sure *how* I feel," Mercy said, grabbing a bag of salad fixings. "And besides, he hung up before I had a chance to respond."

"That's right. He did, didn't he?"

Thankfully, she'd faced the kitchen window to shred let-tuce into a bowl.

"Well, no problem. I'll retire early and give you plenty of time—and privacy—to tell him how you feel once we've had our dessert. What are you making, by the way?"

"Chocolate cheesecake."

"I approve, heartily!"

"I aim to please."

"And the main course?"

"Beef Wellington."

"Aren't you a darling to make my favorite!"

"Well, you *are* my favorite brother."

He kissed her cheek. "Well, sister dear, I'm headed upstairs for that much-needed nap. You've worn me out, I tell you, with all your back-and-forth lovey-dovey chatter!"

Halfway up the stairs, he stopped, and, leaning over the rail, said, "Would you mind awful much if I invited my lovely redheaded friend to dinner?"

Mercy gasped. "Does she have green eyes?"

"As a matter of fact, they're nearly as brown as yours. Why do you ask?"

How ridiculous, thinking Leo's redhead and Flora's might be one and the same. The jealousy that surged through her at the possibility? Even more ridiculous! "Oh, no reason," she said. "Go ahead and invite her," she said, breathing a sigh of relief. "The more, the merrier."

"Thanks, Mercy. I'll ring her up right now."

"No thanks necessary," she said, dicing a tomato for the salad. "Now, you enjoy that nap!"

A glance at the clock told her she had six hours to prep the meat, set the table, and get herself ready. Five hours, forty-five minutes, she thought, hoping Austin had been serious about arriving early.

17

"The table looks *lovely*, Mercy, simply lovely! In fact, your entire *house* is just lovely!" The redhead clapped, then jiggled her shoulders. "I can't *tell* you how much I appreciate your invitation. What a *lovely* surprise it was when that darling brother of yours called and asked me to dinner!"

Mercy didn't know which distracted her more—Debbie's tendency to over-emphasize every other word, or Austin, standing there looking like a GQ cover model, with hands in pockets and one loafered foot crossed over the other. "I can't remember a time when Leo has enjoyed a visit to the States more," she said, "and since you're partly responsible for that, Debbie—"

"Really? Do you think he's having fun? Oh, I *hope* so," came her breathy reply, "because I'd so, so, *so* like him to come back. Or invite me to come see him in London!"

Clearly, Debbie wanted her opinion, and Mercy had no intention of giving it. "I know this dinner was rather last-minute, so I'm happy you weren't busy tonight."

"Oh, believe me, if I had been, I would gladly have cancelled for Leo. He's *such* a darling man!"

Across the pond, her brother had earned his ladies' man reputation. Charming and handsome, he attracted women simply by making his interest known. Add "doctor to the stars" to the mix, and it wouldn't have mattered to most of them if he dragged his knuckles and summoned them by thumping his chest. Mercy felt a little sorry for Debbie, because she'd certainly put a lot of effort into impressing Leo, and really, what chance did a woman like that have with a man like him!

"Tell me what I can do to help," Debbie said. "It just isn't fair that you're in here all alone, slaving over a hot stove, while the rest of us are out there in your *lovely* living room, sipping iced tea."

Mercy saw Austin's lips form the word "Alone?" A heartbeat later, he pointed to himself and mouthed, "What am I, chopped liver?"

She did her best not to grin, but Debbie saw it. "Goodness," she said, looking at Austin, "I nearly forgot you were here!" And stepping closer to Mercy, she whispered, "I've always been partial to the strong, silent types, too."

Then what are you doing with the likes of Leo? she wanted to know. "Trust me," she said instead, "Austin isn't always this quiet."

"You're *such* a *lovely* couple," Debbie gushed. "How long have you been engaged?"

Leo walked into the room in time to hear them to sputter *"Engaged?"*

"They aren't betrothed, dear sweet *lovely* Debbie." He looked at Austin, then Mercy, and said, "I dare say, I haven't the foggiest notion *how* to describe what they are to one another." Eyeing Mercy, he grinned. "Help us out, sister dear, and define your relationship for us."

She didn't have the foggiest notion how to describe *or* define it, either. Austin rescued her with "We're old friends."

"Really," Debbie said, her voice ringing with skepticism. "I would have bet a plane ticket to London that the two of you were a couple, and that you've *been* a couple for ages and ages."

"See there?" Austin said. "You've just underscored one of many reasons I'm not a gambling man."

"Same here," Mercy said. "Give me a sure thing, and I'm a happy camper."

Debbie's brow furrowed with confusion as Leo offered her his arm. "'Happy camper.' What a peculiar turn of phrase," he said, ushering her into the living room. "You Americans have so many odd expressions." Patting her hand, he said into her ear "I'm hoping you'll give me a lesson."

"Oh, *Leo!* I'd love, love, *love* to!"

Patting her hand, Leo laughed. "I'd love it, too. Why, what man in his right mind *wouldn't* want his very own talking dictionary?" As they rounded the corner, he winked at Mercy.

Once their voices faded, Austin strode up to the island and planted beefy palms on the counter. "Where did your brother find her?"

"At the Walters—or so he claims." Mercy shrugged. "Hand me that pot holder, will you?"

"This purple one?" he asked, tossing her the only one in sight. "He'd better keep his wallet in his pocket and his watch on his wrist."

"She's a bit—" Mercy searched for the right word, "— a bit eccentric, but Debbie seems harmless enough. And Leo seems to enjoy her company."

One brow rose on his forehead. "Right. Company. That's probably what I'd tell you, too, if you were my sister." He held up a hand to forestall her retort. "But just for the record, I'm so, so, *so* glad you're not my sister."

"In med school, I spent a few weeks on the children's ward, and read *Never Tease a Weasel*. If I ever have kids, it'll be on their bookshelf, for sure." Then she launched into a line from the book. 'The weasel will not like it, and teasing isn't nice.'"

"I don't know whether you're saying Debbie's a weasel, or that I'm not allowed to tease you."

Before she could tell him which, he quickly added, "If that stuff in the pot tastes half as good as it smells, my belly is in for a real treat."

"This *stuff*," she explained, "is Beef Wellington. I thought since Leo's only in town a few more days, it'd be nice to fix him a nice meal. Something he wouldn't get in a restaurant. Well, he could, I suppose, but it wouldn't be homemade, just for him."

"I skipped lunch."

"Duly noted."

"So tell me . . . ."

Squinting, he tilted his head, and Mercy waited for another "Leo Question." With any luck, she wouldn't need to remind him that two weeks during summer vacation and every other Christmas hadn't given her much time to bond with her brother.

"How come 'July' is pronounced 'Joo-*lie*' and we say '*doo-lee*, even though it's spelled almost exactly the same way?"

Mercy slid the roaster from the oven to the stovetop and met his eyes. "Um . . . because the English language is almost as confusing and difficult as Mandarin Chinese?"

"I think you and I should catch a movie tomorrow night."

"I don't see any bumps or bruises on your head."

Austin ran a hand through his hair. "Bumps and—"

"How else am I to explain that you've jumped from Leo to the entrée to phonics, and now movies in a span of, what, two minutes?"

She laughed, and when he joined her, Mercy wished she'd been born with a better-developed comic gene. That way, she could crack jokes any time she had a yen to enjoy the delightful sound. "Would you do me a favor?"

He walked around to her side of the island, and, hands on her shoulders, said "Your wish is my command."

"Let Leo and Debbie know that dinner will be on the table in five minutes?"

He grimaced. "Aw, Mom, do I hafta?"

"Only if you want dessert."

He raised one eyebrow. "What did you make? 'Cause if it isn't worth the trip in there—"

She slid the beef onto a deep platter. "Chocolate cheesecake. It's one of—"

"Yeah, yeah, I know, one of Leo's favorites. Is it homemade?"

"Uh-huh. And you haven't called them to the table."

"From scratch?"

"Yes, using a recipe I found on the Internet this afternoon."

"Just like that."

She grinned back at him. "Just like that." And pointing toward the living room, she said, "Please?"

Leaning forward, he pressed a light kiss to her forehead. "I'll be back in two shakes of your serving spoon to help you carry stuff to the table."

And before she could tell him that wasn't necessary, he hustled toward the doorway. Mercy stood stock-still, slotted spoon in one hand, purple pot holder in the other, and caught a glimpse of herself in the polished glass of the microwave door. The sight inspired an embarrassed giggle. *You look like the experiment of a mad scientist who crossed the Cheshire cat with Mickey's pal, Goofy.*

She started to lift the heavy ironstone platter when Austin darted back into the room.

"My eyes, my eyes!" he said, covering them with his fingertips.

Mercy dampened a paper towel and raced to his side. "What happened? Did you walk past the automatic air freshener and take a spritz to the face? That happened to Woodrow once. Ohmygoodness, don't tell me you've developed an allergy to him—"

When Austin came out from hiding, *he* grinned like the Cheshire cat. "No, but I'd take either over what I just saw: your brother and his . . . and his *Debbie*, doing their best to imitate a couple of human pretzels. Why, I'll bet he—" He noticed the paper towel. "Is that for me?"

Mercy clucked her tongue. "Well, it *was*."

"Y'know what?"

"I'm almost afraid to ask."

"You're sweet." He pulled her to him. "And thoughtful. And caring, too."

"Much as I hate to interrupt your admiration recitation, I just have to ask: Did you get a chance to call them to the table before their twining rendered you temporarily blind?"

"No. I did not. But I will. Right after."

"After what?"

"After this." And he proceeded to kiss her, long and slow and sweet, then stepped back and smacked his lips, as if he'd just gulped a tall refreshing glass of lemonade. "Ahh," he sighed. "That oughta hold me 'til dessert."

18

He heard her mantle clock counting out the eleven o'clock hour as they walked onto the terrace. "Your brother's quite a card," he said, settling down beside her on the rattan loveseat.

"Funny, but he said the same thing about you."

"Wouldn't it be a hoot, getting Leo and Bud in the same place at the same time?"

"We'd probably do permanent damage to our vocal cords, laughing at their antics."

He slid an arm around her. "Let's hope not. I love the sound of your voice."

Austin might have said more if she hadn't leaned her head on his shoulder. "How much longer can Leo stay?"

"I think his plane is scheduled to take off day after tomorrow. A red-eye flight."

"I hate those."

"Why?"

"'Cause there you are," he said, his hand emulating a jetliner, "over the inky Atlantic. You know it's down there, but you can't see it. Or anything else." He faked a nervous shiver. "Scary."

"Funny," she said again, "but I can't picture you being scared of anything."

He snorted, "Obviously, you don't know me well enough."

"Yet."

Her one-word reply sent his heart into overdrive. What was it about her that brought out such enormous reactions in him?

"I'll check my schedule. If I'm not on duty, I'll drive you two to the airport."

Mercy only nodded.

"Unless you'd rather be alone to say goodbye . . . ."

She giggled. "He's my brother, not my boyfriend, y'big silly."

For some-odd reason, her remark reminded him of something Leo had said over dinner, about twice-yearly visits to Long Island that stopped abruptly after 9/11. "So what happened after September eleventh? Did he get cold feet about flying?"

"No. At least I don't think so."

"Then why did he quit making semi-annual jaunts to the good ol' U.S. of A.?"

"Because I stopped inviting him."

"Am I being too nosy if I ask why?"

The distant notes of sirens and car horns peppered the steady buzz of city traffic that slipped over the tall brick walls surrounding the outdoor room. Was Mercy's silence her way of saying she didn't want to talk about it?

"Airfare from Heathrow to BWI isn't cheap."

"Please. He could afford his own private jet and an on-call pilot if he didn't want to fly it himself."

"True, but it's still a long flight, and I wouldn't have been a very good host in those days."

He took her hand in his and rolled back the cuff of her blouse. "'Those days,'" he echoed, running a forefinger over her wrist. "Is that when you did this?"

Austin half expected her to snap her hand back. But she didn't. Instead, she said, "Every time I see those scars, it takes a second or two to for it to sink in. Some days, I still can't believe that I did that to myself."

Last thing he wanted was to awaken bad memories. He searched his mind for something else to talk about, to get her mind off whatever had driven her to take such a drastic and desperate step.

"I was pretty close to quitting my job when it happened, so it was a relief when my boss said he couldn't have somebody with such questionable mental stability working with cops who were psychologically shaky, themselves."

He sat quietly, one forefinger gently stroking the back of her hand. If she wanted to talk about it, Austin would listen. And if she didn't? He said a silent prayer, to thank God for saving her. She had survived, and learned to deal with whatever had driven her to it. What else mattered?

"There was this one cop," she said quietly, snuggling closer, "who just couldn't seem to cope with what he'd seen that day. Came to his sessions blind drunk most of the time."

"Hey, wait just a minute, here. We aren't talking about *me*, are we?"

"No," she said, laughing softly, "you never showed up *blotto*."

He thought of the time she'd looked him in the eye and asked him straight out when he'd last consumed alcohol. Ashamed—and afraid of what she'd write in his file—he'd lied through his teeth. Austin had already made his peace with God for it, and one of these days, he'd fulfill the dictates of number nine on the twelve steps list, and make amends to Mercy, too.

"Took me weeks," she said, "but I finally got him to agree that he needed more help than I could give him, and convinced him to sign himself into a rehab center."

He felt for the guy. It had taken Griff two miserable days to talk Austin into making a commitment to AA. How much more agonizing had it been for *that* cop?

"About halfway through his treatment," she continued, "his wife said she couldn't take it any more. Packed up the kids and left him, just like that. He signed himself out of the treatment facility, and by the time he got to my office, he looked like he'd been run over by a city bus. He'd been sober when he told me all about it, but not long enough to go out there on his own." She heaved a shaky sigh. "So I prescribed paroxitine, because it had worked so well for my other patients with chronic depression or PTSD."

Mercy lapsed into another long silence, making Austin feel like a first-class heel for opening the door to the disturbing subject. He looked toward the heavens for help in leading her away from the tormenting memories, when Venus winked her bright light into the inky darkness. Maybe the Lord would see fit to cast a shooting star across the sky, the way He had when she'd had dinner on *One Regret.*

"He must have filled the script on his way home from my office, gone straight home and swallowed every pill, all at the same time."

Austin cringed. "Jeez. That's terrible." He glanced down at her. "But it wasn't your fault. You know that, right?"

"Yeah. But that didn't stop me from second-guessing myself. Maybe I should've given him a smaller dose. A different drug. *No* drugs—" She ended with a raspy sigh. "But that isn't why I did this," she added, holding out both wrists.

Austin tensed. If she started talking about why she had tried to kill herself, should he let her . . . or change the subject?

"I hate to sound like a walking cliché, but my dad's death was the straw that broke this camel's back."

She'd already told him that her father had become a citizen, that he'd converted to Christianity. Austin had a feeling she was about to add to the raw and painful story. Should he let her? Would talking about it be therapeutic . . . or psychologically damaging? "Oh?"

Mercy nodded against his shoulder, and he pulled her a little closer. *Lord, give me the strength to say what she needs to hear . . . .*

"One night at the end of his watch, after his partner went home for the night, I met Dad for supper at his favorite little pizza place, right around the corner from his apartment. We'd barely had a bite when this guy came in, screaming and shouting and waving the biggest handgun I'd ever seen. He demanded all the money in the cash register, and the poor kid behind the counter got so scared that he could barely do more than tremble. Guess he didn't move fast enough, because that animal shot him, jumped over the counter, and helped himself to the money.

"Dad shoved me to the floor and radioed for help, then tried to chase the guy. But he didn't get very far before the robber shot him, too. Point blank."

And she'd seen and heard it all. *Thing like that would mess anybody up*, he thought, wincing.

"He was a fighter, though, and hung on for nearly two months in Intensive Care. And then pneumonia set in." Her voice thick with tears, Mercy wrapped up with "He died in my arms."

Austin didn't know her well, but he knew better than to say anything that smacked even remotely of pity or sympathy. So he sat quietly, patting her shoulder as the fingers of his free hand absently stroked the long white scar on her arm.

"After the funeral, I kind of hit rock bottom, let self-pity do a number on me." Another shrug, and then a nervous little laugh. "So there you have it. The story of 'Why the Shrink Attempted Suicide.'"

The misery in her voice made his heart ache. If only he knew how to comfort her! "So who found you, got you to the hospital?"

"Leo . . . sort of."

"He was in town?"

"No." Another peculiar giggle. "He stayed with me for a few days right after the shooting, got me through the surgery. But he had patients of his own to take care of." Mercy shook her head. "So he started calling every night at midnight to check up on me. When I didn't answer that night, he called out the cavalry. Told them to break down the doors and shatter the windows if they had to."

Austin remembered a few occasions when he'd been forced to do the same thing. Remembered, too, how he'd been just as horrified during the last rescue as he'd been on the first, regardless of the choice of weapon. His heart clenched, picturing Mercy as the victim.

" The paramedics made such a mess that my landlord threatened to sue. But once again, it was Leo to the rescue. While they were patching me up in the hospital, he wrote a check to the greedy old miser. Bought me a one-way trip to London and threatened that if I didn't use it, he'd get on the next plane and kick my butt all the way across the Atlantic." A sad sigh punctuated her sentence. "Turns out he knows me fairly well, despite how little time we were together as kids."

"I ought to go upstairs and wake him up, right now."

"Why?"

Austin turned her to face him, and, bracketing her face with his hands, kissed her forehead and chin and the tip of her nose. Her eyes sparkled with unshed tears, and when she blinked, one slid slowly down her cheek. He caught it with the pad of one thumb, then kissed the shiny track it painted on her skin. "For saving you, that's why."

A sweet, warm smile lifted the corners of her mouth before she snuggled into the crook of his neck.

And that's where she stayed until the clock struck twelve.

19

*L*eo tossed his bag into the trunk. "I thought your boyfriend wanted to drive us to the airport."

"He did, but there's a weird strain of the flu going around, and the station is short-staffed."

"Another peculiarity about America," he said, smirking as he slid into the passenger seat, "everybody seems to catch everything that's going around, all at the same time."

Grinning, Mercy rolled her eyes and revved the motor. "Right. Like the same thing doesn't happen in London."

"Touché. I suppose."

She merged with the early-afternoon traffic and sighed. "I wish your visit was just beginning, instead of ending. That way, you'd be here for Thanksgiving."

"Never have been much of a turkey-and-the-trimmings fan."

"I'd be happy to make something special, just for you."

He reached across the console and squeezed her shoulder. "You could always come to London for the holiday, you know. If not for Thanksgiving, then maybe Christmas?"

There was no mistaking the sad, pensive tone in his voice. "So what do you think of Austin?" If that didn't get his mind off the reasons she'd last gone to London, nothing would.

"Seems a right likable chap. Smart. Good sense of humor. And it's quite obvious that he positively *adores* you."

"You think so?"

"I can't believe you even have to ask! Surely you've seen the way he looks at you. Why, he reminds me of an adoring puppy, following his mistress hither and yon."

Mercy giggled. "Hither and yon, indeed. You've got a lot of nerve, making fun of the way we Americans talk."

Leo laughed, and after a moment of silence, said, "Ah, I'm going to miss you, Mercy m'love."

"Not as much as I'll miss you."

"Such a silly girl. Why would you say such a thing?"

"Because you have relatives in London. And all over England, for that matter. Lots of them. And a few in France, and Italy, and Canada, too. But you're it for me."

Leo nodded. "Yes. I suppose that's true enough, at least where blood-kin are involved. Makes me all the more pleased to know that you'll have this Austin fellow looking out for you."

"I don't need 'this Austin fellow,'" she snapped, "or anyone else, for that matter, looking out for me."

"Now, now . . . I'm only pointing out that I'll rest a lot easier, knowing how much he cares for you. Why, I'm sure it's safe to say that he wouldn't think twice about putting his life on the line for you."

"Austin was a New York City cop, don't forget, and now he's an EMT. Putting his life on the line is second nature to him."

"Oh, the lies we tell ourselves!"

From the corner of her eye, she saw him frown, and tensed in anticipation of whatever tell-it-like-it-is bit of advice he intended to deliver.

"Funny," Leo said, "but that lost-in-love puppy look that's all over the man's face? I didn't see anything even remotely like it on yours."

"I'm a psychiatrist," she defended. "How would it look to my patients if I let my feelings show?"

"To begin with, you're a guidance counselor now, and those drug-addicted brats who come to you for help in choosing the most mind-numbing, time-wasting courses on the docket wouldn't notice if you wore a pirate hat and an eye patch."

"They aren't brats." *Not all of them, anyway.*

"And besides, not even your Hollywood mega-stars can act that well. I don't mind admitting that I watched you like a hawk, and not once did I see so much as a glimmer of affection beaming from your eyes when you looked at him."

"Because I've mastered the fine art of keeping my emotions to myself!"

He started to protest when she pointed at the big green sign just ahead. "Oh, dear. So soon? 'Airport,'" she read aloud, "'next right.'"

"Here's your hat, what's your hurry, eh?" Leo chuckled. "All right, darling, I can take a hint. But just let me say one last thing and then you have my word, the subject is closed: Austin the constable-turned-paramedic is crazy in love with you, so if you don't feel the same way about him, well, it might be kinder to stop seeing him."

She'd never believed Leo meant any meanspiritedness or malice on the occasions he'd put her in an awkward position. Deliberate or not, Mercy had taught herself to ignore his big-brother teasing, because as a rule, the subject matter itself, had been trivial. *This* topic, however, was neither ordinary nor petty. "Who says I don't feel the same way?"

"Omission, sweet sister of mine, speaks louder than words."

Mercy had always taken pride in the fact that she'd never been the "heart on her sleeve" type. Keeping her emotions in check hadn't just been part of doing her job well—it had become a permanent character trait. She might have pointed that out, if his airline's colorful sign hadn't come into view, glowing into the early-evening darkness.

Mercy had barely rolled to a stop before Leo leaped from the car and rapped on the trunk. "Pop the lid, darling girl," he said, meeting her eyes in the rearview mirror.

"Here's your hat, what's your hurry," she echoed, standing on the curb as he retrieved his bag.

"You of all people know how much I hate goodbyes." He kissed her cheek. "Wouldn't want me getting on the plane with all those pretty—and hopefully available stewardesses—all puffy-eyed and weepy, now would you?"

"You're showing your age," she teased, tidying his collar. "They haven't been called stewardesses for years and years."

He rolled his eyes. "Someday, I'm going to learn of a distant island where the natives haven't yet heard of political correctness. And when I do, I'll pack up and move there."

"What? And leave all your celebrity patients behind? Don't make me laugh!"

Leo pulled back his sleeve and looked at his watch. "Good. I can check in and make it to the gate without any fuss and bother. I sat beside a red-faced, sweaty man on the way over here, and I have *no* desire to be that man on the way home!"

"Have a safe flight," she said, hugging him. "Call me when you land. Or, if you're bored, call from the air!"

"Are you daft, girl? Do you know what those air-to-ground calls *cost*?"

With that, he grabbed his bag and rolled it toward the terminal. Mercy ran after him, gave him one last hug. "I'm really gonna miss you, you big nut!"

"Goodness, girl, are you trying to see if a hundred pound, five-foot weakling can knock a former rugby star off his feet!" Then he held her at arm's length and added "If you change your mind about spending Christmas in London, you'll let me know?"

She wouldn't change her mind, but why rehash an already sore subject? "Of course. And if you feel like making the trip back here for the holiday, well, I'd just love that!"

Leo pressed a noisy kiss to her forehead. "I'm proud of you, Mercy, and happy to see you happy."

"Speaking of happy," she said, looking for a way to stall, at least another moment more, "how soon will Debbie be visiting you in jolly old England?"

"Never, if I have any say about it."

"I'm shocked!" she admitted. "You two seemed so . . . so cozy at dinner the other night."

"Apparently, a talent for not allowing one's feelings to show on one's face is an inherited trait. Suffice it to say Debbie is a tad too effervescent for my liking."

Mercy recalled the way the redhead put double-emphasis on just about everything, for no apparent reason. "I love you, Leo, and I'm really, really going to miss you. That big old house just won't be the same without you."

"Love you, too," he said, and, after a final hug, walked into the terminal. Inside, he turned to wave one last time before blending into the crowd of travelers who'd congregated at the ticket counters.

The drive home seemed three times longer than the trip to BWI, and on the way Mercy thought about Leo's assessment of her feelings for Austin. Had she really become so proficient at hiding her emotions that her only brother couldn't read her, at least once in a while? And if he couldn't, surely Austin felt just as confused.

She didn't like the idea of ending things with Austin. For one thing, how would she end something that hadn't officially started? For another, their time together had always been enjoyable. Well, except for his maddening tendency to put *Jesus* into nearly every blessed thing. God had never been there for her. Not when her mother left, or when she drowned. Not when 9/11 tore the nation apart, or as she tried to help those who'd witnessed more death and dying in one day than fifty Americans see in a lifetime. Not when her patient committed suicide, or when her father tried to stop an armed killer, and certainly not when her father died in her arms.

She had no use for a being who, in her opinion, had repeatedly turned His back on her. Mercy didn't even care enough about Him to summon those old, bitter thoughts any more.

Yet something akin to anger smoldered deep in her soul . . . .

Let Austin put his faith in heavenly powers if that helped him when ugly memories rose up and threatened to choke every moment's peace from his life. Mercy had made out just fine without divine intervention—including that bloody little episode with the kitchen knife—and saw no reason to alter her beliefs or her behavior.

The traffic light at Pratt Street turned yellow, and only then did Mercy realize how many miles out of her way she'd driven. She braked, nodding because suddenly, she understood the confusion that sometimes clouded Austin's clear, honest eyes, why he sometimes seemed afraid of getting too close, or saying too much. How much farther might their relationship have progressed if she hadn't held back so much of herself?

"Oh, give yourself a break," she blurted, slapping the steering wheel, "it's only been two and a half months since you reconnected with him! You can't expect to—"

The passenger in the car beside hers met her gaze and raised his eyebrows. Pointing at his chest, he mouthed, "You talkin' to *me*?"

Thankfully, the light turned green, and she wasted no time moving forward. As she turned right on President Street, Mercy grinned. *You must have looked like a first class weirdo to the poor guy!* By the time she maneuvered the circle around Baltimore Civil War Memorial, the quiet giggle had turned into full-blown laughter. She was pulling into her garage on Aliceanna when it dawned on her that Austin was the only person who'd understand why she saw found the whole thing so funny.

Warmth flooded her being and pulsed in her heart. Was as she thought *Maybe you do love him . . .*

. . . just a little bit . . .

20

"If you don't have other plans," Mercy said into the phone, "I'd love for you and Bud to come to Thanksgiving dinner."

Flora's laughter trickled through the wires. "Gracious, girl, that's three weeks off. You do believe in planning ahead, don't you?"

Was it her imagination, or had the poor dear caught a head cold? "Well, I'm not overly fond of last-minute invitations, so I figure no one else is, either. Besides, I didn't want to risk that someone else would snap you up before I got the chance!"

She half expected Flora to say that she and Bud would spend the holiday with their children and grandchildren. "Hold on a sec," she said instead, "while I see what this old buzzard I'm married to says about it."

Yes, definitely something different about Flora's voice. But maybe it only seemed that way because Mercy hadn't spoken with her on the phone before. As she listened to the Callahans' muffled back-and-forth exchange, she recalled her tour of their schooner. In a place that small, why hadn't she seen any photographic evidence of extended family, like pictures of gap-toothed youngsters or photos of newlyweds?

Bud's voice interrupted her thoughts. "I, for one, would be delighted to eat a Thanksgiving turkey that isn't dry as toast, and stuffing that's ain't soggy as a deck mop."

And Flora hollered from the background "Tell her we usually eat out on Thanksgiving, or she'll think I'm the one who serves up slop like that!"

Mercy heard the smile in his voice when he said "I'm sure there's no need for me to repeat that since my lovely wife can bellow like a foghorn." He lowered his voice to add, "One of us will call you in a week or so to let you know for sure. Whether we can come or not will depend entirely on what the docs say after they've read her test results."

As she hung up, Mercy realized this was another bit of information Austin hadn't shared with her. Not that it had been entirely his fault. Between chaperoning before- and after-school activities and delivering Tommy's homework every afternoon, Mercy hadn't been home much in the weeks since Leo returned to England.

Tommy . . . .

The poor kid, she thought, remembering the brittle voice mail message from his mother: "Much as we appreciate all the trouble you've gone to, gathering his books and visiting all his teachers to make sure Tommy doesn't fall behind, his dad or I will do it from now on."

If she'd known that her little speech would inspire such drastic action, Mercy would have made it, anyway. Mrs. Winston needed to hear that her pampering—though rooted in an attempt to keep her boy safe and off the football field—had put him behind at school *and* slowed his recovery. In the days since, his mother stuck to her guns, and, unfair as that was for Tommy, Mercy was powerless to help him.

Frustration mounted when that same week two juniors decided to quit school, and nothing she said could convince them otherwise. Drug-sniffing dogs found pot in one of the seniors' lockers. Mercy pointed out that it was the girl's first offense, but the school board chose to make an example of her. She might have coped with two hundred hours of community service, but the month-long suspension meant she couldn't graduate with her class, and she became the third student to drop out.

Learning that Flora might have a serious condition did nothing to improve Mercy's mood, so she tackled the guest room in the hope the work would get her mind off things. When vacuuming and dusting and putting fresh sheets on the bed did nothing to raise her spirits, she moved to the hall bath. Maybe those chores would leave her exhausted enough to sleep without worrying about the welfare of her students. Mercy was elbow-deep in a bucket of pine cleaner when the front doorbell rang.

Drying her hands on her jeans, she muttered, "Who could that be at this hour?"

If she had glanced through the peep hole, Mercy would never have opened the door, because the last person she wanted to see while covered with suds and sweat was Austin.

Grinning, he held up a big brown paper bag and headed straight for the kitchen. "I wasn't sure if you'd want sweet and sour or barbecue sauce," he said, putting tiny white containers onto the counter, "so I got both."

Mercy slapped a palm to her forehead and groaned.

"Whoa. Don't tell me you forgot our date."

"All right, I won't tell you."

"Is it OK if I pout after we eat? I'm starved."

She didn't even want to think about how she must look, with her hair tied back in a bandanna and her jeans rolled up to her knees. "Just let me get cleaned up a litt—"

"Please. Don't." He flipped on the radio and fiddled with the dial until he found a soft rock station. "The charwoman look is great on you."

The delicious scents wafting from the containers reminded her she hadn't eaten since breakfast. At the sink, she washed her hands, then hopped onto a counter stool and flapped a paper napkin across her lap. "Pass the wasabi, will you please?"

His did, eyes widening when she scooped a generous portion onto her plate. "You're not seriously gonna eat that."

"Of course I am." And to prove it, Mercy dabbed some onto her sushi and popped it into her mouth.

Laughing, he said "Remind me not to kiss *you* on the lips. At least not until you've had plenty of water to wash that stuff down!"

She stopped chewing long enough to try and make sense of what he'd said. Once she figured it out, Mercy grinned. "You don't like spicy foods?"

He was emulating a rock star, bobbing his head and drumming on the granite with his chopsticks when he said, "Well, sure. Just not in megadoses." Then he speared a dumpling. "So how was your day?"

She rolled her eyes. "Please. Don't get me started."

"That bad, huh?"

She told him about the dropouts and Tommy's mom, and the girl who'd been suspended for hiding pot in her locker. "Days like this, I'd like to round them all up and put them each into suspended animation, until I can figure out what to *do* with them."

He shrugged one shoulder. "Good thing Leo isn't here. He's already convinced they're doomed to a life of crime."

"Don't remind me."

"Heard from him since he left?"

Mercy nodded. "Once when he called to tell me he'd made it home safely, once to say he missed Debbie."

"You're kidding."

She shook her head. "Took me by surprise, too. Especially since he told me on the way to the airport that she isn't his type."

"Guess there's no accounting for some people's taste."

"That isn't very nice." She lifted one brow to add. "Isn't very *Christian*, either."

"How do you figure that? 'Honesty is the best policy.'"

"Yeah, well," she said, emptying the contents of a thimble-sized container of sweet and sour sauce over her egg roll, "it's possible to be nice *and* honest, y'know."

"What can I say? I just wouldn't have guessed that redhead is Leo's type." He paused long enough to capture her gaze with his own. "I know she sure as shootin' ain't *mine*."

Mercy pretended that not spilling the sauce required deep concentration because she had no intention of asking what his type was. An open-ended question like that could only lead to . . .

"So how was *your* day?"

"Listen to us," he said, "sitting here over supper, talking about our days like an old married couple."

Now really, she asked herself, why would a little joke like that start her heart beating like a parade drum? "I talked to Flora and Bud earlier."

"Yeah? 'Bout what?"

"Invited them to Thanksgiving dinner."

"And . . . ?"

"And if the doctors say it's OK, they'll come."

Austin shook his head. "Bud's about going nuts waiting for the reports."

"I never did understand why it takes so long. The waiting is probably at least as damaging for patients as hearing the results of whatever the doctors and lab techs are looking for."

"I'm dying to ask what they're looking for," he said as the furrow deepened between his brows.

"Weird."

"What is?"

"I don't know why, but I figured you already knew."

"Just because we're neighbors doesn't mean I'm all up in their business, y'know."

She chose to ignore his biting tone. He'd probably had a far worse day than she had—given what he did for a living—and that was saying something. "How many kids do they have?"

"None. They had a son," Austin said, "a firefighter. He died about five years ago when the roof of a burning building caved in, and took him with it."

The image of it raced through her head, and Mercy grimaced. "That's—that's. Just. *Awful.*" And she meant it, with every fiber of her being. It made her angry, hearing that Flora and Bud had lost their only son—while he was performing a life-saving task, no less. And now Flora might have god-knows-what. "What is it with that *God* of yours?" she demanded.

His eyebrows rose and his eyes widened. "He's *your* God, too."

"Oh, no He isn't, either! What kind of *God* sits up there on His throne, watching, doing *absolutely nothing* while all over the world decent people die in accidents and fires and floods and wars and terror attacks." She was on a tear and knew it, but couldn't stop the breathless flow of furious words. "I can't put my faith in a being that would allow such terrible things to happen to good people like the Callahans and their son. And my students. And your mom and brother. And *my* dad, and—hard as it is for me to get past my lips—my mom, and you and me and—"

"Mercy," he interrupted gently, "God didn't *allow* any of that to happen."

"Oh, please! Save your self-righteous sermonizing for one of your airheaded bimbos. I wasn't born yesterday. I've heard all about how He's 'all powerful' and 'all merciful.' How He works miracles every single day." Both hands flat on the counter, she leaned closer. "Well, if that's true, how do you explain all the suffering and evil in the world?"

Calmly, quietly, he helped himself to another piece of sushi. "Jeez. You weren't kiddin' when you said you had a bad day, were you?"

How many times had her dad warned her not to discuss politics or religion with anyone unless she was one hundred percent certain they held the same beliefs. Too many to count, yet there she sat, spewing ire like a human Vesuvius. She'd apologize in a minute or two, once she'd caught her breath and quit trembling with rage.

"Did the Callahans say when Flora's reports would be in?"

One shoulder lifted and she did her best not to snarl "I gather they're expecting to hear something within the next few days, because Bud said one of them would call about a week before Thanksgiving to let me know if they can make it or not."

Austin only nodded, so she tacked on "If Mohammad can't come to the mountain . . ."

He looked up so quickly, she was surprised his neck didn't pop. And he wasn't smiling when he said "Was that some kind of test?"

Years ago, he'd asked the same thing in her office. Back then, though the question was out of line, it had at least made sense, given his situation. But now? Mercy had no idea what he was talking about, and said so.

"You know, a test, to see if I'd say something anti-Muslim, to retaliate for the way you slammed God just now?"

Mercy hadn't known what he might say, but if asked to guess, it certainly wouldn't have been *that*. She supposed she had it coming, because she *had* torn his precious heavenly Father to shreds just now.

"I'll be perfectly honest with you, Austin. I don't believe in *any* god. Not the god of the Christians or the Jews or the Buddhists or the Muslims or any other religion you can name. Life experiences have made it very clear to me that there is no god. Not in heaven. Not on earth. Not in your heart or mine. None."

How could he sit there so cool and calm while she ranted and raved like a lunatic? For all she knew, he'd already dialed the state's best psychiatric hospital and any minute now, a big white truck with "Shephard Pratt" printed across its side would roll up to cart her off to a padded cell. *If you stop behaving like a lunatic, it'll be your word against his.*

"So no, that wasn't a test. I'm sorry for all the yelling, because it isn't your fault the world's in such a sorry state, and if it makes you feel safer believing there's a great and powerful entity up there in the sky looking out for you, well, this *is* America."

He took a gulp of his drink and said "So what time's dinner on Thanksgiving?"

It didn't go unnoticed that he'd ignored her apology. A good sign, she wondered, or a bad omen? "Three o'clock?"

"Need me to bring anything? I'm told I make one mean spinach dip."

He'd grinned to say it, but only slightly, and Mercy knew it was her fault that the smile never reached his eyes.

"M-m-m. Love the stuff." If she had any sense at all, she'd thank her lucky stars that he still wanted to come to Thanksgiving dinner. But if she had any sense at all, she'd never have allowed their once strictly professional relationship to become such an important part of her life. "Do you put yours in a pumpernickel or rye bread bowl?"

He opened another tiny container of sweet and sour sauce. "I usually just slop it in bowl and serve it with crackers. But I'm happy to hollow out a loaf of bread if that's the way you like it; whichever is your preference."

In the weeks since they'd reconnected, Austin had never sounded—or looked—more stiff and formal as he did now. If only she'd heeded her dad's advice, and sidestepped the whole religion thing! Why had she let her emotions take control over logic?

"Either's fine."

Again, he only nodded, then leaned against the stool's back-rest and patted his flat stomach. "I'm stuffed."

She didn't want him to leave. Ever. "You know how Asian food is," Mercy said, forcing a smile. "You'll be hungry again in half an hour."

On his feet now, he stretched. "Early day tomorrow," he said on the heels of a yawn. "Better hit the road." Then he began stacking empty containers and paper plates from the counter. "What're your plans for tomorrow night?"

"I don't have any." No matter what he suggested, she intended to go along with it. And make it clear she was happy to do it, if it meant spending time with him.

"I promised to grill pork chops for Flora and Bud, with my famous barbecue sauce on 'em. I can throw an extra chop in the grill." He tossed the trash into the stainless can near the sink. "If you feel like making the drive over, that is."

"I'd like that."

"Or I could pick you up," he added, rinsing sweet and sour from his fingers.

"No, that'd be an incredible waste of time and energy." It seemed to Mercy they'd had a very similar conversation in their recent past.

Their past. She had to clean up this mess her big mouth had made, because Mercy would hate it if her outburst turned the phrase into a permanent condition. "And gasoline."

Another silent moment slid by, and then Woodrow flopped onto his side between them and delivered a happy "pet me" chirrup. When they crouched to fill his request, their foreheads collided, inspiring a round of tension-breaking laughter.

On his feet now, he rubbed his eyebrow. "How am I gonna explain a black eye to the guys tomorrow?" he joked.

"Just tell them the truth. You spent the evening with a hard-headed woman."

Gathering her close, he kissed the tender spot above her right eyebrow. "Well, I'll say this for you . . ."

Mercy looked up into his open, honest face and waited expectantly for him to complete his thought.

". . . you sure aren't afraid to tell it like it is."

It's a very good thing, she thought as he kissed her, that people close their eyes when they kiss, because in this instance, at least, the action helped hide her tears of relief that he'd forgiven her tantrum.

21

Heat seeping through his favorite mug warmed his palms, and he downed a gulp of strong black coffee. It would take this—and the rest of the pot—to counterbalance his long, sleepless night.

The weatherman said temps might reach fifty today, but the slate gray sky said otherwise. Austin watched the white vapor of his silent yawn float on the cold November wind, wondering why life sometimes felt like a tapestry of "ifs."

If he'd sewn up that hole in his pocket when it first appeared, the button of his old police-issue jacket would still be in there. And if he'd put the button back where it belonged before stowing the coat for the summer, he wouldn't be standing here now, shoulders hunched and shivering.

If he made a list of things he'd been neglecting, it'd probably give him writer's cramp, because he hadn't exercised, been to the barber's or picked up his dry cleaning in weeks. If he didn't soon get a coat of oil on the tug's brass, he'd spend a month, come spring, buffing away winter's heartlessness. And if he missed another AA meeting . . . .

Austin couldn't think of a time when he needed Harvey Griffin's no-holds-barred logic more.

Well, except maybe for that awful night when Griff bailed him out of jail and dragged him into the rectory, where Austin woke up in a pool of his own drunken drool. He'd never heard the man curse before. Wouldn't have thought a man of the cloth knew *how* to cuss like that. But the drill sergeant-turned-firefighter-turned-AA sponsor-turned-minister held nothing back, not even full-blown brazen blame: "I hope you're happy, because now I'll have to spend hours on my knees," he roared, "begging forgiveness for my gutter talk." Then he'd filled both meaty fists with Austin's shirt and gave him a good shake. "And so will you, for driving me to it!"

Austin hadn't found anything about the situation funny back then, but now, the memory made him grin.

His smile grew as he recalled the day Griff announced that he'd quit his job and packed everything he owned into his beat-up old Chevy van. "If Charm City can't handle me," he'd joked, "it'll be your fault for reminding me of all the city's plusses."

After a week on Austin's lumpy couch, Griff rented an upstairs apartment in Washington Village and shocked every one of his Pigtown cousins by enrolling at the Maryland Bible College and Seminary. The family blamed the head injury, sustained when an I-beam trapped Griff and the woman he'd tried to free from the debris, but Austin knew better. After 9/11, the call to serve God was just about the only thing Griff could talk about.

His relatives hadn't believed he'd finish the program, but Austin knew better. Once Griff set his mind on something, it was as good as done, and Austin was walking, talking proof of that.

How many times during that long, harrowing week had Griff wanted to throw his hands in the air and walk away from his drunken friend? Too many to count.

"Marines don't quit!" he'd said when Austin questioned his tenacity.

"You haven't worn a uniform in years."

"Once a Marine, always a Marine," he'd snarled, and went right back to pouring coffee down Austin's gullet and reading from the Good Book. By week's end, he'd turned Austin into a verse-spouting, born-again believer. Talked him into joining AA, too, and on the way to the first meeting, they'd toasted Austin's new life with back-to-back Boilermakers . . .

. . . and Austin hadn't touched a drop of the stuff since January 8, 2002. Oh, he'd wanted to, plenty of times! But on the occasions when temptation threatened to let go of his precarious grip on self-control, he could always count on Griff to rake him over the coals until he came to his sense again.

His driver's license said he'd come into the world on November second, and he'd given his life to God on May thirteenth, but in his mind and heart, that raw winter day was the only one he celebrated by wearing every pin Griff had ever given him. His favorite? The one that said

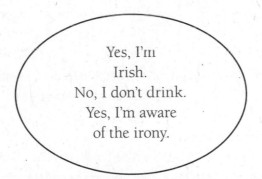

Yes, I'm
Irish.
No, I don't drink.
Yes, I'm aware
of the irony.

Yep, if anybody could help him get a handle on the yo-yoing emotions about Mercy that had been bouncing around in his head, it was good ol' Griff.

Like a mirage, the image of her floated on the frosty fog. He didn't know how long he might have stood at the rail, staring across the Bay, if Flora hadn't called out to him.

Smiling, he threw a hand into the air. "How's my favorite girl this morning?"

"Favorite girl, my foot. I know I've been replaced, you two-timer, you!" Cackling, she pulled her thick robe tighter round her. "I'm fine and dandy. Thanks for askin'."

But she wasn't fine. Austin could tell by the strange tenor to her voice, and the way she moved, slow and stiff—as if each step stimulated immeasurable pain—toward the rail.

"Hear from your doctor?"

"That quack," she huffed, waving his question away. "I heard from him, all right."

Obviously, the news hadn't been good, but Austin could get more details from Bud, later. "Don't forget. I'm making you and Bud pork chops for supper."

"You must have fallen out of your bunk last night."

Maybe he had, because Austin didn't have a clue what she meant.

"A good whack to the head is the only viable reason I can come up with to explain why you don't remember that I've never passed up a chance to eat something besides those nasty fish sticks or chicken nuggets Bud's so fond of!" Another brittle laugh, then, "Your place or mine, sweet cakes?"

Grinning, he said, "Let's do it over here. That way, you won't have to lift a finger."

"Where were you when I was husband hunting!" she shot back, one bony hand pressed to her chest. "Mercy will be joining us, I hope."

How weird that the mere mention of her name had the power to put his pulse into overdrive. "Yeah. But I need to call her, let her know what time. What's good for you guys?"

Flora chuckled. "We're retired, so if it was up to Bud, we'd eat at four. You two are the workin' stiffs, so you decide and that's when we'll be there."

"You got it, gorgeous. Now get inside out of this wind." He stopped himself from adding "before you catch your death." A strange and ominous sensation gripped his heart, and he sent a quick prayer heavenward that she'd be all right.

"Can I bring anything?"

"Only your sassy, beautiful self."

"Be still my heart." Then, "When you talk to Mercy, be sure to tell her how much I'm looking forward to seeing her again."

"You bet." There were three steps leading from the Callahans' deck to their cabin. As she climbed them, the dread inside him grew. Always agile and spry, Flora had never struck him as "old." Now, huddled slump-shouldered in her fuzzy pink bathrobe, she seemed to have aged ten years in the weeks since he'd last seen her. Austin added his concerns about her condition to the things he'd discuss with Griff.

He checked his watch. Too early to call a guy who usually sat up all night talking people out of making "there's no turning back" decisions. Austin didn't have other sponsors to compare Griff to, but he'd been a cop long enough to know a good guy from a bad one. He'd call today and see if *that* good one could meet him for lunch.

After emptying the last of the coffee into his mug, he flopped into his recliner and scanned the channels for a *Three's Company* rerun. "Ah," he said, popping up the footrest, "better than a tranquilizer."

But not better than booze.

Another couple of "ifs" for his list: If he downed enough of the stuff, he could count on two, maybe three hours of uninterrupted sleep. And if Griff hadn't dragged him to that first AA meeting, alcohol would still control every waking moment.

His cell phone buzzed and did a half-circle dance on the coffee table. Its internal clock said six-o-two, and the caller i.d. block spelled out "Harvey Griffen."

"What, you forgot how to tell time?"

"Aw, blast!" came the gravelly reply. "And here's me, about to ask if you forgot how to dial a phone."

"I was gonna call you. Today."

"Yeah, yeah. And I traded my Yankees cap for a pope dome."

"How are things in Pigtown?"

"Well, I miss Babe the pigs."

Austin remembered Griff's story about how the B & O Railroad once herded hogs down the middle of Ostend and Cross Streets to get them to the slaughterhouses in south Baltimore. "You might look as old as dust, but no way you ever met Babe Ruth."

"Whatever."

"Speaking of which, whatever inspired you to call at this ungodly hour?"

"Just makin' sure all my li'l chicks are present and accounted for."

Austin heard the familiar *zing* as Griff flipped open the lid of his Zippo lighter. "I thought you were gonna quit that filthy habit."

"I am. I will. Eventually."

"Yeah, yeah. And I traded my Orioles cap for a Yankees T-shirt."

Laughing, Griff said, "Seriously. How you doin', kid?"

"Doin' great."

"No backsliding?"

"Nope."

His lips popped as he took a puff of the cigarette. "Then why have you been makin' yourself scarce?"

If he told Griff about Mercy, he'd better be ready to get an earful of the damage women can do to a man with a plan. "Mostly working," he said, "and spending time with—"

"Mostly? Uh oh, don't tell me you've got yourself a *girlfriend.*"

"—my neighbors. You met them at last year's Super Bowl party. They're not doing so hot ."

"Aw, that's a stinkin' rotten shame. Nothing serious, I hope. They're a sweet old couple."

"Yeah, that they are."

"Awright, out with it, Finley."

"Never could pull one over on you could I?"

Griff snickered. "Better question is why do you even *try*?"

"I hate talking on the phone, so how 'bout I buy you breakfast."

"Boulevard Diner, half an hour?"

How like Griff to choose a place so near the station, Austin thought as he drove toward Merritt Boulevard. Once there, he saw the rusting brown van in the handicap slot nearest the entrance. Griff lived closer to Mercy's townhouse than the diner in Dundalk. No way he could have made the trip that fast unless he'd called on his way over. Or from the parking lot.

Mercy, the reason he'd wanted to meet with Griff in the first place. But how could he explain things—from therapy back in New York to the secrets and kisses they'd shared—in the middle of a crowded, noisy restaurant?

It didn't surprise him to see Griff, squinting into a blur of cigarette exhaust as he waved from the far corner of the smoking section, far from other patrons.

"I took the liberty of ordering," he said, pointing at two white-ceramic coffee mugs. "Got your usual. Bacon. Toast. Two eggs over easy. Home fries. To save time. Since you're workin' today and all."

"You've got a lot of gall," Austin said, grinning as he slid onto the bench seat facing Griff's. "I had my taste buds all set for French toast."

"Yeah, yeah. And I just traded my pope dome for a welder's mask." He mashed his Marlboro in the ashtray and slid it under the mini-juke box. "What's on your mind, kid?"

"Have you ever in your life beat around the bush?"

"Nope. Least, I sure as shootin' hope not. 'Cause it ain't just a colossal waste of time, it's unnecessarily hard on the shrubbery, too." He chuckled. "You're pretty good at it, though."

Austin raised a brow.

"Somethin' tells me you didn't call just to see my pretty face. . . ."

If he knew where to begin, Austin might have launched into a narrative of his life these past weeks.

"Well-l-l?"

"This. That." He shrugged. "Let's eat. I hate to whine on an empty stomach."

"Oh. Right. Like a full stomach will make it easier for me to *listen* to your whining."

Austin lifted the mug to his lips, more to buy time than because he craved coffee. It tasted bitter, thanks to the sweet remnants of gum still clinging to his tongue. "So how's the leg?"

Griff reflexively fluffed his graying hair, grown long and shaggy to hide the fading red lightning bolt that zigzagged from his left eyebrow to his right cheek. But there wasn't much he could do to hide the limp. "Still gimpy."

"Bummer," Austin said, watching him flip open the one-of-a-kind lighter's lid, then snap it shut again. The metallic echo drew the attention of diners at nearby tables. One old guy, in particular, looked about ready to issue a "Knock it off!" command. So Austin extended his hand, palm up, and wiggled his fingertips. "Hand it over, before you crack its hinge."

"Careful. It was a gift from—"

"Yeah, yeah, I know. From your sainted father, who served bravely in World War II and now sports wings and a halo and plays chess with the angels in heaven."

Chuckling, Griff said, "Nobody likes a smart aleck. Besides, every word is the truth."

Austin had been looking at the thing for years but never saw it up close before. A Marine cap sat on the bony head of the skull and crossbones, and beneath it, crossed rifles. "Mess with the best," said the bold letters to its left and "die like the rest" gave balance to the right.

He closed it quietly and handed it back. "Is that thing the reason you haven't quit smoking?"

A bawdy guffaw preceded Griff's snort. "What! You think I'd rather pollute my lungs than stow this in my underwear drawer?"

The waitress chose that moment to deliver their food, saving Austin from having to reply. And once she'd topped off their coffee, Austin said, "There's somebody I'd like you to meet."

"I kinda figured." Griff slathered grape jelly on his toast. "What's her name?"

"Never said it was a her."

"Didn't have to. It's written all over your face."

Chuckling, Austin offered, "Mercy Samara."

Squinting one eye, Griff used the butter knife as a pointer. "Why does that name ring a bell? Wait. I know—she was the shrink the department made you see after all those brutality—"

Austin cringed. "Sheesh, man, can I maybe get you a megaphone? Make it a little easier for everybody in Dundalk to hear?"

Griff bit the point off his toast. "Aw, don't be so sensitive. Nobody in here gives a fig about anything either of us has to say."

"Maybe. Maybe not. But I don't remember telling you about her."

"I'm not surprised. It's a minor miracle you were able talk at all back then, toasted as you were all the time."

"All right, then, genius, why don't you save us both some time. Tell me what you know about her. Y'know, so I won't go over the same ground twice."

"Good idea. Few things annoy me more than redundancy."

Austin laughed, and, leaning back in his booth seat, said "I swear, Griffin, if I didn't like you so much, you'd be an easy guy to hate."

"O ye master of double speak, would you be so kind as to pass the ketchup?"

After burying his home fries under a thick blanket of red, Griff repeated everything he'd learned on the night he turned Austin's life around.

If only he enjoyed the tale as much as the grumpy old man at the next table.

22

*H*e'd just stepped onto the walkway between his boat and the Callahans' when he noticed her. "What're you doing here?"

"Well, aren't *you* good for a girl's ego."

Austin laughed. "Sorry. Didn't mean to sound abrasive. It's just—"

He'd barely returned from his bare-your-soul breakfast when Bud called to say Flora had just taken a coffee cake out of the oven. Griff had given him a lot to think about, and he needed time to make sense of it all.

She fell into step beside him. "I called to see if they'd heard from Flora's doctor, and find out if they could still come to Thanksgiving dinner. I hate to say this, but seeing you here gives me a really bad feeling."

"Well, aren't *you* good for a guy's ego?"

"Good grief, I didn't mean it that way," she said, grinning. "I just meant if they summoned both of us over here, together, it can't be *good* news, can it?"

"Hate to admit it, but I think you're right."

"Flor-dee-lee, our company is here, right on time!" Bud opened the screen door and stepped onto the deck. "Just pretend you don't notice the way she looks," he whispered as Flora called out "Don't just stand there letting all the heat out, you silly man. Get out of the way so they can come in!"

Austin saw the way Mercy straightened her back and took a deep breath before plastering a bright smile on her face. It wasn't easy, mimicking her expression, especially after he saw Flora in her favorite chair, looking gaunt and pale under a thick quilt. "There's my favorite girl!"

"I think you need your eyes checked," she said, waving Mercy closer as he kissed her cheek. "I declare, you get prettier every day."

Mercy winked at Austin, then said "Aren't *you* good for a girl's ego!"

"Please, please," Bud interrupted, "have a seat. I've got everything ready. Just need to—"

"We'll help," Mercy said, following him into the galley. When he started to protest, she quickly added, "I did a little waitressing to pay my way through college. It'll be good practice, in case I ever lose my job at the high school."

Austin knew the place almost as well as his own, and stacked plates, napkins, and forks on a big wooden tray. He helped Mercy get the cups from a shelf just out of her reach, and handed her the cream pitcher. "I'm the only one of the four of us who drinks his coffee black," he said as she filled it.

Why he'd felt the need to fill the room with small talk was anybody's guess, but he found himself wishing for additional inane banter to fill the endless silence as they sat around the tiny living room, sipping coffee to wash down the dry, tasteless cake. He'd never known Flora to flub up on a recipe, and this bakery fiasco was proof in his mind that Mercy had been right. The Callahans had called them here to deliver bad news.

Mercy finished her cake first—no surprise there, considering the nearly see-through slice she'd put on her own plate—

and asked if anyone needed a refill. Three echoing "no thank yous" sent her to the galley alone.

She wasn't back thirty seconds before Bud cleared his throat. "Well, kids, I'm sure you've been wondering why we asked you to come over here today, and I, for one, think we've kept you in suspense long enough."

"Bud's right," Flora agreed, sitting up straighter. "We wanted you to be the first to know that. . ."

Grinning, she looked at Bud, whose expression couldn't have said "Huh?" any more clearly.

". . . that I'm pregnant."

Bud's eyebrows slammed into his hairline and Mercy's lips parted slightly. As for Austin, he did the only thing he could think to do, and laughed.

"Don't mess with their heads, Flor-dee-lee. At least, not at a time like this."

Nothing like an "a time like this" crack to sober a guy up. Austin glanced at Mercy, who'd started gnawing on the outer corner of her upper lip. The scene reminded him a bit of that day at the hospital, when it took the doctors ten minutes to say "Your mother has a day, two at most, to live." Painful as that had been, he'd understood the legal reasoning behind their stall tactic.

"I have nasal cancer," Flora said.

He'd heard more emotion when the traffic control gal rattled off her list of construction areas and fender benders that clogged the Beltway. As if it didn't hurt enough, hearing it the first time, she said it again, with a little more emphasis this time. "Nasal cancer. Stage IV-C."

Flora calmly launched into a recitation of symptoms, and admitted that her snoring had been just one of many signs of trouble she'd sloughed off as allergies, sinus infections, and head colds. The headaches and blurred vision had been harder to explain, but the lump on the bridge of her nose is what ultimately put her in the doctor's office. After a suspicious biopsy, CT and MRI scans were ordered. "And it appears that a tumor has invaded other tissues," she added, "so the surgeon can't get to it in the OR."

Mercy's eyes widened as her gaze flicked from Flora to Bud to Austin. "Which means they'll start an aggressive chemotherapy-radiation treatment regimen," she said, "*right*?"

"Aw, sweetie," Flora said, patting Mercy's hand, "don't look so worried."

"I'm afraid it's way too late for that, kiddo. Too late for *anything*, except to wait for the Grim Reaper to find time in his schedule." Bud gripped the arms of his chair so tightly that his knuckles turned white. "I told her and told and *told* her to make a doctor's appointment way back when the first warning signs showed up. But would she listen? No-o-o, 'course not, because on top of being the most *stubborn* woman on the planet, she's convinced herself that she's smarter than—"

"Bud. Honey. You promised."

He made a taut line of his lips and hung his head. "You're right. I'm sorry."

The words didn't sound sincere to Austin, but he did his best to contain his exasperation. If Flora were *his* wife? He'd have nagged the daylights out of her! Night and day, day after day, until she got so sick of it, she'd cave in and make a doctor's appointment, if only to shut him up.

Inhaling a huge lungful of air, he clenched his teeth, because he wasn't Bud and Flora wasn't his wife, and he had no business second-guessing the way they dealt with important marital issues.

If only the admission had the power to tame the frustration—no, the full-blown *annoyance*—roiling in his gut.

"Oh, would you look at the mess I've made," Flora said, breaking into his thoughts. She clucked her tongue. "Spilled coffee all over my favorite old quilt."

Austin didn't know what to make of her blasé attitude. How could she be more upset about a stain on a blanket than a diagnosis of terminal cancer, which would take her from all the people who loved her as if she were blood kin!

"Are you sure there's nothing the docs can do?" he pressed. "'Cause, I mean, think about it; we live within an hour of some of the best hospitals in the entire world. There's gotta be a clinical trial going on at Johns Hopkins, or—"

Bud cut in with "Didn't you hear her? It's *stage IV-C.*"

Austin's wristwatch ticked off the seconds that passed before Flora said "Would you do me a favor, hon?"

Bud was on his feet in an eye blink. "You know I will. Anything, anything at all."

Smiling sweetly, she gathered up the quilt. "Fill the tub with cold water and put this in to soak, so the stain won't set, would you please?"

He hugged it to his chest as she added, "And will you bring me the afghan that's draped over the foot of our bed?"

Bending to kiss her forehead, he said, "You got it, sweet cheeks."

Once he was out of earshot, Flora whispered "I have a big favor to ask the two of you." Extending her hands, she beckoned Austin and Mercy closer.

"He does a great 'tough guy' act, but this is going to be really tough on him. Now, I know you're both busy, what with work and volunteering and . . ." She snickered. ". . . and each other, but I'm hoping I can count on you to look in on him from time to time. Because I'm worried if he doesn't have plenty to keep him busy, he'll just roll up into a little ball."

Better than rolling over, he fumed. If she was so all-fired *worried* about the man, then why give in to this thing? She'd fought the marina owner when he tried to sneak extra charges onto their monthly slip rental rates. Fought the fire department when they didn't get her boy's name added to the plaque of men and women who'd died in the line of duty. Fought the phone company when they added a "games" category to her bill, and got her way in every instance. Why not fight *this* with the same mulish determination to win?

Suddenly, he noticed Mercy, blinking so fast that Austin half expected to feel a draft. Having trouble coping with the gloomy news, he wondered, or staving off tears?

"Promise?"

He didn't know which took precedence, disappointment or annoyance that she'd all but given up the ghost. Didn't like knowing that he'd soon lose another loved one and yet again, he was powerless to do a doggoned thing about it.

"Jeez, Flora, it isn't like you to throw in the towel this way. Stop talking this way. You're beginning to remind me of an oxygen tank with a faulty gauge. It *says* 'Empty,' even though it's not." He was on a roll, and saw no point in stopping. "You're too pigheaded to let this thing get the better of you. So don't ask us to do your job for you, because you'll be around for a long, long time. *You* can make sure Bud has plenty to keep him busy."

Mercy's quiet gasp and shocked expression told him he'd said too much, and made him question every word and the attitude that had inspired each. If Flora told him he was behaving like a self-centered, spoiled little boy who'd just found out the Mattel had decided to stop manufacturing his favorite toy, well, she'd have every right.

"See," she said instead, "that's exactly the sort of thing Bud's gonna need after I'm gone!" She drew them both into a hug.

"Promise me," she said, kissing Austin's cheek, "that you'll keep an eye on him for me?"

"Of course we will," Mercy said as Bud walked into the room.

"Will what?"

Flora said "Will be at Mercy's for Thanksgiving dinner at three sharp."

And the women exchanged a self-satisfied glance.

Look at the pair of them, Austin thought, *like a couple of puppeteers, gloating 'cause they've got total control of the strings.*

After decades with Flora, Bud probably didn't even realize his life was being choreographed. He looked at Mercy, hovering near Flora's side, as any caring person would after hearing that a close friend had terminal cancer. *And therein lies the rub,* he thought. Because Flora was no more a close friend than Mercy was normal.

Memory of the disturbing scars flashed in his mind, underscoring his beliefs, and reminding him that he'd need to tread carefully. "You've only had your nose above water for a couple-a years," Griff had said. "Y'don't need a suicidal female dragging you down with her." That advice, coupled with the "don't yoke yourself to an unbeliever" verse in the Good Book made him more certain than ever that he needed to pray. Should he break things off—whatever *things* were? And if he should, when and where should he do it?

"Well, girl," he said, standing beside Bud's recliner, "we're cutting into the lovebirds' TV time. What say we head out, let 'em bill and coo to their hearts' content?"

She gave Flora a gentle hug and followed Austin to the door. "Call me if you need anything, OK," she told Flora, "even if it's only to talk."

They walked the first few yards in silence, and then she stopped at the end of the wooden walkway that led to his boat. "You were great in there."

"Y'think?" Austin growled. "Then what was with that whole 'gasp and big-eyed' show?"

Mercy frowned. "Show?" she repeated. "What're you talking abo—" Then her brow smoothed as she pulled her jacket tighter around her and stared into the velvety blue-black sky. Austin looked up, too, wondering if maybe, instead of believing in God, who'd created the beauty above her, she found her "get out of jams" excuses written on the stars.

He'd once dated a psych major who pretty much drove him bonkers, reading nonexistent meaning and intent into every little gesture and expression. If she were here now to see his stance—one arm folded tightly over the other and shoulders rolled forward—he'd have been subjected to the "Reasons I Think You're Closing Yourself Off from Me" lecture. Mercy was a board certified psychiatrist. Surely she'd read the same books.

Austin leaned his backside against the railing and hooked his thumbs into his jacket pockets. It shouldn't take this much effort to appear at ease, he thought as she said "It caught me off-guard that you told Flora exactly what I might have . . . if I felt I had the right to."

"I don't get it," he admitted.

"I barely know the woman!" She raised a hand traffic cop style. "Don't get me wrong. I like Flora. A lot. And we'd probably become great friends, if . . ." A look of dread and dismay darkened her eyes. "Anyway . . . it . . . I just kept wondering whether to feel honored . . . or pity."

This time, he let his helpless shrug tell her that he didn't understand.

"Honored that she trusted me, a near-stranger, with such intimate information, or pity that she has so few people to share it with." Brows high on her forehead, excitement filled her voice. "Or maybe . . ." Frowning, she shook her head. "No, never mind. That's ridiculous."

"What's ridiculous?"

"Nothing." A nervous giggle bubbled into the air. "Really."

He waited.

Nothing. Then, "I feel so silly."

"Why?"

"Because it's ridiculous."

"What is?"

"The idea I have that she's playing Cupid. Giving us a common bond. Something that'll bring us closer, make us want to lean on one another."

Now that she'd spelled it out—finally—it didn't seem so far-fetched after all. Over the years, he'd introduced Flora to a couple dozen women. She'd felt that one had a wicked smile. Another avoided eye contact. Some were too clingy. And there'd been one who "has the table manners of a chimpanzee." The eye doctor, the bank teller, even the kindergarten teacher inspired a rousing "You've gotta be kidding!" But Mercy? Mercy got the thumbs up so fast that it was a mini miracle that Flora hadn't poked out her own eye.

He wished Mercy *could* be a permanent part of his life. But how could he build a future and a family with a woman who'd turned her back on God?

Maybe she'd change her mind.

Something to pray about, for sure, and Austin intended to start on that, tonight.

23

When she called Austin yesterday to finalize a convenient time for dinner, he'd agreed that a mid-afternoon meal would be best for Flora, given her weakened condition and the pain meds that made her perpetually drowsy. He'd arrive at two, Austin said, in the Callahans' low-to-the-ground sedan, to spare Flora an uncomfortable ride in his ancient pickup. It allowed plenty of time to chat and munch appetizers, too, without taxing the poor woman's cancer-abused body.

Mercy had just given the turkey another butter bath when the phone rang at eleven-thirty. It startled her so badly that she burned the back of her hand on the upper rack. But the pain was blotted out by fear and dread, because she could think of just one reason he'd call at the last minute: Flora's condition had taken a turn for the worse.

"Please tell me she's all right," she blurted.

"Flora? She's tired, but that's par for the course these days."

"Oh, thank God!"

"Interesting thing for an atheist to say, but I agree."

Running her hand under cold water, she ignored his snide remark. Why *had he* called, if not to deliver bad news?

"So, the reason I'm calling. Would it be a problem if I invited a friend to dinner? He lost his wife two years ago, and I hate to think of him, alone on a major holiday."

Mercy pictured the inside of her refrigerator, where bowls of stuffing, sweet potatoes, baked beans, and gravy awaited their turn in the oven. "The more the merrier," she said. "And if your friend wants to bring a friend, that's fine with me. There's plenty of food!"

"Thanks. From him *and* me."

When the doorbell rang two hours later, she'd just grabbed a spoon to stir the gravy. "I'm Austin's pal, Griff," said the long-haired man on her porch. "Sorry I'm early, and thanks for the invite," he said, grinning as he held up a pink-ribboned pastry box.

"I told him you didn't need to bring anything, but thanks," she said, taking it. "It's good to meet you. And I'm Mercy, by the way."

He gave her hand a light shake. "Oh, I know who you are. Austin doesn't talk about much else these days."

"*That* must make for scintillating conversation," she joked, closing the door. "Do you mind joining me in the kitchen? I know they say watched pots never boil, but experience has taught me otherwise."

Mercy noticed the angry scar on his face, despite the attempt he'd made to hide it behind all that wild and wooly hair. She also noticed the slight hitch in his step and wondered where Austin had met this rumpled, wrinkled fellow. In a soup kitchen, from the looks of him, she thought. And not on the serving side of the counter, either. How like Austin to befriend a man obviously down on his luck. "Pull up a stool," she said. "Can I get you some lemonade? Iced tea?"

"Either's fine. But I don't want to just sit here like a wart on a frog. What can I do to help?"

Since she'd spent most Thanksgiving dinners as a guest in other people's homes, Mercy remembered how much more at home she felt when her hosts gave her something productive to do. Trouble was, except for the tossed salad, she'd taken care of today's preparations. "Are you any good at chopping vegetables?"

"Are you kiddin'?" He went straight to the sink to scrub his hands. "I spent years on KP duty before I became a drill sergeant. Hand me a knife and a cutting board, and watch the peelings fly."

Laughing, Mercy lined up what he'd need to make the salad, then slid a big wooden bowl in front of him and went back to stirring pots.

"Austin said you were a knock-out, but he's said that about his women before, and in my opinion, he exaggerated, big-time." Griff grinned. "I gotta say, this time, he earned The Understatement of the Year award."

She'd never been very good at accepting compliments, mostly, because every response felt . . . *wrong:* "Oh, no, my hair is a mess!" or "But I have a zit on my chin" made it seem she was fishing for affirmation, while a simple "Thank you" came across as vain and self-centered. "So how long have you known Austin?"

"Oh, we go way back," Griff said, peeling a green onion. "I was a firefighter in New York, see, when he worked for the police department. Our stationhouses were practically side by side. He's a hard guy *not* to like, and after 9/11—"

Griff's voice faded as he focused on something beyond her left shoulder. "He's a hard guy not to like."

He's a hard guy not to love.

"9/11," he continued, "that's when I got this limp. And the zipper that splits my face in two."

"I'm sorry," she said, meaning it.

"Don't be. I got off easy." He slid the chopped onions into the bowl and carved seeds from the heart of a green pepper. "There are guys who can't work 'cause they inhaled so much ash, and some who'll never walk again. I know a Port Authority cop who was blinded by flames, and everybody who survived that day attended way too many funerals. But the memorial services for first responders who were never found—those were toughest."

Mercy didn't know how to respond except to say, "Still, I'm sorry."

"Easy to see why Austin's nuts about you."

She waited, hoping he'd explain the comment, because nothing on earth could make her *ask* him to.

"You're easy to talk to." Chuckling, he added, "Guess that's why you got into the shrink business, eh?"

Had Austin told Griff how—and why—they'd met? As she grabbed a big spoon from the magnetized utensil rack above the stove, he said, "Not everybody has what it takes to counsel teenagers." Then, "What happened to your hand?"

"Got distracted basting the turkey and burned myself on the oven rack."

"Bummer. 'Cause that's gonna hurt when it's time to do the dishes."

Returning his grin, she said, "Isn't it strange that all three of us made our way from New York to Baltimore after 9/11?"

"I can name another dozen or so who moved here after things settled down. As for me?" Finished with the green pepper, he moved on to the tomato. "Austin is the sole reason I'm here."

"Oh?"

"Every time we talked, all he did was rave about the place. The food, the people, the sights. Made me miss my home town, so when my wife died," he said with a shrug, "I figured, why not leave all those ugly memories behind and start over in the place where I grew up?"

If he wanted to deliver more information about his wife's death, Griff would do it, unprompted. Mercy lifted the lid of a pot and got ready to stir the baked beans as the doorbell rang, and it wasn't until Austin eased Flora onto the sofa that she noticed the spoon, still in her hand.

"Your house is lovely, just lovely, Mercy," Flora said after a flurry of hello hugs in the foyer. "So big and bright and airy. Oh, how I wish I could maneuver the stairs, so I could see the whole space!"

"That's easy enough to arrange," Austin announced, and folded up her wheelchair. He disappeared long enough to bring it to the second floor, then returned for Flora. Bending at the waist, he scooped her into his arms. "Guess I just don't rate with the mistress of the manor."

Griff, Bud and Mercy followed like obedient pups as he carried her up the stairs. "What *are* you going on about?" Flora asked, laughing.

"Well," Austin explained, gently depositing her onto its seat, "I've been here half a dozen times, and *I* never got the nickel tour."

The instant he fixed his gorgeous blue eyes on her, Mercy's heart began battering her ribcage. Hard as it was to break the connection, she stepped in front of them and used the spoon as a microphone. "This, lady and gents, is the guest room," she said, aping Leo's accent. "It has its own walk-in closet and a full bath, complete with a whirlpool tub." A little farther down the hall, she stopped again. "And this is my office. Notice the book-lined shelves—evidence of my brilliance and my well-readedness."

"'Readedness,'" Bud said. "Is that even a *word*?"

Flora giggled. "'Course not, silly man. You're not the only one who gets a kick out of teasing folks, you know."

How good it was to see the smile on her pallid face. Judging by the way her clothes hung from her bony frame, Mercy guessed that Flora had lost twenty pounds in the past month alone. At this rate, she'd waste away by Christmas.

She forced the depressing thought from her mind and continued the tour. "Here," she said, walking backward, "is the master bedroom, with a different view of Charm City."

"Isn't she just *adorable*," Flora gushed, squeezing Austin's hand.

"Oh, yeah," he said. "She's adorable, all right. A regular Vanna White. Only shorter, without blond hair. And with an English accent."

He'd grinned to say it, but the smile never quite made it to his eyes. Was it all in her head, or had he actually grown cool and distant in the weeks? So much for Lady Luck granting her wish that he'd forgiven her for her tirade.

Bud's blustery voice interrupted her worried thoughts. "I'd probably get lost," he said, "end up wandering around for hours up here if I tried to use the head in the middle of the night." He peered into the master bedroom and said "Wait! I know! You have one of those handy map gizmos, don't you, and it's programmed to help you find your way around this huge place."

Laughing, they made their way back to the living room, where Mercy had set out an array of hors d'oeuvres and soft drinks. An Eagles tune thumped quietly from the stereo system. If Austin recognized it as the same song he'd played the night she had dinner on his boat, he gave no sign of it. Another layer of evidence that he had constructed a wall between them, brick by brick, or proof, instead, that her imagination was working overtime?

"I'll just be a few minutes," she said, starting for the hall. "Some fine-tuning of a couple things, and dinner, as they said in those quaint old black and white movies, will be served."

It was a bold-faced lie. She'd prepared everything, right down to matches to light the centerpiece candles, before Austin arrived with the Callahans. He'd never led her to believe they were more than friends. So why had his behavior unsettled her?

Memory of that last kiss hovered in her mind. Eyes closed, she put a spin on the old Don't Drink and Drive commercial, "Friends don't kiss friends that way," she whispered.

"What's that?"

Mercy lurched, nearly overturning the gravy boat on its saucer. "Good grief," she blurted, "You scared me half to death! I'll bet you shaved ten years off the end of my life."

"Sorry. But if it's any consolation, those last ten are the worst years, anyway."

"In that case, thanks. I think."

Austin chuckled. "Need a hand with anything?"

"Actually, yes. Soon as I get all the side dishes into bowls and onto the table, will you slice the turkey?"

It was a simple question, and shouldn't have made him look so out-and-out uncomfortable. Then she remembered Thanksgiving at a sorority sister's house, when the dad handed the carving knife to his oldest son. Mercy didn't remember every word of the little speech, but the essence remained: Turkey carving was seen by some as an honor, a family tradition not to be taken lightly. Maybe Austin saw it that way, too, and her invitation felt more like a shove toward commitment.

"I've never done it before, so no doubt I'd just make mince-meat of it," she said, laughing to hide her embarrassment.

"This is the Callahans' last Thanksgiving together, and I'll do anything I can to make it a happy memory for them. So sure, I'll carve the bird."

It broke her heart to hear the chill in his once-warm voice. What had she done to rile him so?

And then she remembered the night, right here at this counter, when she'd explained why she couldn't put her faith in the being he called God. Her dad warned her that some Christians' devotion to their Lord could never be shaken by dissenting opinions, while others refused to associate with those whose beliefs differed from their own. If Austin shared allegiance with the second group, it was best for both of them to acknowledge the differences now, before she got in any deeper, before her heart was—

"What happened to your hand?"

"Burned it basting the turkey," she said, leaving out the part about how his phone call had been what startled her. "I'm out of regular bandages, and had to resort to gauze and white tape. It looks a lot worse than it is."

"Did you put antibiotic ointment on it?"

She nodded.

"Good. Keep that dressing on it, and the blister won't pop."

"Yes, doctor."

One brow quirked as he studied her face. Looking for signs of sarcasm? she wondered. If so, who could blame him?

"Why don't you show me which bowls to fill, and I'll help you get 'em on the table."

There . . . a glimmer of the warmth she'd come to treasure. Mercy wanted to applaud! Instead, she quickly explained where each side dish should go. Moments later, as she arranged the platters and bowls and lit the centerpiece tapers, Austin rolled

Flora's wheelchair up to the square dining table, still grinning. And this time, the smile reached his eyes.

Clearly, she'd jumped to conclusions. It certainly wouldn't be the first time. As a therapist, she could blame abandonment issues for her tendency to search out the weaknesses in every relationship. And because she'd spent so many years analyzing the behavior of others, she knew full well it was a flimsy excuse, at best. Because it had been decades since her mother had left, then died. Instead of jumping to the conclusion that every cross look or sharp word had some grim connection to her tantrum, why not focus on the possibility that Austin had already begun grieving over the loss of his dear friend? Kindness and understanding as Flora's condition deteriorated would go a lot farther toward closing the gap between them than whiny self-pity!

"Oh, Mercy, the table is pretty enough to be featured on the cover of a magazine. Isn't it just lovely, honey?"

"Yeah, it looks right nice," Bud said, sitting to her right.

Austin stood to her left, poised to slice into the golden bird.

"Wait!" she said, hands raised as if she were the victim of a holdup. "You can't start yet!"

"Why not?"

"Well, because we haven't said grace, that's why!"

He shot a quick glance at Mercy. "I was gonna suggest that, but I didn't want to offend anyone."

Flora laughed as Bud said, "Now, that's just plain silly. Who would you offend? We're all faithful followers here, so put down that sword."

Griff shoved back from the table. "I served as a pastor before—" A guilty look darkened his eyes as he exchanged a quick glance with Austin. "It'd be an honor to say the blessing—" He looked at Mercy. "—but it's your house. If you'd rather—"

"No, no. Please, by all means, be my guest."

Griff bowed his head and closed his eyes. Joining hands, the others followed suit.

"O Father in heaven, we thank you for bringing us together on this Thanksgiving Day, and for giving us one to the other, to make our time here on earth more tolerable. Thank you for granting us the freedom to enjoy the company of loved ones, and the food so lovingly prepared. We pray for your blessing on loved ones who can't be here, and for those who have joined you in Paradise. Thank you for showering us with the strength to live as you would have us live . . . and die with peace and dignity. I ask a special blessing on my new friend Mercy, for she has brought such joy to the lives of two old people. These things we ask in the name of Christ our Lord, Amen."

"Amen," the rest of them echoed.

Amid the din serving spoons and meat forks clanking against stoneware bowls and platters, the people gathered around Mercy's table tossed Thanksgiving trivia back and forth.

"The feast was organized to thank God for answering the Pilgrims' prayers to end the drought," Griff said, "by delivering rain in time to save the crops."

"I read someplace that it wasn't an orchestrated event," Flora added, "but just the end of a regular fasting period."

Austin said, "Yeah, I heard that, too."

"And there's absolutely no proof," Bud said, "that turkey was on the table that day."

Flora leaned forward. "Or pumpkin pie. Wasn't enough flour to make the crust!"

"Well, I'll tell you what *I'm* thankful for." Griff used his fork like a conductor's baton. "That today's Thanksgivings don't last three days." He patted his slightly rounded belly. "One meal like this is more than enough for me."

As the facts and falsehoods continued—from the long lapse between that first gathering to the one in 1623 that followed another severe drought—to Lincoln's proclamation that the fourth Thursday in November should be observed by the entire country, Mercy smiled. It did her heart good to watch and listen as they celebrated long-established friendship.

For a moment there, as she stacked the dinner plates and delivered dessert, she felt a bit like a fifth wheel—but only for a moment.

Because if it hadn't been for Austin, she wouldn't be a part of this celebration at all.

24

Flora hung in there longer than he or Bud would have guessed, and as they drove from Fells Point to the marina, she fell asleep in the back seat, cuddled in Bud's arms.

"She's a real trooper, that wife of yours."

"Yeah," Bud croaked out, "she's that, all right."

He heard the unspoken words in the man's pained voice: It wouldn't be easy, saying goodbye to a woman like this.

"Mercy's 'good people,' too."

"Yeah, she's just about perfect."

"Just about?'"

Bud had enough on his mind without worrying about the roller coaster love life of two crazy ex-New Yorkers. "Griff looks good, don't you think?"

"For a beat-up alcoholic."

A light rain had begun to fall, and Austin turned the wind-shield wipers on Low. Their steady *flick-flick-flick* kept perfect rhythm with his watch and the song ebbing from the car radio. He glanced into the rearview mirror to point out the curious coincidence, and saw that Bud had fallen asleep, his head bobbing in time to the music.

Grinning, Austin eased up on the accelerator and suppressed a yawn of his own. He should have taken Mercy up on her offer to send him home with a travel mug of strong coffee, because if he had to, he'd circle the marina for an hour to give Bud and Flora a little more much-needed shut-eye.

She'd done an impressive job today, and he felt like a heel for not telling her that before packing the wheelchair and the Callahans into the car. Maybe he'd call her once he helped Bud get Flora settled in for the night.

And maybe he wouldn't.

Austin needed time to think about what was best for both of them, and he couldn't very well do that if he had to look into her sweet chocolate-brown eyes, or hear the notes of her beautiful voice. How a person with a heart that big wasn't a follower had boggled his brain. Other unbelievers he'd met had been wickedly selfish, petty and cruel. Not Mercy! Why, she could start a new organization called "Generous Anonymous."

"What're you grinning about?"

Another glance in the mirror confirmed that Flora had awakened. "How do you know I'm grinning?"

"I didn't, but you just confirmed it, you big goof."

Chuckling, he said, "Did you have a nice nap?"

"Wasn't sleeping. Just pretended to so this big goof I'm *married* to would relax enough to doze off."

"How do you know *he's* not pretending right now?"

"I've spent hundreds of nights lying beside him and listening to him breathe."

He didn't know why, but her simple, straightforward reply choked him up. Austin swallowed, hoping to loose the sob in his throat and stanch the tears burning behind his eyelids. It made him lonely for her, even though she sat not three feet behind him, because already he knew that her passing would leave a huge and unfillable hole in his heart.

"This game you and Mercy are playing," she whispered, "it's stupid and silly and a waste of time. And you know how I feel about wasting time."

"What game?"

"Please. I know my brain's foggy from painkillers, but give an old woman some credit, will you? It's plain as the cancer-filled nose on my face that you're crazy about each other, so why not admit it?"

He winced at her cancer reference.

"Sorry, but you've known me long enough that my blunt-ness shouldn't surprise you."

Winced again at her on-target assessment of his reaction.

"Do you love her?"

"Yeah, I think maybe I do."

"You think she loves you, too?"

He remembered how Mercy had put her heart and soul into their last kiss. "Yeah, I think maybe she does."

"Then I repeat: What's with all this pussy-footing around? I'm living—scratch that—I'm dying proof that you've gotta take love where you can find it in this cruel world and hold on tight for as long as you can, because you never know what will steal it from you."

He was mulling that over when she added "Stop. Wasting. Time."

The marina's entrance sign came into view. "Bud," she said, "wake up. We're home."

Thirty minutes later, she was sound asleep on her side of their double bed. "Thanks for driving," Bud said, shaking Austin's hand. "It was a real good day, don't you think?"

"Yeah, I do."

"Thanks to Mercy, I'll have one more good memory to file away." He tapped his temple, then tapped Austin's. "You've got a good head on your shoulders, son. Use it."

He didn't wait for acknowledgment or agreement. Instead, Bud said, "Flora was right. You've gotta take love when and where you find it and hold on tight."

"You were awake that whole time?"

Grinning slightly, he pocketed both hands. "Well, maybe not the *whole* time. Just long enough to know she gave you some good advice."

"I know, and I appreciate it."

"Got time for a cuppa coffee?"

"Sure. Why not?"

Bud nuked what was left in the pot from breakfast, and handed Austin a mug. "Will you think I'm acting like a nosy old woman if I ask what's holdin' things up?"

"With Mercy and me, y'mean."

"No. With that flock of Canada geese that has decided to winter here. Again." He chuckled. "Of *course* I mean this thing between you and Mercy."

His reflection, staring back at him from the surface of the coffee, rippled and wavered, just like his emotions these past weeks. "We both have enough baggage to fill a carousel at BWI," he began carefully. "I'd hate to be the reason she fills another suitcase."

"Y'mean, 'cause of those scars on her arms?"

Bud must have seen them when she rolled up her sleeves to collect the dinner plates.

"Can't help but wonder what would drive a gal like her to do something that drastic," he muttered, shaking his head.

"It's like I said—lots of baggage."

Bud lifted one brow. "You ever try to kill yourself?"

"Not in the traditional ways, but I suppose it could be said all that boozing I did, years back, was slow suicide."

"I suppose."

"Everybody who tries it has their reasons. Or tell themselves they do."

He nodded again. "Takes a lot of faith to survive in this ol' world."

"And Mercy doesn't have any."

"What?" Bud frowned. "That's crazy talk. The girl's got a heart of gold. No way you can convince me she's not a—"

"And that, m'friend, is my Catch-22." He described in as little detail as possible the things Mercy had told him in her kitchen that night to defend the reasons she didn't believe.

"I gotta say, that's a surprise. I mean, wasn't she right there in the middle of the whole 9/11 mess, same as you and Griff?"

"In some ways, she was even more involved, being forced to listen as cops and firefighters and search and rescue personnel bared their souls during sessions in her office. That's a lot of misery for one person to carry around."

"Yep. It is, indeed." Bud drained his mug. "You tried talkin' to her about it?"

"Did you sense any tension between us today?"

"If I'd-a had a knife, I reckon I could-a cut through it."

"Well, there y'go."

"Have you prayed with her?"

"Would *you* if you were in my shoes?"

"No. I don't suppose I would. Take her to a church function, then. Let her see with her own eyes that—"

"Her father was a devout Christian, right up until the end. If that wasn't example enough for her, I don't know how I can change her mind."

"Prayer and time," Bud said. "At least the two of you have that."

Which was more than Bud could say, Austin finished in his mind. The thought roused a wave of guilt, because what kind of self-centered fool would dump all of this on a grieving man's shoulders?

"Did I hear at dinner that Flora has a doctor's appointment this week?"

"Yeah, though it seems a colossal waste of time to me. Takes half the day to get her ready, weak as she is. Then they draw so much blood, I'm tempted to go at 'em with a wooden stake. Honestly? I'm about ready to put my foot down. Because why make her go through all that if—" He plunked his mug onto the coffee table and held his head in his hands.

Austin reached across the space between them, squeezed Bud's shoulder, hoping the gesture would express his grief, underscore the support he'd provide, any time the Callahans needed it, because he didn't think he could get any words past the choking lump in his throat.

"You want me to come with you to her next appointment, maybe keep her busy while you give that quack a piece of your mind?"

"I'll be OK. But thanks for the offer."

On his feet, Austin started for the door. "Early shift tomorrow," he explained. "But you've got my cell number. Use it any time, for any reason. I mean it."

Hunched into a blast of icy November air, Austin hurried over the walkway and into his tugboat. He sat for nearly an hour, flicking a thumbnail against his incisors and staring at the cupboard where he'd stored a brand new bottle of Jim Beam. How easy it would be to yank open the door, unscrew the cap, and let it burn away the harsh reality of dying and death and uncertainty about his feelings for Mercy!

But the fiery liquid would burn more than that. He'd been face-down on the mat as an imaginary referee counted down from ten when Griff showed up and forced him to his feet. If he'd lost that bout, there wouldn't have been an ounce of fight left in him.

Austin stared at the phone, considering his options. He had four choices, as he saw it:

Grab the Good Book and lose himself in its pages . . .

. . . break the seal on that bottle . . .

. . . get Griff on the line . . .

. . . or call Mercy.

Hands trembling, he grabbed the phone, praying even as he dialed her number that she'd be home. Because more than anything right now, he needed to hear the sweet reassurance of her voice.

25

Mercy looked in all of Woodrow's usual hiding places and couldn't find him. When not even shaking the can of his favorite treats brought him running, she started to worry.

Any time an opportunity provided itself, he took full advantage and sneaked out the door. And with all the confusion and fuss of getting Flora out the door with her wheelchair, he'd probably done exactly that.

It wouldn't have caused such concern if she hadn't seen that big black tomcat prowling around on the terrace for the past few days. Woodrow had seen it, too, and the two had stood nose to nose with nothing but the glass of the French doors between them, fur standing on end and tails whipping as they growled and snarled and spit.

As if that wasn't bad enough, the weather had turned raw and rainy. The tabby had spent ninety percent of his life indoors. After a night in this mess, he could come down with pneumonia. Or worse.

She donned her raincoat and grabbed a flashlight and stepped into the downpour. "Woodrow," she called, peeking behind trash cans and shrubs as she moved farther and farther from the townhouse. "Here kitty, kitty, kitty."

"Only an idiot would be out in this deluge," she muttered, bending to shine the beam of the flashlight under a parked car. An idiot with a cat who considered her home a well-decorated prison. What else explained his chronic need to escape!

"Hey, lady—you lost?"

The gravelly voice startled her, and she loosed a tiny squeal. "No," she said, "just looking for my cat."

Three boys—any one of whom could be one of her students—stood shoulder to shoulder, smirking at one another and snickering as they moved closer.

This didn't look good. Not good at all. Just yesterday she'd heard a news report about kids attacking tourists at the Inner Harbor, on Federal Hill, and in Fells Point. Maybe if she showed no fear, they'd pass right on by.

"I have a good excuse to be out in this mess," she joked, "because I have a brainless cat out here somewhere. What're you guys doing out here? On Thanksgiving night of all things!"

"You got a wallet?" said the one in the middle.

"No." She dug around in her coat pocket, came up with a five and two ones. "This is it. Like I said, I'm trying to find my—"

"Get those earrings," said the shortest one. "They look like real diamonds."

Before she knew what was happening, they were on her, around her, punching and slapping and cursing. They tore the studs right out of her earlobes, then ripped open her raincoat and pawed around, looking for a matching necklace. It riled them when they didn't find one, and they jerked her to her feet.

"You live in this neighborhood and all you got is seven bucks and these itty bitty earrings? What are you, some rich man's maid?"

She could barely speak past the sausages they'd made of her lips, couldn't hear much either, above the odd ringing in her ears. Mercy sensed they'd resumed the beating, but she couldn't be sure. She was beyond pain by now, and the only thing holding her up was the big one, who stood behind her, gripping her upper arms.

"Hey," came a voice from one of the houses across the way, "what's going on over there?"

The boys grabbed the flashlight that had rolled under the parked car and used it as a club. After half a dozen blows, the light went out and the plastic shattered to the sidewalk.

"Call 9-1-1, Robert," a woman yelled. "Someone's being assaulted over there!"

"Let's get outta here!" one of the boys shouted. And before they ran off, the big one shoved Mercy into the car. She heard the passenger window crack, and knew it had been her forehead that caused it. Their eerie cheerful cackling was the last thing she heard as she slid into the narrow space between the tires and the curb. Cold rainwater rushed past her head, and a discarded fast food cup bobbed in the rivulet before it came to rest against her face.

Her last hope before the world went black was that Austin wouldn't be on the ambulance that came to take her to the morgue, because with all he'd seen and survived, he didn't need to add this to his memory.

26

She'd never ignored his call before, and he hoped she wasn't ignoring him now.

Not that he'd blame her if she did. He'd behaved like a complete idiot today. In truth, not just today, but ever since that night in her kitchen, when she'd made it impossible for him to convince himself that *maybe*, under her bluster and blow, beat the heart of a true believer.

He'd never been one to jump to conclusions, so why do it now? She'd probably stepped out for milk or eggs, or treats for Woodrow. He'd shower and shave and change into his uniform, and try her again. Surely she'd have returned from running errands by then.

While getting ready, he gave some thought to the way he'd acted. He didn't like admitting that his attempts to step back and take stock had probably hurt her feelings. Bud had been right, suggesting that he could pray, and that he and Mercy had time to make things right—unlike him and Flora. When he finally got hold of her, Austin intended to explain. Apologize. Do whatever it took to ensure that whatever happened between them, she wouldn't hate him.

The possibility of that hit him hard, because she'd already been beaten up by life. He sure didn't want to be the cause of still more pain, just because she didn't see eye to eye with him about . . .

. . . about the most important element in his life.

Still, what kind of example had he been, behaving like a sanctimonious jerk who, over the years, had convinced himself that his way is *the* way.

In truth, though, that's exactly what it was. Still . . . .

He picked up the phone and punched in her number. When she answered, he'd suggest dinner and a movie, so he soften her up before laying his cards on the table. During the second ring, he ran down a mental inventory of possible restaurants. By the fourth, he remembered two movies he'd read about in the Style section of *The Baltimore Sun*. On the sixth, her voice was preceded by a series of clicks: "Hi! Sorry I can't take your call, but if you'll leave your name and number after the beep, I'll get back with you just s soon as I can. Unless you're selling something."

Grinning at her final words, he waited for the beep. "Hey, Merc, it's me, Austin. Call me when you get a minute, will you? Oh, and thanks for dinner. And for letting Griff join us. The whole day was . . . was just great."

Nothing more to do now but wait, because unfortunately, the ball was in her court.

Austin grabbed his keys and cell phone, and as he locked up a deafening blast of thunder rolled overhead. Lightning zigzagged through the sky, each blinding flash lighting the marina with white light that put the sunshine to shame. The wind sent crisp leaves skittering across the walkways and started the boats bobbing like gigantic corks in the water. Rain came down in sheets, and he ran full-out to his truck, praying with every step that when he got home in the morning, there'd be a red light blinking on his answering machine.

The next eight hours raced by as one call after another put them out there in the icy black rain. First, a head-on collision on I-95, then a domestic dispute that left a young mother with cracked ribs and a broken arm. Down on Eutaw Street, a homeless man was discovered by a jogger, unconscious and bleeding after a gang of teens cut the gold teeth from his mouth. Then a brazen robbery at the corner of Holabird and Broening Highway, where a liquor store cashier gave his life to save his boss a whopping seventy-two bucks.

Normally, he and McElroy would grab a coffee at Dunkin Donuts after filling out their reports. Tonight, between the bone-chilling weather and the back-to-back incidents of mayhem, both opted to hole up at home, where it was warm and dry—and safe. The closer Austin got to the marina, the more he looked forward to hitting the button that would allow him to hear the voice that was so easy on his ears.

If he'd really believed that she wouldn't return his call, Austin might have devised a plan to help him cope with the enormity of his disappointment.

The bottle called to him again, and this time, he had three choices: Call Griff, unscrew that cap, or reach for the Bible.

Two hours later, a crick in his neck woke him. He'd fallen asleep reading Psalms, and when he sat up to work out the kinks, the Good Book fell to the floor. He picked it up and slid it gently onto the shelf above the television, grabbed the remote and laid on the sofa to watch the a.m. news.

"And on the local front," said Don Scott, "police are trying to identify a woman found beaten in Fells Point."

Fear gripped Austin's heart as he bolted upright. "No," he grated, "it can't be." There could be a dozen reasons why Mercy hadn't returned his call. Maybe she'd taken the phone off the hook. Or last night's storm killed the power in her house.

"The photo you're about to see is very graphic in nature, so if there are children nearby, we suggest you usher them from the room," Scott continued.

The screen filled with the full-color photo of a badly-beaten woman. "If you know this woman," the anchorman said, "please contact police at—"

On his feet now, his pulse pounded. Even with eyes swollen shut, he recognized Mercy. Why hadn't he paid more attention, because how would he find out which hospital they'd taken her to?

He grabbed the phone and called the station, explained the situation and got the information he needed. Mercy was at Johns Hopkins. In the ICU. Recovering from surgery. Alone.

"Not if I have anything to say about it," he growled, half-running toward the door. He'd call Bud on his way to the hospital, let him know where he could be reached if he or Flora needed anything.

Still in uniform when he arrived, no one questioned his presence in the Intensive Care Unit. He walked the halls until he found her in the last glassed-in room on the left. It broke his heart to see Jane Doe written on the wall outside the door. Teeth clenched, he walked past it and into the dimly lit room.

She looked tinier than ever, propped at a thirty-degree angle in the bed.

A thick white bandage covered her right eye, and a pulley contraption held up her right leg. There was a sling on her right arm, and he'd have been hard-pressed to find a spot on her that wasn't bruised or bloodied.

They'd attached her to just about every monitoring devise at their disposal. He read the screens, relieved that her blood pressure and pulse rate, at least, were normal and stable. It was time to talk to the doctor on call, find out what had happened. Austin headed for the desk, and rapped lightly on the counter to get the attention of the floor nurse.

"The woman in 2424," he said, aiming a thumb over his shoulder. "She's not a Jane Doe. I know who she is."

She sucked in a little gasp. "Good!" She handed him two slips of paper. "Write down whatever information you can on this one, and that's the number we were told to call if anyone identified her. Why don't you get hold of the police while I try and locate Dr. Eversly?"

Austin sat on a bench across the way and dialed the number, explained why he was calling, and pulled as many facts from the duty officer as possible: Last evening, witnesses called 9-1-1 to report that three young men in hoodies, blue jeans, and high-tops were in the process of assaulting a young woman at the corner of Bond and Shakespeare Streets. No weapons were seen, but a broken flashlight had been collected near the gutter where she'd been found.

His mind froze at the word "gutter." What sort of animals would do something so vicious and violent? And why?

"Did they break into her house?"

"No forced entries were reported in the area," said the officer. "But since we didn't know who she was, we had no way of checking out where she lived."

Austin provided her address, and the cop promised to send a squad car to check things out. "Will you call me when they report back, let me know what they found?"

"This woman . . . ." Papers rattled. "Dr. Samara. Is she a family member?"

"No, she's—"

"Fiancée?"

Austin knew where this was going, because he'd been on the asking end of this conversation as a cop in New York. Unless he provided some personal connection, the officer couldn't release pertinent information to him. "Yeah, and she has no one but me." He provided his station and i.d. numbers, then added "I was on duty when this went down. Couldn't get hold of her and didn't know what to think. Then I saw her picture on the news."

"Sorry, bud. That's gotta be tough."

The man had no idea *how* tough. "Well, thanks for the info, but I'd better get back into her room, in case she wakes up."

"Call this same number when she does. We'll send somebody over to take her statement."

He could've kissed the guy for saying "when" instead of "if." Later, he'd drive over to her place, make sure things were buttoned up good and tight, and feed Woodrow. That would take a load off her mind when she came to. And while he was there he'd dig around for her insurance information. Call the high school to let them know she wouldn't be at work on Monday morning. Pick up a few of her personal items—a comb and toothbrush, slippers, a few magazines.

For now, hearing the doctor say she'd be all right was the only thing that mattered. So when he saw Eversly walk into her room, he all but tackled the guy and grilled him until he had the man's word that Mercy would walk out of here, eventually.

"She'll be out of it for at least another day," Eversly said. "We've loaded her up on pain meds to keep her quiet and still so she can recover from the surgery."

It seemed she'd suffered significant internal damage. Infection was a major concern, so they'd loaded her up with antibiotics, too.

Satisfied Mercy could pull through this, Austin thanked the doctor and made his way to the chapel, got on his knees at the altar . . .

. . . and broke down and cried.

27

Mercy's first thoughts as quiet whispering floated on the outskirts of her consciousness were of Austin. Hopefully, whomever told him that she'd been murdered in front of her own house had done it with a modicum of kindness.

What *were* those sounds, anyway? Certainly not angel's wings, because even if she'd been wrong all these years and there *was* a God in heaven, He wouldn't welcome someone who'd vehemently denied His very existence.

Or would He?

"Dr. Samara?"

Odd. The Lord of the known universe—who'd supposedly created her—addressing her in such a formal way? She tried to smile, to open her eyes and say, "Please, call me Mercy." But neither her lips nor her eyelids cooperated.

The questions in her head, the sound of a man's voice, the steady beeps echoing in her ears, none of it made sense, and all of it raised serious concerns about her condition. She'd earned a medical degree before choosing psychiatry as her specialty, and understood only too well that these things were not normal.

"Mercy? My name is Dr. Eversly. If you can hear me, will you open your eyes for me, please?"

Odder still, the disappointment she felt, hearing proof that it wasn't God. *Really,* she tried to say, *I'm not being intentionally rude. I'm trying to respond.*

Evidently, she had survived the attack. That would explain the pain pulsing through her body and a doctor beside her bed.

"I'll be back," Eversly said, "after I've made my rounds."

All right. Don't hurry on my account. It isn't as if I'm going anywhere.

"I'll page you if she comes to."

A woman's voice, now. A nurse, she supposed. Mercy would laugh—if her traitorous body would only cooperate. *How self-centered to think the doctor was talking to* you!

She heard the unmistakable sounds of a pen, scritch-scratching over paper. "I'm decreasing the pain meds. Maybe that'll bring her around."

Then the rattle of the clip-board that held her chart, clunking into place on the hook at the foot of her bed. And except for the monitor that counted her heartbeats, silence.

When she woke up—if she woke up—would the lower dosage be a shock to her system? During her days as an attending, she'd seen a patient go into cardiac arrest because the pain put too much stress on his system. The surgeon had blamed the man's age, the severity of his injuries, and a preexisting history of hypertension for his death. Was she strong enough—physically and constitutionally—to withstand the pain? *That'll depend on the extent of your injuries.* That, she thought, and a real desire to survive.

"Put them over there."

Put what, where? she wondered.

A gentle pressure on her wrist, followed by the sensation that the nurse was fiddling with her IV tubes. "I just love roses," she told Mercy. "They're my favorite flowers, especially white ones. If you don't wake up soon, I might just give in to the temptation to sneak one from the bouquet and tuck it behind my ear!"

And then she left the room and left Mercy wondering how long had she'd been in the hospital? *Long enough for someone to send a get well gift.*

The mattress dipped. The nurse, taking advantage of an opportunity to rest her weary legs? Or Eversly had finished his rounds? If only she could ask what type of surgery had been required, how long before she'd regain control of her limbs— and her faculties!

A warm hand blanketed hers, a soothing, comforting sensation. If only it could cover all of her.

"Holy mackerel. You're as cold as ice."

Austin.

Footsteps, then his voice, coming from farther away. "Nurse, could we get one of those heated blankets in here? She's freezing."

Then the bed shaking slightly as he sat down again. "Don't you worry," he said, sandwiching her hand between his own, "we'll get you warmed up in no time."

Thanks.

"Glad to see the roses arrived."

Wish I could see them, so I could tell you how much I love them!

"You gave me quite a scare, y'know."

Sorry.

"I must have called you a dozen times after I dropped Bud and Flora off. Then I gave up."

Why?

"Thought maybe you'd get it into your pretty little head to call the cops, report me as a stalker."

She heard the smile in his voice.

"And then I saw your picture on the news."

He blew a stream of air through is lips. She knew because he'd done it before. And because she felt the light breeze travel over her hand.

"I wouldn't say this if you were awake, but I hate hospitals. Always have, but never more than when my mom was admitted. With a job like mine, I see the inside of 'em more often in a month than a hundred other people see in a lifetime. I'll never get used to it."

Sorry to put you through this. You don't have to stay. I'll be fine. Really.

"Went to your house."

Oh? Why?

"Had to see for myself that the . . . those . . ."

She could almost picture him, grimacing as he tried to keep a civil tongue in his head.

"They found you a couple blocks from home, so I guess that's why those sorry excuses for human beings didn't get in. Your door was locked. No sign of a B and E."

That's good. A real relief. Did you see Woodrow, by any chance?

"Called the high school and left a message at the office. I let them know you won't be at work on Monday."

Thanks. That was really thoughtful of you. And what about Woodrow?

"Hope you don't mind, but I rummaged in your office, looking for insurance information."

Mind! I'm grateful as I can be! But where did you get the keys to the front door?

"Eversly—he's the surgeon who patched you up—"

Yes, I know. We've met. Sort of.

"—he says you'll be here in the ICU for another couple days. At least 'til you regain consciousness."

Ah, good. That means he expects it to happen. Now, about Woodrow . . . .

"Then a couple days to a week in a regular room."

He gave her hand a gentle squeeze. "You'll probably flip your lid when you're able to talk, but I don't care. When they let you out of here, I'm going home with you. You won't be able to do anything for yourself, at least not at first."

Then wouldn't it be better to hire an in-home nurse, to spare us both the awkwardness of—

"I can change dressings, administer meds—all the medical stuff—but I've arranged for in-home nursing, mostly to see to your, ah, your personal needs? You know, sponge baths, using the, ah, facilities, stuff like that."

If she were a gambler, Mercy would have bet Austin was blushing right about now.

"But I'll be there for everything else. Round the clock. You've got my word on it. And I won't take no for an answer."

Right. With your crazy work schedule? How will you manage that?

"I have a month of vacation time coming, and it begins whenever Eversly gives you the green light to go home."

The offer was so sweet, so thoughtful and caring, that she would have cried—if only her body would allow it.

"Aw, Merc . . . ."

She felt the rasp of a work-hardened fingertip at the corner of her eye.

"Please don't cry, sweetie. Are you in pain?"

Not the physical kind. It was a relief to know her tear ducts, at least, were functioning normally. But not being able to communicate? Yes, painful. Definitely!

"I'm sure you're scared. The most normal and natural reaction to a thing like this in the world. You've been through one heck of an ordeal, but try and remember that you're in the best hospital in the world, and Eversly has an excellent reputation—I know, because I Googled him a while ago. Take my word on it: Everything's gonna be all right. And if anything crops up that isn't? Well, you have my word that I'll *make* it all right."

The bed moved again, a sign he was on his feet.

Don't leave yet. Stay a while longer, OK?

Something soft and satiny brushed her hand, and it brought back memories of brushing her Barbie doll's hair. It wasn't until she heard Austin's trembly voice that Mercy realized he'd dropped to his knees, pressed his forehead to the back of her hand.

"Dear Father in heaven, wrap Your merciful arms around this precious woman. Heal her from the inside out, and if there's any pain involved with her recuperation, let me bear it in her stead."

She'd never known anyone who, with nothing but a few words, could touch her the way Austin could. Never knew anyone who cared this much about her, either, except maybe her dad. Mercy's eyes began to leak again. More proof that the drugs were wearing off, because she felt the tears inch down her cheeks.

"Watch over her, Lord, and make sure she knows how very much she's treasured . . ."

Good thing you're sitting up, or the tears would puddle in your ears, and you wouldn't be able to hear his beautiful voice.

". . . and how much she's loved. I ask all this in Your most holy name, Amen."

It had been a long, long time since Mercy had believed in anything, and after 9/11, she hadn't believed in any*one*, either. But she believed in this man, wholly and completely.

If she believed in the *Almighty*, she'd thank Him right now for bringing Austin back into her life . . .

. . . and then she'd beg Him to *keep* Austin near.

28

*H*e arranged to transport her from Fells Point, two times a week as prescribed for rehab at Johns Hopkins. And to assure the use of an ambulance when needed, Austin had traded favors, swapped shifts, promised to mow lawns and do dishes if he had to. Nothing was more important than getting her home, where she could recover in quiet comfort, without hourly disruptions of her sleep as nurses checked her vitals and new patients were checked in to nearby rooms.

The day after Thanksgiving he'd rooted around in her purse, and after fumbling around in her office to figure out the copy machine, printed out duplicates to satisfy the hospital's billing department and save Mercy from having to deal with money issues upon her release.

Eversly had promised to give him a heads up when Mercy was well enough to leave, so that he could prep her place for a patient with a toes-to-thigh cast on one leg, another that went from thumb to elbow and taped-up ribs. And the instant he got the word, Austin raced to the grocery store to stock the fridge and pantry, then scrubbed the townhouse from top to bottom.

Hard to believe a cat had set all of this in motion. How had Woodrow slipped past her, when she guarded the door like one of those harlequin-uniformed soldiers outside the Vatican? It was a nice cat—as cats went—but nice enough to drive her into the dark, alone, in the middle of a gully-washer?

Austin would just have to wait for an answer to that one. But to put her mind at ease, he'd found a picture of the fat orange feline on her desk. The kid behind the counter at the copy shop had snickered when he saw it. "What's its name?" he'd wanted to know. And when Austin told him, he snickered again. "Looks more like a *Garfield* than a Woodrow," he said before running off fifty full-color leaflets.

Austin brought them to the high school and, with the help of her students, spent an entire Saturday afternoon knocking on doors in Fells Point. She'd gone all weepy on him when he told her no one had seen or taken Woodrow in, but quickly pulled herself together when Austin added that the teens had tacked "Missing" flyers to every shop window, fence and telephone pole in the area.

"He's resourceful," she'd said, blotting her eyes with a paper napkin. "He'll find his way home. I hope."

The only other time she'd gone damp-eyed had been when the doctor removed the bandages from around her head. Eversly had been forced to shave the incision site, leaving a bald spot the size of her fist. She'd tried hiding under her pillow, but gave up when one-handing it proved more than she could manage, thanks to bruises and muscle strain in her good arm.

To her credit, she'd recovered quickly from that, too.

They were less than two blocks from Aliceanna Street when she said, "Have I told you how much I appreciate everything you've done?"

He glanced at his watch. "Not in the last five minutes, you haven't." He chuckled. "You're slipping, missy."

She laughed quietly. "I'll just blame this li'l bump on my head."

Little bump, indeed. The beasts who'd attacked her left a three-inch scar just under her hairline. Skull fracture, subdural hemorrhage . . . another half-inch lower, and they'd have hit her temple. Even Eversly said that her guardian angel had been working overtime that night.

"It'll seem weird, not having Woodrow around. Thanks for all you did to try and find him."

"Maybe we'll get a call from someone who's seen him." He shrugged. "And who knows? He might just make his way home on his own."

"I hope so, because he's been a constant companion, almost from the day I moved in. I'm going to miss him if—"

Her tears prompted him to say "Let's keep a good thought, huh?"

She nodded and let him blot her eyes. "I know. You're right. I just wanted you to know. I think you're really, really sweet, going to so much trouble for Woodrow."

"Not as sweet as you."

She smiled. "And I appreciate all you're doing for *me*, too."

"Happy to do it." And he meant it, too.

"Well, it bears repeating. This is so nice of you. I'm—"

McElroy groaned, met Austin's gaze in the rearview mirror. "You guys wanna save the lovey-dovey stuff for *after* I leave? I haven't had breakfast, and all this sugar is making me wanna hurl."

Austin gave Mercy's hand a gentle pat as his partner wheeled the ambulance into her driveway. "Let me get the door unlocked and clear a path for the gurney," he said, patting it again.

"Don't worry, I'm not going anywhere."

Austin's nerves jangled so badly, he nearly dropped the keys. He could hardly wait to see her reaction to everything he'd done.

The hinges squealed quietly as he swung the door inward. No problem, he thought, pocketing the keychain, because he'd have plenty of time to oil it while Mercy napped.

Once he and McElroy cleared the entry, they rolled her into the living room, where Austin had made up the sofa bed. He hoped she'd like the magazines he'd bought and stacked on the end table beside a box of tissues.

Together, the men gently moved her from the gurney to her makeshift bed, and McElroy wasted no time hot-footing it out of there. "Call me if you need anything," he said, saluting as he back-pedaled toward the door.

And before Austin or Mercy could respond, he closed the door behind him.

"Why don't you try and catch a few Zs," he said, drawing the curtains over the floor-to-ceiling windows. "That ride home had to be tiring. And while you're sleeping, I'll start supper. And oil the front—"

"Austin . . . ?"

"Hmm?"

"When did you have time to do all of this?"

Man, she looked cute, propped against the pillows in her pink PJs and fuzzy robe. One of her former students had heard about the attack, and, seeing what happened to Mercy's hair, volunteered to put her talents to work, camouflaging the bald spot. The stylist clipped it into a chin-length bob and parted in the middle, so that the stitches were barely visible. Yeah, Mercy was cute, all right. He watched her take it in—the lighted pine garland he'd swagged from the railing, the six-foot wreath that twinkled above the fireplace, the ceiling-scraping Douglas fir that dominated the living room.

"You were with me at the hospital almost 24/7. Did you get any sleep *at all*?"

"'Course I did. But don't change the subject, missy. You need to rest up after that bumpy ride home."

"I've never had a Christmas tree before."

"What? *Never*?"

"Well, not one of my own, I mean. Dad always insisted on a tree, of course, and made me help him decorate it, too."

Austin breathed a sigh of relief. Fixing the place up this way had been a risk, considering how she felt about religion in general, and God in particular. But he didn't feel like getting into a theological debate right now. "I'm gonna fix you a cup of herbal tea. What's your preference, orange spice or blueberry?"

"Surprise me." She grinned. "You seem to have a knack for that."

"Back in a jif—"

"Austin?"

What now? he wondered.

"I'm just curious."

He watched her glance around the room again, then focus on his face. "Why did you choose this color theme?"

"Because your favorite color is purple." He grit his teeth. *Oh, Lord, tell me I'm not mistaken.* "Right?"

"Well, yes, it is. But I don't remember ever discussing star signs, or favorite foods and movies and songs, or any of the other endless trivia that usually dominates first—"

If she hadn't cut herself off, would Mercy have said "first dates"?

"How'd you figure out what my favorite color is?"

"Oh, I dunno," he said. "Maybe because your bath towels are purple and your bedspread is purple and even the pot holders in your kitchen are purple?" He paused. "Or maybe I'm just a psychic genius."

"Oh, really. Well, then, Mr. Mind Reader, what am I thinking right now?"

He sat on the arm of the sofa farthest from her and did his best not to blink as she drilled his eyes with those chocolate-brown eyes of hers. The truth? She could be thinking the Percocet had started to kick in, or that she wished it *would*.

Austin grimaced and pressed his fingertips to his temples. "You're thinking that you don't believe for a minute that I can read your mind."

She started to giggle, then winced. "Please. Don't make me laugh."

He handed her the remote. "What *I'm* thinking is you're exhausted. So why don't you surf for an old rerun on that gigantic widescreen of yours. A sitcom, maybe, with a mindless plot that'll make you drowsy." He'd almost made it to the hallway when her soft voice stopped him.

"Austin?"

Grinning, he said it out loud this time. "What *now*?"

She used her chin as a pointer. "Is *that* where you plan to sleep?"

Sensing her need to live an organized and orderly life, he'd taken care to hide the twin-sized cot behind the other L of the sectional. Evidently, Mercy had found the only "can't see it from this angle" he hadn't tested. "Yeah."

"You're welcome to use the guest room, you know. I gave it a thorough cleaning after Leo left for—"

"No way. I'm staying close by to make sure you don't decide to practice your Jitterbug or squeeze in a few jumping jacks in the middle of the night."

She laughed . . . and winced, then said "Blueberry."

Taking care of her would be a lot of things, he thought as he held the teapot under the spigot, but boring wouldn't be one of them.

29

*T*wo days after bringing her home, a Baltimore City Police detective called to see if Mercy was up to looking at a few mug shots. "Will Campbell, Baltimore Police," he said, flashing his badge. "Thanks for agreeing to this."

Austin remembered him from the hospital, when he'd brought a grizzled old woman with a sketch pad and a pencil and freckle-faced kid from the district attorney's office into Mercy's room. While the detective took her statement and the young lawyer snapped pictures, the woman held up the pictures and frowned as Mercy insisted she didn't recognize the faces in the drawings. When the trio left an hour later, they didn't have much more information than when they'd arrived.

Even now Austin had found that puzzling—and disturbing—because all of her injuries had been inflicted head-on. Surely she'd seen her attackers. Was she afraid that identifying them might incite a payback beating, or had the blow to her head knocked all memories of the event from her brain?

"You guys didn't waste any time rounding up those thugs, did you?"

"The mayor's leaning on us, and leaning hard, because more than half the victims have been tourists. With this attack, we're in double digits now—and we've made network news. That ain't helpin' build a campaign fund."

"I don't imagine it is."

"We've picked up a couple dozen of these two- and three-man assailants. Could be the same ones, could be copycats. All we know for sure is that those bozos down at the prosecutor's office can't run 'em through the system fast enough."

Austin gestured toward the living room. "She's in here."

Campbell tucked a mustard-colored envelope under one arm, stuck out his free hand. "Thanks for agreeing to do this on such short notice, Dr. Samara."

"Please, call me Mercy," she said, shaking it. "I just hope I can be of some help."

The detective gave her a quick once-over, and slid a small spiral tablet from his jacket's breast pocket. "How are you feeling?"

"A little achy here and there, but that's all."

"Well, that's no surprise." His clicked his ballpoint into action. "They sure did a number on you, didn't they?" He paused and sat on the edge of the sofa. "Any bad dreams about the incident?"

"No."

A one-word answer, given that fast? It told Austin there *had* been nightmares. Told Campbell the same thing, if his furious scribbling was any indicator.

Mercy sat up straighter and pointed at the folder. "Are those the photos you want me to look at?"

"Yes, ma'am." He opened the metal clasp that held the flap in place and slid a few inches closer to her side. He glanced around the living room, and when his gaze settled on a food tray, he cleared plates and silverware from it. "Mind if I spread the pictures out on this thing? I think it'll make it easier for you to see them, all at one time."

He didn't wait for her to agree. Instead, he shook his wrists and snapped the mug shots onto the tray, looking more like a Vegas dealer than a police detective. "There," he said, gently placing it on her lap. "Now just take your time, and if any of these guys look even a little bit familiar, just say the word."

Austin watched as her brows drew together in a serious frown. Hands trembling, she picked up the photographs, one at a time, then returned each to the tray. He watched her lick her lips, too. "Coffee? Soda?" he asked.

"No, I'm fine."

"How about you, Campbell?"

The cop held up one hand. "Thanks, but I'm meeting my wife for lunch soon as I'm through here." He smiled. "It's our anniversary."

"Really," Mercy said, mirroring his smile. "How long have you been married?"

"It'll be eleven years on Saturday."

She gave a nod of approval. "How nice. Children?"

"Twins. Boy and girl, age seven."

"I don't suppose you carry pictures—"

"Are you kidding?" Campbell laughed. "If I didn't, my mother would forget I'm pushin' forty and turn me over her knee." He withdrew his wallet and opened to the photo gallery. "This is Samantha," he said, pointing at a dark-haired girl, "and Steven."

"Goodness," Mercy said. "They're complete opposites!"

"That's what everyone says." He slid the wallet into his back pocket.

"I hear that happens all the time with fraternal twins."

"Uh huh."

"Sorry if it seems I'm stalling." She glanced back at the mug shots. "This is just—"

Even from Austin's angle—upside down and with the glare of the window obscuring a few faces—the young men looked frightening, soulless, ready to kill at the drop of a hat.

"No apologies necessary," Campbell said. "We're not in any hurry." He met Austin's eyes for a second, then quickly added, "Today." And clearing his throat, he said, "If this is too much, too soon, I can come back another time, when you're feeling a little stronger, because I don't want to—"

Mercy held up a hand. "No, no. I'd just as soon get it over with. I'm fine, really."

But Austin had heard the tremor in her voice, and from the look in Campbell's face, he'd heard it, too. He connected with the cop just long enough to know the man had also noticed her shaking hand.

While Mercy went back to studying the photos, the detective adjusted the Windsor knot of his tie. "How long have *you* two been together?"

Mercy had been holding a mug shot in each hand, and her giggling nearly made her drop both. "You mean, 'together' as in *married?*"

"Yeah."

"We're not!"

He looked from Austin to Mercy and back again. "Could-a fooled me."

To gain quick access to her hospital room, Austin had told the staff at Hopkins that he and Mercy were engaged. It wouldn't matter to Campbell one way or the other, especially now that she'd been released. So why did he feel the need to send the same message to the detective? "We're—ah, I'm workin' on her," he said, surprising himself, and, judging by Mercy's raised eyebrows, surprised her, too.

Campbell shrugged, proof in Austin's mind that mild curiosity and a desire to fill the uncomfortable silence with chatter was the only reason for the man's question. As if he needed more proof, Campbell pulled back the cuff of his white shirt and glanced at his watch. He pointed at the mug shots. "Any of those men look familiar to you?"

"No, I'm afraid not." Mercy traded the pictures for two she'd already studied. "But I'd hardly call them men. Why, from the looks of them, they could very well still be in high school. Barely more than boys."

"If you're going by their birth dates, *maybe*," Campbell barked, "but that's about the only way they're *boys*."

He huffed in disgust. "We have sworn statements from witnesses that indicate *all* of the offenders have been kids. Not just boys, either. Half of the attackers have been young women." He paused. "And believe me, I use the term loosely, because when the girls were involved?" he shook his head. "Let's just say their victims ended up in far worse shape than you." Another huff. "I'd bet my next paycheck that the last one will never be able to move her jaw again."

Austin watched Mercy's eyes widen with a mix of fury and fear. Good thing she hadn't heard what Campbell and his cronies had said about the gang as they were leaving the hospital. He'd been too worried about Mercy that night to be more than mildly curious, but now, he wished that he'd pressed the cop for more details.

Campbell cleared his throat again. "You're sure you don't recognize any of them? I know it was dark and cold and raining cats and dogs, but—"

"No." She shook her head. "I'm positive. Those weren't the boys who—" She bit her lower lip, shook her head again, harder this time. "No. No, I don't recognize any of them."

"Sometimes," Campbell said, gathering up his snapshots, "people remember things long after an assault. Fragments of what happened might come back days, weeks, even months later. That's why I asked if you've been having weird dreams. Maybe you remember scars or moles on the attackers' faces. A tattoo. A piece of jewelry. A baseball cap. A lisp." He stood and dropped them back into the envelope. "If you think of anything, anything at all, call me." He fished a card out of his shirt pocket and handed it to her. "I sure hope your recovery is fast and easy from here on out."

"Thanks, Detective Campbell. You've been very patient and understanding. I'm sure it's frustrating for you that I can't remember much, because all you're trying to do is catch the bad guys so they can't do the same thing to anyone else. I'm sorry I couldn't be more help." She looked at his card, then put it into the basket Austin had placed on the table beside her.

"You have nothing to apologize for. And please, call me Will. If you need to call me, that is." He winked and started for the door, then stopped near the window wall. "Looks like we might just get that winter storm they're predicting."

Austin followed his gaze. Sure enough, dark clouds had gathered overhead, painting the sky an icy gray. "Last I heard, they were calling for a couple of feet."

"I hope we get a full-blown blizzard."

"I love being snowed in, too," Mercy said.

"One good thing, crime statistics drop during snowstorms." He chuckled. "Guess even criminals like to cuddle up when it's cold outside." He tipped an imaginary hat. "Hope the little woman has stocked up on milk and toilet paper. And junk food for the twins. Nothin' I hate worse than the grocery store in Baltimore after the weather bureau predicts bad weather."

"I know," Mercy agreed. "It's as if they believe we'll be snowed in for months!"

"Well, guess I'd best make tracks. With any luck, not literally." Laughing, he walked toward the hall. "No need to see me out. If I can't find my way back to the door, what kind of cop am I, right?"

Once the door clicked shut behind him, Mercy said, "Well, *that* was embarrassing."

He sat across from her. "What was?"

"All those kids in the pictures? What's with those too-hard-for-their-age faces? I mean, honestly, hiding under their hoodies with those gigantic diamond studs and tattoos and eyebrow rings, how's a citizen supposed to tell one from the other?"

"It's no accident that they dress alike. Makes it tougher for victims to identify them."

She growled under her breath and punched the sofa cushion with her good arm. "Well, it's just so *frustrating!* Like when all those first responders came to me for help after 9/11, and there wasn't a doggoned thing I could do but encourage them to talk it out. I felt useless and helpless and—"

"Quit being so hard on yourself. You did what you could then—I'm living proof of that—and you did what you could today."

The reminder of the disaster brought memories of his own to the fore, and for the first time since delivering her home from the hospital, Austin wanted to leave. Just long enough, anyway, to clear his head.

"How 'bout grilled cheese, tomato soup, and a salad for lunch?" he said, standing.

"I'm really not hungry."

"It's lunch time. Hungry or not, you need to eat to keep up your strength. Besides, you can't take your meds on an empty stomach. I can make ham and cheese, BLTs, even an omelet— all with a salad—your choice." He slapped his palms together once and grinned. Not an easy feat, considering the way her cuts and bruises reminded him of the dead and injured he'd unearthed at Ground Zero. Good thing he couldn't get to that bottle of Jim Beam.

"So, which will it be?"

"I need sleep just as much as I need food." She scooted down, into a slightly more prone position. "I think I'll take a nap, instead."

"You'll rest a lot easier with a full stomach." Arms crossed over his chest, he said, "You can make a choice, or I can make it for you."

Mercy rolled her eyes. "All right, then. Fine. I guess I'll have a BLT. At least that way I'm getting the salad and the sandwich all rolled into one, and I can get to sleep faster."

He'd made it halfway to the kitchen when she added, "Thanks, Austin. You're . . . ."

Turning, he waited for her to finish the sentence, and as her dark eyes locked on him, every muscle in him tensed.

". . . I didn't mind at all, finding out that you had fibbed— about our relationship, I mean—to the people at Hopkins. Or that you led Detective Campbell to believe we're . . . um . . . you know . . . ."

No, he didn't know. Did she expect him to finish her statement by admitting he was crazy in love with her? That he'd give anything to stand beside her at an altar and profess before God and all present that he wanted her to share a home and kids and everything else that went into the whole "happily ever after" package?

Leave it to her to further confuse and confound things, because now, in addition to figuring out how he'd tamp down his ugly 9/11 thoughts, he'd have his feelings about her to contend with. Because how likely was any of *that* to happen when she wouldn't share the most important element of his life?

Austin realized he realized he'd been staring, gap-jawed and panting like a dog who'd been offered a pork chop—at arm's length. How could he expect her to profess undying faith in God when *he* hadn't been to church in months, and the only time he'd picked up the bible these days had been to dust under it?

Snapping his mouth shut, he gave a little wave and walked into the kitchen—

—where he burned the bacon.

And the toast.

Nearly hacked the tip of his finger off, slicing a tomato, and bled all over the lettuce.

It took two tries, but somehow he managed to assemble a gorgeous triple-decker sandwich. As he arranged triangle sections around a mound of low-salt chips, he considered snapping photo of it, so he could show it to Bucky over at Captain Harvey's next time he and McElroy stopped in for a quick lunch. Bad idea, he thought, filling a tumbler with ice and lemonade, because Bucky might resent the competition and quit putting extra bacon on his orders.

He reached for the plate and glass, but froze. Both palms pressed on the counter, Austin stared out the window.

What would he talk about when he went back into the living room with her lunch? Gilded invitations and honeymoon packages?

He groaned, as he saw that a steady snow had begun to fall. Big fat flakes floated gently to the ground, melting on impact. Austin remembered what Campbell had said about the weather report. If it kept coming down at this rate, he wouldn't be at all surprised if a couple of feet fell by morning.

The chickadees and sparrows jockeyed for position at the feeder. A blue jay splashed in the heated birdbath, and a squirrel scampered on the ground, scrounging for seeds dropped during the frenzy. He'd read someplace that when birds and animals sensed foul weather, they started eating like there was no tomorrow. Maybe that's what he'd talk about when he got back to the living room.

Or maybe he wouldn't talk at all. Just deliver lunch and announce his intention to move the feeder and birdbath around front, so she could get some enjoyment out of the birds' frolicking. And when he finished that, he'd take down the Christmas decorations.

The chore reminded him that they'd spent the holiday doing pretty much the same thing they'd done every day prior to and after the twenty-fifth. Nobody could accuse him of being a Christmas nut, but they couldn't call him Scrooge, either.

After looking in every nook and cranny without finding so much as an ornament hook, he'd thrown in the towel and gone to the nearest discount store, and filled a cart to the brim with things to brighten up her house. Curiosity made him ask, once he'd made her comfortable that first day, where she'd stored her decorations. And when she said she didn't have any, he'd asked, "You've lived here how long?" he'd asked.

"It'll be five years, this summer."

"And you've never owned *any* Christmas decorations?"

"Nope."

"With all the decorating Baltimoreans do?"

She'd frowned so deeply Austin thought maybe she'd popped a stitch. It surprised him when she followed it up with "It's messy and gaudy and time consuming. So what's the point?"

The *point*, he'd wanted to say, is that tinsel and ornaments and blinking lights—the gaudier, the better—helped put folks in the mood. And what was wrong with that, as long as it didn't detract from the real reason for the day? Pleasant diversions were important, especially in this age when everything happened in an eye blink, and people had forgotten how to make time to stop and smell the flowers. Why, he had Jewish friends who got more excited about the date than Mercy, who shared that her own mom had called herself a "Santa-holic!"

He added it to his mental "Differences and Similarities" list. The fact that the left side was way longer than the right left him with an uneasy feeling, yet he couldn't quite put his finger on *why*.

Austin had known couples who'd spent a long and happy lifetime together, though it might appear to the casual observer that they had nothing in common. Take Eddy and Cora, for example—a self-professed Bible-thumper linked for life to a guy who'd spent weeks after graduating from the academy trying to make his uniform hat fit over his yarmulke.

And what about Bud, who'd traded his diehard anti-church mindset for an usher's pin when he married Flora.

And Griff, who'd converted from Jehovah's Witness to Catholicism to gain the approval of Mary and her parents.

In every case, the relationships had succeeded because the husbands and wives had been willing to compromise. If he and Mercy took things to the next level, they'd both have to give a little. He was willing to meet her halfway, but would she go the same distance?

Flapping wings and angry tweets pulled his attention back to the window. He counted eight perches on the tubular feeder, yet only two were in use by black-capped chickadees. A stark reminder that in nature concessions and negotiations were unheard of policies. Instead, an inflexible "my way or the highway" stance dictated the pecking order in nature, literally.

It explained a lot, from his point of view, about what was wrong with mankind. Wars, divorce, family feuds—all because of humans' need to have their own way, and few things proved that better than the events of 9/11.

As the birds wrangled, gruesome images flashed in his mind's eye. Austin clenched his jaw. He'd better stay plenty busy today if he hoped to keep the grisly pictures from popping back into his head.

He palmed a fork and napkin, and used the same hand to grab the sandwich plate, then wrapped his other hand around the glass. "Start with the bird stuff," he muttered as he aimed for the hall. Because now the birds would be a constant reminder of 9/11.

Maybe he'd oversimplified the cause of the aggressive attack, and maybe he'd hit the old nail square on the head. A scary concept. Equally daunting, the parallels between that situation and the one between him and Mercy.

One thing was certain: The minute Mercy could take care of herself, and he returned to work and *One Regret,* he had a lot of thinking and praying to do.

Until then, he'd better stay busy. The busier, the better, because then his mind wouldn't fixate on the date that changed the entire course of his life . . .

. . . or the woman who'd turned his life upside-down.

30

Mercy's goal, right from the start, had been to get back on her feet as quickly as possible. By the end of the second week, her hours of grueling exercise paid off and her doctor agreed that she no longer needed the in-home nurse or physical therapist.

Cabin fever had set in, and despite Austin's his attempts to keep her entertained with movies and board games, she missed her students and coworkers at Dundalk High. And though he served grilled meats, BLTs, and salads with flair and enthusiasm, the repetition made her miss the cafeteria food, too.

He'd just settled in with the morning paper when she said "I haven't talked to Bud or Flora in days. Do you think we could drive over there this afternoon for a short visit?"

He peered over one corner of the sports section. "How about if we ask Eversly about that when you see him, day after tomorrow? I have a feeling he'll give you a clean bill of health and permission to return to light duty, so let's not push it, OK?"

Two more days stuck inside, with nothing to do but watch TV and fill in crossword puzzles? And two more days of his constant care? Much as she loved spending time with him, and appreciated every hour he'd dedicated to her care and well-being, Mercy needed to get back to the business of taking care of herself.

She needed to get out of the house, too, before the stresses of being inactive, in pain, and cooped up made her say something thoughtless and ungrateful.

"If I'm strong enough to ride back and forth for checkups, then I'm strong enough to drive to the marina." After all these hours alone with him, Mercy recognized *that* expression, and nipped his objection in the bud. "Who knows how much longer she'll have? We need to spend as much time with her as we can, every chance we have."

She watched as his "I'm only doing what's in your best interests" frown softened. Logic, she'd learned these past weeks, went a long, long way with this generous, thoughtful man.

"Good point. And I suppose by now the road crews have cleaned up most of the snow."

"I'll call and give them a heads up that we're on our way, because in Flora's shoes, I'd want to freshen up before people stopped by."

He put the paper down and picked up the phone. "Good point," he said again. "How 'bout if we stop on the way over, pick up lunch. That'll save Bud the bother." He dialed their number. "I'd better find out, first, what she's allowed to eat these days."

"Yeah. How mean would that be, showing up with one of her favorites if all she can do is inhale the aromas!"

"My thoughts, exactly."

Two hours later, they balanced on the edge of the sofa cushions, knees tucked under wobbly TV trays. All but Flora, that is.

Bud had warned them to be ready for a big change in his wife's appearance, but no amount of preparation would have lessened the shock of seeing her for the first time in more than a month. Skeletal and gray-faced, something as insignificant as blinking seemed to require more strength than she had in reserve. Her once-thick, salt-and-pepper hair had turned white as new-fallen snow. Dull and sparse, it made the shadows beneath her sunken blue eyes look darker still.

While caring for her dad during his long, harrowing months in the hospital. Her system for washing and rinsing a bed-ridden patient's hair caught on. Soon, all the nurses in ICU had copied it. After lunch, Mercy thought, choosing a thigh from the bucket of fried chicken, she'd treat Flora to a gentle scalp-massaging shampoo.

If the poor thing could stay awake, that is.

Austin must have noticed her drooping eyelids, too. "We can drag chairs and the TV trays into your room," he suggested, "so you can lie down while we talk."

But Flora was adamant. "I've been cooped up in that dim little room all day, every day, for nearly a week. I've counted every knot hole in the paneling, every flower on the curtains, and every feather on that hideous flamingo print hanging across from the bed *a hundred times*, and I declare, if I have to spend one more minute under the quilt my near-sighted mother-in-law ruined in the clothes dryer a decade or so ago, I might just have to eat it. If that doesn't put me out of my misery, I don't know what will!"

She laughed, which started a coughing fit that lasted nearly five terrifying minutes.

Mercy had spent part of her internship assisting an oncologist, and remembered the symptoms only too well. Flora's cancer had metastasized, attacking her major organs, one by one. At this rate, the poor woman would be gone by Valentine's Day.

When she recovered, Flora tried—but failed—to hide her bloody hanky from Mercy. "I want to hear all about this awful thrashing you took, girl. Bet you were terrified. I know I would've been!"

Mercy would have done just about anything for Flora—except talk about the attack. She hadn't had much cause to put her "put it to the back of your mind" talent to use since 9/11, but the gift came in handy in the weeks since her release from the hospital. The fierce, menacing glares had been scary enough at on the night of the attack. Last thing she needed was to see them in her nightmares. "I'd rather not talk about it, if it's all the same to you."

The familiar gleam that once sparkled in Flora's eyes flashed for an instant as one corner of her mouth lifted slightly. "Never figured you for the type who'd hide from the hard things in life."

Hide? Why, of all the—

"You don't want to hear the details, Flora."

Both women turned their attention to Austin, but it was Bud who asked "Why not?"

"Because she gave every bit as good as she got."

Mercy considered asking him if he'd lost his mind, because she had no memory of fighting back. In fact, all she remembered was agonizing, pounding pain, then thinking she'd drown in the river of rainwater rushing down the gutter. That, and the irony of the filthy little cup that kept the mud and grit from getting into her nose and mouth.

Austin winked and reached over to squeeze her knee, exactly as her dad used to—a private signal between them that meant "Don't take everything so seriously!"

If asked to count how many times she'd compared Austin to her father these past weeks, Mercy believed the number might reach double digits. Though the two men had nothing in common physically, they shared a fierce determination to protect those they cared about.

While pretending to nap on her first day home from the hospital, Austin had tiptoed closer to tuck the blankets up under her chin, just as her father had done when a virus or a cold kept her home in bed. And on Sunday mornings, her dad loved taunting her with a quiet "Hmm . . ." or whispered "Well, I'll be" as he read the headlines, prompting Mercy's inquisitive "What, Dad. What's so fascinating!" And when Austin did the same thing, she'd nearly burst into tears at the sweet memory.

Bud laughed. "Well, good! I'll bet those tough guys won't soon forget *this* li'l gal."

"Yes, good for you, Mercy!" Flora said. "I hope you scratched and clawed and kicked so hard that . . ." She had to stop to catch her breath. ". . . so hard that . . . that the next time they decide to . . . to hammer on an innocent citizen they'll think twice!"

"Aw, will you look at her pretty little face, Flor-dee-lee? Why, she looks terrified, just thinking about what happened. Can't you see that Mercy wasn't kidding when she said she didn't want to talk about it?" He winked at her. "Talk less, listen more. It's better for your health."

Brows high on her forehead, Flora pinched off a piece of her biscuit. "I wasn't talking about it, exactly," she defended. "More like commenting is all." She looked to Austin, hoping for an ally.

Unfortunately, she didn't find one in her next door neighbor, either.

"Well, if this doesn't just beat all," she grumbled, feigning a pout. "Guess I'll just have to hide my curiosity *and* hurt feelings behind my love for buttery biscuits." And she popped the bread into her mouth.

Mercy suddenly felt horribly guilty. "I'm sorry, Flora. Maybe in a week or two, when the bruises have healed and Woodrow has found his way, I can—"

"Woodrow? Your cat is *missing*?"

"Yes. He's the reason I went outside in the first place. I'd opened the front door to tuck a bill into the mailbox, so the letter carrier would pick it up on his way by, and when I did, Woodrow must have made a run for it."

"Why, that ornery, sneaky little ingrate!"

"Wait just a cotton-pickin' minute, here," Bud said. "Do you seriously expect me to believe that you went out in the driving rain, on that bitter-cold night, all by yourself to hunt for that—"

From the corner of her eye, Mercy saw Austin signal Bud to hush. Later, she'd thank him for that. "I never understood why he always tried so hard to escape, when he has a loving home, and food, and vet care and—"

"Didn't you say he sort of found you on the day you moved into the house?"

She didn't remember telling Flora that story, which meant Austin had done it. If he'd relayed something that trivial, what else had he said?

"Maybe he was like that dog from that kids' movie—I forget the title—going going from pillar to post, staying sometimes and leaving whenever he felt like it."

"You could be right, Flor-dee-lee. Makes sense to me." Bud stroked his chin. "Guess he's like so many bachelors these days; hangs around until he's bored, then off he goes."

"Yes," Flora said, "like my sister's fiancé. Here today, gone tomorrow. That man can no more make a commitment than a giraffe can fly." She aimed a maternal glare Austin's way to say it. Aimed a crooked forefinger, too.

She'd dropped a similar hint the evening Mercy met her, and another on Thanksgiving. It had been a relief to hear he hadn't taken any relationships seriously, because that left the door open to possibilities. They'd survived a couple of heated debates, and enjoyed warm conversation, hearty laughter, and sweet kisses, yet he hadn't given any sign that he wanted more. And to be fair, neither had she.

"You know, I never gave a thought to the possibility that Woodrow had another family—maybe more than one—beyond the boundaries of my minuscule slice of the world. Is my face red thinking I had a singular claim to the little bigamist!"

The comment invited a chorus of laughter that drowned out Mercy's aching disappointment. She may never see her precious Woodrow again . . . yet another beloved thing Austin's so-called loving God had taken from her.

"You're awfully quiet," he said during the drive back to her place. "You feeling OK?"

"I'm fine." She didn't have the energy to get into a whole "religion thing" with him again. Besides, last time when their debate ended, he'd gone home. This time, she'd be stuck with his pouting self. "Just tired, I guess, and a little down in the dumps about Flora's condition. And remembering what Bud said about more snow on the way. What if she takes a turn for the worse and Bud can't get her to the hospital?"

"Yeah, she looks pretty bad, doesn't she?"

She didn't comment on the fact that he'd ignored her weather-related observation. Instead, Mercy said "I've only known her a short while, but what I miss most is her vim and vigor. It's so sad, not hearing that 'loving life' music in her voice."

He stared straight ahead, working his jaw muscles and gripping the steering wheel so tightly, it was a wonder it didn't bend. "Did her doctor tell him how long she has?"

Austin shook his head. "Last I heard, they expect her to hang on until summer. Only God knows for sure."

God again. She wanted to shake some sense into him. Because if *God* gave a fig about what was happening to Flora, then why was it happening?

The hiss of tires spinning over the wet pavement seeped into the front seat as they rode the next few miles in silence. "Awful as it was seeing her like that, I'm really glad we went. Thanks for taking me."

Austin grunted in reply.

"I'm feeling lots better," Mercy said. "You wouldn't have to stay. If you want to get back to work. Or anything."

He looked over at her and smirked. "What was that, my 'Here's your hat, what's your hurry' hint?"

"Of course not!" she said, though in her head, that's exactly how she felt. Mostly because she really did feel better, thanks to his nonstop nurturing. "It's just—you've wasted your whole vacation babysitting for me, and—"

"Wasted? What makes you think I see it as a waste of time?"

She'd never heard that edgy note in his voice before. Anger, Mercy wondered? Or had she hurt his feelings? Shame threatened to turn her cheeks red, because she didn't want to provoke either emotion. He deserved better than that. So much better!

"Of *course* not," she repeated, this time with more emphasis. "It's just that I feel so guilty, taking and taking and taking from you. I'll never live long enough to repay you for all you've done."

He swallowed. "I hope you don't think the only reason I stayed with you was to put together a scenario where you'd end up owing me."

How many times did she have to say it? "Of course not. But think about it, Austin. How would *you* feel if I'd given up every moment of my vacation to hover over you?"

"Interesting word choice, 'hover.'"

She'd never known him to be overly sensitive. Or pouty, either. And Mercy didn't much like it now that she'd been on the receiving end of both. "You're right. That was a very poor word choice. Blame it on the pain meds. That isn't how I meant it, and you know—"

"You haven't taken any Percocet in days."

Ack, that's right. How're you gonna wiggle out of this one, Merc?

Fortunately, before she had a chance to respond, he said "Who would have taken care of you if I hadn't had all that vacation time to use or lose?"

"A nurse, I suppose. But I'm the first to admit that no nurse could have pampered me the way you did."

He chuckled. "Pampered. I like that a *lot* better than hovered."

An idea dawned, and it made her smile. "Would it be too big an imposition to ask you to do me one more favor?"

"Of course not," he said, mimicking her intonation. "Anything. Name it, it's yours."

She'd had it with feeling helpless, and with seeing Flora helpless. Even Bud had looked helpless, telling them all about "a typical day at the Callahans." She'd probably never see Woodrow again, and day after tomorrow, once the doctor gave her permission to go back to work for a few hours a day, she wouldn't see Austin until who knew when!

Despite it all, she felt *hopeful* for the first time in ages. Hopeful that Woodrow, wherever he was, had food and shelter and a warm lap to sit in. That Flora would slip into remission and stay there, despite the doctors' prognosis. And that Austin would remain a part of her life, indefinitely.

Her sour mood sweetened, and, feeling a little bit playful, said "Really? *Anything*?"

This time when he aimed that grin her way, one brow rose on his forehead. He spun the radio dial, found a country station and proceeded to bob his head in time to the music. "Why not just throw it out there, and we'll see if it sticks."

Oh, he was one of a kind, all right! "I'd like a silver Ferrari, and a thatched cottage in Ireland, and a Piper Cub to get me 'across the pond.'"

He was grinning when he said "I don't know if a Piper Cub can *make* it all the way across the Atlantic Ocean."

"Oh, well, that's all right. Then I guess it'll just have to be a jet. Like the one they use on that TV show. You know, the one where FBI agents hunt down serial killers?"

"Oka-a-ay. . ."

She laughed, and it felt good. So good, in fact, that Mercy wished there was a way to guarantee the sensation lasted for a long, long time.

"What I really want," she told him on a sigh, "is for you to start thinking of something *I* can do for *you*. A favorite dinner, or I can clean your boat. Do your laundry, even press your shirts." She shrugged, then winced as her shoulder reminded her it hadn't healed all the way. "I want—no, I *need*—to do something for you, to show you how much I've appreciated all you've done for me."

"Mercy, really, I know already know that. You don't owe—"

"No-no-no! This isn't a payback. I don't want to do something for you because I feel as though I *owe* you. Just—" How would she explain that it was important to her that Austin experience, firsthand, a sliver of what he'd given her?

"Don't try to come up with something right now. Take a few days. A week. A month! Promise me you'll at least think about it, and that as soon as you come up with something you'll let me know. OK?"

He breathed in a big gulp of air, and let it out slowly. "All right," he said, nodding. "I promise to think on it."

"I guess I should've known that with a guy like you I need to be more specific. I should have said 'Promise you'll actually *come up with something.'*"

The car engine idled and the turn signal tick-tick-ticked as they sat at the traffic light, waiting to make that last left before pulling into her garage. The blue-green numerals of the dashboard clock said one fifty-nine. Time was running out. She'd have him with her this afternoon, tonight, tomorrow night, then he'd drive her to her doctor's appointment and—

Mercy couldn't bear to finish the thought.

She focused, instead, on the test run she'd conducted day before yesterday, when he ran out to get a few groceries to prepare for the next snowstorm. It hadn't been easy, hobbling around on her crutches with just one normally functioning arm, but she'd made it upstairs and down again without taking a header. She shambled into the kitchen and munched a slice of Swiss cheese, then poured herself a paper cup of water. And because she'd promised to stay put while he was gone, Mercy buried the cup under a discarded paper plate in the trash bin.

The venture proved that she no longer *needed* him—at least, not as her round-the-clock helpmate.

"—that your favorite color is purple," he was saying, "and your birth sign is Taurus, but I have no idea what kind of music you prefer."

"I don't have a preference," she said, hoping to hide inattentiveness behind an exuberant tone. "I know, I know. Lots of people say that, but I really mean it. I like music. Any kind of music. Well, except for rap, because I'm too old to 'get' the beat and the melody. Though I have to admit, I *do* appreciate the poetry and the drama that goes into a lot of those songs."

He hit the button on the visor above him, starting the garage door on its upward roll. "Reason I ask if you like country is, I won tickets to see Marty Johnson, and I was wondering if you'd like to go to the concert with me."

"You won a contest? How exciting! I've never won anything. Unless you count the little glider plane my third grade teacher gave as the prize for getting the most hits with a Paddle Ball."

"Aw, I hated those things. Couldn't hit that ball twice without the rubber band getting all twisted around my hand. Or the paddle. Or the ball coming loose from the rubber band." He switched off the ignition. "How many hits?"

Mercy lifted her chin and assumed a snooty expression. "Two hundred and seventy-three."

"Wow," he said, "impressive."

"That's what Sister Bertina said."

"Wow," he repeated. "I had no idea you went to Catholic school."

"It isn't something I brag about. Those weren't my favorite school years."

"Did you wear a pleated little skirt and a cross-over tie and saddle shoes with ruffly socks?"

"Blue plaid, unfortunately," she said with a groan, "and, yes, a snap-tie. And a matching vest, too."

"How many years?"

"All twelve."

Austin climbed out of the car, walked around to her side and opened the passenger door. "Y'know," he said as she unbuckled the seatbelt, "I don't think I've ever met anyone who went to parochial school and liked it."

"Trust me. There's a reason for that."

He reached into the back seat for her crutches. "The little gilder plane is one of a handful of good memories," she said as he handed them to her. "I think maybe that's why I still have it."

"You do? No kidding!"

She got to her feet. "It's in my keepsake box on the shelf in my closet."

"The rubber-band kind, with the wind-up propeller?"

"No." Mercy laughed. "It's as plain as plain can be."

"Ah-ha. The ones we used to call Amish flyers." A peaceful, happy smile crossed his face as he shoved open the door leading into her kitchen. "Bet I had a couple dozen of those when I was a kid. My grandfather brought one every time he visited. Said he and my dad sometimes spent hours flying them around the yard."

She pictured Austin as a boy, happy innocent face turned toward the sky as he followed the course of his plane. If they had a son together, would he have Austin's golden hair and blue eyes? And near-black lashes that touched his eyebrows when he looked up? She hoped so, because—

Good grief. Where did that *come from!* Mercy clomped down the hall, stood on one foot and shrugged out of her coat. Even managed to hang it on the hall tree, all by herself. "So how'd you win the tickets?" she asked, thump-sliding her way to the sofa. "Wait. Don't tell me. You filled out one of those 'You Can Win' cards at the drug store, didn't you?"

"Nah. I get enough junk mail and annoying sales calls without giving those pests direct access to me." He smirked, then winked. "On the way to the station the other day, I dialed WPOC. Never did it before. Never expected to be their ninth caller, either, but I was, and I won."

"Congratulations," she said,

Had she answered too quickly?

Not if that smile on his face was any indicator.

Once she'd settled on the sofa bed, Austin said, "He'll be at the Convention Center in a few weeks, but the seats are in the nosebleed section. I'm thinking that's way too soon for you to climb all those stairs. It's a sure bet we didn't get aisle seats, which means more climbing to get past the lucky stiffs who *are* on the end. So—"

"I can manage. You'll be right there to lean on—if I need to, that is."

"True. But I found out I can swap these tickets for two more, in September, when he's in New York."

"New York *City?*"

Austin laughed. "The way you said that reminds me of that old sàlsa commercial." The smile faded slightly when he added "*That* concert is part of the 9/11 tenth anniversary services. I thought—" He shrugged. "I thought since we'd both been away for so long, it might be a good time to reconnect, pay our respect to all the first responders who died, and the ones who were injured, and their families."

If anyone else had suggested such a thing, Mercy would have turned it down, flat. Too many negative emotions tied to that date. Too many painful memories. But hers paled by comparison to his. Had he invited her as a friend? Or as a former psychiatrist?

What did it matter? He'd never asked anything of her. And unless she wanted to look like a clown, offering to do something to show her gratitude—then refusing it even before he'd officially spelled it out—

"Yes," she said simply. "It'll be an honor to go with you."

"I was hoping you'd say that."

"It's probably going to be a madhouse up there for an event like this."

"New York is always a madhouse. At least this time, there'll be a method to the madness."

Mercy nodded because he was right.

"Mother Nature's definitely in another snit," he said. "Looks really threatening out there. I have a feeling we're gonna get it big time this time."

"Well, you just restocked the fridge and pantry, so unless we lose electricity, we'll be fine until the plows dig us out."

"I've been freezing empty water bottles and milk jugs, so if the power goes out, we'll be OK for a few days. Plus, I noticed that big stack of firewood on your terrace. I'll build us a roaring fire."

"Gosh. I almost hope the lights *do* go out. Almost."

"I'm gonna fix myself a snack, get something cold to drink. What can I bring you?"

"Whatever you're having." It's what she always said, because Austin always seemed to know just what she'd like.

He bent to kiss her forehead. "Back in a minute."

He wasn't gone thirty seconds before the emptiness set in, deep and gnawing.

Better get used to the feeling, she told herself. Because day after tomorrow, *this is how you'll feel* all *of the time.*

31

The east coast had been slammed by one ferocious blizzard after another, breaking all weather records. By early February, fifty-eight inches had accumulated in three separate events, inspiring the governor to declare a state of emergency.

The National Guard was dispatched, and they loaded into more than a hundred Humvees to make their way to motorists stranded when traffic came to a dead halt, thanks to three inches per hour that clogged every highway.

Baltimore-Washington International Airport called off all incoming and outgoing flights. Schools, malls, businesses, and church services were canceled. Those owning four wheel drive vehicles were asked to help deliver doctors and nurses to area hospitals.

Local TV stations put their news copters in the air to film parades of dump trucks that offloaded the frozen stuff into Baltimore's harbor, inciting heated debates between environmentalists about the potential hazards to marine life, once the salty snow made its way to the Chesapeake Bay.

Unlike the experts, ordinary citizens took full advantage of being snowed in, and turned the clearing of side streets into block party events, while their kids climbed snow mountains higher than any they'd ever seen.

Normally, Austin would have hated being cooped up. But living on the water with three-sided views of the bay tamped down any symptoms of cabin fever. Mercy, on the other hand, had sounded at her wits' end when they talked night before last.

She'd recovered, but not enough to shovel show from her front porch, sidewalk, and driveway. He chuckled, remembering the way she'd grumbled about the neighborhood association. "What are they doing with the hundreds of dollars they charge all of us?" she'd fumed.

Fortunately, she and her neighbors now had an escape route—though she wouldn't go so far as to credit the powers that be in the association office. It sounded to Austin as if Mercy needed the upcoming Super Bowl shindig more than anyone, so it would be a double disappointment if the weather forced the marina to cancel, especially since the managers had decided to celebrate in a bigger-than-usual way when they learned that Flora's cancer had gone into remission.

Plus, Bud had organized a silent auction to raise money for the Cancer Society, and knowing this, Austin had spent hours, fashioning a fancy bird feeder as his contribution to the charity.

And Mercy canceled her trip to London.

She'd wanted to back out of the party, too, when he offered to pick her up. "You live right there!" had been her objection. "Why drive all the way to Fells Point and back again if you don't have to?"

She didn't know it, but Austin *did* have to. Since leaving her house, he'd thought of little else, and a pounding need to see her invaded every waking moment.

After what she'd just been through? Any other woman would have huddled inside, afraid for her life. When he rolled into Mercy's driveway, it surprised him to see her on the porch, alone, in a sassy black hat and matching mittens, and black leather boots that hugged her shapely calves. Make that 'calf,' he thought grinning at the sight of her exposed red-painted toenails. Oh, how he wanted to scoop her up and plant one right on those smiling, rosy red lips!

All in good time, he thought, steering to the far right of her drive. All in good time.

"Thought we'd take your car," he said, locking his truck, "since it's easier for you to get into and out of than this big—"

"But they're predicting more snow. What if they're right? Your pickup rides higher, and I don't have 4-wheel drive."

She made a good point, and, as he unlocked the passenger door, he admitted it.

"What's this?" he asked, taking the black plastic-wrapped package from her.

"My contribution for the silent auction."

"What is it?"

She wiggled her eyebrows, and opened her mouth to answer. Instead, she slipped on the only patch of ice to be found.

Austin one-handed the package and steadied her with his free hand.

"Whew," she said, backing into the passenger seat. "That was close."

"Yeah. That's all we need . . . you, back in the hospital so soon." Trembling with concern, he said, "Buckle up," then slid the parcel into the back. No other woman had stirred his protective instincts like Mercy, and something told him no other woman ever would.

She chattered the whole way back to the marina, about the banner the kids had hung across the school's entrance to welcome her back.

"And there were two phone calls," she said, "about possible Woodrow sightings."

"That's great news. Did either pan out?"

She heaved a disappointed sigh. "No. One was a gray tabby, and the other a solid black cat with enormous green eyes."

No doubt she was worried that the poor critter had frozen to death. And to be honest, that thought had crossed Austin's mind a time or two. "Don't give up hope just yet. You said yourself that he's resourceful, and as Flora pointed out, he might be holed up with another family."

"Oh, I hope so. The image of him buried under a mountain of snow—" She shivered. "Isn't it wonderful about Flora!"

"Yeah. Best news I've heard in a long time."

"I wonder if maybe they made a mistake, with the original diagnosis, I mean. Because how else can her doctors explain that one blood test teemed with cancer cells and the next three were one hundred percent normal."

"Eversly admitted he believes in the power of prayer."

Even if peripheral vision hadn't told him she'd turned to get a better look at him, Austin would have known because he could almost feel her gaze, boring into the side of his head.

"What does *Flora* think?"

"The members of her congregation held a special prayer vigil in her name, and she's grateful as all get-out to every man, woman and child who hit their knees on her behalf." Dare he add the rest, and risk setting off a chain reaction of denials and explanations and rationalizations for her doubt and skepticism? "When she got the good news, she called me over so she and Bud could tell me in person. Squeezed my hand so hard, I thought sure she'd dislocated a couple of knuckles, and thanked me for adding to all those prayers. She'd made her peace and got her affairs in order, but she's grateful that God saw fit to heal her."

He heard her snort of disgust, and couldn't ignore it. "I mean no offense, but I just have to ask: How can you stare a full-blown miracle in the face and still deny God's existence?"

"Coincidence."

That's it? That was her rationale for Flora's cure— *coincidence*?

"So how's the leg?"

She sighed. "If you hadn't changed the subject, I would have. I don't want anything to spoil Flora's special day. And the leg's fine, thanks to—"

"Glad the worse of that ordeal is behind you." It didn't take a genius to figure out what she wanted to say, and he sent a silent thank heavenward that Mercy hadn't finished her sentence.

"Did you get the birdhouse finished?"

"Yep. It's on the back seat."

"I can't wait to see it. From your description, I've been picturing a miniature mansion."

"Well, it sorta *is*." Then, jerking a thumb over his shoulder, asked "What's in the big package back there?"

"A painting."

"Not a bad choice." If he had to guess, he would have said the marina's regular members could buy the place and three more just like it. A few owned sailboats bigger than most people's houses, and he couldn't name one who'd been affected by the recession. "Even if it's a print, it'll probably bring in big bucks."

"Oh, it isn't a print. It's an original."

"Better still," he said, parking in a handicap space near the clubhouse door, "especially if the bidders recognize the artist's na—"

"Hey, it's Tommy Winston and his family!" She pointed at a Cadillac SUV, then pointed again, this time at a Hummer. "And the Healyes!"

Austin jogged around to her side of the pickup and opened the passenger door. "I'll get you inside, then move the truck."

"I can—"

"Probably, but you aren't going to." He called her attention to the stubborn patches of ice still clinging to the wooden walkway. Planting both palms on her slender waist, he lifted her from the seat . . .

. . . and for a moment, held her in mid-air.

Mercy, hands resting on his shoulders, looked down at him. If that wasn't love beaming from her dark, sparkling eyes, he'd settle for whatever it was.

"Austin," she said, grinning, "people are beginning to stare."

"Let them." He brought her closer, pressed a quick kiss to her lips, then put her gently on her feet. "Here," he said, handing her the tickets, "save us a table. Not too close to the DJ's speakers."

"Anything you say."

Anything? he wondered. *Even the promise that you'll at least try to give this whole God thing some serious thought?*

"A guy can hope," he whispered, jogging back to his truck.

Inside, he saw that management had displayed the auction items on long, narrow tables that hugged the walls of the banquet hall. Austin inspected the donations, and it pleased him to see that fourteen people had scribbled their names on the lines beneath the description of his birdhouse. And pleased him more to read the last bid for $51.25.

A little farther down the table he saw Mercy's painting. Propped against the white beaded board wall, it caught the overhead lights and reflected the muted colors of a sunset. His heart nearly stopped when he recognized it as *his* sunset. Well, the view of it from his boat, anyway. Even more amazing —the tiny black signature in the lower right-hand corner that said Mercy S.

He caught her eye, and, with a nod, asked her to join him. Even stumping along on her half cast, she crossed the room in no time.

"What," she said, stepping up beside him.

Austin pointed at the painting, and at the form where two dozen people had tried to outbid one another, so that they could take it home. "That's what."

She glanced at it, then looked back at him. "What about it?"

"I didn't know you could paint."

One brow rose as she smirked. "There's a *lot* you don't know about me, Mr. Finley."

"When did you do it?"

"The weekend after you grilled me steaks on your boat."

"From memory?"

Mercy nodded. "Well, sure. How else?" And then she laughed.

"I thought maybe you'd snapped a picture. With your cell phone camera." He shrugged. "Or something like that."

"No, no," she said, her voice light and airy as the painting's brush strokes.

"You must have a photographic memory, then."

"You two sound like an old married couple . . . ."

Cora . . . and she didn't sound happy. Austin plastered a smile on his face and turned around. "Hey, kids," he said, standing between the boys. "I thought you'd never get here!"

"Is this the lady you were living with?" Ray asked.

"I wasn't *living* with her," he said, laughing. "I was—"

"He's right," Rick agreed. "She got beat up by a gang of bad dudes. He was only staying at her place so she wouldn't take a header down the stairs, or drown in the toilet, or—"

"Boys!" Cora said. "Where are your manners?"

Mercy held out a hand to Cora, and smiled, "It's so good to finally meet you. I've heard so much about you."

"And you must be Mercy."

Cora's smile never quite reached her eyes. Not a good sign. Not a good sign at all. Bookended by the boys, he stood looking at the two most important women in his life, and thought he understood what a slice of lunchmeat felt like right before a lumberjack bit into it.

"So where are you guys sitting?" he asked.

Rick pointed. "Over there. Right next to—"

"Dr. Samara," Ray injected. "Her name is *Doctor* Samara."

"Oh. Right. So anyway, we're over there, right next to that painting she did from your boat."

"How do *you* know that's where she painted it?"

"Pul-eeze. It's, like, the *only* place in the world where a sycamore tree grows outta the water. And there's a sycamore in her painting." Rick looked at Mercy. "Isn't that right?"

Mercy licked her lips, then smiled. "Yes. That's true. But I wasn't on Austin's boat when I painted the scene. I just happened to see the sunset one evening when—"

"You know Austin," Cora interrupted. "He has a girl up there in that pilot house of his every day of the week, showing her" She drew quotation marks in the air and cleared her throat. "—the view."

Bud and Griff walked up them as a cheer rose up from the crowd. Mrs. Healye and Mrs. Winston joined them, too, as all eyes turned toward the wide-screen TV behind the bar. "Saints won the coin toss!" a deep voice shouted.

"Landed heads up!" bellowed another.

Austin's gaze was fused to the screen when he said, "Twenty-second time that's happened."

"What are you," Bud asked, "some kind of walking, talking encyclopedia?"

Griff laughed and clapped a hand onto Austin's shoulder. "Our boy put his free time to good use, wouldn't you say?"

"What free time? I pretty much worked 24-7-365 until my recent babysitting job."

Thankfully, Mercy seemed too involved in her chat with Mrs. Healye and Mrs. Winston to have heard the crack. But he'd better watch his mouth from here on out, though, unless he wanted what her to think he'd been spewing baloney when told her how much he'd enjoyed taking care of her.

But Cora heard it. He knew by the width of her smirk.

During halftime, the DJ tapped his microphone and directed everyone's attention to a second widescreen on the wall opposite the game, where a mini-documentary filmed by his brother and sister in law to honor the victims and survivors of 9/11 and their families, would soon begin.

Austin and Griff exchanged a cynical glance. They'd already seen it all, in black and white and full color and in person. Did they really want to view yet another version of the tragedy?

Mercy grabbed Austin's wrists and looked up into his face, exactly as she had that day so many years ago in her office. "Are you OK to do this?" she whispered. "Because if you aren't, we can leave. Just get in your truck and *go*."

He tucked a loose tendril of hair behind her ear and smiled. "Yeah. I'll be fi—"

Mrs. Winston said "I've seen this documentary before. *This* time, I'm going to ask for a copy, and I don't care *what* it costs.

Because my brother was in the South Tower. He made it out, but went back in to help a woman who'd fallen on the stairs."

It wasn't necessary for her to say more.

Mrs. Healye nodded. "My niece was a passenger on Flight 93. I haven't seen this one, but if it's everything you say it is, I want a copy, too."

A man behind her said, "I had a cousin in the Pentagon that day."

"And our dad was there, too," Ray added.

"All of the money goes to a college fund," Mrs. Winston added, "for kids whose parents died that day. Cops, firefighters, paramedics, people on the planes and in the buildings. All of their children will benefit."

"Count me in," Flora said.

And Griff said, "Me, too." He gave Austin another look, then shrugged. "At least this one's for a good cause."

Yeah, he supposed that was good enough reason to stay.

No doubt the movie would stir up some ugly memories, but at least this time he'd have Mercy at his side.

Cora stepped up and hugged him, then rested her head on his shoulder and began to cry.

Correction, he thought as the boys joined their hug. He'd have Mercy. And Cora. And Eddy's sons.

Chances he'd get a good night's sleep tonight with Eddy and Avery and the rest of this mess running through his mind?

Nil.

Unless he spent the first few hours with his buddy Jim Beam.

32

Mercy had never been a fan of the game, and her distaste for football doubled in the days following Super Bowl Sunday. Everywhere she went, people seemed obsessed about weighing in on the plays, time outs, side judges' rulings, and the final score.

To make a bad situation worse, the Saints' win created a stir on Baltimore's radio airwaves, with half the city's football enthusiasts calling the team's loss "Punishment for Irsay's desertion in '84!" The other half—too young to remember team buses slip-sliding on new-fallen snow during the wee hours—termed the Colts' defeat "The universe making right what happened to New Orleans after Hurricane Katrina."

How easy it would be, she thought, to hide from all of the bickering out here on the terrace, watching the birds as she enjoyed the crisp March breeze!

A quiet meow broke into her consciousness, and she turned toward the distinctly feline sound. "Woodrow?"

Sure enough, he peeked out at her from under a deck chair, looking dirty and rumpled and exhausted. Ignoring his matted, reeking fur, she scooped him up and hugged him. "Where have you been, you crazy escape artist, you?"

He nuzzled into the crook of her neck and chirruped.

"Well, you sure don't sound like your usual peppy self, but I suppose there's a price to pay for living a nomad's life, isn't there?"

Mercy could count his ribs if she had a mind to, heard his rattling breaths, too. She had her suspicions about what had caused his symptoms, "Let's get you inside, out of this cold wind. And while you're lapping up some water, I'll make an appointment with the vet."

Three hours later, after x-rays of his chest and stomach, the ELISA test confirmed her worst fears: Woodrow had feline leukemia.

"How in the world did he get *that?*"

"Picked it up while gallivanting around the neighborhood, I imagine," the vet tech said, "eating out of other cats' bowls, getting into fights, letting an infected cat groom him. Even with inoculations—and I know you've been religious about them—sometimes—"

"Will he need surgery?"

"No, that would only traumatize him unnecessarily. The cancer has invaded his vital organs, so an operation is pointless."

Oh, poor, poor Woodrow! she thought, ruffling his sparse fur. "How long before . . . before he—"

"I've seen cats live two, even three years with this disease. He *might* last that long, but his cancer has invaded vital organs. Plus he's severely anemic."

"So it's hopeless, then."

"Nothing is hopeless." He tousled Woodrow's mangy head. "You're a tough ol' boy, so I'll just bet you're gonna fight this like a tiger."

"That's what I used to call him. My little—" A lump formed in her throat, choking off the rest of her sentence. *You're such a whiny baby! Woodrow is sick, not you. So what're you blubbering about?*

"I'll keep him here for a few days, get him cleaned up and stabilize him. I'll send him home with an antibiotic. An anti-viral, and alpha interferon, too. That stuff won't cure him, but it'll go a long, long way in making him more comfortable until—"

Until it's time to euthanize him, she finished silently. *Chalk another one up for the Big Guy*, she fumed, and added another item to her "God is never fair" list. She thanked the tech and paid the bill, and all the way home, ranted about God's utter lack of compassion.

The part of her that craved comfort yearned to call Austin, who'd turned the doling out of reassurance into an art.

But the rest of her held back.

He'd been standoffish and secretive lately, and Mercy feared that another battle between "The Great Believer" and "O Ye of Little Faith" would only put more distance between them— and less between him and his partner's widow. How many times had she pictured the two of them at the Super Bowl party—Cora, with her cheek pressed to his chest, and Austin gently stroking her hair.

What a horrible, selfish person she must be to behave like a jealous wife at a time like this! *Pull it together, Merc, or you'll lose him to Cora.*

She forced herself to remember that he'd taken *her*, not Cora, to the party. To dinner and a movie for Valentine's Day, too. *She'd* been the one he invited to New York to see the con-cert. And what about those weeks following the attack when he'd cooked and ran errands and did his best to feign interest in those decorating shows on the home and garden channel?

It wouldn't surprise her in the least to find out that he'd done the same for Cora, after Eddy's death. Why, for all she knew, he'd played the hero role to the hilt, dozens of times. And why not, when he was so good at it!

As a little girl, Mercy had wished for a kind-hearted and handsome prince to ride in on a white steed and whisk her away from everything sad or scary in her life. In place of the horse, he'd arrived in a red and white ambulance, and though he hadn't said it in so many words—yet—Mercy believed Austin *was* the hero she'd been dreaming of.

He had it all, from rugged good looks to a brave and caring spirit. So why did his "saved" status matter so much? It wasn't as though he went around spouting Bible verses, or judging those who couldn't—or wouldn't—recite them from memory. He wasn't anything like most Christians she'd known who behaved as if they had all the answers to the world's questions. But if they really had Jesus in their hearts, as they claimed, would they jump at every chance to make unbelievers feel small and stupid?

If his faith didn't mean so much to him, or if she could find a way to believe, even a little, in his God, maybe, just maybe they'd have a chance at a happy life together.

But he'd never turn his back on God, and she couldn't trust the being who'd taken everyone and everything she'd ever cared about, from her parents to America's ability to keep its citizens safe from terror attacks to Flora's near-death experience and the disease that would consume Woodrow one frail cell at a time.

Even without her degree, Mercy would have recognized the feelings for what they were: raw, unbridled rage. Didn't need special initials after her name to know that her fury had festered far too long to expect that they'd fade simply because she'd met the man of her dreams.

Living alone and on her own for so many years had made her self-reliant. And maybe self-centered, too. She needed to put Austin—and what was best for him—first, and she knew of no way to accomplish that except to fade out of his life a little at a time.

He deserved a woman who'd appreciate his finer qualities, who'd share his hopes and dreams, and, yes, even his faith. One who knew every detail of the life he'd lived, and who'd love him because of—and in spite of it.

A woman like Cora, who wore her feelings for Austin like a gossamer cloak. Her boys loved him, too, and he thought the world of them. A ready-made family and a wife young enough and clearly more than willing to give him a child of his own? What man wouldn't want that?

It wasn't easy admitting that as much as Mercy loved him—more than she'd ever loved a man—she didn't love him *enough.* Austin didn't do anything halfway, and if he ever got around to admitting that he loved her, he'd love her with everything in him.

He'd survived aching losses, too, yet each time, he'd risen from the ashes, more determined than before to fight for his peace and happiness, and retain his honor while doing it. That, alone, earned him the right to expect full-blown, unreserved love, and since she couldn't give it to him, it was only right to walk away, so he could find it elsewhere.

At the tender age of ten, Mercy had begged God to change her mother's mind about sailing from New York to Annapolis. When He didn't grant that, she asked Him to keep her safe, yet the nightmares of her childhood were filled with terrifying images of her mommy, gasping for breath as the angry Atlantic gobbled her up.

She'd pleaded with the Almighty to watch over her father, and, after the dreadful robbery that left him bloody and weak, she implored Him to heal the wounds so that he could come home.

Then 9/11 happened, and like millions of Americans, she'd sat mesmerized as the reports rolled in, detailing the fire and smoke and ash that killed thousands of innocent victims.

Afterward, her patients—men and women who would willingly have given their own lives to save any one of them—struggled to grasp even a thread of their former lives. Some succeeded, and others—

Like the firefighter, who, consumed by grief and guilt because he'd survived, tried to kill himself . . . and the cop who had succeeded.

And then Austin walked into her office, all six-feet and two hundred stubborn pounds of him, looking to her to help him find the missing pieces to the puzzle his life had become.

She'd failed him then, despite heartfelt prayers that God, in His loving wisdom, would make things right—and if she didn't leave him soon so he could find the love he so richly deserved, she'd fail him again.

If she could believe for a moment that God *would* answer just one of her prayers, Mercy hoped He'd answer this one:

"Let me be far, far away when he finds it."

33

The stray mutt had been hanging around the marina since the last of the snow melted into the bay, and despite a chorus of advice against it, Austin sneaked food to her every chance he got.

He'd been up on the deck of the pilot house, putting the finishing touches on another birdhouse when he heard her, whimpering on the walkway between his boat and the Callahans'. If he said "Scat!" or "Quiet down!" his hollering would only alert the marina manager, who seemed bound and determined to capture the scruffy half-breed and deliver her to the pound.

She sat on her haunches, head tilted as she watched him wave and mouth "Get lost!" and "Go on, get out of here!" Her big doggy grin gave her away: The pup understood exactly what he wanted from her, and she had no intention of going anywhere until he gave her a pat on the head and a slice of bologna.

The lunchmeat disappeared in one swallow, and Austin laughed. "What's your hurry?" he asked, ruffling her thick salt-and-pepper fur. "You need to learn to enjoy the little things in life, every chance you get."

She rolled onto her back, feet clawing at the air as she waited for a good belly scratching. "Well, as I live and breathe," he said. "You're gonna be a mommy soon, aren't you, girl!"

On her side now, she aimed that brown-eyed stare at him, and grinned a little wider.

The poor thing could barely feed herself; how would she care for a litter of hungry puppies?

Austin couldn't ignore the situation for a moment longer. The birdhouse would just have to wait. "C'mere, girl," he said, patting his thigh. "Let's go for a ride."

The instant his passenger door opened, she leaped onto the seat as if she'd done it a hundred times. If he didn't have such a wacky schedule, he'd give her a name and buy her a collar, and bowls and a bed. They way she'd unquestioningly followed him and watched his every move reminded Austin of Rick and Ray. *They* looked at him with big, soulful "You can do no wrong" eyes, too.

Chuckling, he patted the dog's head again. "You're sure good for a guy's ego."

She responded with a breathy bark, as if to say, "I know. Now *earn* it."

"Don't worry, girl. I'll see that you and your babies will be taken care of. From here on out, you'll have it all."

A home, a couple of kids to run and play with, healthy food instead of the table scraps she'd been eating.

He spent as much time as he could at the vet's office. "Gotta get to work," he told her, "but I'll check on you tomorrow."

She never took her eyes off him as he made his way to the waiting room. And when he got into the truck, he saw that she'd poked her nose through the window blinds to watch him drive away.

"Aw, you're breakin' my heart, girl."

She blinked, and barked. Another silent one, or did this have some *oomph* behind it?

What would Cora say, he wondered, if he offered to get the boys a dog? Not just any dog, but *this* dog. Grinning, he waved and shifted into Reverse. "Say your prayers, li'l mama, 'cause I might just have the perfect home for you."

Thankfully, he hadn't asked the vet to try and find her a good home. Instead, he'd instructed the guy to give her the royal treatment. That meant shots and a teeth cleaning, toenail trimming and a bath. If Cora agreed to this, he'd deliver the dog—and everything she'd need—just as soon as her pups were weaned.

That gave him a couple of months, anyway, to work on Cora. And he'd start at the fundraiser, day after tomorrow. His biggest challenge? Pecking away at her when the Ray and Rick weren't around. Because it wouldn't be fair—to Cora *or* the boys—to open the door to a lovable mutt, only to hear their mom veto the idea.

She'd promised to whip up one of her famous cakes for the bake sale, and if he knew Cora, she'd slide a pie and a plate of cookies onto the table—and bag up a few for him to take home, too.

As predicted, she'd delivered far more than just the promised cake. She'd stuffed a plastic container to the brim with goodies for him, too.

"I declare, woman, if I didn't know better, I'd swear you were trying to make me fat."

"Really now," she said, blushing prettily. "Why would I do that?"

"Because then no other woman will want him."

Austin opened his mouth to tell her how adorable she looked in her long, gauzy skirt and dangly earrings. But Cora beat him to it.

"Mercy! I had no idea that you'd be here today."

She hunched her shoulders. "I'm one of the guidance counselors at Dundalk High. I sort of have to be here."

"Oh? As a chaperone?"

"Sure. But also to relieve the principal at the silent auction table."

"Another painting, I hope?" Austin asked. He didn't know how to explain what was going on between these two, but if asked to describe the sensation, he'd have said "Palpable." That, or "Territorial."

A flattering concept, if he did say so himself, because although he'd had his share of girlfriends, none had found it necessary to hang a "Taken" sign around his neck.

"Another painting," Mercy answered, "but a sun*rise* this time."

Cora's eyes widened. "Y-you've . . . you've been on Austin's boat *in the morning*?" A nervous giggle escaped her lips. "Why, I've known him for*ever*, and not even *I've* been there *in the morning!*"

He'd seen that pained expression and heard the wavering voice enough times to recognize them for what they were: Cora's feelings were hurt. Admittedly, it was fairly easy to accomplish that, but he didn't know for the life of him what had inspired it this time. Unless . . .

Understanding dawned at the same moment as Mercy said, "No, of course not. I was only in the pilot house once, and luckily, in time for a sunset." She pointed across the room, where her painting leaned against a mint green-painted cinderblock wall. "Used my memory of the landscape to—"

"And you?" Cora interrupted. "Did you build another birdhouse?"

"As a matter of fact, I did." He didn't know what was going on here, but it made him uneasy in half a dozen ways. "It's over there, across from the water fountains. Where are the boys?"

"In the gym, I expect, playing h.o.r.s.e."

Several Christmases ago, Austin bought the kids a basketball hoop, installed it above the garage door and taught them how to play one-on-one. It had been one of Eddy's favorite pastimes, and every time they'd played, the boys had asked to hear another "How I Never, Not Once, Ever Beat Your Dad" story.

Times like these, he missed his partner. Missed him a lot.

"I see some parents in the hall who look a little lost," Mercy said. "I'd better get over there before they end up in the boiler room." She snickered. "Catch up with you two later?"

You two? He must have missed something while his mind had locked on memories of Eddy. Either that, or he'd read something in her voice that wasn't there, and read the same error in her body language. Because after all they'd been through together . . . .

He licked his lips, thinking of their last kiss. She hadn't initiated it, but she sure hadn't ended it, either. What had happened to make her think he could ever be interested in anyone but her?

"You're well rid of her, if you ask me."

Austin followed Cora's heated gaze.

"She's not only self-centered, but the jealous type." Laying a hand on his forearm, she smiled up at him. "You've had enough grief in your life without linking yourself to a woman like that who's sure to bring you more."

"You're a true-blue friend, and I appreciate your concern, but I'm a big boy." He grinned to soften the sting of what he was about to admit. "You're dead wrong about Mercy. I've spent a lot of time with her since the attack, and I'd stake my life on the fact that she doesn't have a self-centered bone in her body."

His gaze followed Mercy into the hall, and stayed on her as she smiled and joked with the parents of a student. "I could do worse," he said, hoping Cora couldn't hear his heart, knocking against his ribcage, "a whole lot worse."

"I wonder what Eddy would think of her."

Good question, Austin thought. "Never crossed my mind, but now that you mention it, I think he'd like her."

She waved the comment away. "You can't go by that. Eddy liked *every*body."

"Y'got that right. He liked me, and you know better than most how hard that is."

She responded with a sigh, and a *look* that Austin couldn't define. Maybe lack of sleep had him imagining things. Since viewing that documentary on Super Bowl Sunday, his dreams had been fragmented and disturbing, because instead of the smoking buildings and fiery airplanes he'd grown accustomed to seeing, this film had connected quiet conversations with the men and women who'd arrived first at Ground Zero. In one-minute segments, the interviewer posed pointed questions, then zeroed in on the subjects' faces, allowing viewers a penetrating look into their hearts. The anguish in their eyes had fused to Austin's soul, and echoed in his dreams.

Each time he woke, Austin thought about the bottle of golden liquid that stood in the dark cupboard, waiting for someone to break the seal and release its heat. If Griff knew how close he'd come to doing just that, Austin would probably need hearing aids now.

Or crutches.

"You aren't hard to like," Cora said. "In fact, it's scary how easy you are to be around."

Working hard not to offend her, to make her feel protected and safe, to be her rock and her shoulder to cry on was *scary*? At times like these he admired Eddy all the more, because he'd lived with the woman's uncertainty and self-doubt for years before—

"The boys have missed you."

"Same here. But with work and those back-to-back blizzards, and Mercy's, ah, situation—" Austin shrugged. "I'll make it up to them once things settle down."

"You expect that to happen with a woman like her?"

"What does that *mean*, exactly . . . 'a woman like her'?"

"High maintenance. Jealous. Possessive. And an unbeliever."

Until that last word, she could have been describing herself. "I didn't realize you and Mercy had discussed religion."

"Didn't have to." She lifted her chin. "You can see it all over her face."

"See *what*?"

"Lack of faith. It's . . . it's—"

"Time to change the subject," he said, and none too gently. He remembered that sweet pregnant dog, sitting in a kennel cage at the vet's office. He'd promised to get her out of there as soon as possible. Get her into a good home. And he'd meant it.

"I think the boys need a dog."

"I can't afford a dog."

"It's my treat. Everything. Food, toys, even the vet bills."

"I don't have time for a dog. I barely have time for the boys!"

"It'll be *the kids*' dog. I'll have a talk with them. Make them understand it's their responsibility, even when they don't feel like it. And if they give you any trouble about it, you can call me. I'll come right over and straighten them out."

"Austin—"

"They've been asking for a dog for three years, and you keep putting them off. It's time to give them a chance to prove what good kids they are. It'll be good for them."

Cora sighed.

"I know the perfect dog. She's about to have puppies, so we'll have plenty of time to prep the boys. Once the pups are weaned, and in homes of their own, I'll deliver the mother."

"I don't know. It's a huge commitment."

"So is marriage. And parenthood. You did OK with both of those."

A slow grin spread across her face.

"And just think of this: In a couple years, when the twins are away at college, you'll have something warm and fuzzy to cuddle up with at night."

She threw back her head and laughed. "What? You aren't planning to shave or cut your hair until the boys are college students!"

He wrinkled his brow. "Huh?"

"Oh, never mind, you thick-headed Irishman, you." She threw her arms around his neck. "Fine. Give the boys a dog." And kissed his cheek. "If you think I won't call when things get . . . hairy . . . you're mistaken. Because I will." Then kissed his other cheek.

By now, he'd figured out what her earlier comment had meant, so the hug and kisses were unsettling. Maybe he could pretend that he'd seen somebody on the other side of the room, then politely untangle himself from her embrace. That should buy his freedom without hurting her feelings.

Austin put his hands on her shoulders, fully prepared to hold her at arm's length, when he spotted Mercy, smiling and waving and pointing as she said something about his bird-house. And that's when Cora decided to plant one, square on his lips. In all the years he'd known her, she'd never done anything like it before. So why *now*, he wondered, watching helplessly as Mercy's smile faded and her hand slid slowly to her side.

"Cora," he mumbled against her mouth, "what in the—"

And when he looked up, Mercy was nowhere in sight.

34

*T*he foreman must have insisted that his men take their coffee and lunch breaks in shifts. The up side? Students and staff could expect air conditioned comfort in their brand new building come fall. Unfortunately, it meant cordoned-off halls filled with sawhorses and coils of thick electrical cords, and tool-belted men in hard hats raising clouds of wood and drywall dust. Only a few more weeks, she reminded herself, before the start of summer vacation.

Unable to concentrate, thanks to the oppressive heat and construction noise, she dialed Leo's cell number and tapped her pencil eraser against her desk blotter as a recorded voice said "Please enjoy the music while your party is reached." Seconds later, the velvet voice was interrupted by a head-pounding, ear-blasting guitar riff.

"Leo, what's gotten into you!" she said, laughing when he picked up.

"Most recently? A liverwurst sandwich." He chuckled. "Lovely to hear your voice."

"Sorry," she inserted. "That awful noise distracted me. What's up with that, anyway? I thought you Brits only listened to opera and classical."

"New phone," he explained. "Had the young fellow behind the counter transfer numbers from my SIM card. Guess he thought it would be a hoot to stick me with that frightening greeting, and I haven't had time yet to read the book and find out how to change it." Another chuckle. "So how's my favorite sister today?"

"Good, and I'll be better if you say it's all right for me to come visit."

"Of course it's all right!"

"I was thinking for my birthday next week?"

"Perfect. I'll be home day after tomorrow, so let me know if I can give you a lift from the airport."

"Home? Where are you?"

"Athens, darling. Didn't I tell you? Medical conference. I gave a speech on the proper way to reconstruct nostrils. Then I took a few days to snap a few cliché shots of the Parthenon."

Giggling, Mercy said, "No, you didn't tell me. I'm happy you made time to enjoy the city." Years ago, she'd taken her dad on a Greek cruise. A fond memory, until she remembered they'd gone a mere three months before he was killed. "It's so pretty this time of year."

"So tell me, how are things with your—now, why can't I ever think of his name when I want to?"

"Austin." The image of him flicked in her brain, and she blinked it away. "Austin Finley, and he's fine." *No thanks to the romantic attentions of Eddy's widow.*

"I have a feeling we'll have lots to talk about once you arrive."

As always, Leo managed to sweeten her sour mood, and Mercy hung up feeling good and looking forward to getting away from it all.

Somewhere on her cluttered desk she'd put the ad torn from *The Dundalk Eagle,* detailing the services of a fancy cat hotel near the Inner Harbor. She'd stop by on her way home, and, if the place looked as good as it sounded, she'd book a room for Woodrow. He'd love the scheduled playtimes, and she'd love the video feed which promised twenty-four hour Internet access to her four-legged friend. If the round-the-clock medical care checked out, she'd arrange that, too.

After locking in the dates, she retrieved her suits and sweaters from *"Cleaner than New (and Neatly Pressed, Too!)"*, then sat down at the kitchen island to adjust her Prepare for England list:

Water houseplants – *check*.

Refill prescriptions – *check*.

Arrange for Woodrow's care – *check*.

Pick up dry cleaning – *check*.

Austin –

Her pen hovered above the page as she glanced at the clock—a ticking reminder of the brief voice mail message she'd left, asking him to stop by after his shift ended. "No need to call unless you can't make it," she'd said before hanging up. And since Mr. Punctuality hadn't called, Mercy knew he'd arrive within the hour.

She was halfway up the stairs to freshen up when sadness and regret wrapped around her. Not surprising, really, since she wasn't looking forward to this date. Well, not a *date* so much as a meeting, scheduled for the sole purpose of outlining her intentions to call an immediate and permanent halt to their relationship. Shouldn't be too difficult, since neither of them knew how to classify the relationship. If it *was* a relationship.

That kissing scene at the fundraiser flashed in her head again, and again, she pushed it from her mind. "Seriously," she said to Woodrow, curled up on her pillow, "does he kiss *every* woman he knows like there's no tomorrow?"

The cat didn't move, save the flick of one ear. Mercy kicked off her shoes and climbed onto the bed. "Hey, buddy," she whispered, lying down beside him, "you're awfully quiet tonight."

He puffed out a weak breath and closed his eyes.

"Oh, this isn't like you. Not like you at all." She sat up, leaned on the headboard, then gently gathered him close. "What's wrong, sweetie?" she cooed, stroking his soft, striped fur. "Come on. You can tell Mommy."

Woodrow paw-walked up her chest and put both paws on Mercy's shoulders. For a long, silent moment, he stared, unblinking, into her eyes.

"Woodie," she sobbed, "what're you doi—"

He rubbed his face against Mercy's left cheek, pausing for another glimpse at her face before doing the same on the right side.

"Woodie . . . ."

He'd been a good cat, a wonderful companion, a tidy house-guest who never jumped onto the counters or dug through the trash. He didn't complain when she watched tear-jerkers on the Lifetime channel, and tolerated the mountains of clothes and piles of shoes that ended up in his favorite resting spots every time she got ready for a date.

No judgments were passed if she ate Cheerios for supper; no nagging took place when she skipped breakfast.

It was Woodrow who snuggled up beside her when bad memories made her cry, and he was there, too, when nightmares disturbed her sleep.

He'd been so much more than a pet. With her only living relative all the way on the other side of the Atlantic, Woodrow had become family and best friend, confidant and comforter. She loved him and knew his moods. This warm and cuddly stuff? It was a first, and it scared Mercy to the point of tears.

"Aw, sweetie, soon as I change out of my work clothes, I'm taking you to the animal hospital." And as she made a move to put him down, Woodrow licked the tears from her face, looked into her eyes yet again, and curled up in her lap.

She didn't have the heart to disturb his purring, to move him so that she could change into jeans and a T-shirt, and find a clean towel to stuff into his cat carrier. Her brain wrote a mental list of things she'd do—just as soon as he'd had a moment's rest.

First, call the vet's office from the car, let them know she was on her way over with Woodrow. Describe his symptoms and remind them he'd been diagnosed with feline leukemia, so they'd have the right equipment ready when—

The purring stopped.

So did his steady breaths.

She didn't need to look into his big round eyes to know he'd left her, but that's exactly what Mercy did.

And then she lay down beside him, held him to her breast, and bawled like a baby.

35

Austin stood on her porch, foot tapping as he waited for Mercy to answer the door. When she didn't respond to the bell, he knocked. Then pounded. Rang the bell for the fourth time.

Her car was in the driveway, and lights glowed from nearly every window in the house. He pressed an ear to the front door and heard the TV, and if he wasn't mistaken, The Eagles, singing "Hotel California."

So what was taking her so long to get to the door?

He pulled back his sleeve and pressed the button that lit up his digital watch. Eight-o-five. He'd have waltzed inside at eight sharp if she hadn't kept him out here on the porch all this time.

The slow rain fell harder, and he pulled up the hood of his sweatshirt. OK, now this was getting ridiculous. He'd put up with her chronic tardiness before, mostly without complaint. But did she really expect him to stand here and take a soaking—literally—while she—

What *was* keeping her, anyway?

Austin flipped open his cell phone, and when she didn't answer, worry seeped under his collar along with the wet May breeze. During her weeks of recuperation, she'd told him stories about how her racing around in a perpetual rush had brought about some hilarious results. Like the time she'd closed her hair in her car door, then slammed it—with the keys still in the ignition. And the day she'd locked herself out of the house and got both hands trapped when the window she'd jimmied open fell. If not for the kindness of strangers, she'd said above his laughter, she might still be under that tall bureau that fell on her when she used the drawers to reach a box stored on top of it.

Yeah, those had been side-splitting stories, but at the end of each—once he'd regained his composure—Austin made sure she understood how each could have had disastrous results. What if she was in there now, trapped under a hulking piece of furniture, or inside a cupboard? What if she'd tumbled down the stairs and—

Heart pounding, Austin looked left and right, and, convinced no one would see him, retrieved the key from her secret hiding spot on the trim surrounding the front door. "Mercy," he called, slamming the door extra hard. "Mercy! Where are you?"

Nothing.

"I think maybe there's a short in your doorbell's wiring."

But he knew better than that, because he'd heard the two-note chime every time he'd mashed his thumb on the tiny white button.

"Doggone it, Merc, you're scaring me—" He poked his head into every first floor room, then took the stairs, two at a time. When he saw her curled up in a little ball in the middle of her bed, sobbing into Woodrow's fur, he knew why she hadn't come to the door, why she hadn't answered when he called out.

"Aw, sweetie," he said, drawing them both into a hug. "I'm so sorry."

At first, she only nodded, but then the words poured out in staccato-like bursts, and by the time she finished, his eyes were damp, too. Maybe it wasn't such a great idea to give Ray and Rick a dog, after all. Best case scenario, the cute little mutt would die of old age in eight, maybe ten years. But what if she got hit by a car, or came down with some dreadful disease, like Woodrow had? The boys had no real memory of Eddy, because they'd been so young when he died, but still—

He understood how much Mercy had cared for Woodrow, but he couldn't just let her sit here all night, clinging to the dead cat. "Let me take him, OK?" he said gently. "Maybe you can bring me one of his favorite blankets, and I'll wrap him up, so we can—"

Can *what?* he wondered. She lived in the city, with a brick terrace and a concrete sidewalk. He couldn't very well dig a hole and bury the poor animal for her.

Mercy nodded, gave Woodrow one last kiss to the forehead, and handed him to Austin. "He loved sleeping here," she said haltingly, patting the downy plaid quilt. "I think—" She hiccupped. "I think he'd like being wrapped up in it."

Half an hour later, while she sniffled through her second mug of herbal tea, Austin put her phone back into its cradle. He'd called half the cops and firefighters in his cell phone before finding one who knew the right way to handle a— situation like this one.

It was nearly midnight when she dozed off in his arms. Austin pressed a soft kiss to her temple. How odd that he felt more like a parent than a boyfriend—or whatever his part in this relationship was called—especially considering this wasn't the first time she'd roused that protective, nurturing side of him. He'd never been in love before. Thought he had a time or two, but he'd been wrong, as evidenced by the way things ended up each time. That, and the fact that compared to his attachment to Mercy—

She'd stopped crying hours ago, and her red-rimmed eyes weren't nearly as swollen as when he'd found her. But she'd withdrawn, went all quiet and sad on him, and the only thing he could think about were those long, thin scars on her inner forearms.

He listened to her soft, steady breaths, and thanked God for these moments of peaceful slumber. When Austin thought of all she'd lost and survived in life, it seemed fitting and proper that the Lord rewarded her with gentle dreams.

No sooner did he have the thought than Mercy tensed and began to weep, a soundless sad cry that put a sob in his own throat. Was she reliving the vicious beating, or her last moments with Woodrow? The instant when she learned her mother had drowned, or the awful hour when her father had died in her arms?

None of those, he hoped, pressing a second kiss to her temple. "Shh," he whispered. "You're all right. Everything's gonna be fine. I promise."

Almost instantly, she relaxed. The whimpering stopped and she went back to breathing in and out, in and out. He had a crick in his neck and his arm had gone from numb to achy, but he ignored both. He'd sit here all night if he had to. He'd use a sick day tomorrow, too, because no way he'd leave her in this condition.

36

The Dundalk parade turned out to be everything she'd heard about and more, with colorful floats and noisy marching bands, candy-tossing clowns and smirking politicians. As the largest July 4th parade in Maryland, it didn't surprise Mercy that, days in advance, residents plunked down lawn chairs and sawhorses to stake claim to their own stretch of curb. What surprised her was that they trusted their friends and neighbors enough not to collect them all once the last exhibit rolled by.

Mercy wished she'd worn shorts instead of jeans, because already, the oppressive heat had glued the fabric to her legs, and she still had a back yard barbecue and the fireworks to get through before the day ended!

Cora met them at the door, looking especially pretty in a yellow sundress and sandals. She'd pulled her long blond hair into a curly topknot, erasing ten years from her smiling face. "Come in, come in!" she said, opening the front door wide.

"I hope your boys like chocolate cupcakes," she said, handing Cora a red and white cooler.

"Are you kidding?" Austin answered in her stead. "Those two would eat rocks if you salted 'em first."

Fingers wrapped around her gold cross pendant, Cora threw back her head and laughed, then relieved Mercy of the cooler. "Austin," she said, shaking a scolding forefinger under his nose, "Didn't you tell her that I didn't need her to bring anything?"

"Yes, I did."

"Ah, one of those 'I do things *my* way' women, are you? Oh, how I envy you. I've never had a talent for saying no to the men in my life!" Another giggle, then, "But don't worry. I'm sure your little cupcakes won't go to waste. Not even with the tiramisu and cheesecake I baked. Or the deep dish cherry pie."

She looked at Austin to add, "All Austin's favorites, you know!"

No, she hadn't known all of Austin's favorites. But Mercy smiled politely, anyway.

It seemed to Mercy that time had slowed to a painful crawl, thanks to the heat and humidity and similar comments from Cora. By eight o'clock when they left for the fireworks Mercy wished she hadn't let Austin talk her into riding with him.

Oddly enough, Cora's behavior partnered beautifully with Mercy's plans to play Cupid. As if it wasn't enough that the woman kept a tastefully decorated spotless house, she'd prepared a delicious meal and exquisite desserts, all while looking like a model who'd just stepped from the pages of a fashion magazine, Cora had insisted that Austin say a blessing before they ate and held onto her little gold cross while he prayed.

She was the exact opposite of Mercy, making her the perfect life mate for Austin.

"She means well," he said during the drive back to Fells Point.

Mercy didn't understand what had prompted the comment, because she'd made a point not to react to Cora's remarks.

Made a point, too, of complimenting her at every available opportunity.

"Sometimes she tries so hard to please people that it comes off a little—"

"Annoying?"

Austin grinned. "I was going to say 'driven', but I guess she can be that, too."

"The boys seem to love that little dog. And it looks like they're taking good care of her, too."

He nodded. "Yeah. And if I didn't know better, I'd say Aretha had been with them since she was a puppy."

The mention of the dog's name made Mercy snicker. "I asked Rick why he and Ray chose that name."

"I meant to do that, and kept getting side-tracked."

I'm not surprised, considering you had a blond growth *on your side all day.*

"He said the very first time they let her outside to do her business, she wailed like a soul singer to be let back in."

That inspired a round of quiet laughter. "Man. Y'gotta love the pair of 'em. Eddy would have been so proud."

He rarely talked about his partner, so she never knew whether it was all right to ask about him or not. *You'd think a psychiatrist could come up with a few non-harmful questions.* Just as she had every other time the notion popped into her head, Mercy tamped it down with a quick and firm confirmation of facts: She'd been a lousy therapist, as evidenced by the number of failed cases in her files.

Besides, once she dropped the bomb a few minutes from now, he probably wouldn't even want to discuss the weather. That would break her heart, but she'd survived worse. She'd miss him and grow lonely for him. No question about it. And when she did, Mercy would remind herself she was doing the right thing. At least, the right thing for Austin.

"You OK?" he asked as she unlocked her front door.

"Sure. Why wouldn't I be?"

He shrugged. "You were . . . weird today. What's with that?"

This door, you mean? The one I have no intention of opening until you've driven away? "It was a long, hot day, and I'm pooped." No sense putting off 'til tomorrow. "If you want companionship, Cora's your girl."

Laughing, Austin said "What? I know she behaved like a nut today, with all her fussing and—"

"She's in love with you. And to be honest, I think it'd be a great match."

Now he frowned. "Is that a fact, *Yente?*"

Yente? The matchmaker from *Fiddler on the Roof?* Mercy didn't know which was funnier, that he was familiar enough with the musical to pull a character's name from his memory, just like that, or the fact that he'd zeroed in on her intentions just as quickly.

"Are you denying that Cora is a good woman?"

"Of course not. I love her like a sister." He shuddered, grimaced as if he'd inhaled a nose full of skunk spray. "A *sister,*" he repeated, "which is *exactly* why I could never—"

"Never say never," she warned, one finger ticking like a metronome.

He grabbed the finger and gave it a gentle yank, forcing her closer. Then he kissed it. Kissed the inside of her wrist, her shoulder and neck, and her cheek. Pressing his palms to her cheeks, he touched the tip of his nose to hers. She licked her lips, thinking that if he aimed to kiss her, well, she'd let him. That way, she'd have it to remember him by as she sniffled over the plot of an old black and white romance, clinging to a fuzzy afghan and a bowl of buttered popcorn.

"You think I don't know what you're doing? What you were doing all. Day. *Long*?"

"I wasn't doing—"

"Yes, you were . . . ," he said again, one side of his mouth lifting in a sexy grin. "*Yente.*"

Mercy tried to look away, to step out of the protective circle of his arms, but Austin held tight.

"Dumb idea, but sweet." He chuckled. "My only regret is that I wasn't there to watch the gears turn as that amazing brain of yours came up with this whole crazy plot." He smiled, shook his head and exhaled a big sigh. "I don't want Cora, you goofy li'l nut," he ground out. "The only woman I want—the only one I've *ever* wanted—is you."

Well, she thought as his lips found hers, *looks like you'll have this kiss to remember him by after all.*

That is . . . if she ever developed the courage to let this wonderful, honorable, beautiful man go.

37

"I sure hope those ropes hold," Griff said, dusting his hands.

"They should." Austin tested the knots securing the Callahans' boat to the pier. "We've got 'er double-tied."

"Yeah, but it isn't every day a cat four hurricane blows into the bay."

"Aw, the weather people are wrong more than they're right. Just covering their butts," Austin said, "so they won't get sued if Earl *does* make it this far."

"Happened with Agnes. And Floyd. And Isabel—"

"I could name two for every one of those that was supposed to blow us to smithereens—and didn't." He started for his own boat. "You gonna help me get my craft battened down, or we gonna stand here all day talkin' hurricanes?"

"You're welcome to stay at my place. Just in case."

Austin laughed. "I'll be fine, right here."

"OK, so I'll help you tie 'er down. And then I'm going straight to Sheppard Pratt to book you a padded cell."

"Why don't you call Bud and Flora, instead? Tell 'em not to worry."

"You better do it. I'm not that good of an actor. How much longer will they be in Wisconsin, anyway?"

"I didn't ask, they didn't say."

"Well, it's good they went." He snickered. "I could think of a hundred places I'd rather be than *Milwaukee,* but," he shrugged, "it's their money."

The men finished securing *One Regret,* then Griff said, "Better run. I'm supposed to serve supper at 'Helping Hands', and it's a good half-hour drive from here to McElderry Street."

Austin wished his friend would leave stuff like that to younger, more able-bodied men. But he'd learned through experience that saying so would only waste his breath and Griff's time. "Well, be careful down there, y'hear?"

"Not to worry, Finley m'friend." He aimed a thumb toward the menacing gray sky as the clang of the halyard threatened to drown out his assurances. "I've got the Almighty watchin' over me."

⁊ℰ

With every step of his flip-flopped feet, Griff chanted "Father, protect him, Father, protect him."

Austin had always been stubborn, but lately, he'd given new meaning to the word. What was he thinking, hanging around when a powerful storm was inching up the East coast? He'd insured that old bucket of bolts to the hilt, so why take the chance that Earl might work up an appetite for green-and-yellow tugboats?

He chased two cats and a pigeon away from his van—a rusting old clunker that still wore a blanket of colorful flower stickers. A gust of wind whipped into the front seat, flapping the hem of his fringed jeans and ballooning the peace symbol in the center of his tie-died T-shirt. Squinting as his gray ponytail slapped his left cheek, he smirked. "What's the matter, haven't you ever seen an aging hippy before?"

LOREE LOUGH

The cats darted under a nearby car and the bird flew away.

"Guess not." He chuckled. "Your loss."

The drive to Eastern Avenue was quicker and easier than he'd expected. Maybe, he thought, because intelligent human beings had holed up inside their homes, safe from the impending storm. Unfortunately, the homeless only had a handful of soup kitchens and shelters to wait it out, and Griff was only too happy to do his part to make the waiting more bearable.

If not for a grizzled old preacher, he'd be among them. A couple dozen times he'd been tempted to conduct a poll to find out exactly how many of the men and women who lived on the streets were there because 9/11 had turned their worlds upside down . . . and they hadn't met up with a living, breathing guardian angel who'd helped right their lives.

He wheeled into the gravel lot behind the crumbling old church and pocketed his keys without locking up. If somebody wanted to crawl into the van to get out of the wind and rain, so be it.

"Yo, Griff!" called the big-bellied man behind the counter. "You's late. Again!"

Technically, he'd arrived early, since supper wouldn't be served for another hour yet. "Take a hike, Sherman, you old codger."

"They's 'maters in the sink fo' you to wash up an' slice. An' when you's done wiff dem, dump some pickles in a bowl."

"Who died and made you boss?" Griff said, untying the man's apron.

"You know well as I does that the gub'nor give me this job after I kep' his boy from gettin' mowed down by a school bus."

Yes, Griff knew. So did everyone here. The story made national news when Sherman put his own life on the line to save the governor's son. After a week in the hospital and another month in a cast, the state's highest official made a mission of seeing to it that this big-hearted man would never have to worry about food or shelter again.

"Dunno why these fools come in here so many hours 'fore we serve up the meal," Sherman said from the corner of his mouth. "It's like an oven in here, and them big ol' fans don't do nothin' but blow hot air around."

"We're all the family most of them have. The heat is a small price to pay for feeling as though they belong."

In the wintertime, the subject changed from heat to cold, the only alteration in the dialog he and Sherman exchanged daily. And, as on every other day, they talked sports scores and politics. They prayed for the Orioles. Prayed that their elected officials would remember they'd each been blessed with a conscience. Today, Hurricane Earl made it into the conversation, and they prayed for the safety and well-being of every city along the eastern seaboard.

It was Sherman's turn to light the burners that would keep hot foods hot, and dump ice into the bins that would hold cold dishes. Griff, meanwhile, made sure the salt and pepper shakers were filled to the brim, then stuffed napkin-lined baskets with plastic flatware.

Nearly every chair at every table was filled, and even though they hadn't put out the meat and potatoes yet, a scraggly line had formed along the cinderblock wall. "Don't mean to compare 'em to critters," Sherman said, "but dey remind me of a dawg I had once't. I knew when foul weather was afoot without listenin' to the weather report, 'cause he'd develop a powerful hunger that no 'mount of food could satisfy." He nodded toward the tired-eyed, shuffling men whose shoulders slumped under the weight of every shirt and coat they owned. "Breaks my heart, Griff, yes it do."

Griff nodded. He'd thought the same thing from time to time. "All we can do is keep praying for them, friend. Praying and making sure they get at least one good meal in their bellies every day."

"Lawd, that is the truth, for—"

Shouting and shoving interrupted Sherman's sentence. "Hey, won't be none o' dat in here," he shouted, lumbering toward the scuffle. "Y'all behave proper or you won't get fed."

"He cut in front of me in line," said a gap-toothed old man.

"You're a liar," said the man behind him. "That, or you're blind, and didn't I was here first."

They went back and forth that way for another moment, and then the shoving started up again.

"Now y'all listen, the *both* of y'all," Sherman bellowed, and grabbed the second man's shirt. "I done tol' you once't we don't allow none of this here. Now, you come with me to the back of the line."

"Get your fat greasy hands off me," he snarled.

Griff stepped between them. "C'mon now. There's no need for—"

The man pulled a pistol from his coat pocket. Griff saw the flash of silver, followed by a deafening explosion and a flare of bright yellow-orange. For a split second, the only sound in the room was the quiet *whir-squeak-squeak-whir* of the big oscillating fan in the corner. Then chairs squealed across the linoleum as the diners shouted and shoved and scrambled for the door.

Sherman hit the floor, and Griff knelt beside him as a blood-stain grew across the front of his white apron. He whipped out his cell phone and dialed 9-1-1. He'd barely barked out the soup kitchen's name and address before a second shot sounded.

"H-he done got you, t-too," Sherman stammered, pointing a bloody finger at Griff's chest. "Guess I . . . guess I weren't wrong, callin' *some* of 'em animals." Then his head lolled to the side, and he fell silent.

It took a second to sink in: He'd taken a bullet, point blank to the chest. The fact that he felt nothing—not fear or pain or anger—told Griff this was it, the day he'd meet Jesus in person.

Still on his knees, Griff sputtered, "Put the gun away, son, before somebody else gets hurt."

He heard the clatter of metal, then watched the gun spin in a slow circle before coming to a stop. Sirens wailed in the distance, and he became aware that two men had pinned the gunman to the floor as a dozen others hovered above him.

"You be OK, Griff," said a gravelly voice he didn't recognize.

He nodded. Yes, he would, because any minute now, he'd be free of the misery that had been his world since 9/11, misery that had only deepened when he lost his sweet wife. Sadness spread through him as his lifeblood puddle around his knees. *Austin.* When news of what had happened reached him, it would hit him hard. "Be with him, Lord, and keep him strong."

"What he sayin'?" said the voice he didn't recognize.

"'Be strong' or somethin'," said another man.

"Crazy talk," said the first.

"'Cause he be dyin'," said the second.

A wave of dizziness wrapped around him, and he sensed, rather than felt, hands, several of them, easing him to the floor.

"Don't you dare die on me, you crazy old hippy."

He knew *that* voice. Of all the dumb luck! Why did it have to be *Austin's* ambulance that answered his 9-1-1 call? This would have been hard enough on him, without seeing with his own eyes that—

"I'm not kidding, Harvey. You snap out of it, you hear?"

In all the years he'd known Austin, he'd never called him that. Griff recognized it for what it was: a last-ditch effort to hold his attention, keep him from slipping into unconsciousness. One of the oldest tricks in the book! He prayed for the strength to say something. Anything that would keep his good friend on the straight and narrow, because while Austin had come a long way, he wasn't invincible; if there was an alcoholic out there who didn't need a hand, now and then, sidestepping temptation, Griff hadn't run across him.

Would Austin find someone to help him remember what was important, make sure he never slid back into that black hole where Griff had found him, nearly dead and begging to die?

Griff grabbed Austin's hand and whispered the first responders' prayer:

"Father in Heaven, please make me strong when others are weak, brave when others are afraid, and vigilant when others are distracted by chaos—"

Griff gave a grateful nod when Austin choked out the final words:

"Provide comfort and companionship to my family when I must be away. Serve beside me and protect me as I seek to protect others. Amen."

Just a little more strength, Lord, just a little more . . . .

"Now listen here, you thick-headed Irishman," he wheezed, "if you screw up, I'll come back down here and kick your butt. I mean it."

"I know you do." Austin sniffed, then swallowed. "Now shut up, will you, so we can—"

"No, *you* shut up." Ignoring his friend's shaky grin, Griff jabbed a finger into his chest. "I put a lot of time and effort into getting you back on the straight and narrow . . . ."

"I know you did, and I'm grateful."

"Then I want your promise."

"Anything. You've got it."

"Stick to the program, no matter what, no matter who."

When Austin nodded, Griff closed his eyes and went home.

All the way home.

38

Strange that in all the years they'd been friends, Griff had never mentioned how he'd like things done should the unthinkable happen.

Well, the unthinkable had happened, and with only dirt-poor cousins and elderly aunts left behind, the thorny duty fell onto Austin's shoulders.

Griff hailed from a long line of proud Irishmen who'd served the country as soldiers, sailors, cops, and firefighters, and every last one of them had asked for pipers who'd play *Amazing Grace* over their graves.

Weeks after 9/11, while attending the funeral of a fellow first responder, the mournful music started up, and Griff leaned in to whisper "If I have to listen to just one more minute of nasal whining from those confounded bagpipes, I swear, I'll jump into the coffin with the man!"

That's why there'd be no bagpipes for Harvey Griffen.

But with nothing else to go on, the best he could do with the rest of it was to give his friend the kind of send-off like he'd want for himself: simple, quiet, and brief.

So he pulled together a few trusted friends who attended an early-morning mass at St. Ambrose's church, where for the past eight years Griff had served as usher, choir director, sermon-writer, deacon, and handyman. The parish priest—a freckle-faced fellow in his sixties—sniffled all through the service. "He'll be missed," the father said, "by all who knew him."

At the cemetery, standing shoulder to shoulder with the handful of men who'd known Griff best, Austin held his breath. It was the only way he knew to control his powerful urge to blubber like a baby. He knew better than to shed a tear, because if he could, Griff would throw open the lid of that plain brown coffin and slap him silly. "I sure hope there won't be any weeping and wailing over *my* grave!" he'd say, right before launching into a homily about how he hoped to take over, leading the choir of angels.

Austin grinned, picturing it, then swallowed the sob, aching in his throat. He didn't have time for self-pitying malarkey. There were calls to make and papers to sign. Besides, there'd be plenty of time for tears, later. Tears and moaning and some fist-shaking at the heavens, because Austin didn't know how he'd survive without his substitute brother. Ironic, he thought, that every other time he'd experienced a loss, Griff had been his go-to guy. Man, he was going to miss the guy! Both Griff and Austin were longstanding AA members, but when they weren't working or volunteering or home recovering from both, the men loved hanging out at McDoogle's Pub, where construction workers and big shot lawyers forgot, for a few hours anyway, where they'd gone to school as they tipped a few as equals. All but Griff and Austin, that is. "Man doesn't need to imbibe to enjoy things like that." If Griff had said it once, he'd said it a hundred times.

"Wish I could have afforded a pricier casket," Austin said on the way to dinner in the Poplar Inn's banquet room.

"I didn't know Griff very long and definitely didn't know him very well," Mercy said, "but I have a feeling he'd be very happy with what you did. Especially under the circumstances."

Circumstances, indeed, he thought, gritting his teeth. "Ironic, isn't it, that he survived the Gulf War and 9/11, only to die dishing up dry meatloaf in a soup kitchen?"

"I heard him say once that he was most content when serving others."

Translation: Griff had died happy. Or, at the very least, satisfied.

"Thanks for driving," he said. "My brain's been kinda fuzzy this past couple of days."

"I'm happy to do it."

Maybe he'd get lucky, and she wouldn't add "after all you did for me last fall."

She parked on the Wise Avenue side of the restaurant. "Looks like everybody you invited is here."

He nodded.

"That's good."

"Why?"

"Because I'm hoping they'll tell lots of Griff stories, that's why."

He noticed that she had to half-run to keep up with him. Not an easy feat, even before the attack. Austin slowed his pace. "Yeah. That'd be cool."

The room was bright and airy with plenty of long narrow tables arranged in U-fashion, just as he'd requested. That, too, had been a decision inspired by Griff. "Nothin' more annoying than going to a shindig, only to try and make conversation with the back of somebody's head."

The waitresses handed out Griff's favorite meal—lasagna with extra sauce, salad, and garlic bread, served with sweet iced tea—and kept people busy and relatively quiet for the first half hour. It wasn't until after apple pie ala mode and coffee that the tales began to spin. Laughter and tears and sighs of remembrance floated around the room, and through it all, Mercy stayed at his side.

Afterward, as they crossed the parking lot to her car, he said "Don't know how I would have gone through that without you."

"It wouldn't have been easy, but you would've been all right."

He thought about that as she steered onto the Beltway. "I'm not as tough as you think I am. It's all an act. And not a very good one."

"'Tough' and 'strong' are two very different things." She braked at a red light, and grabbed his hand to add, "I've never met a stronger man."

Fortunately, the light turned green, because if she had kept looking at him that way—as if she really believed what she'd said—Austin might have lost it.

"How like him to duck out right when he did."

Her voice, like spun honey, soothed his frazzled nerves. "What do you mean, 'duck out'?"

"Right before—" Austin swallowed, then started over. "He'd been at the marina, helping me tie up Bud and Flora's boat, and mine, too. Started in on me about getting out of there in case the hurricane decided to suck my boat to the bottom of the bay."

He saw her tuck in one corner of her mouth. "I don't understand."

"I'll never get to say 'I told you so!'"

Nodding, she laughed. "Sure you will. Don't you Christians believe you'll all meet up again in the afterlife?"

You Christians? Austin would have said it out loud, except he just didn't have it in him tonight to get into a big religion thing with Mercy. Again. Instead, he said, "You're right. I just hope I remember to hit him with that line when he meets me at the pearly gates."

She pulled into the slot beside his truck in the marina lot and unbuckled her seatbelt. "Now, don't take this the wrong way, but—"

"Whoa. If that isn't an attention grabber, I don't know what is." He exhaled a loud breath. "Go ahead. Lemme have it."

Her lips pulled into a tiny smile, but her eyes glittered with regret. Of course she was sorry that Griff was gone, even sorrier about the way he'd left this world. Was she feeling down about that? Or feeling sorry for *him*?

"I don't want to leave you alone tonight."

Yep. It was pity, all right, and after her "you Christians" crack, Austin didn't know how he felt about that . . . or if he *wanted* to be alone with her.

"Since Woodrow died, there's really nothing for me to do at home, except wander around, wondering how you're doing over here. I won't get in your way. I promise." Her hand formed the Scouts' salute. "I can bunk down on the sofa. Make your coffee and scramble you some eggs in the morning." Mercy glanced at the dashboard clock. "Scramble some eggs *now*, since it's nearly suppertime."

What did she think he'd do, throw himself overboard? Empty that bottle of Jim Beam? Stick his head into the oven?

That inspired a grin, since she didn't know about the booze—or his troubles with it—and his oven had never worked.

But what would they do, all alone for hours on end? Things between them had been—strained, to say the least, even before Griff's death. Austin shrugged one shoulder, thinking maybe this would push things in whichever direction God intended.

"I don't think I have any eggs."

"How about this: I'll worry about what we'll eat, and you worry about how you'll get it down without making me feel totally inept in the kitchen."

"Galley."

"Excuse me?"

"On a boat, the kitchen is called a galley."

"Oh."

"And the bathroom is a head."

"Right."

"Living room is 'the cabin.'"

"I see."

"And the place where I sleep is the stateroom." He paused, and reached for her hand. "Pay attention, because there will be a quiz—"

"And if I fail it?"

He didn't tell her that if there really was a test, one of the questions would be "Do you think you might *ever* change your mind about faith, about God?"

"I'm gonna start praying, right now, that you pass with flying colors."

Because cliché or not, if she didn't, tonight would be the beginning of the end.

39

September 9 2011
New York City

*H*e liked to drive, and she didn't.

Mercy hated trains, Austin loved them.

She had never taken a bus anywhere, except to school, and that's how he'd gone from the Big Apple to the Windy City with Avery, half a dozen times while they were both in college.

Riding the Greyhound from O'Donnell Street to New York's Penn Station wasn't half as bad as she'd expected. The only thing smaller than the disinfectant-scented bathroom had been the movie screen hanging above the first passenger seat, but since she'd seen *He Said, She Said* half a dozen times, it didn't matter.

The ride north had been uneventful, without so much as rush hour traffic to foul things up. It took standing at the hotel registration desk to accomplish that, because despite confirmation numbers and email printouts to verify that they'd booked two rooms, only one suite was available.

The clerk fired up his computer to hunt for available rooms at other hotels, but thanks to half a dozen conferences and conventions, and 9/11 ceremonies, the closest was in New Jersey.

A gal who didn't belong to the "you Christians" set, getting all riled up over a thing like that? It made no sense to Austin, and he might have said so—if she hadn't looked so all-fired cute, fussing at the clerk about the inappropriateness an unmarried couple, sharing a room.

He stepped up to the counter and said under his breath, "How big is this suite?"

"King bed in the guest room," the buttoned-up fellow said, "and a pull-out sofa in the sitting room."

"Is there a door between the rooms?"

"No, sir, I'm afraid there isn't." He brightened a bit to add "But there *are* double entrances to the bathroom."

He looked at Mercy. "See there? Problem solved. You'll take the guest room, and I'll bunk down on the sofa."

She sighed loudly. "I guess that'll just have to do, since there are no rooms to be had in this. Whole. Entire. Enormous. City."

Well, if he had to suffer through this tenth anniversary reminder of the tragedy, at least he'd do it with Mercy, who, without even trying had already made it a memorable trip. Austin tucked both key cards into his shirt pocket, then grabbed their suitcase handles and rolled them toward the elevator.

As the car whooshed up, he took a huge gulp of air and held it, and stared as the numbers lit up above their heads, one by one. When at last the doors slid open, he exhaled.

"Very good," she said with a wink. "I don't even see one bead of sweat on your brow."

Sometimes he forgot that she'd seen him at his worst during those early days after the tragedy. Obviously, she couldn't say the same, but with any luck, the perps who'd been on the receiving end of his temper before quitting the force had put it out of their minds.

"It's almost six," he said as he unlocked their door. "We have a lot of restaurants to choose from. What're you in the mood for? Italian? Asian? French?"

"Good old American is fine with me. A pink-inside burger with catsup-covered fries would really hit the spot."

"Sounds good." He scrubbed a palm over his face. "Think I need to shave before we head out?"

"Why bother? People will think you're going for that 'Hollywood scruffy' look."

She giggled, and he smiled, thinking how lucky he was that since he had to be stuck in the same room with her for three days, Mercy wasn't the type to hang on to a bad mood for very long.

The small talk that started as they walked to the diner continued over dinner, and during the walk back to the hotel, too. The waiter had mistaken them for husband and wife, and oddly, neither of them bothered to correct him. Austin didn't know about Mercy, but he rather liked the easy rapport they'd established as she recovered from the attack. Already, they'd spent more time together than most couples had after years of marriage. They'd probably do just fine, linked by vows and a license and an address—if she shared his spiritual views. Or if she'd given him any reason to hope that she'd at least *try*.

The Callahans had called him stubborn and agreed when Griff said "Where's your faith, man?" He didn't even try to explain how many hours he'd spent, asking for Divine Intervention, or how every time he hit his knees, he felt more certain than the time before that God wanted him to remember that it had been his faith that saved him, literally and figuratively. Much as he loved her, Austin didn't know how he could share the future with a woman who'd repeatedly disrespected his God. Let them underscore what he and Mercy had in common. Without faith, how would any of that stand up under the pressures of life?

Maybe when he put it to her that way—and that's exactly what he planned to do when they got back to Baltimore—she'd mull it over and decide he was worth giving faith a try. If not, he hoped they'd always remain friends, because God help him, he loved her right down to the marrow of his bones, and always would.

They were racing across the intersection when she said, "You know what?"

"Hmm . . . ."

Once they reached the other side, she stopped and looked up at him, and when he saw that twinkle in her eye, it was all he could do to keep from scooping her up and kissing her, right there in the middle of the street.

"I lived here for years, but I never took a carriage ride through Central Park."

That made him laugh. "You know what?"

"What?"

"Neither did I. What say we do it tomorrow, right after dinner?"

Mercy hailed a carriage, and, fishing two twenties and a ten from her pocket, said, "Life's short. Why wait?"

She'd climbed up onto the seat before he could agree or disagree, so he joined her. If she realized how rare it was to flag a driver and get an empty cab, that fast, *then* would she believe in God? Austin chuckled. "Why not?"

It was a beautiful night, with balmy breezes and a clear sky. The lights of the city were mesmerizing, and he doubted either of them paid a bit of attention to the Irish brogue of their driver. They passed the Bow Bridge and a gorilla statue, and the fountains spouted water that glittered in the lamplight. The steady clop of the horse's hooves on the pavement lulled him into a tranquil state, and he found himself struggling to keep his eyes open.

Leave it to Mercy to rouse him.

She leaned forward and asked the driver "What's your horse's name?"

"Marmeduke."

"Well, he's just beautiful. Especially his thick mane. And I love his bangs!"

"Better not let Marme hear you callin' her a he!" He plucked a rose from the vase near his elbow. "For you, m'lady, on the house."

Giggling and blushing, she held it to her cheek and thanked him. Austin had never seen her happier or more animated. Maybe, just maybe, there was hope for them after all.

September 10, 2011
New York City

He slept deeply and without dreams, which would have been unusual at home in his own bed. But here, with the noise of the city floating up to his window and the sofa bed's bar digging into his spine? Austin didn't know what to make of it, so he simply thanked God.

He'd wanted to get an early start, partly to map out their route to and from the World Trade Center, and partly so they could get the touristy stuff out of the way before tonight's concert.

He grabbed her purse straps, thinking to make it easier to climb out of the taxi, and, unprepared for its heft, nearly lost his balance. "What's *in* this thing?" he asked, handing it back to her.

"Just Milk Duds, Whoppers and Junior Mints, and a couple bottles of spring water."

Too stunned to comment, Austin stared.

"Don't look at me as though I've lost my mind," she teased, grinning. "They charge an arm and a leg for this stuff at events like this."

So she was frugal, too. He returned her grin, thinking he couldn't love her more. But on the way home, when her voice creaked from having sung every song at the top of her lungs, Austin added yet another item to the list. Maybe Griff and the Callahans were right. Maybe he *could* learn to live the rest of his life with an unbeliever.

⌾

Mercy held tight to Austin's hand, not so much to keep from getting lost among the crowd, but because she couldn't shake the feeling that he was slipping away from her with every tick of the clock.

He'd printed out a dozen articles, each outlining the city's plans for Ground Zero, and during the bus ride to New York, he read every one to her.

The memorial boasted more than four hundred trees, dug up from the field in Pennsylvania, and near the Pentagon, and around New York. They now stood stately and tall, a symbol of rebirth and growth.

Beneath the verdant canopy, two enormous granite pools— representing strength and stability—lay in the footprint of the towers. Softened by leafy groundcover and supple mosses, the pools collected the powerful spray of the country's largest manmade waterfalls . . . and the names of every victim, etched into their walls.

Mercy and Austin made it through the tour without too many tears, but when the ceremony began with the unfurling of Old Glory as trumpets blared and choirs sang, Austin cupped a hand over his eyes, and silently wept.

Then came the speeches—a dozen or more—delivered by politicians, Hollywood stars, and Nashville singers. Powerful and riveting as they were, not one could compare to the simple, straightforward stories about the victims, as told by the loved ones who remembered 9/11 in their own unique way.

Then the thousands who'd gathered slowly went their separate ways, where jobs and school and neighborhoods awaited them. They'd arrived with heavy hearts, expecting to view and relive the stark reminders of that terrible day, expecting, too, to return bent and bowed and for the most part unchanged.

Instead, they left with spirits renewed and heads held high, for what they had seen and heard was evidence that America had risen from the ashes of grief and sorrow. The respectful crowd now had a reason to believe, and hope, for those who'd died on this honored ground would never be forgotten, and neither would their sacrifices.

When Mercy looked into Austin's eyes, she saw that the ghosts that had haunted him these many years were gone. In their place, the quiet calm that comes from knowing who you are and what you want.

One thought echoed in her heart:

Please, Austin. Please want me.

40

January, 2012
Dundalk, Maryland

Like every morning, Austin woke to the screak of gulls and waves, gently lapping at the hull, and thanked God for his hard-earned peace of mind. He treasured this boat, and the briny scent of the Chesapeake, and the job that made him feel whole and useful and needed.

Over time, he'd even grown comfortable with his memories—the good ones and the not-so-good—of his mom and his dad, of Avery and Eddy, and as proof, the bottle of Jim Beam still stood unopened in the companionway cupboard. Griff would be proud.

Last week, as he scraped and sanded the fading, peeling letters on the tug's stern, her name echoed in his head, reminding him why he'd chosen it. That call from Avery—the one he'd ignored on the morning of 9/11, then listened to a thousand times over the years—had been the source of his greatest regret.

Time had healed that wound, and though he'd found peace from the nightmare, he'd replace the name, because these days, it had a whole new meaning.

Yes, he'd reached a blissful, blessed point in his life, and had even come to terms with the heart-wrenching decision, made on that sultry September day when he finally put the question to Mercy, who was and always would be the love of his life:

"Do you think you might *ever* change your mind about faith, about God?"

She'd said no.

And that, he admitted as he stood at the rail, hoping to catch a glimpse of the elusive green flash, had become his one regret.

Discussion Questions

1. What expectations did you have for Mercy and Austin's relationship when they first met?

2. List three of Austin's PTSD symptoms.

3. Do you feel that Mercy displayed PTSD symptoms? If so, what were they?

4. What were Austin's character strengths?

5. And his weaknesses?

6. What were Mercy's most positive traits?

7. And her character flaws?

8. Why did Austin have such a hard time admitting his anger?

9. Do you feel Mercy overcame resentment toward her mother?

10. Which of the two main characters did you most closely identify with, and why?

11. Who's your favorite secondary character, and why?

12. If you had to select one "faith theme" from this novel, what would it be?

COMING SOON
from
Abingdon Press

The Search for Honor

Book Two in Loree Lough's First Responders series

*Q*uiet and serious, Honor Mackenzie was forced to leave the fire department when a misunderstanding about a platonic relationship with her lieutenant threatened his career and hers. The two heartbreaking romances that followed left her with a sour attitude toward love. So when she meets Matt when training SAR dogs, she can't decide who's more immature . . . the ten year old twins or their dad.

They become a team, both still confused about the exact nature of their friendship. Then Matt receives an urgent call from Honor's boss: Honor hasn't reported in since heading out to look for a missing child; anyone who knows her understands three days without a word from her is a very bad sign . . .

We hope you enjoy this except from chapter 1.

1

The beams of high-powered flashlights crisscrossed the sleety fog and shimmered from herringbone ripples on the river's surface. The eerie wail of a lone coyote hung in the wintry air, and overhead, trees creaked as the wind whistled through the woods, intensifying the gloom of the night. Shivering, Honor tightened the string that cinched her parka's hood tight around her face, praying they'd find the secondary crash site soon, and that when they did, they'd send more people to the hospital than to the morgue.

Heavy boots crunched over frosty moss as Elton, her boss, jogged up beside her. "Hey, Mackenzie . . . is it just me," he puffed, "or is that gas I smell?"

Grinning slightly, Honor Mackenzie took care not to aim her light too near her boss's eyes. "Either that or you've sneaked a gulp of whiskey to take the chill off—"

Up ahead, a voice she didn't recognize bellowed, "Over here!"

"Watch for the flare," hollered another.

As they followed the red flash, the scent of jet fuel grew stronger. Honor thanked God for the icy rain. Yes, it added to the ten-man team's discomfort, but if it doused embers, hidden by the wreckage, well, small price to pay.

And then, in a small clearing a few yards to her left, Honor spotted the tail section of the airliner that had plummeted onto I-95 at the height of rush hour. Emergency personnel had shut down all lanes in both directions to enable Medi-vac copters to airlift passengers of the airliner—and those it had crushed on the highway—to Shock Trauma, but not before eyewitnesses reported seeing fiery bits of the plane falling a few miles north of the explosion. Moments later, Honor got the call to round up a team and head for Patapsco State Park.

Like a beached whale, what was left of the plane teetered belly up on the Patapsco's bank, one mangled wing pointing skyward and twin witch-finger pillars of smoke spiraling upward, as if reaching for the treetops in a last feeble attempt to free itself of the muck.

A small pink palm slapped against a window, and beside it, the bloody and frightened face of a boy appeared, startling Elton so badly that he lost his footing in the slimy sludge. Arms windmilling, he staggered backward a step or two. The instant he regained his balance, Elton roared, "Donaldson!"

From somewhere to their right, that same powerful baritone repeated, "Over here!"

"Fire up that radio of yours. We need fire equipment. And ambos, on the double!"

Honor climbed onto the tail fin and pressed her own palm to the boy's. She could almost feel his panic, pulsing through the glass. "Help is coming," she told the boy, doing her best to look and sound like she believed it. Not an easy feat while peering over his shoulder to do a quick head count. If he'd survived, maybe others had, too.

"Mackenzie, get down from there."

Usually, Honor would have obeyed instantly. But the poor kid's terrified, teary eyes had locked with hers, seeking reassurance and hope, and she couldn't bring herself to look away, let alone walk away.

In the reflection of the window, she saw Elton, pointing toward the biggest column of smoke. "I'm dead serious, Mack. *Get down from there*," he repeated. She didn't have to look over her shoulder to know he'd said it through clenched teeth.

Then, as if on cue, glimmers of yellow and orange flickered to her right. The boy saw it, too, and cut loose with a weak, trembly wail. "I know you're afraid," she told him, "but don't cry, OK? Help is coming."

The fire's heat penetrated her down-stuffed jacket and warmed her cheek. Please God, she prayed, squinting into the choking smoke, *let it come soon.*

Want to learn more about author
Loree Lough and check out other great
fiction from Abingdon Press?

Sign up for our fiction newsletter at
www.AbingdonPress.com/fiction
to read interviews with your favorite authors, find tips
for starting a reading group, and stay posted on what
new titles are on the horizon. It's a place to connect
with other fiction readers or post a
comment about this book.

Be sure to visit Loree online!

www.theloughdown.blogspot.com
www.loreelough.com